WHEN WE LIED

NEW YORK TIMES BESTSELLING AUTHOR
CLAIRE CONTRERAS

Copyright © 2024 by Claire Contreras
All rights reserved.

No part of this book may be reproduced in any form or by any electronic or mechanical means, including information storage and retrieval systems, without written permission from the author, except for the use of brief quotations in a book review.

ISBN: 978-1-7330411-9-5

Edited by: Gina Licciardi
Proofread by: Brittni Van at Overbooked Author Services
Formatted by: Champagne Book Design
Cover Design: Hang Le

Dear Reader,

When We Lied is NOT a dark romance, but on the next page you'll find the content warning. I hope you enjoy reading this book as much as I enjoyed writing it. If you're able, please leave a review when you're done <3

Xo,
Claire

CONTENT WARNING

Suicide (off page)
Loss of a parent (off page)
Death of a sibling
Hostage situation

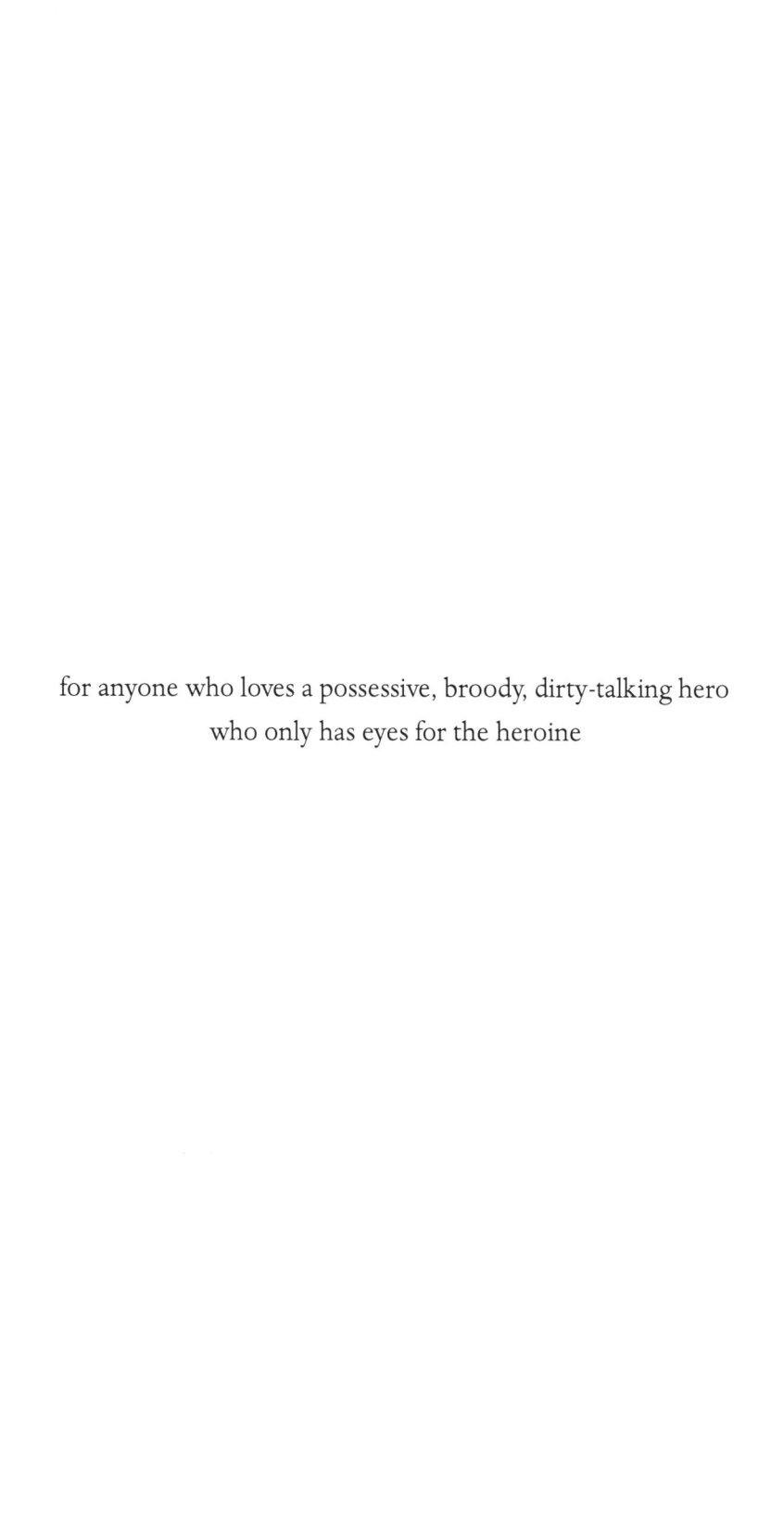

for anyone who loves a possessive, broody, dirty-talking hero who only has eyes for the heroine

Chin up, darling.
They'd kill to see you fall.

WHEN
WE
LIED

CHAPTER ONE

Finn

3 years ago

I don't know who the woman in the hot pink dress is, but I want her screaming my name by the end of the night. My own thoughts give me pause. It's completely out of character for me to notice, let alone think that about anyone in Fairview. Thanks to my father and his friends, I adopted a "don't shit where you eat" mentality when it comes to sex. It shouldn't apply to me since, unlike them, I'm not married or in a relationship, but it's been years since I hooked up with anyone from Fairview, and up until now, I planned to keep it that way.

Fairview has been growing substantially each year, our social circle is small and incestuous. You'd be hard-pressed to find someone that a friend of yours hasn't already fucked or tried to fuck. This woman isn't one of them. She's talking to my sister, so I assume she's around the same age. If that's true, she went to my high school, and would have been a freshman when I was a senior. It's doubtful that I wouldn't have seen her around back then.

I wouldn't have forgotten if I had. Not with a body like that. And that face. Fuck. I want to see it up close. Preferably looking up at me while she's on her knees. She's beautiful, but a lot of women are. Yet, something about her demands attention. Maybe it's the way she smiles like she means it, or the way she throws her head back, unrestrained, when she laughs.

I can't remember the last time I saw someone act so reckless with their feelings, so free. That's what emotions are in our world. Reckless. It's another lesson I learned from a young age, and one I won't soon forget. Movement catches my attention and I glance over to see Gracie Davis walking over with a determined look on her face. *Fuck my life.*

"Hey," she says when she reaches me.

I don't say anything as I scan the room for my asshole friends who were just here a moment ago. It shouldn't be hard to spot them, since, unlike most nights, the lights aren't turned off and this place isn't at capacity. Pure is a nightclub, but because it's my sister's birthday weekend, we're allowing her to use the first floor of the three-story club.

The first is the general nightclub, the third is the VIP lounge, and the lower level is what my cousin turned into an exclusive speakeasy sex club, which is completely off-limits to Mallory. Before I signed my first professional contract, my cousin roped me into investing money in this place. Much to my financial advisor's disapproval, I agreed. On paper, I co-own it, but I've only stepped foot in here maybe three times, if that. This is Lucas' baby, and he treats it as such. I'm more of the absent father who only comes around when he has time, which in my case, is never.

My sister thinks I'm here because it's her birthday—and she definitely went a little extra hard with the guilt trip this time. Unbeknownst to her, I'm only here because some friends are in town and wanted to discuss a lucrative business opportunity. Otherwise, I would have stayed away from Fairview like I have the last two years. Year one in the league, I came home during the summer. Year two, I took the summer off and went to Europe. This year, I'm standing in my own nightclub, trying to avoid conversations with stage-five clingers like Gracie. I finally spot Ella on the other side of the room, and she has the audacity to smirk.

"Are you having fun?" Gracie asks.

"Not particularly."

She laughs. "Do you ever have fun?"

"Not particularly."

"We can have fun *downstairs*." She sets a hand on my bicep and I cut her a glare that instantly makes her drop it. "It's just … I haven't seen you in so long and I know we'd be good together."

"*We* wouldn't be anything together."

"I think I can change your mind about that." She arches her back slightly, making her tits, which are nearly spilling out of her top, brush against my arm.

My eyes drop to them briefly before I look away. I could, of course, walk away from her or go upstairs and watch the festivities from the comfort of the private office that overlooks the club. I won't, though. I promised my sister I'd be here, and I'm staying until my phone buzzes in my pocket to tell me I've been here a full hour.

I look around again to see if I can find Hammie. He's the one she should be talking to. They've already fucked, but I have no doubt he'd have another go at her. As I'm scanning the room, I hear a laugh that beckons my attention. The mystery woman. My sister's smiling at whatever she's saying. I'm not sure what surprises me more, the fact that I'm drawn in by this stranger or that my sister's smile is genuine.

As if feeling my attention on her, Mallory glances over, sees Gracie standing with me, and makes a disgusted face as she looks away. The mystery woman turns slightly and my eyes snag on her ass again. Since I don't live here, fucking her wouldn't be completely breaking my rule. I've never seen her before tonight. Chances are I'll never see her again after. My thought is interrupted as I watch a guy walk over and whisper something in her ear that makes her frown. I hadn't even considered that she might have a boyfriend.

"I hate her," Gracie says suddenly. I cast her a blank look. "The brunette in the tight pink dress. I can't believe your sister likes her."

"Who is she?"

"Josslyn Santos." I ignore the disgust in her tone.

Josslyn. The name suits her. I can't stop myself from asking, "Why do you hate her?"

"She's a bitch." Gracie's lips pinch like she tasted something sour. Probably the taste of her own bitterness. "She played varsity basketball for Olympia, so I used to see her when we'd go cheer for the guys."

"Basketball?" My brows furrow as I examine Josslyn. Even in heels, she's not what I'd consider tall. "Really?"

"She thinks she's hot shit."

"Is she?"

"No."

"Have you seen her play?"

She scoffs. "She's mediocre at best."

"Sounds like you're jealous."

"I'm not." Her eyes narrow on Josslyn.

The guy—who looks a little familiar though I can't place him—pauses mid-sentence when a few girls walk up to Josslyn. Whatever they're saying makes her smile widen. One of them hands the guy her phone to take a picture of them together. The others follow suit.

"For someone mediocre, she sure has a lot of fans."

"I can't imagine why. She has like four hundred thousand social media followers." Gracie sucks her teeth. "I didn't realize Mallory was one of her groupies."

I cut her a look that makes her back straighten. I pull out my phone, see that I have twenty minutes left, and figure I might as well kill the time by finding out who my sister has been hanging out with. Without saying another word to Gracie, I move toward them.

CHAPTER TWO

Josslyn

FINNEAS ALEXANDER BARLOW IS A WALKING THIRST TRAP. TALL, hot, and broody. Tousled brown hair, chiseled jaw, alluring hazel eyes, perfect teeth, well-groomed beard, broad shoulders, and lips that look good enough to bite. He looks like a Disney prince, if the prince was a broody asshole. At least, that's what I've gathered from interviews I've seen and people who know him or of him. Which, in Fairview, is everyone.

He plays professional hockey and won the Calder Memorial Trophy his debut year, and the Conn Smythe Trophy two years in a row. Which, according to Damian, is a huge deal. Then again, everything Finn does impresses my stepbrother. And everyone else, for that matter.

On paper, Finn is the total package, which is why I don't understand the reason he's been watching me all night. The moment Damian walks away, the hairs on the back of my neck stand up. I chalk it up to the cold air coming from the vents above us, but when Mallory stops talking and looks at the person who just joined us, I instantly know he's the reason behind this feeling.

Mallory frowns. "Are you leaving already?"

"Not yet."

The low timbre in his voice makes my stomach dip. It dips again when my eyes meet his. No picture or interview clip could do this man justice. The storm brewing in those dark green eyes of his should be a clear indication of the destruction he undoubtedly leaves in his wake. Not wanting to get caught in the storm, I look away.

"I'm so happy you're here." Mallory smiles, then looks at me. "Oh my God! You two haven't met. This is the girl I told you about! The one who broke the record for triple-doubles."

Having her drop my accolades on someone who can fill this club with trophies and medals makes me bite the inside of my cheek to keep from blushing, but I manage to look at him again.

"No kidding," he says. "I bet you're going to miss playing."

"She still plays," Mal says, laughing. "Do you not pay attention when I talk to you?"

"Not really."

I press my lips together and look at Mal, who rolls her eyes and then groans when someone calls out her name. "Don't forget about tomorrow night," she says, shooting me a stern look before she walks away.

"'I'll be there," I smile.

"What's tomorrow night?" Finn asks.

"Nothing," I say too quickly but then add "girl's night," so he doesn't suspect anything.

I look at the floor and hope by the time I look at him again he doesn't ask me anything. I'm a terrible liar. Plus telling Mal's brother that she's taking us to an underground sex club isn't something I want to disclose to him. Going to the club isn't my usual thing at all, but Mallory has been showing off about being able to get in even though we're not even twenty-one yet. She insists that we need to see it for ourselves.

"So you still play?" he asks.

"Yep. I got a full ride to Fairview."

"They have a good program." He looks at me the way my

parents' friends look at me when they're about to ask me whether or not I'm any good.

I get it. From my stature, it's obvious I can't dunk—which is something many people, even ones who are six feet tall, can't do. It doesn't help that I'm a girly girl and always sharing my love of makeup with the world. Most of the time, I like being underestimated, which is Gracie Andrews' specialty.

"Let me guess, your girlfriend Gracie told you I suck."

"Not my girlfriend. Not my *anything*," he says. "I just figured with your height…"

"I know. I'm so glad they were able to overlook my height long enough to appreciate my skill set."

He barks out a laugh that seems to surprise him and frowns at me like I've done something wrong. He continues to study me like he's trying to figure me out, which is kind of funny since most people think I'm an open book. I mean, I document most of my waking life on my vlog, TikTok, IG, and Snap. Hundreds of thousands of people have formed strong parasocial relationships with me, which is cool, but can be strange sometimes. His eyes drop from my eyes to my mouth and continue lower in a slow perusal that makes me feel naked.

"What, you didn't get your fill when you were watching me from the corner like a creep?"

"You noticed me looking at you?" His eyes shoot back to mine. "I'm sure you liked knowing my eyes haven't strayed from you all night."

My stomach dips despite the arrogance in that statement. I manage to raise an eyebrow and say, "I bet you thought I would."

He tilts his head. "You're telling me you weren't dying for me to walk over and introduce myself?"

I let out a huffed laugh. *The nerve of this guy.*

"If I wanted an introduction, I would have walked over there. Maybe I would have, but you looked like you were a little busy."

"Just biding my time and trying to figure out if I should get a picture with you, since you seem to be the most popular person in the room."

I laugh. "Let me guess, you're used to being the center of attention."

"Maybe." He searches my eyes. "So, you know who I am."

"Obviously." I signal in the direction Mallory disappeared to. "Besides being Mal's brother."

I hesitate. I don't need to feed his already overinflated ego, but telling him I don't know who he is would be a huge lie, so I decide to go with the things I've heard from everyone. "Finn Barlow. Number one pick in the NHL draft, center for Vegas, and notorious womanizer."

He raises an eyebrow and tucks his hands in his pockets. "You've been keeping tabs on me."

"Please," I scoff. "You'd have to live under a rock to walk around Fairview and not know those things."

"How have we never met?"

"What do you mean?"

"I mean, how have I never seen you?"

"I don't know." I shrug. "Divine timing, I suppose."

"Divine timing," he repeats, still studying me. "Where'd you go to school?"

"Olympia."

"All four years?" he asks, and when I nod, he adds, "You met Mal at Fairview?"

We're in different social circles, so I can see why he'd find it difficult to believe that I wouldn't know his sister from a high school party or something. Even though most kids at Olympia are from upper-middle-class families and it's known as the "rich kid school," it's public. I can't imagine the Barlows even considering sending their child to a public school. They didn't even go to a regular private school. They went to one of those international private schools that cost as much as a Ferrari.

"Olivia Nassir is my best friend. We met through her," I

explain. Livie went to Olympia, and her family isn't Barlow-rich, but their parents do business together.

"My sister isn't the most welcoming to outsiders," he says.

"Trust me, I know." I smile thinking about how Mal treats most of the friends we've introduced her to.

I don't like to say she's a bitch, but she's extremely uncomfortable around people she doesn't know. From what I know about their upbringing and how many of her friends, including Gracie, have stabbed her in the back, I don't blame her.

"We should make up for lost time," Finn says.

"Meaning?"

"Meaning, leave with me," he says, eyes smoldering.

My breath seems to pierce out of my lungs. I'm beginning to understand why everyone is enamored with him. He hasn't looked away from me all night, and the way he's talking to me … being the center of Finn's attention provides a certain kind of high. A high I can't afford right now, or ever. Nevertheless, I remain nonchalant.

"You don't even know my name."

"Josslyn Santos."

My heart skips. "So you've been keeping tabs on *me*."

"Is that a yes?"

"About going home with you?" I take a small step back, heart pounding in my ears. "No."

"I should clarify that we wouldn't even have to leave the building."

"Really?" I let out a breathless laugh. "You have a private room ready for you?"

"As a matter of fact, I do." He watches me for a moment, then adds, "A very private room downstairs."

"How pragmatic of you." I bite my lip and tear my gaze away from his in hopes of calming the hell down. "The answer is still no."

"Because you don't fuck strangers?" He squints ever so slightly. "We can get to know each other if you want."

"Really?" I ask, even though I should cut this conversation. "When exactly?"

"Preferably when my fingers are buried in your pussy."

Oh my ... my body clenches in a way I've never experienced before. *Who says stuff like that? And why is it hot?* Probably because he's so damn hot. Coming out of any other man's lips, that line would be revolting. God, why am I even stalling and acting like I'm considering this? I need to seriously stop this conversation. Walk away, Josslyn. Walk the hell away.

"I can't believe you just said that." I lick my lips and swallow. "I'm kind of dating someone."

"*Kind of* dating someone?"

"It just started getting serious."

Like *yesterday,* but I don't say that part because it sounds ridiculous. Since it's a recent development and Tate never acted jealous while we were keeping things casual, I'm sure he would forgive my indiscretion, but it doesn't feel right. From the way Finn is looking at me, I can tell he doesn't really care if I have a boyfriend, and I can't help but compare him to Tate, which is ludicrous since they're so different. Tate is the kind of guy you take home for your mom to meet—charming, well-mannered, blond with blue eyes. Finn is the opposite—broody with chestnut hair, and an *I'll fuck my neighbor's mom in my Gucci flip-flops if I want to* attitude.

"How long ago is 'just started?'" he asks finally.

I hesitate and look away. "Yesterday."

"You're kidding."

"I'm not." I meet his eyes again.

"Two days? Technically, you wouldn't even be cheating."

I shake my head, laughing lightly. "I would hate to be *your* girlfriend."

"I'm not asking you to be my girlfriend. It's a one-time fuck. I don't do more than that, which I'm sure you've heard since you've been keeping tabs on me."

My eyes narrow. "You're so freaking arrogant."

"I wouldn't say that."

"I would." I cross my arms. "Why me, anyway? Why not Gracie? She looked like she was trying pretty hard to get your attention."

"And as you saw, when you were pretending not to notice me, she didn't have it."

"I still don't understand why you're wasting your time with me." I put a hand up to add, "I'm not fishing for compliments. I genuinely don't get it."

"Why you?" he muses as he looks at me. I hold my breath. Finally, he shrugs. "I have no fucking idea."

That makes me laugh. I know I said I didn't want a compliment, but what the hell? I open my mouth to respond just that, when someone bumps into me from behind, making me crash into Finn. We both inhale sharply as my hands land flat on his chest, and he puts his hands on my elbows to steady me.

I push away, inhaling his delicious cologne as I fully straighten and look into his smoldering eyes, committing the brief moment to memory. One day, I'll think back on this as "that time Finn Barlow propositioned me and then caught me when I was falling." As jarring and memorable as the experience might be, it solidifies one thing…

"I definitely can't have sex with you," I say shakily once I take a step away and find my voice.

"I definitely shouldn't want to have sex with you."

"Joss, we need to go." The voice comes from my stepbrother, who breaks the weird spell I seem to be under.

I turn my face and watch as he does a double-take when he sees Finn standing there. When he reaches us, he wipes his left hand on his black slacks in front of Finn.

"Sorry to interrupt. Damian Fletcher."

Finn looks at his hand for a moment before shaking it. "Finn Barlow."

Damian chuckles. "Yeah, I know. We met at The Stable. Well, more like you obliterated the team I was rooting for."

"Fletcher," Finn says, almost to himself, as he appraises him again. "You're the one who was being recruited for football and hockey. You were the youngest one on that team, right?"

"On every team," Dame says, and I stifle an eye roll as he does little to hide the smug expression on his face.

Finn is a much more skilled hockey player, but my stepbrother has reason to be cocky about his athletic prowess. Finn doesn't seem very impressed by him, and just nods before he turns to me again. With the weight of his full attention, my heart skips so many beats, making it hard to breathe. He's searching my face like he's looking for something to say, but I beat him to it.

"It was great to finally meet you, Finn." I smile wide because I really mean it. It was intense and strange and wonderful. "Congratulations on your success."

"Yeah." His gaze drops to my lips briefly. "It was nice to meet you as well."

I turn toward Damian and slide my hand into the crook of his arm to hold myself steady as we walk away. We're a few steps away when Finn calls out my name. I stop walking, forcing Dame to stop as well and glance over my shoulder. Finn's expression is unreadable, but the way his eyes rake over me sends a thrill up my spine.

"Fuck divine timing."

We stare at each other for a second, until I can't take the fire in his eyes a moment longer, and force myself to walk away.

"What the fuck was that?" Dame asks.

"I have no idea."

"How was he?"

I glance up at Dame. I know he's asking because he's been a fan of Finn's for years. "Intense."

"Yeah, Will Hamilton introduced us once, so I know for a fact he knows who I am," Dame says.

"Why didn't you say that then, you weirdo?" I shoot him a look.

"I didn't want to be the loser who remembered everything about our past interaction."

"Who cares?"

"It doesn't matter," he says. "He was trying to make a point by introducing himself and acting like he didn't know me."

"What point?"

"That he doesn't care who the fuck I am, because he's going to have you anyway." He lets go of my arm to get his phone from his pocket as he walks up to the valet.

My pulse seems to be everywhere as I stand there waiting. I realize I never said Dame's my stepbrother, and with the way we walked away arm in arm, he'd have to assume we're together … *right?* I shake the thought away. Mallory had mentioned that Finn's leaving tomorrow morning, so what Dame's suggesting is obviously not the case. The valet goes to get the car while Dame walks back over to me.

"What the hell does that even mean, Damian? You can't just drop that on me and walk away."

"It means what I said. He's used to getting his way."

"I literally just turned him down, and he's leaving tomorrow, so I probably won't see him again until … who knows when. If ever."

His expression turns serious as we watch his car approach. "I'm just telling you what I've heard. He's a one-and-done kind of guy who takes what he wants and leaves a trail of broken hearts behind."

"So, sort of like you, then?" I swallow hard, wishing my heart would stop pounding so erratically.

He shrugs. "Not that my opinion will make a difference, but I think you should stay away from him."

"I have a boyfriend now, remember?"

"Don't remind me." Dame scoffs as he takes a step forward when the car reaches us. He opens the door for me and walks around the car as he speaks. "I can't believe you're seriously dating that loser. You know he's only with you because Dad…"

I set a hand on the door as I step into the car, and his words are drowned out by the pulse in my ears when I see Finn standing outside. He's looking at his phone, and there's a woman by his side taking a selfie and smiling like she just won a prize. I don't understand the sudden hollow in the pit of my stomach, but it's what I feel as I get in the car and pull my seatbelt on. It makes no sense. I don't even know him. We had *one* conversation. But as I lay in bed, the unbidden image of that woman at his side returns, along with the hollow feeling.

CHAPTER THREE

Josslyn

WE HAVEN'T EVEN FULLY STEPPED INSIDE OF ONYX AND I ALREADY feel like I'm out of my element. That alone is a feat, considering I rarely feel uncomfortable anywhere. I take my eyes off the picture of a man kneeling in front of a man dressed in only leather chaps and study the small cut on the back of my hand. Seeing it makes a wave of anger bubble up inside me, but I push it down.

The cut doesn't bother me as much as the reminder of the argument Tate and I got into while we were fixing the old red pickup truck he decided to buy and restore. We were unofficially together for almost a year and never argued, but this morning—our first official morning together—he started acting like a jerk.

"I can't believe I finally got you to come here today," Mallory says, breaking me out of my thoughts.

"Well, it's your birthday," I say, smiling. "Who am I to say no to the birthday girl?"

"Still." She looks at Tate and I can tell she's trying to smile at him, but can't out of loyalty to her family. "Thanks for coming. I know she wouldn't be here without you."

"No problem. I'm curious about this place." He looks around at the art of dominatrixes that line the deep burgundy walls of the entrance.

Mal excuses herself and tells us she's going to check in and make sure we're on the list. She's been talking about this place for months, and even though I've been curious about it, I never actually find myself here before. I definitely didn't think it would be the first place Tate and I would go as a couple, but he already told me we could leave if I get uncomfortable.

Tate leans over. "You know, if you want to play with other people, you just have to say the word."

I pull back, my gut twisting. "I don't want to have a threesome."

"It doesn't have to be a threesome. I'm just leaving the option open, so you know you can play in there if you're curious."

I wanted to check this place out, but I'm not *that* curious. He knows this, which only leaves one other option.

"Do you want to play? Is that why you're suggesting this?"

"No! But I figured I'd give you free rein in here," he says. "Well, to a certain extent."

"To a certain extent," I repeat, dumbfounded. "What does that mean?"

"No fucking other people."

"That's it? Like no p and v sex?" My brows shoot up when he nods. "So if someone touches me or goes down on me or vice versa, that's okay?"

"Sure, why not?" He shrugs.

"Are you into watching? Is that it?"

"I'm not opposed to it." He turns my body toward him and kisses me. "You're four years younger than me, babe. I know it doesn't seem like a lot, but I don't want you going into this relationship and wishing you'd done more."

"*Going into it?* I thought we were already in it." I pull away from him to put distance between us. "You said, *and I quote*, 'I want us to stop fucking around and be exclusive already' and I agreed, but if you changed your mind or didn't mean monogamous…"

"I meant monogamous." He reaches for my hand and brings it to his lips. "This is forever, Joss, so yeah, if you want to do those things with someone *in here just tonight*, I'm okay with it. Do you want to? Are you not okay with me doing something with someone else? Is that what you're worried about?"

"I mean, I wasn't." I tug my hand away again. "But now that you're saying all these things…"

"Would you be jealous?" He grins. "If you saw me with another woman?"

I chew on that. I've never really been a jealous person, and I don't think we've been together long enough for me to care, but I haven't been put in that situation, so I answer honestly. "I'm not sure."

I've seen him flirt with the women who work at my stepfather's law firm, and I've never cared. But we hadn't decided to "make it official" then, and even if we were, I don't think he'd be stupid enough to fuck someone there. I think about the hollow feeling in my stomach last night and become even more confused.

"We're here!" Olivia says loudly. I walk away from Tate and throw my arms around my best friend's neck.

"I'm so fucking happy to see you."

She kisses my cheek and laughs as she pulls away. While she says hi to Tate, I turn to Devon, the guy she's been sort of seeing. He plays for the Fairview basketball team, but I'm not sure where he and Livie stand relationship-wise. She's a hopeless romantic, and most of the guys we know seem to just want an easy fuck.

"I'm shocked you guys are here," Livie says to Tate. "Now that you finally decided to make it official and all that."

"We have an agreement while we're in here," Tate says, looking at me. "Only for tonight, though. When in Rome and all that."

"Really?" Livie's brows furrow. She glances over at me, but I have nothing to give her. She must read something on my face, though, because she frowns deeply.

"I think she needs to get whatever is in her system out before I ask her to marry me," Tate says, smiling.

"To … marry," Livie sputters, eyes wide on me, then on Tate. "Have you even asked her what she wants?"

"Let's go!" Mallory says, interrupting our conversation.

She walks over and gives each of us a tiny manila envelope with our name on it. Inside, there are two different color wristbands.

"What? No masks?" Livie asks.

"You want one? They're optional," Mal says, turning back to the hostess, who pulls out a silver box and sets it on the table. "The masks don't mean anything, so you can pick any color."

Devon grins at Livie as he reaches for two dark purple masks. "We're doing this."

"We can stick together, or you guys can go off and play together," Mallory says. "I've heard it's a great place for couples."

I don't love the sound of that, but I grab a mask. Tate and Mallory follow suit. We follow Mallory down the hall to the massive ornate silver doors that look like they belong in a castle. Even though the club is exclusive and they've already run background checks, they make us go through a metal detector and check our bags into lockers. Once we're done, two people dressed like cats push the doors open and lead us inside.

CHAPTER FOUR

Josslyn

THE LIGHTS ARE DIM, BUT UNLIKE A REGULAR NIGHTCLUB, THERE ARE no strobe lights or a visible DJ, though music is playing. The middle is an open square that has strips of aerial silk with performers twisted around them. Naked performers. Well, they appear to be naked, anyway, and are somehow coordinating their seductive movements with the music playing.

"It's a lot like the one my cousin owns downtown," Mallory says as we walk. "But theirs is child's play in comparison. If you're looking for a specific kink, this is the place to be. Some can be intense, which is why you signed all those waivers."

Anticipation rolls through me as we walk down the hall, and I reach for Tate's hand again. He's weird about hand-holding, but he lets me as Mallory opens another beautiful door. My grip on his hand gets tighter when we step inside and there's a full-on orgy with at least fifteen people on display. There's EDM music playing in here, but it does nothing to drown out the moans, slaps, and screams. My entire body heats up from the sounds alone.

I glance up at Tate, whose eyes are glossy as he looks at them.

He licks his lips and lets go of my hand. He's still looking at them when he says, "I'm going to the bar. You want something?"

I shake my head and keep staring at the scene in front of us when he walks away. I find myself taking a step forward, fascinated by everything they're doing. Admittedly, my sexual experience is fairly limited, but even if I was experienced, I don't think I'd be prepared for that. I watch the three closest to me. A guy with a porn-worthy penis is sucking a woman's nipples while the man behind him kisses his neck. They're both thrashing, begging for more. It's intense.

"You can join," Mallory says, her breath in my ear making me jolt. She laughs and sets a hand on my waist, pulling me toward her as she stands beside me. "There aren't many rules, which is what I like, and they keep it simple with the different colored wristbands."

I look at my bands—one white and one red. I hadn't realized we weren't all wearing the same ones. "What do these mean?"

"White means you need to ask about relationship status, so that'll be the first question they ask you." Her eyes sparkle as she brings her face closer to mine. "The red means safeword, so, well, do with that what you will. They used all of the questions you answered to pick the right colors for each of us."

"Oh."

I look at hers. One red, and the other white with black stripes. Then at Livie, who only has a red one. Devon's is the same. I look around until I spot Tate at the bar, smiling at something the woman pouring drinks is saying. I can't see his from here, but I think I remember what he had. I glance at Mal's arm again.

"What does white with black stripes mean?"

"Threesome, or rather, multiples, but most people just go with threesomes." She tears her gaze from me and looks at the scene in front of us. "Or this."

"*Oh.*" I turn back to the orgy in front of us.

She'd told me recently that she liked to experiment, but I didn't think she meant this. She's Mallory Barlow, and while she may not have been born into that family, it doesn't make her any less one of them. They're always so ... proper. Mal is definitely the black sheep, but even still, she doesn't publicly do anything that'll bring shame to her family name.

A wave of heat sears through me when I glance at Tate again and get a glimpse of the white and black band on his arm. I bite my tongue for just a second. I don't understand how someone can go from begging for me to give a serious relationship with him a real shot, and talking about marriage in the freaking lobby, to wanting a threesome and telling me to go "have fun."

"What's wrong?" Mal asks, gripping my waist.

I bite back a laugh and look around quickly to see if I spot Olivia. I don't, but I know she would probably be laughing her ass off if she could see me. She swears Mallory has a crush on me—which is ridiculous—and told me I shouldn't show her too much affection. Which is also ridiculous and not the easiest thing for me to do. I come from a long line of people whose love language is touch. For us, hugs, kisses on the cheek, and hand-holding are natural. With friends, with partners, with parents. It's just how we are. And Mallory, well, she's starved for affection.

"Joss?"

I blink. "Tate has a threesome band on."

She drops her hand from my waist and pulls away, frowning as she looks at my bands again. "I thought you guys discussed tonight?"

"We did, and in the lobby, he all of a sudden decided he wanted me to 'go have fun.'"

"Maybe you should then."

I bite my tongue so I don't say anything that might offend her. While this may not be my scene, it is Mallory's, and it took her a while to admit that to herself and to us. The last thing I want is to shame her in any way. I take a deep breath and look at her.

"I respect that you like this. I think it's super cool that you're able to let yourself go and actually enjoy it," I say. "But you know it's not my thing."

"I can't imagine why. If I had a body like yours…" She shakes her head. "I would take full advantage."

"What are you talking about? You're perfect."

She smiles sadly. "I went to therapy for years and was told that over and over, but you're the only person who's actually made me believe it."

I grab her hand and squeeze it.

She sighs heavily. "There's a bar down the hall. It's beautiful and it's fun. No one will be naked or doing anything in there that might make you uncomfortable. Go have a drink, or water, or whatever." She pulls me into a tight hug, smothering me with her Chanel No. 5. "If you want to leave, I totally understand."

"I'm not going to leave. We said we'd go for pizza after, remember? Besides, I want to be here," I say, which isn't a complete lie. "You go have fun. I'm going to head to the bar."

She gives me one last long look before she leaves. I look down at my wristbands again and think about my conversation with Tate last night. He seemed curious, but not overzealous about coming, so I figured it would be perfect for us to check the place out and watch without actually participating.

Now that I know he only has a white and black wristband, I take a deep breath and step away from the partition, ready to tell Livie about this, but she's gone. As are Devon and Tate. I look around as I head to the bar Tate was just at. The woman who had been there just moments before is gone, replaced by a man wearing a bow tie and the shortest and tightest black briefs I've ever seen. He smiles wide when he sees me.

"Cocktail of the night?" He points at the small digital board that displays a picture of the drink and its contents. "It's included in the admission."

"In that case, yes. I have a feeling I'm going to need a little liquid courage."

He grins. "First time?"

"Yeah." I look around again. "I already lost the people I came with."

"That happens here." He starts pouring things into a shaker. "It's kind of like going to an art gallery. Everyone has their preferences, so groups rarely stay together."

"How many rooms are there?"

"Ten if you count the pools."

My eyes widen. "There are pools?"

"Indoor pools, but they're not for swimming." He winks. "There's even a little forest outside. No animals, of course, but if you're into the whole 'caveman, catch me if you want to fuck me' vibe, it's available."

"What the—how big is this place?"

"Big enough to fit approximately one hundred and fifty guests without having them run into each other. We cap it at eighty, though, so reservations are highly encouraged." He shakes the drink and pours it into a small tumbler with ice. "Don't waste your time looking for your friends. Go have some fun!"

"Yeah, I will." I thank him as I take the drink and walk away.

They couldn't have gone too far. If I'm being honest, I'm more upset with Livie than I am with Tate. We have a buddy system, and no one is supposed to get left behind. I walk into the next room, and the next, and then over to some that are locked. I whirl around and gasp, almost crashing into a blonde woman dressed like a bunny. She's gorgeous, has a name tag that says Scarlet, and beams a smile that puts me at ease.

"Can I help you find something?"

"I lost my friends, so I went looking, but now all I find are locked doors."

"Those are private." She points up at a red light on top of the door. "If it's red, it means it's completely private. If it's green, you're allowed to watch or join if they give you permission. Most of the time, they're red."

"Oh." I look down the hall and see a series of red and a couple of green lights. "That makes sense."

"The doors have small windows, like in a classroom." She walks over to the door behind me and presses the screen next to the door, which illuminates with the word "private." "This window is shut since it's private. The green ones will be open, so you can peek in without actually going inside."

"That's so helpful." I smile wide. "Thank you so much. They should really say all of this at the door."

"They assume you're already a member or are with one," she says. "If you need anything, ask for me."

I thank her again, and we walk in opposite directions. I go straight to the first door I see with a green light up top, and sure enough, there's a window. I look inside and see a man with a black mask on his face. There's a woman kneeling between his legs pulling his pants down, and another unbuttoning his dress shirt.

My heart pounds hard when I see the cursive Carpe Diem tattoo on his right pec, confirming that it's Tate. I'm not sure if it's jealousy or anger for not telling me about this, but my heart plummets just the same. He did say he wasn't interested in playing, didn't he? I take a step back and crash into someone behind me. I automatically start to apologize as I turn around, but the person presses up against me and keeps me from moving.

CHAPTER FIVE

Josslyn

"I HAVE A PRIVATE ROOM IF YOU JUST WANT TO WATCH, *Josslyn*."

His roughly whispered words skate through me, causing a shiver to go down my spine. I turn around quickly, my breath catching when our eyes lock. He's not wearing a mask, which doesn't really surprise me. Finn doesn't seem like the type to care about others discovering his hidden kinks.

"I…" I set a hand on my heart, willing it to slow down before it punctures a hole in my chest. "How do you even know it's me? I have a mask on."

"I have my ways."

My mouth opens, shuts, and opens again. "I thought you were leaving?"

"I was." He looks down the hall and back at me, his eyes falling to the wristbands for a second before meeting mine again. "What are you doing here? Don't you have a 'boyfriend?'"

"I … yeah. It's complicated."

"A two-day-old relationship is complicated?" His brows raise. "That sounds promising."

"When was the last time you were in a committed

relationship?" I narrow my eyes at him, as I set my empty glass down on the table beside me.

"It's been a while." He searches my eyes, and though it's gone quickly, I think I see a spark of humor in his. "You look surprised."

"I am."

"Because you heard I'm a womanizer."

My knee-jerk response is to glance over my shoulder again to where Tate is almost completely naked now, though the mask remains on his face. Everything that's happened tonight is making me question my willingness to be in a relationship. I should've listened to my gut when I met him. He was too proper, too perfect, and smiled too much. No one smiles that much unless they have something to hide. My mom insisted that Tate would be good for me. And my loneliness outweighed my hesitance. And now, here I am feeling foolish. My jaw clenches. I cross my arms as I turn away.

"The plot thickens," Finn says, making my eyes snap back to his. He quickly looks at the window behind me and back at me. "That two-day in there?"

Two-day. I snort. "Maybe."

"He didn't invite you to join?"

My response is to purse my lips and tear my eyes from his. I stare at the acrobats moving up the silks.

"Huh. He didn't then," Finn says, demanding my attention again.

"In case you haven't noticed." I bring my arm up to show off my bands. "I'm not interested in threesomes."

"Yet it's the only one he has on."

"This is none of your damn business."

"Nor do I care about any of it, if I'm being completely honest."

"Then why…"

"Because I'm still here, and I'm bored, and my offer remains," he says, shoving his hands in the pockets of his slacks.

My heart gallops, but I ignore it. "The offer remains because you're bored?"

"I'm here because I'm bored." His eyes scan my face. "The offer remains because I still want to fuck you."

I swallow and drop my gaze from his, taking him in. He's wearing a light blue button-down, brown slacks, and matching sneaker-style dress shoes. Everything fits him as though it's tailored to show off his impressive body. And it does. It definitely does. I blink away to stare at the aerial silks again, in an attempt to calm my nerves.

"Then I'm sorry to inform you that there are rules," I say, my eyes still on the silks. "No fucking."

"As in, I can't put my cock inside your pussy?"

My breath catches again, but I force myself to look at him. "Pretty much."

His eyes gleam but he says nothing, as he takes his hands out of his pockets, brings a card out, and turns around. "Follow me."

He doesn't wait for my response. I watch him swipe a card and push the door open, waiting for me to follow. I do, despite the voices in my head that tell me not to. The room is completely dark until he pushes a button and dim lights appear above us. Though the lights are dim, they're enough for us to go up four steps, where another door awaits. He slides the card again and steps inside, holding it open for me.

Four movie theater chairs are facing dark floor-to-ceiling windows. Finn walks over and crosses his arms as he stands in front of them, watching the scene as if it's there solely for his entertainment. I finally let go of the door, and when it clicks shut behind me, Finn uncrosses his arms and turns around to face me.

"Do you own this place?" I ask, suddenly feeling ten times more nervous than I did outside.

"A friend of mine does."

"And they just let you have a key card?"

"They do." He takes me in slowly like he did last night, but unlike last night when I felt like I was on the defense, the lust in his eyes makes me feel wanted. Special. He waits until he reaches my eyes again before he speaks. "If you come in here, you're consenting to whatever happens."

My heart stops. I don't know what that means, but I want it. I've met a lot of guys, but I've never met one as intense as Finn. Something about that, about the way he looks at me, is intoxicating. Last night, I'd said no because of Tate, who's now doing god-knows-what with multiple people in the next room.

"I signed the papers." I take a step forward.

"I know what you signed, and I know what you think you want." His eyes fall to my wrist briefly. "I'm asking for your consent, because once you give it to me, you're mine for the night to do with as I please."

I let out a shaky breath. "Okay."

"Just like that?" He raises an eyebrow. "You don't even know what I want to do to you."

"I don't care," I say on a shaky exhale. "I just want you to do *something*."

His eyes flash, and for a moment, I think he's going to tell me to watch my tone or something. What he ends up saying is much more shocking.

CHAPTER SIX

Josslyn

"**G**ET ON YOUR KNEES."

"Wh … what?" My eyes widen. I'm pretty sure I heard him say…

"I want you on your knees."

I stare at him with a frown on my face, but something about the fire in his eyes makes me slowly sink down. The hardwood floor is cold, but I remain still, waiting. What the fuck is wrong with me that I'm on my knees for a man? I don't know, and I don't care. If Tate asked me to do this, I'm pretty sure I'd laugh in his face, but Finn…

He swivels the seat closer to me, his eyes on mine the entire time as he sits and leans back against the chair. His long legs are in a wide stance. The illuminating light above makes him look almost sinister.

"Crawl to me," he says in a low growl.

I don't even hesitate. I freaking crawl. I stop when I'm at eye level with the bulge between his legs. A very large bulge. My breath hitches again, knowing that it's because of me. I sit back on my heels and look up at him. He leans forward slightly, bringing his hand to my face. As he runs the tips of his fingers from my hairline to my chin, I shut my eyes. The calluses on his fingertips make me bite my lip to keep from moving. He cups my face and brings his thumb over my lip, making me release it from my teeth. My eyes pop open and I nearly pass out at the way he's looking at me now, as he swipes the pad of his thumb softly over my lips.

"This is a one-time thing."

"I know."

"I mean it." He tilts my chin up slightly. "No asking my sister about me, no calls, no texts. Nothing. Just this, tonight, and that's it."

"I know. I get it." I hold his gaze as my tongue darts out of my mouth and rolls around his thumb, making him hiss.

He puts his thumb inside and fucks my mouth with it, his eyes darkening with each lick and bite I give him. All too soon, he pulls it out and widens his stance even more.

"Stand up."

I comply.

He puts his hands on the backs of my thighs and bends his head slightly, my knees hitting the front of the chair he's sitting on as he pulls me closer to his face. He runs his rough hands up my legs slowly, hitching my dress all the way up to my waist, leaving my lace thong exposed. His left hand slides to the front of my thigh, and he uses the same thumb that was just in my mouth to swipe over my mound. I set my hands on his shoulders to keep myself from falling.

"That feels so good." I let out a shaky breath.

His hand stops moving but remains there as he glances up at me. I don't know what he sees or what he's thinking, but he seems to make up his mind about something, as he helps me slide my panties off. He lets me take my heels off and brings me right back to where I was, sliding my dress up slowly as he plants kisses on my thighs, my hips, and my waist, until the dress reaches my head. He pulls away to lift it over my arms and head, exposing my naked chest.

"Fuck." He squeezes one of my breasts and runs that same finger over my sensitive nipple.

I shiver hard at the motion and yelp when he pinches it. He doesn't let me get a word out, because his mouth is back on me, sucking my abdomen and biting me right underneath my breasts. My eyes fly to the window, at the people slightly beneath us who are all over the couches, chairs, floor, and chaises fucking and doing other things. I look away quickly before my eyes find Tate. Finn pulls back, looks at the window, and then at me.

He starts turning his chair so he's facing the window, and I walk with him as he does, still between his legs.

"Turn around."

My breath falters. "No."

He raises an eyebrow. "Anything," he reminds me.

"But not ... I don't want to see..."

"Turn around, Josslyn." He slaps my left ass cheek, making me jolt up. "Now."

Oh, fuck. I turn around slowly. I could just close my eyes and not look at the people. I could pretend no one I know is down there.

"Put your hands on the glass."

I do.

"Spread your legs."

I do, holding my breath when his lips meet my right ass cheek, then the other. He spreads them apart, and I shiver at the feel of his breath between my legs.

"Fuck," he whispers. "I want to fucking ruin you."

My arms shake a little as he slides his fingers up and down my folds. I bite my lip and close my eyes, throwing my head back as he continues his slow torture. His hand disappears and he starts to gather my hair, wrapping it around his fingers tugging lightly. My arms shake again.

"Do I need a safe word?"

He lets go of my hair. "Do you want one?"

"I don't know." I glance at him over my shoulder. "I'm not sure what you're going to do to me."

"Have you ever used a 'safe word?'" he asks, not bothering to hide his mocking tone.

"No." I swallow. "But I don't know what you're going to do."

"Now you want to know what I'm going to do with you? After you crawled to me? After you showed me this glistening pussy?" he asks. My breath catches at the things he's saying, at the way he watches me. His mouth tugs slowly into a smile. It's not kind. It's cocky and filled with filthy promises. I gasp when he runs the back of his finger up and down my inner thigh. "Did you forget that you gave me permission to do whatever the fuck I want to you?"

"Except…"

"Except fucking." He squeezes my ass cheeks with both hands. "Trust me, I'm well aware of that stupid fucking rule. If you don't like something, tell me to stop and I will." He holds my gaze for a moment to make sure I trust his word, and I don't know why, but I do. I nod. He slaps my ass hard. "I want you to look out there and find your little boyfriend, so you can remember how it feels to have a real man eat this pussy."

At the feel of his tongue swiping from my clit to my ass, I already know he's going to make good on his promise.

CHAPTER SEVEN

Finn

1 year ago

"Can someone explain what I'm looking at?!" My mom's voice is shrill, as she continues to toss papers at us like they're bills for a stripper.

"We don't know, Eliza." My father sighs heavily, rubbing his eyes before putting on his reading glasses and picking up one of the pages.

His lawyer just went home.

Growing up, I never wondered whether or not these two were good parents. Maybe I would've questioned it if I'd had other kids' parents to compare them to, but I didn't. It wasn't until I left Fairview for good and unwillingly met other people, that I came to the realization that *holy shit*, my parents sucked. Or maybe it was the parents who were overly involved in their kids' lives that sucked. I couldn't say. Nevertheless, I was eighteen years old when I realized my parents and everyone in their social circle only had kids, not because they wanted them, but to continue their legacy.

"You." Mom points at me, her normally composed expression cracking with anger, with grief. "You knew about this place."

I shut my eyes and focus on breathing. I've had a brick sitting on my chest for the past week, and it doesn't seem to be going anywhere. When I open my eyes again, I do as my father did and pick up one of the pages she's thrown at us. They're all photocopies of the evidence the police took with them. They're already calling it a tragedy, but all I see is wrongdoing. My molars grind as I look down the list of times she'd been there.

Not only did I know about this place, I stupidly let her join—though "let her" is a stretch. I couldn't dictate anything Mallory did. My parents adopted her when I was just shy of six years old. She'd been born into an abusive household and had seen things that my worst nightmares couldn't conjure. When she moved in with us, her wires were already crossed, and no amount of recircuiting could reset those fuses. She went from that hellhole to high society, where she was expected to look, breathe, talk, and act a certain way.

While I'd been solely focused on grades and hockey all through high school, Mal had been a wild child, sneaking out and getting high. If I couldn't get through to my little sister then, I don't know how my mother thought I'd be able to change her ways when she was a twenty-three-year-old woman. Besides, they were here, while I was focused on my career two thousand miles away. I wouldn't point that out though. Not while they were in the thick of it.

"Finneas, answer me!" my mother bellows.

"I knew about it, but I didn't know *this*. And you know I couldn't dictate what she did." I pick up a pile of pages that have been stapled together and frown as I go through them.

"That's her gratitude journal," Mom says, her voice shaking. "The police are saying…" She licks her cracked lips. "They're saying she could have done this to herself."

My chest squeezes. I don't want to believe that, but my mother's right. We failed her. I push the thought away. No. She wouldn't have. Someone did this to her. Someone knows what happened.

"You need to rest," Dad says, standing and walking over to her. "Let's get you the medicine the doctor gave you."

"No!" she yells, her delicate fists hitting Dad's chest as he wraps his arms around her. "We failed her, Rick. We promised we'd take care of her and we failed that little girl! Oh, God. She told me I was too hard on her. I should've listened."

"I'll need to call Jerry and figure something out. I don't think Mallory would want everyone finding out about this."

I stare at them as they leave the dining room. Of course, he's already thinking about ways to make this disappear. God forbid the Barlow name is tarnished in any way. I sigh and go back to the pages. None of the journal entries have dates, and she didn't seem to write more than one or two sentences.

I'm thankful for the air I breathe.

I'm thankful for the roof over my head.

I'm thankful for my new best friend, Joss, and for her family. They feel more like a family than mine ever have.

That one gives me pause. I move a little faster as I read them.

Joss invited me to Titus' bday dinner. I almost felt guilty telling my dad I wouldn't spend his bday with him, but they'll be on their yacht in Martinique. I doubt they'll notice.

He picked me up today. He promised not to say anything to Joss, so I'm grateful for that.

I messed up again. He fixed it though. So glad to have him.

I want out. I want OUUUTTTT of <u>all of this.</u>

The bday dinner was strange. There were so many people there but he still kept looking at me across the table. Everyone was talking about Dame leaving college for the NHL next year so they were busy, but still.

Mom brought it up again. The matchmaking thing. I hate it. I hate them.

OMG! Joss' boyfriend is the WORST. I hope she opens her eyes and sees it. So thankful for her. She's a good soul.

I told him I want to stop. Stop or come clean. I can't do this to Joss anymore. He reminded me I was the one who started it. I hate this.

I saw him again tonight. He took me to a secluded farm and we lay on the bed of his truck. I love the way he makes me feel. FML.

There's a spot in their yard that the cameras can't get to. It's become our secret cove when I go over and 'go to the bathroom.' I hate myself so much. I know I need to stop.

I need to stop. I need to stop. I need to stop. I need to stop. I need to stop.

I want to tell someone about this but I can't do that to T. Olivia saw us together but she was drunk out of her mind so I doubt she'll remember.

I really want out. Of here. If I can't see them I won't want them.

I flip to the last page.

We're meeting at Onyx. I fucked up last week and gave everyone a scare, so J is forcing me to take her w/me. She says she'll drive me and wait for me to finish. I really don't want her to be there. I feel like the **worst person in the world.**

I haven't heard from Josslyn since that night at Onyx. It's what I always demand from women, but most of the time, they go out of their way to "coincidentally" run into me. Not that Joss could've done that even if she wanted, as I've only been back twice since that night. Still, I thought she'd call or text, or maybe ask Mal about me. Then again, she was a busy girl and very much sought-after. The thought of what she's been up to all these years ... of *who* she's been with ... makes my mood sour. I wasn't planning to reach out to her, but after reading these, it looks like I'll have to. I pull out my phone and call my cousin first.

"What's going on, man? Are you okay?" he asks, sympathy bleeding through the receiver. I grind my teeth but force myself to not be an asshole right now.

"Yeah. I need any videos we can get of Onyx that night." I look at the papers in my hand. "And I need a PI on Josslyn Santos and her family."

"A PI on..." He pauses. "Who's Josslyn Santos?"

"He's a PI. He'll figure it out."

"Okay. I'm on it. If you need—"

I hang up before he can finish that sentence. I want answers, not sympathy.

CHAPTER EIGHT

Josslyn

Present

Fairview Owls Sign Finn Barlow to Three-Year, $37.8 Million Deal

The Athlete first reported on this a few years ago when Hat Trick Sports Group came to our attention. Read the original article here: (3 Stanley Cup Winners and 1 Super Bowl Champion: The Powerhouse Behind Hat Trick Sports Group).

A few years ago, when rumors swirled about who was behind Hat Trick Sports Group, the world seemed to stop. It's not uncommon to hear about a group of former athletes doing business together, but three former Stanley Cup winners and one Super Bowl champion? That's something we hadn't seen before.

When Hat Trick Sports Group announced that they were building a brand-new NHL team from the ground up, it quickly turned into a media frenzy and speculations swirled about what city the team would belong to. No one expected Fairview. With a little less than half the population of Brooklyn, NY, it's not where you'd expect to have an NHL team, though the city's inhabitants would beg to differ.

"We live and breathe hockey," one local said. When asked how they *thought this would affect the turnout for Fairview University's top-tier hockey team, they said, "It would be unfair to compare NHL and college, but I don't think the Blaze have anything to worry about."*

"We'll go to both, alternate if we have to," his partner added with a laugh.

Needless to say, the Fairview Owls haven't even played their first game and are already the most talked-about team in the league. It's only been a few hours since it was confirmed that defenseman Finn Barlow—number one draft pick six years ago, Calder Memorial and Conn Smythe Trophy recipient, and Fairview native—is joining the team, but the team website already crashed due to the demand for pre-order jerseys.

When asked about his latest acquisition, Duke said, "It's a brand-new team and we have a lot to prove. We know he'll help us do that."

"We've already signed talented guys from the AHL, and now that Barlow is on board, we're starting off with arguably the most solid blue line in the league," Fitzgerald added during their press conference this morning.

Also noted in attendance were Nolan Astor, David Banks, and billionaire mogul Henry Duke, who is rumored to be a silent investor in Hat Trick Sports Group. They've remained mum on whether or not this means Barlow is also part of their company, and Duke's lawyer Prescott Sanders declined to comment.

With all of these ties to Fairview, the Owls are hopeful that...

My stomach coils so tight that I'm grateful to be sitting in a parked car. This information may be news to the world, but it isn't to me. When my Aunt Nina married Lyla Marichal's father, Albert, I gained a cousin who turned out to be the big sister I'd always wanted. Our families hit it off from the moment we met, and both Lyla and her husband Lachlan have been an integral part of my decision-making for all things basketball, including sponsorships. Lachlan and his friends own Hat Trick Sports Group, a sports entertainment firm in charge of many NIL deals. It was their primary focus until they decided to bring a professional hockey team to Fairview.

When they started talking about the team they wanted to

put together, Finn's name kept coming up, which is understandable. Who wouldn't want the face of their brand-new team to be a Stanley Cup winner? That he's a Fairview native is the icing on the cake. Every time his name comes up, I pretend not to hear it. Sometimes I leave the room altogether. My "if I can't see it, it doesn't exist" mentality is the only thing that gives me peace of mind. I'm not sure how to feel now that it's come to an end and I'm being forced to accept that it's actually happening.

On paper, it shouldn't matter that he's here. Fairview is big enough that we wouldn't run into each other. It helps that hockey is on at the same time as basketball, which means we'll be busy with our respective sports. But he's playing for my cousin's team, which increases the chance of us seeing each other. And worse, it's summer, which means neither of us is currently playing, so we both have more free time than usual.

It shouldn't matter. It wouldn't. But last year, Finn proved to be the asshole everyone said he was, when he implied some pretty awful things about me that I'd rather forget. Having him here won't do anyone any good. With a heavy heart, I pick up my cell phone and shoot Mallory a text. It's not like she'll ever read it. Her phone was amongst the things that were never found.

CHAPTER NINE

Josslyn

I'M NOT SURE WHY PEOPLE ARE SO ADAMANT ABOUT RIPPING EACH OTHER apart when we do such a great job of it to ourselves. I don't normally dwell on things people say about me, but having hundreds of thousands of people discuss my breakup on multiple social media platforms isn't ideal. The broadcast hurts more than the betrayal itself. We hadn't been together very long this time around, and the last time we broke up, we'd ended things on good terms.

>SarahB: did tate really cheat on you?
>
>PipaGrant: tate is an idiot
>
>Mike67: you can come warm my bed any day
>
>10m8: tate finally opened his eyes and moved on from this slut
>
>SarahB: @ 10m8 if you feel that way get off her page
>
>Ryan007: marry me i swear i'd never cheat on you @ PatMK this is the girl i was telling you about
>
>PatMK: @ Ryan007 wifey material fr fr
>
>PipaGrant: @ Ryan007 @ PatMK - get in line

> Ryan007: @ PipaGrant does she even like girls?
>
> PipaGrant: @ Ryan007 idk but i'm going to shoot my shot anyway *wink*

As I'm reading comments, I get a series of texts from Olivia. I let out a tired laugh as I scroll through.

> Livie: DON'T LOOK AT ANY SOCIAL MEDIA TODAY
>
> Livie: I mean it. You're not going to like what you find
>
> Livie: if you need me to tell you what it is, call me and I'll fill you in
>
> Livie: please don't look at anything
>
> Me: too late, but thanks

The phone rings with a call from her, but I send it straight to voicemail and text again.

> Me: at Lyla's watching Theo. I'll call you later

With that, I put my phone away and rub my temple with both hands. I wish I could set all of my accounts to private for a while, but I don't have that luxury. Brands sponsor me, teenagers look up to me, and haters watch me closely to see how I'll react to the latest drama in my life. I refuse to set a bad example for my followers, and I won't crumble under the scrutiny of haters. The only "good" thing about this is that Tate's been on a family trip to Sweden for the last week, and he isn't due to come back until next weekend. While we've had the "official break up conversation"—if you can call screaming at the top of my lungs and hanging up a *conversation*—we haven't seen each other in person since pictures of him making out with another woman were blasted everywhere.

The worst part is that after our breakup, I promised myself I would never, ever get back together with him. And then I did. I didn't even like him *like that* anymore, but I was sad and lonely, and he was ... safe. It took him TWO WEEKS after convincing me to give him a second chance to publicly humiliate me. I sigh deeply and get back to reality, my eyes on the most adorable six-year-old in the world, who's currently drawing a picture.

"Done." He sets his blue crayon down like a gavel and slides the paper over to me.

"This is so nice, Theo. It's your best work yet."

"Mommy's belly looks like a big basketball." He puts his hands over his mouth as if to keep from laughing as he says it.

I smile. "She looks beautiful."

He drops his hand and grins. He wrote his name up top and drew a stick figure picture of his family—him, his mom, his dad, and a baby—and a girl I'm assuming is me, since there's what looks like a basketball by her feet, and she is holding his hand.

"Why's your baby sister in the corner again?" I ask, to see what he'll say this time.

He shrugs, and I bite my lip to keep from laughing. Theo's a momma's boy through and through, and he's having a hard time accepting that he'll have to share her. He's a lot like his father in that sense. The thought makes me laugh.

"Your baby sister should be included, Thee. You're going to be her favorite big brother in the whole world."

He purses his lip. "Yeah, but she's gonna potty *a lot* and I don't want to get pee-pee on me."

"Theo." I admonish lightly with a laugh.

He ignores me and points a finger at another stick figure. "And that's you. You're wearing a basketball jersey."

"I see. That's so sweet." I squeeze his cheek lightly and he smiles, hazel eyes twinkling.

"You're there because you're my girlfriend."

"Well, I'm honored to have made it into the Duke family portrait." I smile, setting the paper down and standing up. "Are you ready for lunch?"

"Yes!" He hops off the chair. "Dad says I can have ice cream."

"For lunch?" I raise an eyebrow and take his little hand as he leads me to the kitchen. "When did he say that?"

"Before he left. You probably didn't hear him since you were talking to Mommy."

"Really?" I squint at him as I let go of his hand and open the fridge. "That's funny since there are two containers here labeled for lunch."

"That was Martha. She didn't know 'bout the ice cream either."

I have to bite my lip to keep from laughing. Theo is very serious about his ice cream. And his lies, apparently. He sets up the step stool by the sink, and I rush to set the containers down and stand beside him, without making it obvious that I'm trying to help since he's "a big boy who knows how to wash his own hands." I wash mine at the same time and try to dry them before he hops off.

"Theo, what did we say about jumping off the stool?"

"That I shouldn't do it," he says with finality in his voice. "But Dad lets me."

I turn my back to hide my eye-roll. I highly doubt his helicopter father lets him do anything of the sort. I've been babysitting Theo since he was one, and family or not, if there weren't former Marines outside guarding the place, I wouldn't be left alone with him. I can't blame his parents for having security. They even stuck security on me for some time after what happened last year.

"Mommy says we might be here for Christmas," Theo says. "Do you think Santa will know we're here?"

"Of course." I smile.

"But how will he know?"

"Because Santa knows everything." I ruffle his hair. "And your parents will tell him."

"But how will they tell him?" He stops twirling and glances up at me with a frown on his face. "Do you talk to Santa?"

"Nope. Only grown-ups can speak to Santa."

He waits until he finishes chewing and asks, "Do you love basketball?"

"I do."

"Why?"

"Because I do."

"But why?"

I take a moment to think about it. What am I supposed to say? *It's what my dad and I bonded over, and as long as I'm dribbling a* basketball, I can trick myself into believing he'll show up to one of my games? Instead of saying all of that, I go with another truth.

"Love is inexplicable."

"Inex ... what?" His brows furrow.

"Inexplicable. It can't be explained." I point my fork at his Toy Story plate. "Keep eating. I don't want to tell your mom you weren't listening to me."

"I *am* listening." He shoves some spaghetti in his mouth, chews, swallows, takes a sip of his water, and looks at me again. "Were you sad when you couldn't play last year because of your boo-boo?"

"Yes," I say, offering him a small smile.

Theo had many questions about my boo-boo, and was very confused when I explained he couldn't see it. He's too young to understand the worst injuries are internal.

"Can we go watch *Cars* now?" He pushes away his plate.

"Only because you did such a good job and finished your food."

I take our plates and stand up, while he wipes his face and hands like his parents taught him. The movie has barely started when Theo snuggles into me and I realize he's sleeping. I lay my head on his and keep my eyes on Radiator Springs.

CHAPTER TEN

Josslyn

MY EYES POP OPEN WHEN THE DOOR ANNOUNCES SOMEONE'S OPENED it, and Theo lifts his head and hops off the couch. I yawn and follow along, reaching them just as Lyla bends down to hug and kiss him, while Lachlan pockets his phone and opens his arms to pick him up. Theo starts quickly filling them in on everything we've done in the few hours they've been gone.

"Sounds like you've had a great time," Lachlan says, kissing his son on the top of his head and setting him down. He glances up at me. "I bet you didn't think your birthday would include hanging out with a five-year-old."

"I didn't, but it's been the best part of my day by far." I grin and look at Theo, who's hopping from one marble tile to another, careful to miss the grout.

"I'm sure you have plans tonight," Lyla says, shooting me a pointed look. "I hope you do, so you can make one of those get-ready-with-me posts."

"I'm sure Lang already called to advise you to go on, business as usual," Lachlan adds, "If he hasn't, that's what he'll say. Besides, there's no bigger 'fuck you' than for Tate to see you're doing better without him."

"I'm always better without him." I shake my head and try not to let my disappointment show. "It's fine. It's not like I was in love with the guy."

Lachlan offers a sympathetic smile and looks at Theo, who's still hopping. "You ready to go to the rink with me and your grandpas?"

"I thought we were going to meet new friends?" he pouts.

"You're also going to meet new friends," Lachlan says. "One of them will be here soon."

My stomach tightens. It could be anyone, but knowing my luck … I push down my nerves. No. The universe wouldn't be so cruel.

"Yes!" Theo says, snapping me out of my thoughts as he pumps his fist in the air. "Are you coming, Mommy?"

"Mommy's tired, buddy. We'll go get ice cream when we're done and bring one back for Mommy," Lachlan says.

Theo shoots me a smug look. "I told you Dad lets me have ice cream for lunch."

Lyla raises an eyebrow. "For lunch? That's news to me."

"Theo, that's not exactly true," Lachlan says.

"It is true. You said Mommy would be mad at you if we told her we had it for lunch."

Lyla glares at her husband, who looks like he wants to crawl into a hole right now. As he should.

"It was one time," Lachlan argues.

"This is the second thing you keep from me. That I *know of*." She shakes her head as she starts walking toward the kitchen.

"She's hangry," Lachlan mouths behind her. "Let's get you cleaned up, Theo."

"I want Mommy to help me."

"Theodore, we talked about this," his dad says in his stern dad voice.

"Apparently, you talk about a lot of things when I'm not

around," Lyla comments as we all walk into the kitchen. "Maybe I'll start keeping secrets with this baby. See how you like it."

She opens the fridge and starts taking things out to make her usual granola bowl, when Lachlan walks over and grabs her by the shoulders to turn her to face him.

"I let him have ice cream for lunch once, and it was the day you had ice cream for lunch because you couldn't stomach anything else," he says.

"It's not about the freaking ice cream, Lachlan." She pulls away from him and shuts the fridge. "The other day it was 'don't tell Mommy you fell at the rink and got a boo-boo.' Today, it's ice cream. Who knows what will be next? I don't like this little 'let's keep secrets from Mommy' BS."

"Jesus Christ." He runs a hand through his hair. "He fell and scraped his knee. I didn't want you to worry for no reason. It's not like we're starting a boys-only club without you or something."

I start busying myself with the dirty dishes and pretend I'm not here. She's usually only this upset with him when she's hangry, but she's 36 weeks pregnant and paused her life for the baby and her husband's hockey team. It's a lot. Luckily, Lachlan always knows how to appease her.

"You're my best friend, Lyla James. I tell you everything," he says quietly, wrapping his arms around her from behind. Whatever he's whispering in her ear works, because when he turns her to kiss her, she looks lighter than she did a second ago.

"Fine, I believe you. Stop crowding me," she says, nudging him, but she's smiling at him.

Lachlan grins and walks back to Theo. "Let's go get ready."

"Why do you always kiss Mommy?" Theo asks as they walk out of the kitchen.

Lachlan chuckles. "Have you seen Mommy? If it were up to me, I'd kiss her all day."

"That's just weird."

We share a laugh as I dry my hands. They're not perfect by any means, but they share a love unlike anything I've ever seen before.

"How are you *really* feeling?" Lyla asks as we walk to the door.

"I'm fine, really. It's not what I wanted to deal with on my birthday, but it is what it is, right?"

"Have you spoken to him?"

"Once." I sigh as we stop at the grand foyer. "Honestly, I think I'm all out of tears. I'm more upset about who he cheated with than the fact that he did it … which is kind of sad. "

"The Gracie girl?"

I purse my lips. "Yep."

Lyla sets a hand on my shoulder. "You deserve better than him. I hope you know that."

"I do. Thanks." I smile a little and set a hand on her stomach, laughing when I feel a little kick. "She's definitely going to be a soccer star like her mom."

Lyla huffs out a laugh. "I just want her to be in my arms already. My back is killing me."

The doorbell rings as I grab my bags and keys.

"Call me if you need anything," I say as I reach the door and unlock it.

"I will," she says. "Have fun tonight."

"I will."

I smile as I pull the door open, but it falls—along with my heart—when I find Finn Barlow standing on the other side.

So it begins.

CHAPTER ELEVEN

Josslyn

BEHIND ME, I HEAR THEO AND LACHLAN'S FOOTSTEPS AND FORCE myself to open the door wider to make way for him to walk in—and hopefully, for me to step out quickly.

"We're just about ready, but come on in, man," Lachlan says.

"I'm waiting for a call, so I'll step…"

"Hi," Theo says loudly when he reaches us, interrupting Finn's response. "Mommy, is he a stranger danger?"

I look at Theo, whose neck is tilted all the way back to look at Finn. They say animals and children are the best judge of characters, and in this case, I have to agree. I don't want Finn anywhere near my Theo. Or Lach and Lyla, for that matter, but obviously it's too late for that. God, I can't even picture them being friends. Even though his expression is soft, he's not even smiling at Theo. You have to be a major asshole to not smile at a child.

"No, he's a friend of Daddy's," Lyla says.

"I'm gonna go." I kiss the top of Theo's head and ruffle his untamed hair. "I'll see you soon, buddy."

"Wait!" Theo grabs my hand and looks at Finn, making me

meet his gaze *again*. God, I'm going to be sick. Theo gives my hand a little squeeze. "This is my girlfriend, Joshlyn."

"Your girlfriend, huh?" Finn makes a slow perusal of my body that makes my heart pound harder in my chest.

It stops when his gaze meets mine again, and my entire body reacts, core clenching, nipples tightening. I guess my body doesn't care that he's a jerk. Not that it matters. Finn means it when he says one-and-done, and even if he didn't, I wouldn't let him touch me again.

"Have you two met?" Lachlan asks, causing me to take a step back.

"We had the *pleasure* of meeting once," Finn says.

My eyes narrow at his response. There's no way anyone with a brain would miss the way he said that. *Asshole.* This time, when I drop Theo's little hand, I say goodbye again quickly to the three of them and head back to the door. Finn's saying something to Lachlan, and he steps outside behind me. Of course, he does.

"What are you even doing here?" I hiss when he catches up to me.

He raises an eyebrow. "Don't tell me you didn't know I was back."

"I don't think anyone can miss your stupid face all over the bus stops," I snap. "I mean *here.*"

When he shoots me a look, I roll my eyes and pick up my pace. I turn the corner, only to see that my car is being blocked by a sleek black sports car that I'd probably stop and admire under different circumstances. How is he even blocking me? This property, and the parking area, are huge. God, he's annoying.

That's on the tip of my tongue as I whip around quickly and nearly crash into him. There are so many things running through my mind, that I don't even know what to address next—his idiotic parking choice or what he said inside. I go with that, since it's what's pissing me off the most.

"Also, the *pleasure* of meeting once? *Really?*" I ask.

"I was trying to spare you from being called a liar in front of your—"

"Family," I snap. "And I am not a liar."

"I beg to differ."

"Whatever. Nothing I say will change your mind, so this is a pointless conversation." I turn around and keep walking to my car. "Move your car."

"Don't I get a 'please,' Josslyn?" he asks, his impossibly deep voice causing a shiver to run through my body.

"Leaving already, Joss?" Patrick, Lachlan's head of security, asks loudly as he's walking by.

I shoot him a shaky smile, grateful for his presence. "I'll be back before you know it. With ice cream," I say with a wink.

He chuckles. Instead of walking away, he idles by until Finn moves his car and I'm able to leave. It isn't until I reach the stop sign at the end of the road that I realize my entire body is shaking. I hate him for calling me a liar, and I really hate that he's right.

"It took Lachlan a year to let me come over, and I'm your best friend." Livie rolls her eyes. "But, of course, Finn gets a free pass."

That amuses me. "Apparently, they're actually friends, not just work friends."

Her lips flatten. "Do they know what happened with his sister?"

"What part?"

"The freaking part where his sister was strangled at a club after we left her there."

My stomach sinks. *We* is too many people. The words are at the tip of my tongue, but I don't voice them. It's something I know she still feels guilty about. I mull over her question. Lyla and Lach were in Chicago when it happened. They may have heard about it in passing, but the Barlows made sure any mention of their daughter was wiped out. Even today's best sleuths can barely find information on the matter. I know because I've tried.

"Yes. I mean, not all the details, but enough."

"Friends or not, I doubt Finn would talk about that with anyone," she says. "And the Barlows tried to wipe everyone's memory of what happened to Mal."

I huff out a watery laugh. "I wish they'd done it to me. Maybe I wouldn't feel so damn guilty all the time."

"You couldn't have known it would happen. What happened was awful, but Mal was hanging out with a lot of weird people at the time," she says, pressing her lips together. "You have to know it's not your fault."

I nod, swallowing to rein in tears. Maybe one day, I'll actually feel that way. Taking a deep breath, I set my hands on the area I have set up for my social media content and focus on the video I'm about to make. If I dwell on that night any longer, I'll throw up and cancel this entire outing. It's stupid. I know if the tables were turned, I'd want Mallory to celebrate her birthday without feeling this way, but I can't help it. I take another deep breath, then turn on my camera with a huge smile on my face. Fake it till you make it, right?

CHAPTER TWELVE

Finn

E VERYONE WEARS A MASK, BUT NONE WEAR IT QUITE AS WELL AS Josslyn Santos. It's a feat, considering how much of her life she posts on social media. The entire world seems to think she's their best friend. As a popular athlete, it's something she's been able to capitalize on. She's not the best college basketball player out there, but she has more NIL deals than anyone *I've* ever heard of. She spends a chunk of her money funding non-profits she started—one builds basketball courts at schools in underprivileged neighborhoods, and the other provides mental health options to those same neighborhoods.

For those accomplishments, she gets a lot of respect, even from me. She was already popular when I met her, but she's the internet's "it girl" at the moment, which comes as no surprise since she's fucking gorgeous. Probably the most beautiful woman I've ever laid eyes on.

Especially when she lets that mask drop, as she did in the newest pictures my PI sent me. She was on a date with some idiot from the Fairview basketball team and she was smiling. A genuine smile that reaches her eyes. I guess that happiness wasn't worth much, since she dropped him the moment Tate Foster came running back. Tate fucking Foster. I couldn't believe it when I discovered who *two-day* was. My only regret was not fucking her at Onyx that night. The only thing I'd done was wait until the masked man looked up to take the blur off the glass window, so he could see her on her knees with my cock in her mouth. Neither of us had a mask on by that point, and I knew the moment he saw us from the way he pushed off the woman who'd been doing the same to him. He had two women between his legs, but I had the only one that mattered on her knees in front of me.

We both knew that, and to further prove my point, I'd grabbed the back of Josslyn's hair, demanded she touch herself, and grinned at the fucker. I'd put the fog back on the window before either of us came, because I didn't want to give anyone the privilege of seeing that, and I never looked back out there. I didn't need to. Funny thing is, I didn't even know it was Tate, and once I found out, it tasted like sweet victory. Just for a moment, because in the end, he had the girl and I only had the memory.

Not that I wanted more from her, though I had to admit it would have been a nice addition to our family feud. Our fathers have been at war for as long as I can remember, which I always thought was beneath me. It wasn't until Tate personally attacked me that I got involved in that bullshit. I let him get in that one blow, but in the end, I had everything—the lifestyle, the hockey contract, and the women. I'd come home twice since that night at Onyx, and had seen them together once. When he spotted me, he made a show of being with her. The only thing that bothered me about it was that he was under the impression that I gave a fuck.

I've had her followed for a while now, so I have pictures from my PI of the moment she found out about his cheating. In the pictures, she looks upset but not distraught, as if expecting something like that from him. Cheating with Gracie, of all people, was quite possibly the worst birthday present Tate could've given her.

I drop my phone and exhale heavily. I don't know how I'm going to get her to cooperate with me, but I need to figure it out before training starts. As it is, I've been inundated with team meetings. My days are numbered, though, and I need her to admit that she lied that night. I need her to tell me what she's been covering up. The bad news is that she's rarely alone and I'm sure her posse will be with her more than ever after the cheating scandal. The good news is that the Fairview Owls picked up her stepbrother in the NHL draft, and he's a new teammate of mine. It helps that the guy idolizes me.

At the sound of the door opening, I sit up straight and pick up my drink from Lucas' desk.

"Holy shit. It is so crowded out there, you'd think they're anticipating Taylor Swift or something." Ella's eyes are wide as she lets out a deep breath.

"Or Drake," Hammie adds, as he walks in behind her.

"Or Bad Bunny," Lucas says, walking in behind him and shutting the door. "I haven't had a chance to look her up, but she must have a lot of fucking followers."

My cousin takes his phone out of his pocket and sits down in one of the chairs across from me. He doesn't even try to kick me out of the chair he sits in every day.

"Fuck, we've already made double what we made last weekend, and it's only been two hours." Lucas' wide eyes meet mine briefly.

"She's a hot commodity," Hammie says.

"She's hot alright," Ella adds.

I sit back and take a sip of my old fashioned, ignoring my annoyance at their words as I set my right ankle over my left knee. It's not like they don't know what I know. I showed them the same footage of Josslyn leaving Onyx with her stepfather in tow. From the way she's flailing her arms in the video, it's clear that they were arguing. At the end of the clip, she leaves, and he goes back inside for another ten minutes before he walks out with a group of guys. For some reason, she comes back and goes inside the club again, right before all hell breaks loose. I have a PI on her stepfather's tail as well. The truth about him will come out sooner or later. For my sake, I hope it's sooner.

"Why did no one tell me Josslyn is hot as fuck?" Lucas asks.

I shoot him a glare. "You're too old for her."

"I'm…" He pauses, sputtering out a laugh. "No, I'm not. My last girlfriend was twenty-one."

"You were too old for that one too."

He scoffs. "I'm not even thirty."

"You will be soon," Hammie says, pouring himself a drink and walking up to the floor-to-ceiling window that gives us the perfect view of the downstairs area.

"You should pay her to come every weekend," Ella suggests as she joins her brother by the window.

"Fuck yeah, I will. I'll pay her for a lot of things," Lucas says, still scrolling through Josslyn's posts.

I bite back the annoyed growl that forms in my chest and stand up to walk over to the windows. There's no way I'd be able to spot Josslyn in the sea of white. Who the hell chose this white-party theme anyway? I'm about to turn around, when, as if I'd summoned her with my thoughts, Josslyn walks inside. A few women who had been waiting by the door spot her and flock to her right away, asking for selfies.

I've been in the public eye for a while now, and I get recognized a fair amount, but never like this. Even Hamilton, who played for the Blaze up until last year, said the attention stopped after a while. I guess once people get used to seeing you in the real world, you lose your luster. Not Josslyn, though. She's as dazzling as ever.

"She definitely can't be wearing anything under that," Hammie muses, causing me to nearly choke on my sip.

"I can't wait to see how her ass looks in it," Ella whispers.

"She's here?" My cousin practically jogs up to us and stands beside me. "Well, fuck. I think I'm in heaven."

Can they be any more annoying? I make myself focus on

breathing as I track her. She walks through the crowd, surrounded by friends who hold their arms up to part the path for her like she's the fucking Pope. When they finally reach the bar, I try to get a better look at her, but it's impossible with Damian hovering over her. If I didn't know any better, I'd think her stepbrother has a hard-on for her, but I know that's not the case. Everyone around her treats her like she's made of glass.

"Fletchie needs to get out of the way," Hammie says.

"You guys have the weirdest fucking nicknames." Lucas mutters. "When I played football, we went by last names, and we sure as fuck didn't shorten them to shit like 'Hammie' and 'Fletchie.' What the fuck are you, five?"

Hammie shoots him a glare but goes right back to looking downstairs.

"Thank god this glass is tinted," Ella says.

Damian finally moves out of the way, and my breath catches as I get a view of that god-forsaken dress. A bright light flashes over her and for a split second I see the way her flawless golden brown skin stands out against the white scraps of fabric she's wearing. Her entire back is exposed, and Ella was right about her ass. I'm instantly reminded of how it feels in my hands, under my palm, between my teeth. I bite my tongue and force myself to look at the rest of the crowd. There must be someone else I can focus on.

"Jesus," Ella says. "I tried on that exact same dress at Cult Gaia in New York last week, and it did not look like *that* on me."

"Maybe you should do more squats." I look at Josslyn's biteable ass again.

"True." Ella snorts out a laugh. "Did you hear she's single now? That idiot cheated on her."

"Who was she dating?" Lucas asks.

"Tate Foster."

My cousin sucks his teeth. "Damn." He glances at me. "Did you know that?"

I don't say anything, because it's irrelevant. I don't care

about her love life. I just need her to tell me what happened at Onyx the night she went with my sister, and I want to fuck her so I can quench this annoying thirst I get whenever I see her. That's it. Ella answers for me anyway and tells him I knew. While they discuss all things Josslyn, I walk back to the bar and scan the bottles I've looked at five times since arriving here. I'm normally not much of a drinker, but being around Josslyn, even if she doesn't know I'm here, has me on edge.

"Finn, did you hear me?" Ella asks as they walk over to me. "She's single now."

"I heard. I just don't understand why the fuck you think I'd care." I stare at the amber liquid I'm pouring.

"Because sparks flew when you met."

"Sparks flew." I scoff as I set the bottle down and cap it.

She's talking about the night we were here. I never told a soul about our night in Onyx. I'm not a kiss-and-tell man, but even if I was, that night was different. It left me wanting more. Probably because I didn't get to fuck her in the traditional sense. At least, that's what I tell myself when I'm in the shower, with my dick in my hand as I recall her moans, her face, and the taste of her pussy. Fuck. I push those thoughts away quickly.

"You laughed with her. Finn Alexander Barlow laughed at something. *In public.*"

"Yeah, right," Lucas scoffs. "I'd pay to see that."

I lift my middle finger off the glass. "I laugh. It's not my fault none of you are funny."

"I heard *you* approached *her*," Hammie says, ignoring what I said.

My eyes flash to his. "Do people have nothing better to talk about?"

"In Fairview?" He lifts an eyebrow. "In our inner circle? No."

"Whatever." I look away. "She's not even my type."

"No one is your type," Ella says. "Or maybe I am, and that's why you take me as your date to all your public events."

"Please. If you were my type, I would've fucked you by now."

I take a sip of bourbon. "I take you because you like going, and I don't want to give the women I fuck the wrong impression."

Ella laughs. "Remember when we tried to hook up?"

"Can you not?" Her brother groans.

"Wasn't that hookup what convinced you that you were a full-fledged lesbian?" Lucas asks.

That makes me bite back a laugh. Fucking assholes.

CHAPTER THIRTEEN

Josslyn

AFTER THE FOURTH CELEBRATORY SHOT MY TEAMMATES MAKE ME consume, I decide to take a break. Thankfully, I'm buzzed but not enough that I can't walk straight, and I don't have to go far to get to the bathroom. I'm almost there when I see a familiar face that makes my heart drop into the pit of my stomach. He looks like someone I'd save on a Pinterest board, wearing a white button-down with the sleeves rolled up and the two top buttons undone. His hair looks like he's already run his fingers through it a million times, and even though I can't see his eyes well in this lighting, I feel them piercing right through me.

One of the people sitting with him—a really attractive guy I've never seen before—waves me over, and I comply. Ella Hamilton, who's sitting right next to Finn, smiles wide as I approach. I've never formally met her, but I've seen her in endless pictures with Finn. Seeing her sitting close to him now makes a stupid, uncomfortable feeling settle in the pit of my stomach. Ella and the man who waved me over stand up as I reach them.

"Hi, happy birthday! We've never met, but I love your content.

I'm Ella Hamilton, and that dress looks incredible on you," Ella says, smiling as she sets her hand out for me to shake.

"Thanks so much." My smile is genuine as I shake her hand. "I see the resemblance between you and Will," I say and turn to the man next to her, who's even more handsome up close.

"Lucas Barlow. I own this place," he says, as we shake hands. Barlow. My eyes fly to Finn, and the man holding my hand chuckles. "We're cousins, but I'm much less of an asshole."

At that, I laugh, my eyes flicking back to Finn, whose glare is set on the hand his cousin is still holding. I try to pull away, but he holds it. There's a spark in his light brown eyes when his gaze flicks briefly to Finn that tells me he's doing this on purpose. The idea that it's to piss off his cousin excites me, so of course, I go along with it.

"Thanks for having me," I say. "I always have a good time here."

"You're welcome here anytime you want, and you're not allowed to pay for anything. I'm putting you on my personal list."

"Oh, wow. Thank you so much. I feel so special." I smile.

"As you should." He lifts my hand to his mouth, eyes full of mischief when he kisses it and says, "Let me know if I can assist you with *anything*. And I do mean anything."

I don't hear the glass slam on the table, but I see it and practically jump away from Lucas, taking my hand back quickly as our heads whip to Finn, who's scowling at us. Lucas smirks, and my heart skips a beat at the mere idea that Finn is actually reacting to this. That he might be … jealous? It's impossible, I know. The man either has no feelings or masks them well, but the idea of it still thrills me. I open my mouth to greet him, but he sits back and whips his phone out. So much for the idea that he was jealous a second ago.

I smile at the two people with him and say goodbye, thanking them as they wish me a happy birthday. I walk away, silently fuming. Thankfully, the bathrooms here are huge, each with its own sink, so it'll give me time to compose myself and think about something other than strangling Finn before I go back out there. I find an empty stall and practically slam the door shut.

If it weren't for the way my entire body heats up when he looks at me with that intense gaze, I would think the night at Onyx had been a fever dream. I read once that attraction is like a drug. The levels of dopamine are so heightened that it makes you feel high. Seeing Finn doesn't make me feel high. It makes me feel like what I imagine an addict feels when they're coming down and crashing. After a few moments to myself, I take a deep breath and head to the sink. I don't even need the bathroom, I'm just here to wash the salt off my hands from the last tequila shot I did.

After washing my hands and using the wet wipes to freshen up, I hold onto the edge of the counter and look at myself in the mirror, focusing on my calming breathing exercise. It's something I've learned to do when I feel my anxiety climbing. Unlike what I portray to the world, I'm not *always* down for a party. For the most part, I love being around people for a few hours at a time, but by the end of the night, I always feel depleted. I don't get hangovers from alcohol; I get emotional hangovers, which are much worse. The following day, I'm practically glued to my bed, so I've learned to alternate between water and drinks. I take one last deep breath and smile at my reflection.

When I open the door, I freeze in my tracks at the sight of Finn, who's leaning against the wall across from the stalls, staring at me like I stole his lunch money.

CHAPTER FOURTEEN

Josslyn

"What do you want?"

He straightens suddenly, and my heart thunders when he takes a step forward. He stops when he's at the halfway point between me and the exit.

"What if I told you I have proof that you lied to everyone, including the police?"

The last shot I took climbs to my throat. I clear it and manage to respond, "I'd say you're the liar."

"I don't lie." Another step toward me.

"What do you want me to do, Finn?" I ask.

Someone walks into the bathroom and we both look in their direction. The man glances over at us and walks into the first stall he sees. When Finn and I lock eyes again, it takes me a moment to remember what he just accused me of. The last time he cornered me like this, I remained silent and let him verbally attack me.

He was confused, pissed off, and grieving, and I knew from experience that he wanted—*needed*—someone to yell at. It's in our nature to look for someone to blame when we're hurting. Especially when inexplicable things happen. I'll never forget the fierceness in his eyes or the way he seethed, "So strange that you were there that night and nothing happened to you," as if I should've done something. I won't let him berate me again.

"What do you want me to do?" I repeat. "I can't go back and undo what happened. I wish I could. Trust me, I do, but I can't. I'm sorry, okay? I'm so fucking sorry about that night…" My words catch, and I pause to swallow the ball of emotion in my throat that seems to keep growing. "You can hate me all you want, but it won't change what happened."

He doesn't take his eyes off mine as he strides toward me. My brain wills me to move, but my feet won't cooperate. His eyes are dark and inscrutable as he reaches me, and when he sets a hand on my hip, all of my wires cross. My body obeys when he walks me backward into the stall I just came out of. With his free hand, he reaches back to shut and lock the door.

Despite my muddled thoughts, my lips finally part to question him, but when my back hits the wall next to the sink, and he leans his face down to mine, the only thing I can do is gasp. I shut my eyes and brace myself for the kiss. My pulse spikes when his hold on my hip tightens, and I feel his breath against my lips. When he doesn't do anything, my eyes fly open.

"I don't hate you, Josslyn. I hate that despite everything, when I think about you, I only remember the way your pussy clenched around my fingers and the sounds you make when you come."

He brings a hand up and cuffs it around my neck, moving the other slowly from my hip down to my thigh. He grips me there and squeezes my throat as he leans in. The combination of his touch and his light beard prickling my cheek sends a sharp shiver through my entire body. He nips my earlobe, eliciting a soft moan from me, and my body arches, pressing his thick length hard against my stomach. He hisses at the movement, grip tightening. With the fury I see in his eyes, I should probably be afraid he's going to strangle me to death. Tit for tat and all. Somehow I know he won't, and honestly, I'm not sure I care if he does.

"I hate that I can't remember what you taste like, but I know having your pussy against my mouth is the closest to heaven I'll ever get." His grip loosens and I gasp in a breath. "I hate that I want to do it again." His grip tightens again. "Do you ever think about that night?" He pulls back slightly, searching my eyes. The smug expression on his face tells me he clearly knows the answer. "Do you get wet thinking about the way you choked on my cock?" He squeezes my throat and lets go again. "Answer me."

"Yes," I whisper.

A ghost of a smirk tugs his lips. "Did you ever shut your eyes and pretend it was me you were fucking instead of your boring boyfriend?"

My eyes squeeze shut, my breath coming out in soft pants now. I hate how much I crave it. When he squeezes my throat and lets go again, my eyes fly open and I glare. "Yes."

His dark chuckle vibrates through me. "I bet you're soaked right now."

"Finn," I plead shakily. "Please."

"Sweet, perfect little Josslyn. Do you even know what you're begging for?" His grip loosens, and I realize he's right.

I don't know what I want. It's definitely not for him to let me go. I want him to do … something. Anything. That's always been my problem in the bedroom. I don't really know what I like, and men … well, men are naturally selfish beings. They usually don't ask. Finn didn't ask either, though, and everything he did to me was utter perfection. I realize he's waiting for an answer from me, but I don't know what to say. I just want him to do something to alleviate the throbbing between my legs.

"Please."

"You're going to have to be specific." His grip tightens again when he brings his mouth a breath from mine. "Do you want me to walk away?"

I shake my head as much as his hand will let me.

"Do you want me to finger your pretty pussy right here?" he rasps, as I bite my lip to hold back a moan. "Do you want me to taste it?"

"Yes," I pant, back bowing at his teasing words. He pulls back, raising an eyebrow. "Yes to any of it. *All* of it. Please!"

His eyes darken, and he makes a satisfied hum in the back of his throat. He moves his hand from my hip to the bottom of my dress and slips it underneath, inhaling sharply when he finds me bare. He pinches the hood of my clit and my entire body shudders.

"Fuck, birthday girl. I knew you were naked under this, but I didn't expect you to be soaked." His fingers leisurely move between my folds. When he flicks my clit, I gasp loudly, bringing my hands up to grip his bicep. "Were you like this before I walked in here or is this for me?"

"For you," I breathe, hating myself for admitting it, for being this wanton.

"I should drag you downstairs right now." He bites his lip for a moment, sliding a finger between my folds.

"Oh, fuck." I grind against him, and he makes that satisfied sound again, dropping the hand around my throat to replace it with his mouth.

"I should fuck you in front of all your stupid friends, so they can watch the girl they treat like glass shatter around my cock." He flicks my clit again, sucking and licking the dip between my clavicles when I moan and throw my head back. "You'd like that, wouldn't you?"

I bite my lip, trying and failing to keep another moan from escaping. I've never been to the speakeasy sex club here, nor have I heard anything about it. It's that secretive. I've definitely never been interested in having an audience watch me have sex, but I can't deny that his words turn me on even more. Suddenly, his hands leave me and he takes a step back.

I set a hand on my chest as I try to catch my breath so I can plead with him not to leave me like this. It's embarrassing, but right now I don't care. He drinks me in slowly, biting his lip like he's savoring the sight of me like this. His throat moves as he visibly swallows, and that alone makes my core clench.

"Hike your dress up to your waist."

My pulse spikes again. I look down and do as he says, slowly, careful not to rip any of the delicate strings it's made of.

"Fuck," he says quietly. "Set your foot on the counter."

"I…" I hesitate as alarm bells go off in my head.

Suddenly, I'm very aware of where I am. I've been gone for a while now. Soon enough, someone will start looking.

Finn's eyes darken. "Set your foot on the fucking counter."

I don't know what it is about his commands that make me—the person who would rather die before I let a man control me—instantly comply. I grab onto the counter and lift my foot carefully. I'm so thankful I wore these block heels, and that I used those wipes earlier. He lets out a huffed laugh, shaking his head as he takes in the sight of me and walks back over.

"You should be illegal in every fucking continent." He steps between my open legs and pushes me against the wall, gripping my thigh and waist. My hands fly to his shoulders as his eyes meet mine. "Relax, I won't let you fall."

I don't trust this man for a second, but right now, falling is the last thing on my mind. If I fall, I fucking fall. My eyes screw shut when he leans in and kisses the side of my neck, his lips moving slowly down my body, gently, slowly, like we have all night to do this.

When he reaches my breast, he bites my nipple lightly over the fabric and lets out a breath that makes me shiver. "Another time."

Another time? I'm not going to ruin this by reminding him of his own rule. As it is, this is our second time. Or does he not count it unless we're actually fucking? His lips on my inner thigh drown all of my thoughts. My grip tightens as he moves lower. When he crouches in front of me, I'm forced to let go. He nips my inner thigh and presses a wet kiss over each spot. He repeats this until he's directly in front of my pussy. I sink my fingers into his hair and throw my head back when he licks me. He groans against me, the sound vibrating through me as he licks and sucks my clit.

"Oh, fuck," I whisper-shout, legs shaking slightly when he does it again.

"Josslyn?"

We both freeze at the sound of Damian's voice. My head lifts from the wall and Finn rocks back. I take my hands off his hair and try to straighten as he stands, but he grips my hip and thigh, keeping me splayed open for him.

"Get rid of him."

"How?" My eyes widen. "I can't."

Finn's eyes narrow as he steps between my legs and grinds against me, the friction making me bite my lip. I fight to not throw my head back again. What I wouldn't do for him to just fuck me already. When Dame says my name again, I grip Finn's arm in warning, but he grinds again.

"Get fucking rid of him," he whispers harshly, bringing one hand between my legs. "Unless you want him to hear you screaming my name."

"Joss?"

I clear my throat, heart pounding harder now. "Yeah. I'm in here."

"Are you okay?"

I open my mouth to respond, but I shut it and bite my lip hard when Finn crouches between my legs again. He licks me, then flattens his tongue against my clit, keeping it that way as he grabs my hips and moves me against it. I grip two fistfuls of his hair as he does this, my stomach clenching with the friction.

"Josslyn, what the fuck? What's taking so long? Are you taking a shit?"

"What?" I squeak. "No! I'll be right there."

"I'll wait for you."

Finn's eyes spark with amusement as he glances up and starts swirling his tongue over my clit, through my folds, and into my hole. My head hits the wall behind me with a thud as my legs wobble. He's trying to make me scream. He really doesn't give a fuck.

"No. Don't wait," I shout. "I'm okay, really. I'll be right there."

"Tate is here."

Finn stills, pulling back as I let go of his hair with shaky hands. "What do you mean he's here?"

"He flew back early," he says, and I hear him, or someone, peeing in a stall nearby. After the toilet flushes, Dame continues. "He's trying to get into the VIP area. I guess you posted a video and he saw it."

Great. I knew my live posts would come back to bite me in the ass one day. I open my mouth to say something, but Finn's mouth is on me again. A powerful shudder flows through me and makes me forget my words. He moves one of his hands to join his tongue, pushing two fingers inside me and curling them in a way that makes my eyes roll back and my breath shudder.

"Oh, fuck, right there," I whisper, unable to hold back. I grip his hair again. "Get him to leave. I'll be right there," I shout, bucking against Finn's mouth.

"All right. Text me if you need anything," Dame responds.

He's not an idiot, he knows I'm not alone. I know he's waiting for a sign that I'm in distress. When I don't give him one, he finally walks away and leaves.

I inhale sharply and tug Finn's hair hard, earning a deep groan from him that really shouldn't turn me on even more. "Finn. What the hell!?"

He pulls away with a raised eyebrow. "You want me to stop?"

"No," I growl, annoyed at myself and this entire situation, but he lets go of me and stands up. "Seriously?" I squeak, lowering my leg to stand up straight against the wall. This time, he lets me.

Finn pulls out his phone, which pisses me off even more. I'm two seconds from making myself come, but for some inexplicable reason, I wait. He types furiously. When he puts his phone away, his hungry eyes rake over me.

"I didn't tell you to lower your leg."

"I … you…" I take a shaky breath. "You were on your phone!"

"And?" He closes the distance between us again and presses his lips to the sensitive spot underneath my ear, where my pulse is undoubtedly out of control. "You didn't think I was done, did you?"

He gives himself enough space to grip my ass and lift me onto the counter, making an appreciative sound when my legs spread open automatically.

"Good girl." He spreads my folds with his calloused fingers and licks his lips. His eyes flick to mine briefly. "Now, don't fucking move."

He dives right back in between my legs and devours me like his life depends on it.

CHAPTER FIFTEEN

Finn

I've had Josslyn's phone number for a while, but I hadn't put it to good use until this morning when I sent her the footage I have of that night at Onyx. It's confusing and brings more questions than answers, but it's enough. I don't like that I'm still waiting for her to respond two hours later. It's ten in the morning, though, and with the night she had, I wouldn't be surprised if she doesn't see the text till noon. The image of her legs spread in the stall last night makes me palm my now hard dick over my boxer briefs. I've already jacked off twice to the memory, which is as many times as I made her come before we went back to the party separately.

By then, security had already escorted her ex out of the lounge, and I wasn't planning on sticking around much longer, but then she entranced me with her dancing. The way her tits bounced and hips swayed made me wish I could drag her downstairs and make good on my suggestion. Every movement, every smile, every laugh all put me in a mood. The way she lives inside my brain puts me in a mood.

I've never gone down on a woman twice and gone out of

my way to make sure we saw each other again. On the contrary, my M.O. is to fuck people I know I'll never see again. Yet there I was, watching her take pictures with people and fend off guys who seemed to have a fucking death wish with the way they were touching her. Every time a new one approached her, she glanced over at me. Whatever she saw on my face made her smile, which is ludicrous considering I'd crafted and honed my blank expression. Nevertheless, she'd take one look at me and shut down their advances.

When did I start caring about such trivial things? I don't know. She confounds me. She always has, which is why I fucking knew from the day I saw her that I shouldn't have touched her. I also knew it would be impossible to deny myself that. When Lucas offered his "services" to her last night, the need to claim her consumed me. I should've fucked her and put an end to this madness. Instead, I took my time eating her pussy. God, this is madness. I rub my hands hard over my face and snap back to the present.

I need to fuck her soon and find someone else to fuck right after. I don't normally do that. People paint me out to be a notorious playboy who fucks every chance I get, and maybe when I was younger, I was deserving of that title. Nowadays, I go weeks, sometimes months, without sex. After Josslyn, I know I'll need a quick palate cleanser to get my shit together.

I look at my phone when it buzzes, and a meaningless text from one of the detectives working on the case pops up. Every so often, he likes to remind me that it's still an ongoing case, but the police aren't doing shit. They're convinced it was a tragic accident, and my parents are happy to accept that. I'm not. There isn't much in my life that can make me feel guilty, but what happened to Mallory has haunted me.

In her journal, she mentions "T" a few times, and even though there are endless people with a name that start with that letter, Titus is the one that stands out the most. Mallory spent a lot of time at Josslyn's house and practically wrote in code about each time she went. She also spoke very highly of Titus a few times, which wasn't the norm for her. That can't be a coincidence. My phone buzzes as I walk through the practice facility where I'm meeting Hamilton for a workout, and I come to a full stop when I see Josslyn's name on the screen.

> **Josslyn: How'd you get my number?**
>
> **Josslyn: NM. how do you have this video?**
>
> **Me: not your concern. It's evidence that you're a liar**

I watch the bubble of her text disappear a few times before my phone vibrates with a call from her.

I hit the green button. "I'm surprised you're awake."

"What do you want?" she asks, her voice raspy and sexy as fuck.

"I want the truth."

"Oh my God." She lets out a deep frustrated groan that makes my dick hard. "I didn't lie. I know how this looks, but I didn't freaking lie."

"I think you're lying right now to cover up for your stepfather."

"Oh my…" She pauses, then laughs. "You think Titus had something to do with this? *Are you insane?*"

"I have proof."

"Yeah, right." She snorts. "Proof of what, exactly?"

"Proof that he had a motive."

She's quiet for a moment. "Look, I don't know what you think you have, but I'm telling you that he had nothing to do with this."

"Why was he there?"

"I can't say."

My jaw clenches. "How convenient."

"It's not like that. *He's* not like that," she says, clearing her throat though her voice remains hoarse. "He wouldn't do that to my mom, and if he did, he would never sleep with a girl my age, let alone my friend."

I feel my face pull in confusion. I want to yell, "HE WAS AT A SEX CLUB!" but I reel myself in. "Yet I have proof."

"You're wrong."

I pause. "This can go one of two ways. You can help me, or I can speak to every judge and attorney in town and stain your stepfather's reputation."

"His reputation precedes him. No one would believe you."

I roll my eyes. "I think you forget who you're talking to."

She's silent for a very long time before saying, "Unbelievable," and then screaming, "UNFUCKINGBELIEVABLE!"

I bite the inside of my mouth to keep from speaking. Perfect little Josslyn Santos sounds hot as fuck when she loses her temper. When I say nothing, she continues talking like I knew she would.

"No wonder Mal looked for a family elsewhere," she says calmly. "The one she had was clearly a piece of shit."

Her words hit me in the chest. My mother was right. Mal deserved much better than the life she was thrown into. When they adopted her, they provided her with an abundance of luxuries that, unlike me, she hadn't been born into. I always figured the exposure to different people that hockey gave me was the reason I was conscious about the things we were afforded, but maybe it was Mallory. Maybe it was the innocent way she used to balk every time she walked into opulent rooms. In my parents' minds, they were doing her a favor by bringing her into this life.

It makes me think of the time a puck bunny I met told me that since all men were trash, she'd rather be a doormat trophy wife to a wealthy man than an equal partner to another. *"If I'm going to cry anyway, I'd rather wipe my tears with money than rags."*

For so long I thought Mallory was a little brat for demanding so much from our parents. She couldn't just accept their lavish gifts. She wanted their attention, and worse, affection. It's just not the Barlow way. Not unless you're Lucas and Asher, who won the mom lottery. At some point, Mal must have realized that, because even though she must have felt unworthy of it, she started leaning into the Barlow name and lifestyle. Everything became a competition.

That's something that's never sat well with me about her friendship with Josslyn. My sister was riddled with jealousy. She'd always found it difficult to make friends with other girls, and rarely had kind things to say about them. She wouldn't have written all of those wonderful things about Josslyn. She certainly wouldn't have spent that much time with her family if there wasn't more to it. Unless Titus was seducing her, or vice versa. It wouldn't matter if it was the latter. Between their age difference, her daddy issues, and her need for affection, she would have been easy prey for someone like Titus. I inhale, exhale, and decide to switch my tactic.

"Does your mother know where he was that night?" I ask, taking her silence as confirmation. "I can only imagine all the places her imagination would go seeing her perfect little daughter leaving a sex club with her stepfather."

"Oh my … Jesus Christ, Finneas!" she growls, and fuck me, I want to hear her say that again.

And again. And again.

A vision of me flipping her over and spanking her ass and her pussy until she comes, screaming those words, plays out at the forefront of my mind. I take a breath and shift my legs to fix my now rock-hard cock.

"Does Damian know you were both there?"

Another pregnant pause. When she speaks again, she sounds a little defeated. "What do you want from me? Just tell me what you want, and I'll do it."

Well, there's a loaded question if I've ever heard one. "I want you to help me prove Titus did this."

"But he didn't," her voice shakes, and I think she might be crying.

"You know that for sure? You'd be willing to stand in court and swear on a bible?" I open my mouth to continue, but Hamilton turns the corner with his equipment bag over his shoulder. "Think on that."

I don't wait for her to respond. I hang up and look at my screen, clicking the text message she just sent.

> **Josslyn:** FYI I DON'T BELIEVE IN THE BIBLE AND NEITHER DO MOST PEOPLE WHO STAND UP THERE AND PUT THEIR HAND ON IT SO WHY DON'T YOU THINK ON THAT?!
>
> **Josslyn:** AND FUCK YOU
>
> **Josslyn:** FUCK. YOU!!!!

I put my phone in my pocket just as Hammie reaches me.

"Are you ... are you smiling?" He frowns deeply, his blue eyes searching my face.

I'm not smiling. Am I? If this is the kind of shit that makes me smile, maybe I am an asshole. I turn and walk toward the dressing room. He follows me with a laugh.

"Tell me you didn't ask Josslyn for her number last night."

"I didn't." I shoot him a look that warns him not to start that topic with me.

He shrugs and plops down on the bench to change his shoes, while I head to where my jersey is hung up next to my brand-new gear.

"Are you coming to the pool party?"

"No."

"You're such a bore. It's fucking summer. We don't even have to be here right now."

I look over my shoulder. "That's the kind of mentality that's going to fuck us up on the ice."

"It's summer. Half the team is in Europe right now," he says, which is true. Only a handful of us are in town, and they're mostly here settling their families down before they leave on their vacations. "I think Joss will be at the party."

My heart, that little bitch, skips, but I ignore it. "So?"

"I'm just saying. Josslyn in a bikini." He puts his fingers together and kisses them like he's an Italian chef or something.

"You think I'm going to go just to see her in a bikini?" I shoot him a blank look and smother the urge to kick the bench he's sitting on. I turn back around and admire how dope the jersey looks.

"I heard Tate is going."

I whip around to face him. "Why would he even be invited?"

"Ah, so you *are* interested." He raises his brows and stands up, grinning. "Dame says he's only doing it to try to win Josslyn back."

I scoff. "He really is a dumb fuck if he thinks that'll ever happen."

For the fourth time since I got home, I click the video of the lobby at Onyx that night. My sister looks nervous as she speaks to the hostess, which is unlike her. Behind her, Olivia and Josslyn are smiling as they talk. Seeing her there shoots a wave of possession through me that makes me wish I could jump through the screen and drag her out.

For bullshit reasons, the owner, who's an acquaintance of my cousin's, didn't want to give us the footage from inside the club. It took some convincing, but he finally turned over this video saying it was, "The only footage that survived the fire." I highly doubt it, but I'll take it. I hit play and watch as my sister hands over two masks. It was an all-black mandatory mask night, which means everyone was wearing the same fucking mask. I keep my eyes on the three of them as they step inside, when suddenly my sister says something and keeps walking down the hall, while they stay behind.

Olivia and Josslyn walk to the main bar—a safe space where sex is off-limits. There, people can drink, flirt, and give and receive invites to hook up without getting too forceful. The girls take a seat by the bar, and my eyes move to the frame my sister is in. She walks down the hall until she reaches one of the private rooms, which she disappears into. I keep my attention there for a moment, and when nothing happens, I look at the bar again. Two men have now joined the girls, and I watch as Olivia smiles at one of them. The other man is leaning against the bar as he speaks to Josslyn.

I look back up at the hallway my sister was in and still see nothing. When I glance back at the bar again, Olivia is walking out with the man she was just speaking to. The sight of the other man taking the seat Olivia vacated makes my blood boil. As he goes to the bar to get drinks, a blonde woman wearing a bunny outfit walks up to Josslyn.

From the way they're talking, I can't tell if the woman is hitting on her or if they know each other. I take my eyes off them and scan the camera that points to the hall, where I see Olivia and that guy leaving the club. I look back at the door my sister entered and shortly after, see a man in a black suit walking in. I replay and watch him walk around the corner and go into the room.

I rewind it again. And again. And again. He has a very similar build to Titus. Very similar. Too similar. He's wearing a mask, though, so I already know this won't count for anything. I replay it one more time, then let it play out. A few minutes after he goes in there, the feed goes dark, along with the rest of the cameras. *What the fuck?*

I play it again, and finally, go to my next email, which has the latest pictures my PI sent me. In one of them, Titus is walking out of his downtown office with a man and woman who look a little older than him. The note from my PI says, "Two days ago. Old friends of his. They own a construction company." I don't open the rest of them because I've learned that my PI notes ones I might take interest in, and this wasn't one.

The next picture is Josslyn running at the park wearing a neon green sports bra and tiny matching biker shorts. The note from the PI reads, "This morning. Ran at the park and played a pickup basketball game." This time, I click to see the rest of the pictures. I'm shocked she was there this morning. Was it before or after I spoke to her? She's the only woman on the court, and some of the guys are well over a foot taller than her.

I can't imagine why she thought it would be a good idea to join them. In some of them, she's shooting the ball. In others, she's crossing it over and getting past the tall guy covering her. In one, he blocks it easily and grins at her as she sticks her tongue out at him. In the next, she falls and visibly scrapes her knee. In the one that follows, the same guy is leaning down and inspecting her knee. That's where the pictures end. Who is he? What happened next? Did he take her somewhere?

A strange feeling comes over me as I keep scrolling. It's clear that they know each other. That, or they hit it off at the park this morning. For some reason, I can't stand the thought. After the tenth one, I stop looking and log onto the first social media icon I find. My heart leaps to my throat when I see a pre-recorded video of Josslyn wearing a black bikini. A *tiny* black bikini. Miniscule. She's talking about the pool party she probably won't go to, but asks them to vote for the outfit she should wear if she decides to go. My fingers itch to type "NOT A BIKINI," but I don't.

She doesn't need to know I've watched every single one of her videos, or that whenever this question comes up, I have to fight the urge to demand she not wear certain outfits. I'm all for women showing off their bodies, but for some strange fucking reason, that doesn't apply to her. She tries on the one-piece and walks back to the camera, looking sexy as fuck in it as well. I tilt my head back and blow out a long, deep breath.

My phone buzzes and I see a text from Damian pop up that nearly makes me drop my phone. Maybe divine timing doesn't suck after all. Damian became friends with Hamilton when they were both playing for the Blaze. They're close enough that Hamilton took him along when he'd visit me sometimes. I wouldn't call Damian and I friends, per se, but I know enough about him and the kind of man he is to cross him off my list of suspects.

Damian Fletcher: my parents are having a bbq on Thurs. Ham is coming. Open invite

From what I can tell, Josslyn and Damian are "WWJD" poster children, with the way they accept and include everyone into their home. I guess they haven't learned that not closing doors is a sure way to let in snakes. Someone should probably warn them about that. *After* they let my Trojan Horse in, of course.

Me: I'll be there

I open the pictures I took of my sister's journal and flip through some pages, picking a random one to land on.

"There's a spot in their yard that the cameras can't get to. It's become our secret cove when I "go to the bathroom." I should stop, but it feels so good.

Part of me doesn't want to believe my sister would do this, but I grew up around men who groomed their now wives. Men who hide behind their distinguished titles. Men like Titus.

CHAPTER SIXTEEN

Josslyn

Fuck Finn for making me relive every memory I have of Mallory. As if it didn't hurt enough to experience it all in real time. As if I hadn't already gone through the shock, sadness, anger, pain, and guilt of the loss a million times. Looking back on all of it now, I'm not sure how to feel. So many things stand out that I hadn't thought about or noticed before.

Despite everything—the pain seeing Mallory caused me those last few months, the awful things she'd said, the hopelessness in her eyes, and the utter pain I felt when they told me what happened at that club—I don't regret being her friend. The one thing I can console myself with is that I was a great friend to her and tried to make her days brighter.

"Did you tell Damian about this?" Livie whisper-shouts after I show her the footage Finn sent me.

My eyes widen. "God, no."

"You're not going to tell him?!"

"It looks bad, Liv." I look at my phone even though the screen is blank. "Finn can paint any picture he wants with this and call it evidence."

"Damn," she whispers, brows creasing with concern. "Did you tell Finn his sister wasn't in her right mind?"

I bite my lip hard and shake my head.

"Really, Joss?" She sighs heavily.

We both glance away when two guys who just arrived through the back doors walk up to the bar. The mixologist is busy making drinks for a few others, so Livie excuses herself and walks over there. There's always an influx of customers at Olivia's parents' bar in the summer. What started out as a place for Mr. Nassir to hang out with friends has turned into an exclusive bar for people to grab quick drinks and get back on their yachts.

"Are you at least going to tell Dame that you're with Finn?" Livie asks as she walks over to grab two bottles of liquor.

"I'm not with him."

She rolls her eyes. "Hooking up with him."

"I'm not doing that either."

"You hooked up twice. It might happen a third time." Livie raises an eyebrow and moves out of the mixologist's way, as he reaches underneath the counter for something. She shoots him an apologetic glance and clicks on the screen until she finds the recipe for whatever she's making.

"I can't keep letting things happen between us." I press the heels of my hands to my forehead even though the only headache I have is Finn. "He thinks I know something."

"But you don't." She frowns. "And Mallory was..." She shakes her head as she walks away.

At least the look of disgust she used to say those words with is gone and replaced with sadness. Olivia may have been the one who officially introduced me to Mallory, but they hadn't been on speaking terms for nearly a year before that night. There was a lot of animosity there on both sides, and Livie only went that night as a favor to me. The sick feeling that accompanies me whenever I allow myself to think about that night settles in my bones again. Finn can call me a liar all he wants, but I don't remember a thing about that night.

I remember going, of course. I remember Mal and Livie acting cordial. I remember Mal's annoyed face when Livie held onto my arm as we walked toward Onyx, and I remember Livie leaning over and whispering in my ear. It was the same thing she'd been whispering for years. *"Mal is jealous of anyone who gets near you,"* she'd said. *"She hates that we're best friends."*

I remember the words Mal said to me as she walked away—and out of my life forever—that night. "Enjoy your time with your *best* friend." It was catty and harsh, and not the first time she'd said things like that, but it was when I realized she hadn't been joking. My only true memory is waking up on my couch to the sound of pounding on my door and seeing Titus and two uniformed police officers standing on the other side. It was almost unbearable to hear that there had been a fire at the club and that Mallory had been stuck there. She'd been so badly burned that they had to use her teeth to identify her.

That night changed a lot of things, including my friendship with Livie, and that hurts worst of all. I've since forgiven her, but things just aren't the same between us. She was supposed to stay with me. She knew I was only there to ensure Mal got home without endangering herself or anyone else on the road, the way she'd been doing for weeks.

After Liv left, I'd been drugged. There was no doubt in my mind about it. That, or I'd become a master of memory repression.

"Tiago's here!" Livie says, making me jolt. As she smiles and waves, she glances at me with an apologetic smile. "I told him you'd be here."

Her apology makes me frown. We hang out with him all the time. We hang out with a lot of the athletes at school, especially the basketball players. I saw Tiago this morning at the park. I'm about to question her apology when she gives me an apologetic look that I can only assume means one thing.

"He texted earlier and asked if he has a shot with you, and I kind of encouraged him to find out." She flinches a little. "But that was before you told me about you and Finn."

"There is no me and Finn," I say, tearing my eyes from her to glance over my shoulder just as Tiago reaches a spot where the ceiling lowers and he has to duck his head to avoid hitting the rattan lamps.

"Why don't you go on a date with T then?"

"Because we're friends," I say, turning to look at her again. "And he's too nice for me."

"I think it's cute that you're so protective of him. He's not an innocent virgin, you know?" she says.

I don't respond. Tiago is basically Olivia in male form. They're both in love with the idea of love, but neither has the discipline to keep it once they have a shot at it. Livie is a strong woman, though. She knows what she wants, understands her worth, and has an attitude that'll crush anyone who tries to hurt her. Tiago is … too kind-hearted. Since I met him four years ago, I've witnessed his heart break countless times.

He may be a big deal in Fairview—and all around the country after doing so well during March Madness last year—but he's a small-town momma's boy at heart. He doesn't make any decisions, about business or life, without speaking to her first. Not his lawyer, or his friends. *His mother.* He's not meant for today's fast-paced dating world. At one point, I thought Mallory was interested in him and I was quick to talk her out of it. Not only was he not her type, but he didn't have the bank account Mal required from the people she was interested in.

"I knew I'd find beautiful women at the bar tonight," Tiago says, as he quickly hugs me and leans over to kiss Livie on the cheek.

"You smell so good," Livie says.

He grins and glances over at me. "How are you doing after this morning's loss?"

Heat instantly sears through me, and I glare. "Don't."

"You lost?" Livie shouts. "Damn it, Joss. You didn't tell me that! We were on a streak!"

I groan loudly and clench my fists. We've been taking turns

playing him one-on-one and had beaten him three weeks in a row, which makes my loss to him even more maddening.

"I didn't lose," I say through clenched teeth.

"I dominated," Tiago says.

"You did not *dominate*." I hop off the barstool and push him lightly, making him laugh harder. "You won by two points when it should have been *one* point, and you called some technical bullshit on the two I'd scored five minutes before, so no, you didn't win."

Amusement lights up his brown eyes. "You're being a sore loser."

"I'm not being a sore loser. You didn't freaking win," I argue.

"Did you cheat?" Livie demands as she looks at him. "You're the worst kind of cheater, T!"

"What!?" He rears back. "I don't have to cheat! We adjust the game accordingly for you two to even stand a chance against me."

"That's bullshit," I mutter.

"And we've been winning," Livie says, eyes narrowed.

"You change the game whenever it's convenient for you," I add.

He rolls his eyes and starts speaking again, but we're interrupted.

"Whoa, whoa, whoa. What are we fighting about?" Will Hamilton's voice startles me.

My heart drops hard into the pit of my stomach when I turn to face him and see Finn standing beside him. He's wearing a white dress shirt and a navy sports coat. His hair is mussed and he's sporting somewhere between a five o'clock shadow and a beard. As usual, he looks too fucking hot for his own good, which renews the constant tug of war my body and mind have when he's around. *"I want you to help me prove Titus did this."* His words come back to me, and a wave of discomfort accompanies them. I look away quickly, wishing I could summon the anger I felt when he spoke to them over the phone, but I'm too pragmatic.

I've had enough time to process it and my anger has already been replaced with understanding. Not that I'm willing to entertain his accusations or anything, but I get it. He's angry and hurt and needs someone to blame.

"Hey, Finn," Livie says. "Hey, Wi—"

"Olivia Nassir," he says, interrupting.

Her brows rise and she responds, "William Hamilton."

Finn greets me, Liv, and Tiago with a cordial nod, which we return, as well as Will's fist bumps as he speaks.

"When are we going to have our big Indian wedding?" he asks, grinning at Livie.

"You wouldn't survive an Indian wedding, and your mother would never let you marry me."

"My mother likes you." He frowns deeply.

"Sure, but she wouldn't want me to *marry* you," she points out. "What are you two doing here anyway?"

"Our agent is meeting us here in a bit," Will explains. "But we saw you three engaged in a riveting conversation. We walked straight over here to make sure we didn't need to break up a fight."

I don't need a mirror to know Livie and I are instantly wearing the same annoyed look on our faces. Tiago laughs and takes it upon himself to tell them about our game and our bet. Livie pipes up to expose his cheating ways.

"What park, and at what time?" Hamilton asks. "I'll be there tomorrow."

Tiago tells him the park we play at and looks at me. "Nine?"

I shrug, still annoyed.

"You're really going to the park the one time I can't go?" Livie argues.

"I'll go watch you next time as long as it's before the season starts," Will says with a wink.

"Please take a video of tomorrow's game," Livie says.

"Why, so you can study my game and try to beat me?" Tiago asks.

I roll my eyes. "More like to have proof of your cheating."

"You're ridiculous," he says, grinning at me, and despite

myself, I feel my lips twitch into a smile. It's hard not to smile back at Tiago.

"Can I get you guys an old fashioned?" Livie asks.

"It's the only drink she knows how to make without screwing up," I explain when the three of them look at her like they can't figure out why she's not giving them a menu.

I'm shocked when I hear something that sounds like laughter coming from Finn, and I glance over quickly. A rush of heat spreads through me when our eyes lock for a moment too long, and I force myself to look away. Tiago starts speaking about the fundraiser coming up and encouraging them to donate things to auction.

"Suicide among student athletes is skyrocketing and the Alma Organization is helping provide mental health support," Tiago says proudly as Livie mixes our drinks.

"Is this Fletch's non-profit?" Will asks.

"Dame helps a lot," Tiago says, "But it's actually Joss'."

"Really?" Will's eyebrows shoot up. "That's impressive."

I smile and glance away, hating the sudden attention. I can sit here in a bikini or sports bra talking sports all day, but I always feel exposed and get tongue-tied when I talk about the Alma Foundation.

"I signed a puck and stick last year, and got him to do the same," Will says, nodding at Finn.

"Thank you," I say with a smile. "It's only the third year, but it's made a big impact already."

"I'll probably go this year since I'll be in town," he adds.

"I'm sure you're busy, with the Owls being a brand-new team and all, but you should come as my plus-one if you can spare a few hours," Livie says, looking at Finn as she sets our drinks in front of us, "We're 'encouraged' to take dates."

Something akin to jealousy coils inside me. Olivia would never make a move on a guy I've hooked up with, but the discomfort in my chest remains. Something about him makes me feel territorial, which is absolutely ridiculous since Finn Barlow doesn't belong to anyone but himself. Hamilton snorts like he knows there's no chance Finn will be interested in attending.

"When is it?" Finn asks.

God, *his voice*. It's as smooth as the bourbon in Liv's old fashioned and sinks into me with the same warmth.

"Next week." She takes her phone out. "I don't think I have your number. Joss can text you the details."

She says it nonchalantly, but my face heats anyway. I stare at the drink in my hand and ignore her statement.

"Who are you taking?" Tiago asks, turning to me. "Not Tate."

I make a face. "Hell no."

"Why are you encouraged to take a date?" Finn asks.

"Well, not just any date. People who will drive more attention to the cause. Preferably athletes," Livie says.

"Don't fret, Barlow," Hamilton smirks. "Everyone knows about your aversion to dates and having your picture taken with women."

"Random women," Finn corrects.

Hamilton's brows rise. "Which … are all of them when it comes to you."

I bite my tongue and focus on my drink. Finn doesn't argue, and I don't dare look over to see what his expression looks like. Not that I'd be able to decipher it, as confusing as he is.

"What does that mean? Do you not date at all, or is it the pictures you don't want?" Tiago asks.

"I don't date," Finn responds.

"Ever?" Tiago asks, raising his eyebrows.

Livie snorts. "Not everyone wants to find love, Prince Charming."

Tiago shoots her a look, then looks at Finn. "So you just never date?"

"He had a bad experience his first season in the NHL," Will explains.

"With the woman who snuck into your apartment?" Livie asks.

"She'd been there the night before and thought she should

surprise him by being there when he got home from a game," Hamilton says.

My jaw drops. Finn scowls and looks away, the muscle in his jaw feathering like he's over this conversation even though he hasn't even said a word.

"Don't they have a fan account that tries to figure out the identities of the women you're seen with?" Livie asks.

That leaves a sour taste in my mouth. I'm not surprised she knew all of this and hadn't told me. She'd have no reason to mention any of it to me, but it still irks me that she knows and I didn't.

"Joss deals with crazy shit, but thankfully no one has ever snuck into her house," Tiago says with a scowl on his face.

"Are you taking a plus-one?" Hamilton asks, glancing at me. "Or are you the exception to the rule since you have more followers than everyone in this bar combined?"

"That's quite the exaggeration," I say, and feel myself smile. "I don't think I'm taking anyone."

"But Tate is still going," Livie says, concerned. "That's what Dame said."

I shrug. "I'm sure most of Titus' staff is going."

When Titus mentions things like this around the office, people take interest. It's how I met Tate, to begin with. I take a large gulp of my drink to wash away the memory of that entire relationship. I'm pretty sure Tate only wanted to get back together with me because he thought it would help him get a major raise or get him closer to becoming a partner now that one of the guys is retiring.

As if that would make a difference to Titus. Then again, my stepfather treated him like a son. The way he treated *all of our friends*. The thought brings an uncomfortable feeling to my chest, and I instantly glare at Finn for his implications. My stepfather is known for being a shark in the courtroom, but everyone knows he's a huge teddy bear and genuinely cares about people.

"You didn't tell me Tate was going," Tiago says beside me.

"I'm not sure that he is. It's just what everyone assumes since he always goes."

"Maybe we should go together. I mean, the internet is always trying to figure out whether or not we're dating," Tiago suggests.

Livie snorts. "I'm sure that's why you want to go with her."

I shoot her a warning look. I feel eyes on me and look at Finn, who looks pissed off as he studies Tiago.

"Our agent's here," Hamilton says, shooting back his drink, and setting the empty glass on the table. He looks at me and Livie. "Let me know about the fundraiser."

"We will," Livie says.

"Thanks for the drink," Finn says, setting down his empty glass.

He looks at me one last time before walking away. I stare at their backs as they go, and notice the people around them halt mid-conversation to look. It doesn't matter that they're all wealthy or distinguishable. The rest of them aren't Hamiltons or Barlows. I let out a breath and continue speaking to my friends. An hour goes by before I announce I'm going to leave. Tiago agrees that he should go as well, since he doesn't want me to be more well-rested than him tomorrow morning. I make it a point not to look in Finn's direction, but I swear I feel his eyes burning into me as we leave.

CHAPTER SEVENTEEN

Josslyn

Finn: did you go home with him?

BUTTERFLIES TAKE FLIGHT IN MY BELLY, BUT I INSTANTLY PUSH THEM away, ashamed of their presence. He must have texted after I switchped my phone off. I should respond and tell him to go to hell. It's where he deserves to be. Instead, I ignore him and silently curse my mother, who ingrained the mentality "Be kind, everyone is going through something" in my brain. I grab my water jug, keys, and phone, and start walking toward the door just as the doorbell rings. I open it and smile at Tiago.

"Impeccable timing."

He winks. "Something I'm known for."

I laugh as I walk out and lock the door. "That, and your humility, no doubt."

"Humility is overrated."

"Apparently, it's a hot commodity these days," I say.

He squints as we reach the elevator. "Is it?"

"Considering no one I know has much of it, I'd say it is."

We normally jog to the park, but today, we decide to walk. As we do, I snap pictures of us and post them in my stories, and he does the same.

"Coach will be proud," I say, smiling as I respond to some private messages.

Tiago laughs as he types out a caption for his post. Coach Ogwumike loves it when we play against the men's team. She says our game improves tremendously each time we do it, and we all agree. It helps that we're all competitive and have major shit-talkers with chips on their shoulders on both our teams.

Tiago stops bouncing the ball suddenly and says, "I guess Hamilton wasn't kidding about coming to watch us."

I glance up from my phone and see Damian, and sure enough, Hamilton's there, but it's Finn's presence that makes my heart drop. I left him on read, and now I'm walking up to the court with Tiago. He's definitely going to think we slept together. Maybe it's better that he gets the wrong idea. It'll make him leave me alone and move on quicker. That thought really shouldn't make my stomach turn, but it does.

"You brought a crowd," Tiago says as we reach them.

Finn's eyes lock on mine, and what I find in them makes me hug my water jug closer to my chest to fight a shiver. I greet everyone the way I always do, with a quick hug. My pulse thunders in my ears as I reach him. The scent of his cologne hits me first, and it takes everything for me not to inhale deeper as I lean in.

Quick hug. Quick hug. Unlike the rest of the guys, who set their hand on my back and pat it once when they return the hug, Finn's arm wraps around my waist. I inhale sharply, grateful for the water jug between us. I use it to pull away from him. My heart's thundering in my ears when I meet his gaze. As I move to turn away, he grabs my wrist, and even though he lets go quickly, the look in his eyes makes my stomach flip.

"I texted you."

I take another step back. "I know."

His jaw tightens and he looks over my head, toward the court. I turn around and head over there, determined not to let him make me feel any type of way about this. I shake my arms and legs when I reach Tiago and get into competition mode. I always want to win, but knowing these people are here to watch sets me on fire. We establish the usual rules, and I run the ball down the court.

"Half court," he says behind me.

I shoot it, make it, and raise an eyebrow at him. "Fine, but the shot counts."

"Like *fuck* it does. That was full court and we're playing half."

"I swear to god, T, if you don't count that shit, I'm never playing with you again."

"You are such a poor sport." He laughs, and then laughs harder when I launch the ball at his chest.

"What happened?" Dame shouts as they walk around to stand closer to the court.

"Nothing," I say, at the same time that Tiago says, "Unsportsmanlike conduct."

I narrow my eyes at him and growl when he starts dribbling again and bumps me with his shoulder. Unsportsmanlike conduct, my ass. He's a damn cheater and he knows it. It's comical since the man is better than me, but I can beat him one-on-one. I'm shorter than many of my opponents, and since I rarely jump to block a ball, I have to rely on other skills. Dad taught me that skill isn't useful without quick thinking. I'm good at reading my opponent's body, the way they move, the way they handle the ball, and I'm always one step ahead. When I get the ball back, I shoot a three. Tiago takes it and starts going back to the other side, but I manage to steal it from behind and score another three. We go back and forth like this until I score 21 points and beat him by one.

"One point," Tiago says, hands on his knees, as he takes a breath.

"A win is a win," I say mockingly, the way he did yesterday.

I laugh and run away when he lunges at me. I manage to dodge him, only to run right into Finn, because *of course*. He grabs my shoulders to keep me from falling back, and when I look up at him, it's not the expected scowl that I find, but an expression of respect and appreciation that makes my heart skip a few beats.

"You've got a killer three-point shot."

"Thanks." I grin.

"You didn't answer my question," he says when I take a step back and go to turn.

I stop and look at him over my shoulder. "Does it matter?"

"Does what matter?" Hamilton asks, walking over.

We both ignore him, and Finn says, "Yes."

My heart skips another beat and I force myself to tuck away the emotions that threaten to consume me. Pretending nonchalance, I uncap my bottle and drink water.

"It shouldn't," I say, looking at him as I'm capping the water again.

"But it does."

I stare at him, wishing I could read whatever is going through that complicated head of his. Finally, I shake my head. For a split second, I think he's going to say something, maybe apologize for trying to blackmail me, but Damian walks over and interrupts.

"I told you she was good," he says proudly.

"I'm going to buy your jersey," Will says.

I smile. "I expect to see you at one of my games then."

We all talk for a while. The only one who doesn't contribute to the conversation is Finn, who's watching me and Tiago like a hawk. A part of me wonders how long it'll take for him to get bored of this little game and move on. The idiotic side of me hopes he never does.

CHAPTER EIGHTEEN

Finn

I'VE SPENT THE LAST TWO DAYS ANTICIPATING THIS MOMENT, AND THE shocked look on Josslyn's face when she opens the door of her parents' house and finds me standing on the other side is worth it. I don't text women, and this one has left me on read for two fucking days. Not only that, but she straight up didn't answer the question when I asked her in person. I should take the hint. She left the bar with that fuck-face Tiago and walked to the park with him the following morning.

It's more than just a hint, really, but something inside me doesn't want to accept it. Maybe it's because I've always gotten my way. Maybe it's that I haven't had her, not fully. Regardless of the reason, thinking about her with someone else twists me up inside, and I don't like it. It further proves that I need to fuck her and move on. As she steps outside and shuts the door behind her, I take a second to take her in fully. *Fuck.* How is she even real? I've never had a type, but if I did, Josslyn would be it. She's wearing a dress with flowers on it that manages to make her look both sexy as fuck and innocent. It's very short, leaving her toned, tan legs on display. It's obvious she didn't know I was coming over, and the thought of her prancing around like this in front of whatever guys are here makes me feel a certain type of way. Especially Tiago.

"What the fuck are you doing here, Finneas?"

My brows shoot up. She's the only woman who has ever called me by my full name. *Twice* now. The first time she was mid-orgasm—which was the hottest thing I've ever witnessed—but hearing it in this raspy voice is just as much of a turn-on. Her lips are glossy, and the thought of how they'd feel around my dick … She snaps her fingers in front of my face and I blink, trying to remember what the fuck conversation we're having. Surely it wasn't about me choking her with my cock. She huffs, grabs my arm, and pulls me to the side of the house until we're in front of the three-car garage.

She narrows her eyes. "Why are you here?"

"I was invited." I lift the bottle of wine in my hand.

"No, you weren't."

"How else would I know this address?"

"Please." She scoffs. "You're a Barlow."

"So? I don't use my last name for gain."

"Yeah, okay." She laughs, a real one, and I'm mesmerized until she adds, "You need to leave."

"No."

"What do you mean no?"

I quirk an eyebrow. "What happened to the cordial Josslyn from the other day?"

She flashes me a smile. "I can be cordial. I just don't want you anywhere near my family."

I stare at her. She crosses her arms and stares back. I don't regret sending her the footage, and I don't regret telling her I want her help on this. But a small, miniscule part of me regrets being aggressive about it. It's the same small, minuscule part of me that wanted to revolt when I saw her smiling up at that Tiago fuck-face. *Who she's most likely fucking.* My molars grind as I push that thought aside.

"I'm not here to cause trouble." I lift the bottle of wine. "Sincerely."

"Sincerely." She snorts out a laugh. "Who even says that?"

My eyes trail down from the bit of cleavage the dress shows to the white sandals she's wearing. She has pink polish that matches the flowers on the dress. My eyes remain glued to the hem of her dress on her upper thighs. I don't know where she gets her clothes, but I want to find out and crash their fucking website.

"This dress is obscene," I say, more to myself, though I'm sure she hears me.

"Finneas," she snaps.

My eyes fly back to hers, and I take a step forward, pressing her back against the garage door. I place the hand holding the bottle against it and use the other to tip her chin. She inhales sharply but doesn't try to move away. I like that about her. She's strong-willed and unbreakable, but she bends to *my* will. Maybe it's stupid of me, but somehow I can't imagine her being this way with anyone else. Her eyes widen when I lean down until our noses are touching. I'm sure she thinks I'm going to kiss her, which I haven't. I'm not sure why, or if I will before I'm done with her, since I'd rather do other things with her mouth. I won't do it now because I won't be able to stop once we start.

"From the moment you opened the door, I've been wondering what you're wearing underneath that dress." I push up against her, so she feels how hard I am. "I don't give a fuck if you're hooking up with that basketball player. If you keep saying my name like that, I'm going to slide my hand underneath your dress and find out."

She seems to stop breathing for a moment, and that gives me a sense of satisfaction. Finally, she tips her chin up a little higher, a mix of defiance and lust swimming in her beautiful brown eyes.

"It's a romper, not a dress," she says shakily as she pushes me away.

I stare at her for a moment, replaying that comment over before I start laughing. My amusement caught in my throat when she brings her hand up to my face. The feel of her fingertips against my jaw makes me want to simultaneously lean in closer and pull away, but the softness in her expression holds me captive. Josslyn, with her smiles and laughter and fiery attitude, is dangerous for me to be around. I've known that from the start, yet I can't seem to get enough. Even under the circumstances, she makes my chest feel lighter.

Still unable to look away from her, I lower her hand. Brows slightly furrowed, she pulls away and crosses her arms as she tears her gaze from mine. I instantly regret the loss of her attention, but I ignore it and remind myself that this is how she makes everyone feel. Millions of people follow her just to feel like they have her attention, even if it's from the other side of a screen. It's what drove my sister, who wasn't friends with many women, to befriend her. It's why the fucking idiot Tate will keep trying to get her back. It's why *I* can't stay away.

"Are you going to answer my question about the other night?" I ask, unable to help myself.

Her eyes flash to mine again. "Only if you tell me why you care."

Ha. *I'm so not going there.* I don't even *know* why I care or how to explain my need to possess her. As much as it's killing me to not have confirmation on whether or not they went home together, I change the subject.

"Damian invited me, and I'm going to remain completely unbiased while I'm here," I say. It's not a *complete* lie. "Will that be a problem for you?"

"Would you leave if I said it was?"

"Only if you leave with me."

"What?" Her eyes widen and she lets out a shaky laugh as she uncrosses her arms. "You're the most confusing person I've ever met in my life."

I don't bother telling her that she's the one who makes me this way, since it's yet another thing I can't explain.

"Fine. Whatever." She sighs heavily. "Maybe you can meet Titus and see for yourself that he's not the monster you think he is."

Or I'll prove that he is.

"Like I said, I come in peace." I lift the bottle once more.

She searches my face for a couple of seconds and walks past me. It takes everything in me not to pull her against my chest and slide my hand up her *romper*. I'm still staring at Josslyn's ass as she opens one of the large front doors and holds it for me to follow. The house is nice. Minimalistic without feeling cold.

The only splash of color comes from the paintings on the wall, some of which are probably worth more than the house itself. Not very smart, in my opinion. My parents have a lot of their art displayed, but they live in a house three times the size of this one, and it's surrounded by twelve-foot walls, an iron gate, and armed security.

The smell of food hits my nostrils as we walk into the kitchen. I'm not sure what I was expecting, but it wasn't Josslyn's mother chopping up ingredients and dropping them into a red pot. The only time I've ever seen my mother in the kitchen is to taste food and assess the plates the staff is using. Her mother is obviously in her element, humming along to the unfamiliar song playing on the small speaker and wearing an apron that reads "Fluent in food & Spanglish."

If I didn't already know so much about her, I'd think she was Josslyn's older sister. Like her daughter, she's beautiful and has an aura about her that makes starved people like me want to feed off of. When she sees us, she stops humming and smiles at me. She taps the wooden spoon on the edge of the pot and sets it down. Josslyn makes no sort of introduction as she walks to the sink and washes her hands. Her mother scowls at her and wipes her hands on the apron, as she walks over.

"Mom, that's Finn. Finn, this is my awesome mother, Jacqueline," Josslyn says in a surprisingly pleasant tone as she dries her hands.

"You can call me Jackie," her mother says, surprising me by standing on the tips of her toes to give me a kiss on the cheek. "Nice to meet you, Finn."

"It's nice to meet you as well." I offer her the bottle of white wine, which she takes with a smile as she thanks me. "Thanks for letting me crash your barbecue."

"Oh, please. The more, the merrier." She looks at the wine and back at me with wide eyes. "Oh, wow. Thank you. You didn't have to do that."

"You're welcome," I say, smiling and inwardly patting myself on the back.

My mother often had a sommelier come to the house when I was growing up, and even though I didn't drink wine, I was forced to sit through the lessons. It's the only reason I know white is the only acceptable option for a daytime barbecue. I never buy it, though, so when I saw a bottle of my mom's preferred Château La Mission Haut-Brion Blanc, I grabbed a bottle.

Jackie turns to Josslyn and hands her the wine, "Make sure this stays cold, Josie. We'll open it during lunch."

Josie. My eyes fly to her as soon as the nickname leaves her mother's mouth, and she shoots me a pointed look—as if telling me not to call her that—which, of course, makes me want to do the opposite. After doing as her mother says, she begins lifting every single piece of foil covering the meals to see what's underneath. One of the dishes in particular makes her lick her lips in a way that forces me to hold back a groan.

"Whatever you're making smells incredible," I say, taking my attention away from her daughter.

"Oh, Titus and Damian handled most of it," she says. "I'm just making white rice and black beans."

"Mom thinks a meal is incomplete without rice and beans," Josslyn says as she sets the wine in the fridge.

"Joss! I'm going to use your room." A male voice says behind me, and I instantly feel murderous.

"Oh hey, Finn," Tiago says, lifting a peace sign as he holds his phone to his ear and rushes down the hall.

TO JOSSLYN'S FUCKING ROOM. Thank fuck, I'm the master of my emotions and able to swallow back my annoyance.

"Everyone is outside," Jacqueline says, walking back to the pot. "Will you show Finn the way?"

"I thought we were going to make croquetas?" she asks with a pout that makes me bite down on my lip to quench the need to walk over and bite hers.

"Your aunt and Albert are coming over this weekend, so I'm saving those," she says and smiles. "I think they're bringing little Theo."

"This weekend?" Josslyn's shoulders sag.

"It'll be an incentive for you to come back." Jackie winks and looks at me. "You're also welcome to come back."

"Mom!" Josslyn says. "Stop inviting more people to eat my food."

"Oh, Josie." Her mother laughs. "Don't worry, I'll save you some."

"You said that last time, and I got *one* croqueta," she says, pursing her lips.

"I didn't know Lyla and Lachlan were coming over that time." She shrugs. "Now, enough about this. Be a good hostess and take him outside."

"I'm not hosting him," she grumbles under her breath, but when her mother shoots her a warning glance, she smiles wide, showing off her perfect teeth and that cute little dimple on her left cheek.

She keeps that smile on her face as she looks at me. "Let's go, *Finneas*."

I bite my tongue.

She's so going to pay for that.

CHAPTER NINETEEN

Josslyn

APPARENTLY, MY STEPFATHER HAS A LOT TO SAY ABOUT MY EX-boyfriend, which is funny, considering he'd been Team Tate for a while. I've lost count of how many times I've locked eyes with Finn during Titus' rant. Each time I do, the fire in his gaze licks through me and I feel like I might combust. He *really* shouldn't be here. We've always had mutual friends, but this is a bit much. And flashing my mom that charming, sexy-as-hell smile? Complimenting her cooking? Bringing a bottle of wine that costs as much as a month on a luxury car payment? I know this because after my mother reacted the way she did, I Googled it.

He glances away and points at the grill, where Damian is cooking burgers and hot dogs. Whatever he says makes my stepbrother laugh. My chest tightens. Dame's been through a lot. I've been through a lot. This *family* has been through a lot. Obviously, Finn doesn't know that, and they don't know about his little theory, but knowing them, they'd still invite him over to break bread. I hope being here makes him feel like an asshole.

"Joss." Titus' voice snaps my attention back to him.

"Yeah, no. I don't want you to fire Tate," I say quickly. "He's a good associate and he works hard..." I pause, finding that I can't think of any more redeeming qualities about the asshole. "Look, we're adults. I genuinely don't care."

And I find that I'm telling the truth. Maybe it's because I hadn't fully opened up to Tate this time around, or that I've been so busy thinking about Finn and that whole situation, but when I think about running into Tate, I don't feel anything. Even when I envision running into him with Gracie, I don't care.

He exhales. "You'll tell me if that changes?"

"Of course."

"What's up with this Barlow kid?" he asks suddenly, glancing over there.

My heart stops. "What do you mean?"

"Why's he here?"

"The Owls signed him. He's supposed to be..."

"The face of the franchise, I know. I mean, why is he here in *our house*?"

That makes my scalp prickle. Titus always has questions for our guests and I swear he enjoys making the guys I invite over uncomfortable, but this is new. Both the disapproving tone and the question. I glance back at Finn, hoping to hide my confused expression. Not much gets past Titus, and even though over the years I've tried to pick up on his tricks for reading people, I've never been good at being on the opposite side of the coin.

"Dame is friends with him," I say after a moment.

Titus frowns. I can see the wheels in his head turning. Mallory rarely spoke about her brother, but if she did it was usually quickly, to brag about how great his hockey seasons were going. When we were at the dinner table, she'd keep conversations about her family to a minimum, and when Tate was around, she never mentioned them at all. Not that she came around much when he was here. Livie told me it was out of respect and loyalty to her family, which I understood.

"Huh," Titus says after a moment. "I thought Mallory was the only Barlow you guys were connected to."

When he says her name, his expression cracks slightly to reveal sadness. It doesn't mean anything, though. Like every other parent in Fairview, Titus was heartbroken when he heard the news of what happened. He'd even offered the Barlows his services pro bono in case the Barlows wanted to sue the club—not that they couldn't afford his rates. That's who he is, though. When things go wrong, he steps in.

"Hockey. You know Will Hamilton took Damian under his wing when he was playing at Fairview, and Will is best friends with Finn, so…" I shrug.

He gives a nod. "And now they'll be teammates on the Owls."

"Yep."

"He hasn't taken his eyes off you."

My stomach dips. "Yeah, because we keep looking over at him."

"It's not that. He's been watching you," he says, with that serious expression that terrifies people. I follow his line of vision and see Finn staring right back like he's unfazed. I wish I could slap him silly. Titus looks at me again. "I'd be cautious with that one."

"I…" I feel myself frown. "There's nothing to be cautious about."

"That family has a difficult time accepting the word 'no,'" he says. "And from the looks of it, you're what he wants."

I bristle. "Finn's not like that."

The words leave my mouth before I can stop them, and Titus glances at me again. This time, he looks at me like he's staring into my soul. If anyone can, it would probably be him. I don't back down or look away, though. Finn might be an asshole who is demanding and dead-set on getting what he wants, but I know if I ever said the word 'no' to him, he'd immediately stop what he was doing. I *know* it.

"He'd never force himself on anyone," I say, licking my lips.

"I didn't say he would. I haven't heard much about Finn, but I know enough about the Barlow men. When they're determined to have something, or someone…" Titus' brows furrow. "I just don't want you opening yourself up for another doomed relationship. You're too great of a woman to be some man's mistress."

My heart twists at that. Thankfully, my mother shouts my stepfather's name. He gives my arm a light squeeze as he walks away. I breathe a little easier when he walks away, but as I walk toward the group, I remember Damian's warning the night I met Finn. It makes me wonder what the hell it is they see when they look at him, at us. It hits me when I sink deeper into my memories and remember Tate once telling me that families in that social circle have certain expectations. Having over a million followers may bring lucrative opportunities and help expand my financial portfolio, but it doesn't change my background or last name.

I push those thoughts away. There's no denying the attraction between me and Finn. He's the opposing pole of a magnet I can't seem to pull away from. Even now, when he's deep in conversation with Livie, Dame, and Hamilton, I can't look away. But ultimately, none of that matters. Once we sleep together, we're done, and even if there was a small chance we weren't, it could never be forever. At the sight of movement in my peripheral vision, I tear my gaze from him and watch as Tiago jogs over to me. From the look on his face, I can tell the call didn't go how it was supposed to.

"What happened?"

He shrugs, exhaling. "The call wasn't terrible."

"No?" I ask, heart still in my throat.

"She'll need to do a few more sessions of chemo, but they say it's gone," he responds, eyes still sad. "I'm going to stay with her for a couple of days next week just in case."

I reach for his hand, squeezing it in solidarity. I hate the sadness in his eyes. Even though he's already been told his mom is going to be okay—thanks to the early detection of her cancer—I understand why it's hard for him to see her that way.

"You're a good kid, Tiago Lewis." I offer him a small smile. "If I ever have a kid, I hope he's just like you."

At that, a slow grin appears on his face. "I'm willing to give you one."

I laugh, taking my hand back and shoving him playfully as he laughs. When we reach the group, Livie hands me a berry-flavored seltzer and taps a *cheers* with hers before we take a sip.

"What'd Titus say?" she asks.

"Nothing, just his usual show-of-support speech." I take another sip and look at the guys who are standing around Dame talking about restoring an old Mustang.

We all follow Dame toward the table. When he sees me there, he gives a nod. "Did you tell my dad Tate's not welcome at the fundraiser?"

"She's too nice to suggest that," Livie says, raising an eyebrow in challenge.

"I'm an adult," I say, taking another sip of my drink.

"Adults know how to ask for help," Livie responds.

I roll my eyes. "Moving on."

She laughs and changes the subject to this year's new uniform.

"By the way," Tiago says. "You lost the other day, so I'll be seeing you in my uniform soon."

I smile. "And I'll be seeing you in mine, since you lost the rematch."

"You guys should wear them to the pool party," Livie suggests with a snicker. "Some of the girls from our team will be there."

"And guys from mine," Tiago says, grinning. "They're going to wish they were me."

I scoff. Livie laughs. There's no point in telling them—*again*—that I'm not going to the pool party. I love my friends and appreciate that they're trying to take my mind off things, but I know myself. I won't be able to do anything remotely fun that day. Tiago directs us to one side of the table, where he sits between us. Finn ends up directly in front of me, with Hamilton and Damian to his left and my mother to his right. Everyone falls into conversation pretty naturally as we eat. Titus asks Hamilton and Finn questions about the Owls. When he starts going into personal territory and directing the questions at Finn specifically, I shoot him a look that he thankfully catches.

"I've already asked Will this question, and I'm curious to know if your answer is similar," Titus starts, "Why would a guy from a wealthy family, who has everything laid out for him, pursue professional hockey?"

Finn takes his time sipping his wine before he answers, "Why not?"

"Because your future is laid out for you," Titus repeats. "Was your father okay with your decision?"

Finn's expression doesn't falter, but for some reason, his question bothers me. Maybe it's because I've heard enough about his parents to know they're very set in their ways. For them, everything is by the book, and the rules of the book are archaic. We all play a part, and our roles change depending on the scene. People like them don't seem to get much of a choice in anything. Mallory had to dress and act a certain way when she was with them, which tormented her. I couldn't blame her. I can't imagine that Finn, as the firstborn male, would have it any easier. Mal only mentioned his choosing hockey once, and she said something along the lines of, "Our parents blew a gasket."

"You don't have to answer that," I say, clearing my throat and earning Finn's attention. "Titus loves to badger people with questions, and sometimes, when his defense attorney side comes out, it can get really intense."

"Good to know," Finn says, his eyes so intense that I feel he's sucking the air out of my lungs.

"Stop pestering him, honey. He provided this delicious wine," Mom says, snapping us out of the trance as she lifts her glass. "A toast to sharing food with a new face."

Everyone mumbles something in agreement, lifts their glass, and takes a sip of the wine, which is ... fine. I'm not sure what I expected. I know nothing about wine, but at that price tag, I thought it would be, "Oh my God-good."

"Do you have any content to shoot or anything going on this weekend?" Mom asks me after a moment.

"Not really," I say. "I'm recording a training session, but that's mostly because people keep asking me for an updated one."

"A training session that she's forcing me to be a part of, by the way, even though we're going to train with some of the girls the day after," Livie says.

I laugh. "Stop whining."

"You sound like Finn," Will says, smirking.

My heart skips. "How so?"

"He trains for fun."

"I train for excellence," Finn says.

"You should do a basketball versus hockey player training video," Dame says. "People would be surprised to see we do a lot of the same things."

"That would be fun," I agree. "Are you volunteering?"

Dame chuckles. "I mean, I guess I can."

"Finn should do it."

"Are you my spokesperson now, Mr. Hamilton?" Finn asks, raising an eyebrow, but he doesn't look or sound upset about it.

From the way Will laughs, and as quiet as I know Finn can be, I get the feeling he normally does this.

"Do you have anything else going on, besides recording content?" Mom asks.

"We're going to a pool party," Tiago says, smirking at me.

"*You're* going to a pool party. I already told you I'm not up for it."

"Is it on Saturday?" Mom asks softly, then offers a gentle smile when I nod.

It'll be the fifth anniversary of my father's death, and even though the years keep passing, the loss still plagues me. Not just the loss, but how I lost him … how I found him. I take a large sip of what's left of my wine and chase the thoughts away. Thinking about death is triggering for me, as it's not something I like to talk about. Maybe if I were familiar with less traumatic deaths, things would be different, but I'm not. It's yet another reason I've tried so hard to leave Mallory's death behind.

"I'll come over and watch a movie with you," Livie says quietly. Dame curses, his eyes going wide. "I'll bring food."

"I'm fine." I put a hand up and smile at both of them. "Really. I appreciate it, but I'm totally fine."

They look like they don't believe me, and I can't blame them. They've seen me break down time and time again. I don't even bother to acknowledge Finn, Tiago, or Will. T knows how difficult that day is for me, but he's never actually been there to witness me at my lowest. I've never let him.

"A party might be fun," Mom says, trying to sound cheerful.

"When does practice start again?" Titus asks, changing the subject. I shoot him a grateful look, and he smiles softly.

"October, but we're going to start conditioning next week."

We're not allowed to practice until October, but our coaches get around that by having us run plays off school property. They're not actually there when we do it and since it's just a group of girls playing basketball, it's technically not breaking any violation.

"God, it's going to be so hard getting back into conditioning," Livie says.

"That's why you should never stop," I quip.

Hamilton snorts. "You *really* sound like Finn."

I finally glance at Finn, who's staring at me with a raw need that makes my pulse race. Every time I'm around him, I feel like I'm back in middle school waiting for my crush to look my way. *God, this is bad.* From the corner of my eye, I see Titus watching us, so I take a deep breath and focus on my food. I don't know how I'm going to sit through an hour of this.

CHAPTER TWENTY

Josslyn

"Dad, you need to make sure Tate doesn't go to the fundraiser," Damian says suddenly.

"Really, Damian?" I shoot him a glare.

"Honey, it's okay if you don't want to see him yet. I'm sure he'll understand," Mom says.

"I genuinely don't care if he's there," I say, picking up my hot dog.

"He's trying to get her back," Livie says.

"That's not true," I respond before taking a bite of food.

We wouldn't know if he's trying to get me back. He just got back in town, and I blocked his number and unfollowed him everywhere. The only reason I didn't block his accounts on social media is that I know he'll just go and get a burner account. His only option is to show up at my apartment, and I already took him off my list of visitors, so he can't even do that.

"He'd be an idiot to think he could," Tiago responds.

"Have you seen all the comments he's been leaving on your posts?" Dame asks, scowling.

"Is that what you do in your free time?" I ask. "Scroll through my comments?"

"Sometimes, they ask where your hot brother is." He shrugs.

That makes me laugh, because he's not wrong, and his already inflated ego feeds off it.

"Tate will back off if you take a date," Mom says. "I'm sure Damian can get one of his Blaze teammates to accompany you."

My jaw drops. "I don't need Dame's help to find a date, thank you very much."

"She really doesn't. As it is, some of them are already calling Dibs on her since I won't be there to threaten them." Dame shoots me a pointed look. "Stay away from Nate Crawford."

I snort. "Nate's the only cute one."

Not that I want him calling Dibs on me. The hockey team has this stupid, disgusting game called "Dibs" where they have a number of people they need to sleep with. If they find one in particular who interests them a lot, they get to call Dibs and no one else can go after her. At least, that's how it was explained to me.

"Is Nate popular?" Mom asks.

"For the wrong reasons," Hamilton says.

"I'll go with you," Finn says out of the blue, making everyone at the table go completely silent.

"That would be interesting," Dame says slowly, eyeing me the way he did the night I met Finn all those years ago.

"That…" Will blinks, shaking his head, unable to form words.

"It would be incredible," Livie says.

"Would you let us advertise you'll be there?" Mom asks.

My head is spinning. It takes me a long moment to start a sentence, only to be interrupted.

"You'll be photographed together," Tiago says and looks at me. "I think we should go together. People—"

"I think we can all agree that my being there with her will get more attention," Finn says, interrupting.

My brows shoot up at his blatant arrogance, but he's not wrong. Finn doesn't abide by anyone's rules. He'd rather pay fines than speak to the press, he doesn't give interviews, and he hasn't been very public since he got here, so I'm sure people are dying to speak to him. I wouldn't be surprised if the entire Fairview Blaze team somehow got together to buy a table just to fawn over him.

"You'd bring enough attention by getting a table," Tiago argues.

Finn smiles, though it's cold and frankly, a little scary. After a second, he says, "I'll donate the cost of a table, but *I* will be accompanying Josslyn."

Tiago lets out a low chuckle, shaking his head. "Just like that? Without even asking her?"

"I'm sure she knows this is the right move," Finn says, his eyes flicking to mine briefly.

I remain silent. I'm not sure what to make of his offer, but he's right. If he goes with me, the media attention would be intense. Which is why I don't understand why he's even offering.

"We all know it'll get more attention if Joss and Finn arrive together," Livie says, then raises her brows at Finn. "*A lot* more attention."

"It's smart," Titus adds, which shocks me.

"If we start feeding the rumor mill, more people pay to watch the live feed," Mom adds, and shrugs when I stare at her in shock. "What? It's the publicist in me."

Hamilton isn't even bothering to conceal his surprise, looking at his friend like he's grown three heads.

"I don't know..." I start but am once again interrupted by Tiago.

"Did you hear that part about having your picture taken?" he asks, dumbfounded.

Finn's expression hardens. "Loud and clear."

"It's not just your picture," I say, shooting Tiago a quick warning look that says I'll hurt him if he interrupts me again. "I know you have a large fan base, but most of them are just hockey fans—"

"And puck bunnies," Hamilton quips.

"And puck bunnies," I add, rolling my eyes. "The people who follow me are very loyal—"

"Psychos," Livie pipes up.

"Can you guys let me fucking talk?"

Finn's mouth twitches. "Don't worry about them, sweetheart. I'm listening."

My stomach does a summersault. *Sweetheart.* OH MY FUCKING ... I've always thought that was the corniest endearment, but holy shit. God. Who even am I?

"Don't call me sweetheart," I manage to say, though my complaint sounds as weak as my knees feel. "My followers genuinely care and are invested in my life, and it may not seem like it, but I'm a private person…"

Everyone at the table laughs loudly, and I turn my glare to each of them. Finn is the only one who's not laughing, but he definitely looks amused.

"I am!" I argue. "I only share what I feel comfortable sharing!"

"She's not lying," Livie says, wiping away tears of laughter. "She didn't even post pictures with Tate this last time."

At the mention of his name, Damian and Tiago groan and mumble things under their breaths. I ignore them, as usual.

"It's true. I'm never posting a guy on my grid unless I'm one-thousand-billion percent sure of him," I say. "I may have to wait until I'm married." I ignore them and address Finn. "You value your privacy, especially when it comes to your love life, so I think you should think about it."

Hamilton snorts. "Love life."

Finn shoots him a look before glancing at me. "I'm aware of the repercussions."

"All right," I shrug. I'm not going to turn down this opportunity or what it could mean for the foundation. "Your funeral."

Everyone resumes conversations, which is a huge relief. I manage not to look at Finn the rest of the time.

Long after we're done talking about it, Tiago leans over and says, "I'll go with you if Finn backs out."

I lift my eyes in time to see his jaw set as he shoots daggers. I don't know if he can hear what T is saying or if he's upset that he's near me. Either way, I can't fight the warmth that his reaction spreads through me. Something is *seriously* wrong with me.

"I'm going to grab another bottle," I say, folding my napkin and picking up the empty one as I push my seat back.

"May I use your restroom?" Finn asks, tossing his napkin on the table as he stands up.

"Of course," Mom says, smiling. "Josie, show him where it is, please."

My heart feels like it may burst out of my chest as I head inside. My stomach is coiled tight and every nerve in my body is hyper aware of him walking behind me. We're quiet as we walk past the kitchen and through the living room. When we reach the hallway and are completely out of everyone's line of vision, the thick silence between us becomes too much.

"Why'd you volunteer to go with me?"

"It's for a good cause," he says, the rasp in his voice causing my heart to ricochet.

"That's fair, but just so you know, you don't have to go *with* me." I stop in front of the bathroom and turn to him.

"I know I don't."

"Okay," I say, meeting his eyes and nearly losing my breath when I see the blatant lust in them. I swallow and point at the door. "Here's the bathroom."

He stares at me for a moment before saying, "I want to see your room."

I turn my back to him quickly and nearly say no, but for some reason I want him to see it. "You have two seconds," I say quietly as I push the door open.

He walks in and looks around until his attention lands on my shelves where the trophies and medals are. It's comical seeing a man with a million trophies looking at each of mine—from the spelling bee in third grade to my youth league—as if they hold equal importance to his.

"Impressive," he says quietly, as he touches the trophy I earned last year.

I snort. "Says the two-time recipient of the Conn Smythe Trophy."

One corner of his sinful mouth lifts as he faces me. "Still keeping tabs on me, Josie?"

My heart skips even as a wave of heat rocks through me, though I'm not sure if it's annoyance or something else. "Don't call me that."

He lifts an eyebrow.

I let out a breath and start ushering him toward the door. "You need to get out of here."

"Why?"

"My mom's old school. She still doesn't allow guys in my room."

He stops walking and turns around. The look on his face makes me take a step back.

"Tiago was in here earlier," he says, his voice so low and quiet it's impossible not to think he's upset.

I stare at him for a moment and laugh. "Seriously?"

He doesn't look a bit amused. "Are you hooking up with him?"

"That's none of your business." I turn around and walk to the small vanity. "But what if I am?"

I gasp when he wraps an arm around my middle and pulls me against his hard chest. He presses a kiss so soft and gentle to the back of my ear that I shiver violently in his arms. He makes a sound of approval in the back of his throat and licks the spot, sending a wave of heat between my legs.

"Finn," I breathe.

"If you are, you should get rid of him, or I will."

"You…" My voice is a weak exhale. "You can't do that."

"Watch me," he murmurs, as his lips trail down my neck to my shoulders.

"We really shouldn't be doing this right now," I say even as I'm tilting my neck to give him better access.

"Because of *him*?" he asks. I'm about to tell him it has nothing to do with him, but the hand he has on my stomach begins to trail down and thoughts vanish. "No. I don't think you'd let me do this if you were serious about him." He moves my hair and keeps raining soft kisses on the back of my neck, as his calloused fingers slide underneath the wide leg of my romper. "Then again, you've done it once before, haven't you?" He rubs me over my underwear and I arch my back with a gasp.

"That was different," I say, my voice shaking when he hits a sensitive spot. "Tate and I had an agreement."

"Right. The agreement," he murmurs, sliding his lips to the other side of my neck and sucking the spot underneath my ear.

"Finn," I say, a plea as my knees wobble.

He takes his hand back instantly and turns me around to look me in the eye. "Are you actually hooking up with him?"

"Are you actually jealous?"

"Is that what this is about? Making me jealous?" He splays a hand over my throat and leans closer, so our noses are almost touching. "Do you want me to tell you that every time I think about you going home with him, I'm blinded with rage?" His eyes narrow as he moves his hand to the nape of my neck and squeezes. "Would you like me to tell you how many times I envisioned myself breaking his shooting arm while he touched you today?"

My eyes widen. "You wouldn't do that."

"There's very little I wouldn't do to eliminate my competition," he says, tugging my hair to pull my head slightly back before his mouth crashes down on mine.

It's a searing kiss that makes my heart pound and my entire body sing. He kisses me desperately, like he's been waiting for this moment forever. That's how it feels to me, like every kiss before this one was just practice. Everything pales in comparison. His hands are wild on my body as he lifts me onto the vanity, pushing the chair aside as I open my legs wider for him. I wrap them around his waist and sink my hands into his hair. That earns me a low rumble that makes my core tighten. He pulls back, nibbling and sucking my lower lip into his mouth.

"Fuck," he breathes, setting his forehead against mine.

My heart is still jackhammering as I lower my arms and set them over his forearms, gripping his biceps as I catch my breath. I lean further into him, relishing how I feel in his arms, wanting to live in this moment forever, feeling the heat of his body against mine as he holds me like I matter to him.

"There is no competition," I whisper after a moment.

"Good." His exhale makes my heart skip. He presses another kiss against my lips, and another.

After a moment, I pull away from him. "We need to go back out there."

Hesitation and a slight frown forms on his face. "I don't like him touching you."

My heart skips. "He's just like that. I'm like that. It's a Latin thing. Some of us are touchy-feely, but it doesn't mean anything."

"Is that what you like?" he asks quietly.

His question takes me by surprise. I search his eyes. I've never thought about it before, but I guess affection is a love language I crave. I answer with a nod. Tate wasn't very affectionate. And despite his jealousy, I don't expect Finn to be either. I'm not sure I can even picture Finn in the kind of relationship that would require expectations.

He looks at me for a long moment with that inscrutable expression I can't read, and takes a step back. He watches my every move as I fix my romper and locate my sandals, which flew off at some point. When we finally walk out of my room, he presses his hand to the small of my back and leaves it there until we reach the kitchen. Only then, does he fully pull away from me.

CHAPTER TWENTY-ONE

Finn

"Wʜᴀᴛ's ʏᴏᴜʀ ᴄᴇʟʟʏ ɢᴏɪɴɢ ᴛᴏ ʙᴇ ᴡʜᴇɴ ʏᴏᴜ sᴄᴏʀᴇ ᴛʜᴇ ғɪʀsᴛ goal?" Lundy asks, as he skates up.

"I've known Barlow since I was born and I've never seen him celebrate anything." Hamilton laughs as he shoots the puck into the goal.

"Is that right?" Lundy takes his shot.

"I'm here to win, not dance," I say, skating around Lundy, who's trying to block me, and shoot the puck in.

"This fucking guy," he says, shaking his head with a laugh.

"We're supposed to go golfing soon," Ham says to Lundy as he skates around me to get the puck. I steal it from him before he can get in a good scoring position. He glares. "You motherfucker. I forgot how sneaky you are with it. Do it again."

I do. And again. And then to Lundy, who thinks he's going to outmaneuver me somehow.

"All day," I say and wink.

"Already showing off, Barlow?" Peter shouts from the other side of the glass as he walks by.

"Just warming up." I nod a greeting to the coach, who laughs.

"You work on your celly yet?" Damian asks, skating up to us.

"We haven't even played a game yet and you two are focused on celebrating." I shake my head.

"Nah, my head's in the game," he says, skating away.

He slows down and does a few turns in the middle of the rink, looking up at the stands. I never played in college, but I've been to the arena the Blaze play in, so I know this is impressing the fuck out of him. The arena is impressive—period. It's brand new, and they seemed to think of everything when they built it.

We keep trash-talking, and when more of our teammates join us, we introduce ourselves to the ones we don't know and start passing the puck between all of us. After a few minutes, Coach Petey comes back with skates on and starts going over general items. While we've all reviewed our playbooks, we'd never been on the ice together before.

A couple of guys have never played professionally, and only two of us have played for Petey in the past. It'll take time for us to learn how to play together, but that's what this is for. And there's always preseason. I'm confident in our coaches and I like everyone's style, so I feel good about this team.

"You get your workout in?" Hamilton asks Damian, as we skate off the ice when we're done with practice.

"Joss made me get up at five in the morning," Dame says, rolling his eyes. "So I feel like I got two workouts in."

At the sound of her name, I feel my body go rigid. I haven't stopped thinking about that damn kiss and how she felt against me. In the shower, in bed, in the kitchen, on my drive here. I swear she's bewitched me.

"As long as your workout wasn't *with* her, if you know what I mean," Hammie jokes.

I feel my jaw clench. I force myself to keep my eyes on the ground. I've always been good at keeping my emotions off my face, but the amount of rage I feel at his little joke is making me see red. As they go back and forth shooting the shit, I grind my jaw and tune them out. Josslyn's a beautiful woman with an immense following, and that's something that doesn't bother me, but thinking about her with someone else is fucking torturous. I keep telling myself that I only feel this way because I haven't had my fill of her. Maybe it is that, but after yesterday, I'm not so sure.

"That's my sister, fuck-faces," Dame says, pushing Hamilton.

"Fuck! I'm kidding," Hamilton says, laughing as he hops away from Dame.

"She was a suggested follow on IG the other day," Lundy says, looking at Dame. "I didn't click follow. Cassie loves her posts, but she'd probably fucking kill me if I follow Josslyn's account."

"She posts some damn good pics," Hamilton says.

This time, I do chance a glance at him. He's looking straight ahead, but I swear he's doing this to provoke me. Knowing that should encourage me to shrug it off, but the anger remains. As we walk to the locker rooms, I take a deep breath. Soon, I'll want to cover my nose every time I come in here, but for now, I enjoy the smell of brand new.

"That was cool of you to offer to go with her to the fundraiser dinner," Dame says to me as we start taking off our pads and walk to the bench.

"It's no big deal."

"It kind of is," he says, sitting beside me and unlacing his skates. "She won't be upset if you back out, you know? I think she's kind of expecting you to."

My stomach tightens. "Why would I back out?"

We both stop messing with our skates and sit upright, facing each other.

"You know why," he says, frowning.

"The pictures will be everywhere," Hamilton says as he sets his gear down. "Hey, maybe it's a good time to grow up and actually try to date."

"Date?" I scoff. "This is for a good cause. It has nothing to do with dating."

Hamilton shoots me a look.

Dame shrugs. "I'm just giving you an out. T doesn't mind going with her."

A dark, amused chuckle leaves my lips before I can stop it. "I bet he doesn't."

Hamilton's brows lift. Dame shrugs again, then stands to put his stuff away.

"You going to the pool party?" Hamilton asks Dame.

"I ... Maybe." Dame scratches the back of his neck. "I have to check on Joss."

The way he says it makes my skin prickle, and I realize I don't like being left in the dark about what's happening with her. Her mother and Olivia also seemed worried about how she'd be doing today, so it must be something big. Whatever it is, she didn't post about it on social media.

"What's going on today?" I ask. "Why's everyone worried about her?"

Dame stops what he's doing and looks at me for a long moment. "It's the anniversary of her dad's death."

"Oh." I blink. Not what I expected. "Were they close?"

"Very," he says. "He was her favorite person. Total daddy's girl." He smiles softly, then clears his throat. "So, yeah, I need to check on her."

Even as I nod, I feel myself frown.

Once he's gone, Hamilton turns to me and makes a face. "What the fuck was that?"

"What?"

"What's up with all the questions?"

I shrug. "They treat her like she's fucking breakable, and I want to know why."

"Why do you care?"

I stand up and keep sorting my stuff. "Don't read into it."

"Oh, I'm reading into it," Hamilton says behind me, laughing again. "This just gets better and better."

"Fuck you, Hammie. Don't make a big deal out of it." I shoot him a look.

"Don't..." He laughs again, as he brings up his hand to start counting off, "You're going with her to the fundraiser. You want to know personal details about her. And you're moving into her apartment building..."

"Because they're working on my apartment, and my dad happens to have a penthouse in her building," I respond.

He snorts. "Don't give me that shit. Your dad has a penthouse in every fucking building in the city. *You* own other places you can stay at."

"They're being rented out," I say.

He rolls his eyes, and I don't know why I feel the need to explain myself, but I try.

"Maybe I want to keep a closer eye on her family. Sue me for trying to get to the bottom of what happened to Mal."

"Finn," he says, opening his eyes the way he does when he calls me out on my shit. "You've had an investigator trailing those people for over a year now, and nothing has come of it. I get why you're looking into Titus, I really do. I don't agree with it, but your theory makes sense," he says, pausing to take a deep breath as he runs his fingers through his blond hair. "But fuck, man. What's your excuse for following Josslyn? You *know* she had nothing to do with it."

"She was dating Tate. I haven't ruled him out."

He stares at me for a moment and laughs, shaking his head as he turns to start walking again. He mutters something under his breath about Tate being too much of a pussy to do anything like this and how I'm out of my mind. Maybe I am. I don't know. I decided to move to that apartment building last night, and I'm not lying about people working on my place.

Sure, it's only a cleaning company and a few plumbers changing the toilets—neither of which requires me to move—but

I don't like people in my space. And yeah, I could've moved into one of the places not currently being rented, but her apartment building is the closest building to the Owls' arena. It's not so far-fetched that I'd want to move there. A couple of guys on our team live there. Damian lives there. The more I think about it, the more justified I feel.

CHAPTER TWENTY-TWO

Josslyn

I COULDN'T SLEEP FOR A NUMBER OF REASONS—THE MAIN ONE BEING Finn. Last night, I was riding high, but then it all sank in and I realized that what happened in my room was probably a mistake. Each time I see him, my brain turns to mush and my body relies on senses that can't be trusted. It wouldn't be such a big deal if Mallory had not cast such a huge shadow over both of us. But the situation is so messy and Mal's secrets never stop, so even if I wanted to help him in this, there's no telling what she was doing leading up to that night.

For months after it happened, I was struck with guilt, wondering if I could have prevented what happened that night. By then, I'd had many talks with her and practically begged her to get help for her self-destructive behavior. I blamed myself for not contacting Finn or trying to get in touch with her parents. There's no doubt in my mind that if I'd done that, my friendship with Mallory would have been over. Back then, it seemed like a high price to pay.

After it happened, I went back to Onyx and asked employees questions that still remain unanswered. When Titus found out what I was doing, he forced me to let it go, and I did. Not because

I no longer cared, but because it was the only thing I could do for my own mental and emotional well-being. Maybe if Dad hadn't died by suicide, I wouldn't have been so triggered by what happened, but he did and I was. I swallow the knot in my throat and focus on my breathing exercise. *There's nothing I could have done differently. It wasn't my fault.* I repeat those things over and over until I sort of believe them again. I don't think I ever will. I lie back down and let myself cry until I'm out of tears and my throat is hoarse.

Maybe Finn coming to me with this is a sign for me to face this trauma. Doing that would mean immersing myself in Mallory's world, which would mean speaking to *those* friends ... the ones she made me swear on my life I'd never mention to anyone ... and I haven't. I'm not sure I can even get in touch with them, but now that the idea is in my head, I know it's not going anywhere. I rub my face over my hands and push the thought away for now. When I finally check my phone, I see a slew of notifications and texts.

Unsurprisingly, I see some notifications from Tate, who's been leaving comments frequently on each one of my posts. I don't understand why, with the way people attack the hell out of him each time he does it, and today is no different.

> Tate: photo cred
>
> Gemma11: @Tate ARE YOU SERIOUS?
>
> PantherP: @Tate GET OFF HER PAGE. YOU LOST ANY RIGHT TO SPEAK TO HER
>
> CarlaM: @Tate YOU MESSED UP ASSHOLE
>
> BlazeBunny: @Tate F. U. CHEATER !!!!
>
> Gemma11: @PuttingQueen CAN YOU BELIEVE THIS GUY!?
>
> PuttingQueen: @Tate you're an idiot. Stop trying so hard. She doesn't want you!!

I click on my private messages and find some from him as well. I stare at his name but don't open the thread. He started sending them the night I saw the pictures and videos of him and Gracie together, which was also the night I called him and sent him to hell before blocking his number. Blame it on the usual sadness and helplessness I feel today, but I finally unblock his number. Now that he's back in town and I'm much calmer about the whole thing, it's better that I deal with him.

> **Me:** pls stop commenting on my posts. You're making things worse.

His response is immediate.

> **Tate:** can you please tell security to let me go up?

My heart drops.

> **Me:** you're here?
>
> **Tate:** I need to see you.
>
> **Tate:** please

I bite my lip and stare at the phone when it starts buzzing with a call from him. I send it to voicemail quickly and text back.

> **Me:** I'll come down

I shut my eyes and take a couple of deep breaths, trying and failing not to think about my father. It's not like I don't think about him each day, but it's as if my body remembers and grieves his death extra today. By the time I get out of bed, my chest is aching, but I push it aside and focus on what I'm going to say to Tate when I get downstairs. There really isn't much, but I want to make sure to keep the peace, even if it's just for Titus' sake.

I get ready quickly. After the fastest shower I've ever had, I throw my hair into a bun and put on sweats and the first t-shirt I find. I find my slides by the door, grab my keys, and head downstairs. As I stare at my reflection in the elevator doors, I realize that despite my best attempt, I still look like I just rolled out of bed. When I step out of the elevator and turn the corner, I spot Tate holding a bouquet of roses and my stomach turns.

I haven't so much as looked at a picture of him after what he did. Since my brain has been filled with thoughts of Finn, I didn't think seeing Tate would make me feel anything, even disgust, but here I am, feeling. He's wearing khakis and a white button-down with the sleeves rolled up, his blond hair perfectly slicked back.

That's one thing about Tate, regardless of what's happening, he's always going to look put-together. When he sees me, his blue eyes brighten, and he begins to walk over.

"Thank you for agreeing to see me," he says, handing me the bouquet, which I take and smell.

"I figured I'd have to see you sooner or later."

He flinches and glances at the sitting area. "Can we sit and talk?"

"As long as you don't apologize."

His face falls. "But…"

I level him with a look. "If you apologize, I'm out."

"Fine." He sighs.

If he does, I'm done with the conversation. I may not have been in love with him, but I don't want to think or talk about the fact that he cheated on me with the one person in the universe I would actually fight. I follow him to the couches and sit across from him with the roses on my lap. I touch the petals and stare at them while I wait for him to speak.

"I know this is going to sound like bullshit, but I was drugged that night," he says.

My head snaps up. His cheeks are pink, and he looks like he's holding his breath as I stare at him. I don't know if it's because he's embarrassed or lying, but I can't imagine he'd make something like this up. Not Tate, who has a superiority complex. Besides, he may be a lot of things, but he knows how personal this topic is for me, so I don't think he'd lie about it.

"By whom?"

"I don't know." He swallows and looks away before looking at me again.

"Do you remember…" I clear my throat and push my shoulders back. "Do you remember kissing her?"

He lowers his head, sighing heavily as he rubs his eyes with his thumb and forefinger.

"So you do remember," I say, jaw clenching.

"I remember her flirting with me, but that's it." He straightens again.

"It wasn't the only time you cheated on me," I say quietly as I search his face.

He swallows hard and looks at the floor. "No."

I fight the wave of discomfort that accompanies his admission. I'm not sure why hearing it feels like such a blow. *I knew he'd cheated, didn't I?* When we were together and he'd go to lunch with that paralegal, Amber, I just knew. One thing is having a feeling, or thinking you know something, and another is actually having confirmation.

"If you didn't want me, why would you stay?" I ask quietly.

"I did want you." He glances up quickly. "It had nothing to do with that."

"Then what?"

"*You* didn't want *me*, Joss," he says and has the gall to look upset. "You didn't prioritize me."

"Oh, do not turn this around on me," I snap, glaring at him. "And to think I thought of you as the 'safe bet.'"

"Maybe that was the problem," he says angrily. "That's how you treated me. You were never really into me."

"That's bullshit."

"You never even told me you loved me!" he shouts, then lowers his voice.

"*That's* your excuse?" I ask, bewildered, and laugh harshly. "Your stupid choices aren't going to make me question my worth, so you're trying to gaslight the wrong fucking person." My eyes narrow. "And I did love you."

His expression crumples. He may not have made me feel the things that I feel when I'm around … I stop the dangerous thought before it blossoms. My mom always told me butterflies were overrated. She said love manifested in many ways. Sometimes your heart doesn't gallop when you're with the person you're supposed to be with. Comfort, safety, and friendship should override the butterflies that will one day die anyway.

It was how she felt with Titus, and she was genuinely over the moon happy with him. So, maybe I wasn't butterflies in my stomach in love with Tate, but I did love him, and I had enough respect for him to never have done what he did.

"Josie…" He flinches and looks away.

"Don't fucking call me that," I say through clenched teeth.

He never called me that, because he damn well knows only my parents are allowed to.

"I don't know why I did that." He exhales. "Look. What I did was wrong, and I'm sor—"

"Don't." I glare at him. "Even if the video hadn't gone viral, what you did was disrespectful. The least you can do is be a man and own up to it. Even your apology is *for you* because you want *me* to absolve *you*. What did you come here for? Let's get it over with so you can get out."

His eyes widen. Of course, he's surprised. The only time I've ever yelled at him was on the phone after I saw the videos. I didn't let him get a word in, so he apologized over mine. I'd been the perfect partner for him, always catering to him, because that's what I saw my grandmother and mother do. I'd settled because that's what they did.

But I'm not them. It took all of this for me to realize it. I wasn't put on this earth to serve anyone. I love helping people and making them smile, but I can't live my life walking on eggshells to make that happen. I won't. And I want the butterflies. Even if they fade over time, I deserve to experience it.

I hold my breath when my eyes shift behind him as the lobby doors open and Damian walks in. He's engrossed in his phone, but he's standing in my line of vision, and I know the moment he looks up, he's going to see us. This is the worst possible time for this kind of interruption. Damian has been looking for a reason to fight Tate for years now, and if he sees him here, I know he'll try to start something. Tate looks over his shoulder and curses as he straightens again.

"He'll leave us alone," I say, and as if the universe hears me,

Damian walks to the elevators without ever looking up from his screen.

I'm about to let out a relieved breath when the doors open again and Finn freaking Barlow walks inside. *Oh, fuck.* My heart does about a million flips. Unlike my stepbrother, he's not distracted, and as soon as he steps away from the revolving door, he lasers in on me. His expression darkens when he sees who's sitting across from me. For a split second, I think he's going to ignore us and follow my brother upstairs, as he should, but instead, he starts walking over.

"I'll be right back," I say, scrambling to my feet and practically sprinting over to Finn. I exhale. "Please don't."

"Why the fuck is he here?" he asks, his angry gaze on Tate.

"He just wants to talk," I say.

His eyes flash to mine. "And you're going to listen?" His gaze drops to the roses in my hands, and his jaw tightens. "He gave you fucking flowers?"

"He works at Titus' firm. I'm going to have to see him sooner or later, and I'd rather it be here than in public. I'm going to have a civilized conversation and hopefully never speak to him again."

His angry eyes flash to mine. "He doesn't deserve a second of your attention."

"What's going on over here?" Tate asks, coming up behind me, and Finn's entire body goes rigid.

"That's exactly what I'm trying to figure out," he says. "Why the fuck are you here?"

"Why the fuck are *you* here?" Tate counters.

Finn's eyes sparkle with mirth. "I live here, asshole."

I frown, taken aback by that. "Since when?"

"Since yesterday," Finn says, still looking at Tate. "You need to leave."

Tate stares at him for a moment and then laughs in disbelief as he looks from me to Finn and back. "Oh ... Josslyn ... tell me there's nothing going on between you two."

"That's none of your business," I snap, overshadowing

whatever words are about to come out of Finn's mouth. I shoot him a look telling him to stay quiet. He just glares.

"If you think *I'm* a liar and a cheater, then you certainly have a type," Tate spits, then adds. "What, you haven't fucked her yet? Is that why you're still interested?"

"I'm going to give you one minute to get out of here before I destroy your fucking face," Finn growls and takes a menacing step forward.

"Finneas," I snap. He glares at me. "Just stop."

"Is there a problem here?" the security guy asks as he walks over.

"Yes," Finn says, at the same time Tate and I say, "No."

"We were just going to step outside," Tate grits between his teeth as he looks at Finn.

He grabs my hand and I'm forced to take a step as he starts pulling me. I don't get to take another before Finn pushes him so hard that I stumble before I'm able to yank my hand back.

"Don't fucking touch her," Finn seethes.

"This is unfuckingbelievable." Tate grinds his jaw and puffs his chest as he looks at me. "You know he's only using you to piss me off, right? He's using you to get back at me because he—"

"I suggest you keep your baseless comments to yourself, Ford," Finn says through his teeth.

"Sir, I'm going to need you to…" the security starts.

"I'm going," Tate snaps, fixing his shirt and walking toward the door. He looks at me. "I'll be in touch."

Finn chuckles, and even though he doesn't say anything, it sounds like a warning. Once Tate is out of sight, I whirl around to face Finn.

"What is wrong with you?" I hiss, looking around the lobby to make sure no one is recording. "Do you realize that could've been caught on video?" I shake my head and start walking, leaving the bouquet on a table as I walk past it.

My arms are crossed as I stand in front of the elevator, only unfolding to stab the button more times than necessary. I don't know what I'm more upset about—Tate for reaching out even though he knows I don't want to talk, myself for accepting the invitation, Finn for the way he acted, Tate for suggesting Finn's only interested in me to get some sort of revenge on him, or the idea that there could've been someone taking video of it all. The wheels in my brain start turning as I try to figure out what my response will be if it comes to that. I run a hand down my face. I can only imagine the things people will say online. Personal drama is catnip for them. I drop my hand and take a breath. From the corner of my eye, I see Finn approaching.

"I am not sharing an elevator with you right now." I stab the button again.

He says nothing, but his face is a mask of anger. When the elevator door finally opens and I find it empty, I begin to step inside but turn to look at him. "Take the next one."

Surprisingly, he listens. I watch him start pacing as the doors close between us. As I ride up, I bury my face in my hands and realize I'm shaking. When I get to my apartment, I find Damian standing outside with a box of donuts. My feelings are chaotic and the last thing I want is company, but I know he's not going anywhere, so I push my emotions aside. He glances up from his phone, when he senses he's not alone.

"Yo, where have you been?" he asks. Whatever he finds makes his expression harden. "What happened?"

I shake my head, walk inside, go straight to my water bottle, and start drinking. It's shaking so hard against my lips that water starts running down my chin. I set it down.

Damian tosses the box on the counter. "Joss, what the hell happened?"

"Tate was here."

His expression darkens. "What did he want?"

"He just wanted to talk."

"What the fuck did he say to make you this angry?" he asks and brings out his phone. "I'm going to kill him."

"No!" I yell, then repeat quieter. "No. It's fine. Finn got here and they had a little altercation."

The last thing I need is for Dame to go after him as well.

His brows shoot up. "They got into a fight?"

"It was a very heated argument," I say, sitting on the barstool and setting my elbows on the counter with a sigh.

"About what? I've seen them in a room together and each usually pretends the other doesn't exist."

My exhale is a shaky laugh. "Yeah, that didn't happen downstairs."

I focus on the box of donuts, opening it and looking at each of them. I've known my stepbrother since I was eight years old. Unlike some stepsiblings, we never had an awkward stage. When we met, it was as if we'd always been brother and sister. Our dynamic has never changed throughout the years. If anything, after the loss of my dad, we became closer.

We always share when we're seeing someone, even if it's casual, but for some reason, I can't bring myself to share this. Maybe it's because I've heard the way Damian and his friends constantly make jokes about the puck bunnies who "think they have a golden pussy that'll make Finn want a repeat." It's disgusting, but unfortunately, it's the kind of talk I've gotten used to. Not that the women's locker room is much better.

"I didn't even know Finn had moved here," I comment, shutting the box again.

Damian opens it and grabs a strawberry-frosted donut. "Yeah, he mentioned that. They're working on his apartment, so he needs to move temporarily."

I stare at the box of donuts, but in my head, I'm thinking about the way Finn looked downstairs and the things Tate said. Now that I'm reviewing it, I realize he said a lot. Tate's self-centered, so of course, he'd say Finn is only showing interest in me to get to him, so that doesn't really bother me, but everything else … The joke is that Finn is a one-and-done kind of guy, but Tate's right. He hasn't actually fucked me yet. It makes me wonder how many women he's done this with. *How many has he acted jealous over until he gets them in his bed?* Is that his thing? And why do I even care?

Damian gets my attention again and spends the next hour trying to talk me into going to the pool party. I refuse and encourage him to go ahead. Even if I wasn't feeling down today, I would have passed up on it.

"We only have one week of freedom," he says.

"I know, and my week is booked."

"Would you want to go skating at the new arena?"

"Pass," I say quickly. The last time I skated, I fell on my ass twice.

"Fine," he grumbles. "Want to work out at our training facility?"

That makes me perk up. *"That* I'll do."

He pushes off the counter. "Tomorrow."

I follow him to the door, and when he opens it, he nearly trips on something. He picks it up, and when he turns around, he has an arrangement of sunflowers in his hand. My heart starts pounding hard as he hands it to me. Even though I can barely wrap my head around it, deep down, I know who they're from.

"Who are these from? Your mom?" he asks.

"Probably," I say, gripping the vase a little tighter as I step back inside my apartment. "I'll see you tomorrow! Have fun at the party!"

"You're not going to read the note?"

"In private," I say, and he rolls his eyes with a sigh, but walks away.

I lock the door and set the flowers on the counter, plucking the note.

These made me think of you. - F

My heart feels like it's going to beat out of my chest as I set the note down and pick up my phone.

> **Me: idk how you managed to get these so quickly, or why, but they're beautiful. Thank you. PS. this doesn't excuse your tantrum.**

I watch the little bubbles that say he's typing back appear and disappear twice before his text finally comes through.

Finn: I know

That's it. It's all he says. I wait a little longer and when nothing else comes in, I put my phone down and take the flowers to my coffee table. Olivia texts to let me know she's bringing pizza, so I start picking up the apartment, and it's only then that something hits me ... *How does Finn know where I live?*

CHAPTER TWENTY-THREE

Finn

"You're so fucking petty," Lucas says, laughing as he pours himself a drink.

"I never said I wasn't."

I focus on the stack of papers in front of me, while my cousin walks around the penthouse telling me what he likes and doesn't like about it. The penthouse he currently lives in is in the building beside the one I'm remodeling, but unlike me, he met with the builder and had a say in every detail of his.

"Do you ever wonder what it would be like to just give in and work for our dads?" he asks as he paces.

I stop everything I'm doing and look at him. "No. Do you?"

Our fathers were born with silver spoons in their mouths and gained access to their inheritance when they turned twenty-one. While my dad made smart investments, Lucas' blew threw a lot of it, something that's very difficult to accomplish considering the amount of zeros in his bank account. It may have been for the best. My uncle married someone outside of our social circle, which is practically unheard of, and Lucas and his brother Asher were raised in a very normal household. As normal as growing up in a high-class household could be. My aunt was a homemaker and very present in their lives—in mine as well—and kept them grounded. She was my biggest cheerleader when my career took off, and still is.

More often than not, when I was growing up, I wished I'd lived with them. But I didn't, and because of that, I had no qualms about walking away. It's not like I was going to gain access to my inheritance if I hadn't. The way things are set up now, only our money managers can touch that money until we're thirty-five. Not that we need it. We've both received money since we were born just for existing.

Even if I didn't, there's no way I'd ever work for my father, and he hates that. He hates that I've paved my own way, doing something I actually love. I used to hate him for it, until I realized he was probably envious of me since he didn't do the same. It never occurred to him that it was an option, so he couldn't get out from under my grandfather's thumb. He couldn't marry the woman he actually loved or do whatever it was he would have done if he hadn't been born a Barlow. That's on him, though.

"Why would you even consider it?" I ask after a moment. "You have everything you want and more. You've built it."

He huffs out a laugh. "Is that what you tell yourself? Our monthly allowance—"

"Yes, fine, you started out in a much better financial situation than most, but it's not like you can survive off of our monthly allowance forever."

He laughs. "If my mom hears you say that, I think she'd slap you."

"She probably would." I feel my lips tug. "She's always been the most normal of us all."

"What happens when they die?" he asks. "Our dads, I mean. We'll have no idea what to do since we've never paid attention to any of it."

"I don't know, Luke, but we have a lot of lawyers, so I wouldn't worry about it. You've been your own boss your whole life. Do you really want to answer to someone, let alone our dads?" I ask, brows raised.

I can't imagine he would. I sure as hell wouldn't. I start sorting everything into individual stacks—one stack for my real estate, one for anything that has to do with the Owls, and a third for things about Mallory. My phone buzzes with a text from Tom, my private investigator, and I open it to see pictures of Josslyn sitting at a coffee shop across from Tate. White heat spreads through my body in an instant.

I knew he'd find a way to speak to her again, but I didn't think it would be so soon, and I definitely didn't think she'd give him the time of day. The fact that she did annoys the fuck out of me, but that's not even what annoys me the most. She's wearing Tiago's basketball jersey. I wish I could reach into the screen and rip it off her. I don't know what the fuck it is about this girl that makes me feel this way, but the most insignificant things make me see red.

Why the fuck should I care that she has another man's jersey on? She already confirmed that they're not hooking up, but seeing his name on her back and knowing it's a jersey he actually wears grates on my nerves. The sound that escapes my lips is typically reserved for times on the ice when my team is losing, so Lucas stops walking.

"What the hell happened to you?"

"Nothing." I wave a hand. "Go back to being a nosy fuck and ignore me."

I keep looking through pictures. Josslyn looks nonchalant, lounging on the chair. She's wearing shorts underneath that huge jersey, and her smooth tanned legs are crossed as she listens to whatever fuck-face is saying. Tate, on the other hand, reeks of desperation, with the way he's leaning over the table. I keep scrolling through the pictures and find more of the same.

When they're finished with their little meeting, they face each other, and Josslyn says something before she turns around and walks away. At least, she didn't do something stupid like hug him. I inwardly groan. I just need to fuck her and get this over with. In the next picture, she has her phone pressed to her ear as she walks down the street with a smile on her face that makes me wonder who the hell is on the other end of that call.

I exit out of the text messages and open up the first social media icon I see. She's permanently in my search history, so I don't have to type out her name anymore. She's the only thing in my search history, I realize. That gives me pause. I click her name and look at her feed.

Her last post was this morning and it's a video of her wearing the jersey. I glance around to make sure my cousin isn't here, and I click it. Josslyn's wearing a sports bra and tiny shorts, and she smiles at the camera as she lifts up Tiago's jersey.

"You guys remember the bet I made with T?" she asks, pouting. "It's my turn to pay up." She puts the jersey on and fixes her hair as she sits down in front of the camera. "I'm only wearing it for a few hours. That was the deal." She glances down at herself and shrugs. "I'm just going to pretend it's mine." Her eyes sparkle, and my chest squeezes. "To be fair, he's wearing mine today, as well, so stay tuned."

I feel my jaw set. He's wearing her jersey? What kind of bullshit bet is this? Josslyn goes on talking about her day as I exit out of the app and find her name on my phone, my fingers flying before I can process what I'm doing.

> **Me: you need to come up with a better bet**

I watch the little bubbles as she types back.

> **Josslyn: why? You don't like me wearing another man's jersey?**

I grip my phone tighter, a part of me wishing I could take back my words, but I can't help it. If I don't say something, my head is going to explode.

> **Me: you know I don't**

> **Josslyn: are you this possessive over every woman you hook up with?**

I frown and lower my phone. What am I supposed to say?

That she consumes my every thought? That no woman has ever made me feel these … emotions before? Fuck no. The fact that I'm even thinking those things pisses me off. I lift my phone and answer honestly.

Me: no

I set down my phone and shut my eyes as I lean back on the couch.

"I don't think she's going to be a one-and-done," Lucas says out of nowhere.

I sit up straight. "Yes, she is."

He laughs. "You sent her flowers!"

I bite my tongue and pick up some papers. "Flowers have nothing to do with me fucking her one time and being done."

"To you, maybe." He cocks his head. "You're going as her date to a charity event."

"For charity."

"You sent a woman flowers, are accompanying her to an event, which is unheard of, and almost got into a fist fight with a guy." His brows lift. "Damn, saying it out loud…" He tilts his head. "You like her."

"I'd *like* to fuck her."

He chuckles. "Keep telling yourself that."

Am I just telling myself that? *No.* I'm attracted to her and I know she's worthy of more than a douchebag cheater who doesn't even know what kind of flowers to buy her. That doesn't mean I like her *in that way.*

I sigh heavily. "I sent her flowers because I *am* petty. Roses don't even match her personality, and I'm going to a *charity* event with her. *For charity.*"

"*Don't match her personality…*" he says with a quiet chuckle.

"You're making something out of nothing."

"If you like her, you need to at least call off your hounds. What do you think she's going to say when she finds out you've had someone following her for over a year?"

I shrug. "I genuinely don't give a fuck what she says. I have my reasons."

"I'd drop it. She's not hiding anything. Not that there's anything to hide."

I lower the papers and stare at him. "You still don't believe someone killed Mallory."

"No, I don't." He takes another sip. "What happened was awful, but I think you need to make peace with it and let it go. For your own sanity."

I push back the anger that threatens. "She's my sister."

Every time I say that, I feel unworthy of the title. I was a shit brother to her. We all know it. I may be a lot of things, but I'm self-aware enough to know that's the reason I'm seeking justice. I should've done more when she was still here. She was younger than me, so we didn't have the same interests or friends. By the time she got to high school, I was on my way out, and things were so hectic that year, I barely had time to see her.

Still, we kept in touch. When I left, I made sure she knew I was still there for her. Not that she ever needed me. She'd call, though, when she was bored, to tell me about her day and her friends. It was usually a one-sided conversation, but I didn't mind. Growing up, I had my friends—Ella, Hammie, and a few other guys I've lost touch with. Mallory didn't have that. Her friend group was full of vipers waiting to strike. And still, she must have liked them. Even after she got closer to Olivia and later, Josslyn, she never stopped hanging out with the other girls.

When she started college, I noticed a change in her, but I never thought to question it. It was college and she liked to party; there was nothing wrong with that. She never told me about Onyx, though. I knew she'd been there the night I hooked up with Josslyn, but I'd scrubbed that from my memory. I didn't know she went there as often as she seemed to. There are a lot of things about my sister that I should have known, and would have known if I'd been paying closer attention. So no, I can't just "let this go." I'm going to find out what happened that night. Mallory deserves that much.

"Did you talk to Donnie about the building across from the arena?" I ask, changing the subject.

"He said it's not for sale."

I shoot him a look. "Everything is for sale."

"That's what I told him," he says, smirking. "Did you meet with the architect?"

"Not yet, but I need to this week."

"You've said that about your entire to-do list."

"Because practice starts soon, and only two of the guys have played together in the past."

"Are you worried about it?"

I nod my response. They're good, but we haven't had a chance to hang, outside of meetings, which isn't ideal. Things flow smoother on the ice when you click with the person skating beside you. We're going golfing together for charity, and Lachlan suggested a barbecue at his house—as long as Lyla is comfortable and hasn't given birth by then. They're just more things on my to-do list, but I can handle it. Josslyn is the only thing on that list that's making me crazy, and I plan on checking her off very soon.

CHAPTER TWENTY-FOUR

Josslyn

The longer I stare at the flowers, the more I begin to question Finn's motives. I'm not a petty person, so that wasn't my first, second, or even third thought when I first got them, but now, I don't know ... Did he do it to one-up Tate? He hates him and it's obvious that he was bothered by the flowers. Deep down, I know they're probably just apology flowers and I'm reading too much into it, but even that makes my heart flutter, because Finn isn't the apology type and this ... is a lot coming from him.

My heart does a little flip when I think about the way he reacted to seeing me with Tate. I've never been with someone fiercely protective of me—and I'm not sure if that's what this is, or if I'm just a toy he's possessive over until he gets sick of me—but it feels good to feel wanted by him. I shake the thoughts away. I need to focus on what's important. I check to make sure I'm signed up for the correct class, Social Work Research II, and exit the school portal. It'll be my first on-campus course in four years, and even though it's the last few credits I need to be done with school, I feel like it'll be my first day all over again. So much so that Olivia and Damian have agreed to go to the mall with me so I can get an outfit for the day class starts. It's not just that. We also need to pick up Dame's tux and get dresses for the fundraiser that's looming—and spinning more out of control by the second.

Every other comment on my post is someone asking if it's true that Finn is going as my date. Of course, the follow-up question is, "Are you together?" which … I can't answer. I know neither one of us is hooking up with anyone else. I also know he doesn't want other guys touching me. But that's it. We've never gone on a date or gone to each other's apartments. We've never hung out alone at all—the times we've hooked up don't count.

It's a sucky realization, but thinking about it reminds me that I want to get in touch with Scarlet, my only friend and connection at Onyx, to ask her a few questions, so I do that.

"Time is just a man-made construct," Livie says.

I snort out a laugh but keep my comments to myself. Every time Olivia and Damian smoke together, they turn into dollar-store versions of Socrates and Plato. Their nonsense makes a twenty-minute car ride feel two hours long, especially when I'm the one driving. By the time I pull up to the mall, I feel like my head is going to explode.

"So is money," Dame says, as I park and turn off the car.

"If money is a man-made construct, why don't they just print more of it?" I ask, knowing it'll take them a while to think of the obvious answers, but at least they'll shut the fuck up while they think.

We're pretty efficient at the mall. I find my new outfit—sneakers and cute cotton shorts with a matching crop top and hoodie. It takes us an hour to get our dresses for the Alma Foundation fundraiser, but even that seems to go by fast. We leave Damian's tux for last, since it's near the food court and we want pretzels.

"Who's F?" Damian asks out of the blue.

My head snaps up while my heart drops a little. "Why?"

"The flowers," he says. "Is it Barlow?"

"That starts with a B," I try lamely, which earns me a look. "Fine. It is but it means nothing."

His brows hike. He's quiet as we walk, pensive, and I hate it. Livie, on the other hand, starts chatting away about the meaning of different flowers and how Finn definitely did his research.

"I don't want details," Dame says. "But I'm confused by the gesture."

"Welp," Livie says. "If you want to ask him yourself, you can in about a minute. He's headed our way."

My heart does a full drop now as I see Finn and Will walking with bags from Neiman Marcus. I nearly roll my eyes, because *of course*, those two shop there. Someone stops to take pictures with them, then another stops them for autographs, and finally, they reach us.

"Fancy meeting you here," Will says.

"I was thinking the same thing," Damian says. I pinch his arm, which makes him hiss and look at me.

Thankfully, the expression on his face tells me he's not going to ask Finn about the flowers. When I dare to look at Finn, I find him watching, checking me out. I feel my face heat and bite my lip, as our eyes lock and his expression darkens. I'm wearing one of Damian's old Fairview t-shirts with a pair of shorts.

"What'd you get?" Livie asks and starts walking, so we all move with her. "Come with us. We're getting pretzels."

"Not much," Will says, lifting one of the bags. "Underwear, socks, and some other stuff."

Laughter bubbles out of me. "You buy your underwear and socks at Neiman?"

"Sometimes." He shrugs. "What's wrong with Neiman?"

"Nothing," I say. "I always thought guys bought that kind of stuff online or at like TJ Maxx or something."

"Hammie's probably never been there," Damian quips.

Will shoots him a look. "I've been there several times."

"You went *once* to pick up your grandma while you were on vacation in a cabin in the middle of nowhere," Finn says.

"*Twice*," Will counters and looks at me, eyes lit with amusement. "Where do you buy your underwear?"

I look at Finn, whose eyes are locked on mine. He looks tense as he waits for my response. I tear my gaze from his and look at Will. "It depends what kind of underwear we're talking about."

"Lingerie," he says, his eyes doing a quick sweep of my body.

My eyes fly to Finn again, and I note the clench of his jaw and the glare he shoots at his friend before he pulls his phone out of his pocket and focuses on that.

"That depends on what kind of lingerie you're talking about," Livie says and even though sometimes it annoys me when she does that, right now, I'm so grateful I could kiss her.

"Oh god. I'm gonna go get our pretzels," Dame says, and we all turn in that direction.

"I can't even remember the last time I came to the food court," Will says.

"Probably the last time you picked up your grandmother at TJ Maxx," I respond, smiling up at him.

Livie and Dame laugh. Will laughs and shakes his head, but it's the sound coming from Finn—somewhere between a laugh and a cough—that makes me smile harder.

"I'll get a table," I announce.

"I'll come with," Livie says.

"Fletcher, get me a lemonade," Finn says as Will and Dame walk to the pretzel stand.

"Don't forget my water," I add, and he nods.

Livie, Finn, and I make a beeline for the first large empty booth we see. Livie sits across from me, and of course, Finn slides in beside me. He scoots closer and crowds me with his large body and amazing smell. Even the way he breathes is sexy, which is ridiculous but true. When his arm brushes up against mine, I tense, feeling like my heart might just beat out of my damn chest.

"Dad's sent me five texts mansplaining inflation to me," Livie says, laughing as she looks at her phone. "Oh god. Now he's sending me links to articles in the NASDAQ."

I laugh. "He would."

"You're almost done with college and you don't know what inflation is?" Finn asks, frowning slightly.

"She took an edible and has been philosophizing about man-made constructs," I explain, my eyes flicking from his to Liv. "What'd you ask Papa Nas?"

The sound of Finn's laugh makes my heart skip. "I bet Dr. Nassir just loves that nickname."

"He actually does," I say, grinning. My heart skips again when I glance over and catch him staring at my lips. I look away so fast I almost give myself whiplash.

"I asked him what would happen if they printed more money," Livie says and laughs again. "Oh my god. He just sent another article." She looks at Finn. "I'm not even going to ask you what you think would happen if they printed more money."

That makes me laugh. "I don't think that's a good question to ask a billionaire trust-fund baby." I look over at Finn again. "Especially one who buys his underwear at expensive department stores."

His mouth twitches. "Did you also take an edible?"

"Nope. I'm the chauffeur."

"She's for hire," Livie says. "As long as you buy her sneakers. That's the price I paid."

I laugh. "You are such a liar! You bought me sneakers because you lost the ones you borrowed from me last fall."

"Still for hire," she quips.

"I'd hire you," Finn says, his voice dropping as he moves closer.

I feel like I'm going to die—from the proximity, his delicious scent, and the way he's acting with me in public. His gaze drops to my mouth and I instinctively lick my lips.

"Fuck," he says. It's a breath, barely a sound.

Everything around us disappears as he moves his face closer

to mine. He brushes his nose against mine and the butterflies in my stomach riot.

"Finn," I say quietly, a warning, a plea.

As if remembering where we are, he pulls back and looks around. Only then do I let out the breath I was holding. I clear my throat and glance at Livie, who's looking at us with a shocked expression on her face, but quickly goes back to her phone. I start drumming on the table and stare at my white nails. I'm dying to check my phone, but I don't want to do it in front of him.

All day I've been expecting a text from Scarlet at Onyx—which is exactly how she's saved on my phone—and I'd rather Finn not see it. Knowing him, he'll jump to conclusions and call me a liar again, which … I guess I technically am. The thought makes my stomach coil. Mallory's no longer with us, and she's still a pain in the ass. God, I miss her.

"I'll be right back," Livie says, standing and walking away.

I watch her go, knowing I'm going to get *such* an earful about this later.

"Whose shirt are you wearing today, Josie?" Finn asks, his voice deeper than it was before and his eyes so dark my heart skips another beat.

"Don't call me that," I whisper, swallowing. "And it's Damian's."

He makes a low grunting noise. "Do you need me to take you shopping for clothes?"

My brows rise. "I have clothes."

"Why do you keep wearing other men's shirts then?"

My mouth twists. "Okay, first of all, you can't tell me what I can—"

"I would never tell you what to wear."

"—and can't wear." I shoot him a look. "Secondly, this is my stepbrother's shirt, so—"

"I don't like seeing it on you."

I blink. "—you can't possibly be jealous."

"Seeing you in other men's clothes is fucking maddening, Josslyn," he growls.

My heart stops, but I don't take my eyes away from his, and the longer we stare, the hotter the fire in his eyes burns into me. I resist the urge to ask why, but it's clear Finn doesn't even know what he's feeling. Suddenly, he pulls back and straightens. When I look forward, I see my stepbrother and Will grabbing pretzels and cheese and turning to walk over. We spend the next hour talking shit and eating pretzels, and even though we're not alone, it feels like we are in our own bubble as we joke back and forth. If I completely tune out the other three people with us, I can almost pretend it's a date.

That's the first sign that I'm treading in dangerous waters. I shouldn't be thinking about dates with this man, but it's impossible to decipher what the hell we're doing. And I don't want to be *that girl* who asks, "What are we?" after being told the rules of the game, even though it feels like he's totally obliterating them. I'm going to let it play out a little longer, but I just might have to be *that girl*.

CHAPTER TWENTY-FIVE

Finn

I'M NOT FOLLOWING JOSSLYN ON PURPOSE. WE WERE DRIVING IN THE same direction and I happened to be two cars behind her when she turned into Onyx. Of course, I pulled into the lot and parked the car in a spot where I could see her. *My sister died here.* What the fuck is Josslyn doing here? I look at the time, hoping to somehow pause it. I left my house early, and now I'm going to be late for dinner with my parents, but I don't care. I'll cancel if I have to. This is much more important.

I watch her get out of her car, lock it, look around a few times, and walk to the side door. *The side door.* Unease grips me. As she waits, I check her out. She's wearing black heels and a little black dress that hugs her hips. She looks mouthwatering, which makes me even more annoyed that she's here. She texts someone, and the door opens a few seconds later. I can't get a clear view of who opened it, but the moment it shuts, I'm out of my car.

My gut twists as I head to the front door. Inside, a pretty red-head greets me and asks for my name and ID, which I give her. I'm not in the mood for conversation, so I'm glad she doesn't say much as she hands me a mask and an assortment of wristbands. I only grab the white one and go inside. In the middle, their usual exotic show is going on, but I don't take the time to admire it. I channel all my focus on walking to the bar and finding Josslyn.

I spot Josslyn right away. She's at the other end of the bar speaking to a woman I've seen here before. As close as they're sitting, they're either going to make out or they're having a very private conversation. That woman better hope to God she doesn't try the former while I'm here. I take a deep breath, let it out, and adjust the stupid mask on my face. I ask for a drink and sip it slowly, as they have what seems like the longest conversation in history. They have to be discussing Mallory. There's no way Josslyn is here for anything else.

I watch a man in a suit walk up to them. He has silver hair and no mask on. He looks old enough to be my dad. He grins and says something to them that makes them both laugh. Josslyn's smile remains on her face as she listens to him speak, and I decide I don't like it—not the undivided attention she's giving him, and definitely not the smile. He crosses his arms and plants his feet like he's going to be there a while, so I lean back slightly and get comfortable.

The woman says something that makes the guy laugh and look at Josslyn again. I clench my fists as he uncrosses his arms and reaches for hers to examine—or make the point—that she doesn't have a wristband on. The biggest downside to my being here is that I can't say anything to her about this. Then again, what would I say? That she should've been wearing a white wristband? I've made it pretty clear that I won't share her, but she didn't agree to exclusivity, did she? Big oversight on my part. It doesn't matter anymore. I'm giving myself a deadline to seal the deal and rid myself of this possessiveness I feel when it comes to her.

Josslyn lowers her hand and says something that makes the man clutch his chest like she hurt him, which I like. He turns and looks toward the entryway and says, "John!" loud enough for me to hear, and a man wearing jeans and a sports coat walks over. This one is much younger. The older one introduces him to Josslyn, who surprisingly doesn't smile at him. He looks serious as he says something to her. My stomach tightens when she hands him her phone and I decide I can't stay here any longer. I shoot back the rest of my drink and signal the woman who took my order so she can bring the check.

While I wait, the two men finally leave, and Josslyn and the woman talk some more. They stand suddenly and Josslyn grabs her things. I shoot a look in the direction of the server, hoping she catches it and understands I'm in a rush. She brings the check and I hand over my card quickly as I watch Josslyn and the woman walk out of the room. Jesus Christ, how long does it take to charge a twelve dollar drink? The woman finally comes back, and I get up as quickly as I can.

Josslyn is down the hall, turning toward the exit, and the woman she was speaking to walks in my direction. She smiles at me as she passes. I've definitely seen her. I stop before I reach the lobby and look down the hall in the direction that Mallory went the night she died. They've remodeled the wing. You can't even tell there was ever a fire here. It's as if nothing ever happened, which serves as a reminder as to why I'm doing this. Mallory can't just be forgotten. Before I turn to leave, I catch sight of the John guy coming out of one of the rooms.

I don't think. I head his way and take him in fully. He's much shorter than I am, but I can tell he works out a lot. From experience, I know that doesn't mean much in a fight. I consider it, but I know it won't do me any favors. Instead, just as he's about to walk past me, I get closer.

"Hey, I hope you don't mind me asking," I say, making him stop walking. "I saw you talking to a woman in a black dress earlier. Long dark hair, tan skin…"

He frowns slightly. "What about her?"

"Are you involved?"

His brows shoot up and understanding replaces the suspicion on his face. "Not yet," he says, smirking. "You interested?"

My heart pounds hard against my chest. "Would you be able to make that happen for me?"

"Maybe." He shrugs. "For a price."

I cross my arms to keep from reaching out and choking him. "How much?"

"I run an exclusive group and she's thinking about joining," he says. "There's a membership fee, but if you want to get to know her, you should check it out."

"Do you have a card?"

He fishes out a card from the inside pocket of his jacket and hands it to me. I take it and glance at it briefly. "Call me and we'll set something up."

I give a nod and walk away. On the way to my car, I text my cousin about John Petrov and Google to see what information I can find. I'm not surprised to find Josslyn's car is gone. I call my mother to let her know I won't be making it to dinner and promise her I'll come next time. Most likely, she told some woman that I'd be there and was hoping I'd magically become interested in her. As soon as I hang up, my phone vibrates with a call from Lucas.

"Why the hell are you talking to that guy?"

"Who is he? The card says nothing but his name and number."

"He's the one who ran the underground club with the fifty-thousand a month membership. The cops were called once because a wife showed up here after finding out her husband was a member. Stop me when any of this sounds familiar…"

"I vaguely remember it," I respond, frowning.

He laughs. "Jesus, Finn. The wife tried to sue us."

"When did this happen?"

"Last May."

I remember him telling me about the incident. "I was in the middle of playoffs."

"Right. Well, John doesn't conduct business here anymore."

"He does at Onyx."

"I heard. He's good friends with the owner there, so it doesn't surprise me," he says, pausing when someone starts speaking to him. "Were you at Onyx?"

"What are the underground groups like?" I ask, ignoring his question.

"They're mostly for swingers or high-profile people who really want to keep their shit private and are willing to pay to ensure no one finds out about them."

Huh. I stare at the card as I flip it between my fingers. I think about Josslyn's meeting with that woman and her interaction with those guys earlier. I know this has something to do with my sister. Most likely, this is her trying to get information that'll prove her stepfather's innocence to me. Does that mean Mallory was involved in these? *What the hell was she thinking?*

"I gotta go," I tell Lucas.

"We're still on for golf, right?"

"Yeah." I hang up and shut my eyes as I lean against the headrest.

Hypocritical as it makes me, I don't like the idea of her being in contact with any of these people. On the drive back to my place, my stomach churns when I think about Josslyn in a room with men like John. The feeling frustrates me more than it should but it proves that I need to put an end to this madness ASAP.

CHAPTER TWENTY-SIX

Josslyn

Instead of meeting Livie and some of our teammates at the bar like I was supposed to, I decide to head home. My head is spinning from everything I just learned from Scarlet and the men she introduced me to. I knew Mallory had a group of friends she met with there. I think about the man we saw at a restaurant one night, and Mallory's strange reaction to him saying hello. He looked like the typical rich, older man. From the way he greeted her, I figured he had to be a friend of her parents, but her panicked face and shaky hands when we walked out said otherwise.

Naturally, I asked her about him, and of course, she lied. I think discovering how much she lied is the worst part of all of this. After parking my car, I grab my phone to text Mallory, as I've done so often.

> Me: Your brother is a real pain in the ass, but i don't think he's wrong about what happened not being an accident. He's bringing Titus into this now, and I KNOW he had nothing to do with it but he has footage that could incriminate him, which means I'll have to prove him wrong. God, Mal. This is so fucked up. I wish I could go back to that fight and

make you see reason. I wish I would've tried more before that night. And after.

I put my phone in my purse and wipe the tears from my face. Twenty-four hours after her death, her parents put a gag order on everyone—Mal's friends, the employees at Onyx, the cops, the media. Days later, their lawyer sent everyone another document stating we needed to take down all photos and posts of Mallory. She hadn't even been dead a week and they were already erasing her as if she'd never existed. That's how it felt, anyway. In a way, I did the same thing after my dad died, so I guess I can't blame them. It's easier to deal with loss if you compartmentalize and file it away. After a moment, I make myself get out of the car and head into my building.

I smell him before I realize it's him, and my nerves instantly go haywire. Somehow, I'm able to act nonchalant as I take a step back. He's wearing navy slacks, a white shirt with the top button undone, and a sports coat. The shadow of a beard gives him a rugged look, and his hair is a little out of place, but I can tell he'd had it slicked back earlier. He looks so fucking hot. Even more so as he drags his hooded eyes over me from head to toe and back.

"Are you going out or getting back from somewhere?" I ask and clear my throat to compose myself.

"Just got back," he says, giving me another heated once-over. "You?"

"I met a friend for drinks," I say, hoping my voice doesn't sound as shaky as I feel.

It's technically not a lie, but for some reason, I feel like it is. Finn makes an acknowledging sound that does nothing to calm my nerves, and we start walking to the elevator. We find a group of people waiting for it when we get there, and when the doors open and they step inside, I take a step forward. Finn grabs my elbow and holds me back before I get very far, letting the elevator doors close. Before I can question him, he lets go of my elbow and the next set of elevator doors open. This time, when I start walking, he's right beside me and doesn't stop me. We step inside and he moves toward the panel.

"You seem to know mine, so I'll let you press the button," I say, making it sound like a joke, though I'm hoping he explains himself.

He doesn't. He pushes the button for his floor, which is four above mine, and when he glances at me, the look he gives me makes my heart stutter. It takes him two strides to close the distance between us. When he's finally in front of me, I stop breathing.

"You're coming home with me tonight," he says, voice gravelly as he slides his long fingers into the hair at the nape of my neck and tilts my head up.

As I stare into his eyes, I consider telling him where I was and what I found out, but think better of it. I won't actually have information on the people his sister used to hang out with until I go to one of the meetings they have planned next week, so there's nothing to tell. Instead, I nod my agreement, because there's no way I'm going to turn him down.

He brings his mouth down on mine and uses my surprise to his advantage as he sweeps his tongue into my mouth. He pins me against the wall behind me, bringing a knee between my legs and pressing where I'm most sensitive as he brings his other hand to cup my breast. An onslaught of sensations shoots through me and my knees buckle. I grip his arms to keep myself upright as I get lost in the kiss. The elevator doors open, and without breaking away from me, he walks out and pulls me with him.

Finally, he breaks the kiss, his eyes wild as he searches my face for a moment before his lips are right back on mine. He wraps an arm around me to keep me steady as he walks me toward his apartment. When he pulls away again, it's to punch the code, open his door, and lead me inside. My breath leaves me as he pushes me against the closed door, his mouth back on mine. And then, we both snap. My hands yank off his jacket as he's hiking up my dress and dragging his mouth along my jaw and neck. I'm tugging his shirt out of his pants and working on his belt buckle when he suddenly grabs my hands, pulls away, and sets his forehead against mine.

"I've waited too long to fuck you. I'm not about to do it against a door," he says between breaths.

I let him pull me away from the door and lead me through his apartment—which is ten times bigger than mine. He doesn't ask if I want something to drink. Makes no small talk. And he definitely doesn't let me wrap my head around the idea that I'm in his home. In his room, he turns on the bedside lamps, giving us just enough light. Then he turns to me again, his eyes alight with lust as he takes me in once more.

"Turn around," he rasps.

Butterflies swarm my belly as I do. Behind me, I hear him wrestling with his clothes, but I stare at the closet straight ahead. I jump when I feel his breath on my neck, followed by soft kisses and nips as he begins to lower my zipper. My stomach somersaults so hard, I feel off-kilter and squirm with each graze of his fingers.

"I don't know what it is about you," he says quietly, as his lips trail down my neck to my bare shoulder.

He pauses the kisses and focuses on getting my dress over my hips and the curve of my ass.

"Jesus Christ, you're going to kill me," he mutters, dropping his mouth on the curve of my neck and biting down hard enough that I jump with a yelp.

He gives me an open-mouthed kiss there and lifts his head to continue. I glance over my shoulder as he slides down my underwear, lowering himself to a knee and grabbing and kneading my ass. I stiffen when I see him lean in, and he glances up to meet my eyes as he bites one ass cheek and then the other, earning another jump and yelp. Once I'm naked, he stands, turns me around, and lets his eyes trail over me slowly. He bites his bottom lip and shakes his head.

"You are my walking wet dream."

My heart skips, and I set my hands on the first button of his shirt. "My turn."

I undress him just as he did me, then inhale sharply when I take a step back and take him in. I shake my head in disbelief. I've been with athletes in the past and I've seen my share of shirtless men, but this is Finn, and just as he said about me, he's my walking wet dream. His body is a work of art. He even has that perfect V that disappears into his boxer briefs, and the tent in them takes my breath away. I hook my fingers into the elastic of his briefs and peel them down his legs, helping him get out of them.

I inhale sharply as I look at him. I've seen him before, but it's been too long, and it feels like the first time. He's thick and hard, and I can't help but wrap my hand around him. He hisses and leans over to kiss me again as he grabs two handfuls of my breasts and twists my nipples. I moan against his mouth and he pulls away and lifts me.

I wrap my legs and arms around him, and squeal as he turns around and drops me on the bed. I land with an oomph and laugh as I look at him, but it's cut short by the smile that breaks out on his face. Finn is the most gorgeous man I've ever seen in my life, but when he smiles, he's deadly. His eyes light up, then heat as he lowers himself and sets a knee on the bed. His lips meet mine again in a slow, deep kiss that makes my toes curl. He sucks and kisses his way to my breasts, and then lower. By the time his tongue swipes against my clit, I'm already shaking with anticipation. At my reaction, he growls and pushes my legs open further.

"Everything about you is fucking addictive," he says, nipping the inside of my thigh.

He feasts on me, licking and sucking like it's his job. When I feel the pressure building in my core, I grab his hair and tug, arching my back and moaning loudly as I come. He doesn't let me recover before he pushes his fingers inside me and rubs my clit with his thumb, pulling another orgasm from me until I'm writhing and panting. And before I recover from that one, I hear him opening a condom.

Going up on shaky elbows, I cup his balls as he slides it on, and relish the deep groan that escapes his throat. I bring my hands to his muscular thighs and scratch his abs as he lowers himself over me. He growls as he lifts one of my legs and grips my thighs to hold them apart, as he pushes inside me ever so slowly, making me feel each bit of him. I bite down hard on my lip to keep from crying out, as he stretches me and holds my breath until he's to the hilt. He stops moving then, groaning deeply as he drops his forehead against mine and exhales a harsh breath.

"Fuck, Josslyn," he rasps, pulling out an inch and groaning again as he thrusts completely in again. "Fuck."

"Please move," I gasp, my nails buried into his sides as I lift my hips to make him move.

He grabs my face so I look at him, his eyes alight with something that makes my stomach clench. "You're not in charge here."

I narrow my eyes and open my mouth to argue, but he begins to thrust in and out of me hard and deep, and the only thing that comes out is a sob. His hand comes down between us as he moves, and I feel my body clench again.

"That's it, baby," he says, pinching my clit. "Come for me again. Just like that. Fuck yes."

I squeeze my eyes shut, wrapping my legs tighter around his waist as I explode around him, screaming his name as I come.

"Hottest thing I've ever seen," he growls and pounds harder with abandon. My stomach swoops when I open my eyes and find him looking at me with an expression that's both awed and confused.

"Finn," I choke out as he slows down and circles his hips to hit a spot that makes me see stars.

"I love the way your pussy grips my cock," he says, picking up speed as he hits that same spot, and once again, I spiral. "Fuck. Yes," he growls as he comes undone.

When the haze lifts, I open my eyes and blink away tiny spots in my vision. He's still holding himself over me, his hair hanging over his face and his eyes closed as he catches his breath. My heart skips a few beats. He's always beautiful, but right now, with no worried lines or arrogant looks on his face, he's breathtaking.

Unable to help myself, I raise a hand, tuck part of his loose hair behind his ear, and trace his full mouth with the tip of my finger. His eyes pop open and he looks at me, his gaze so intense, I think he's about to tell me to stop. Instead, he lowers himself and presses his mouth against mine in a slow, lingering kiss that makes my toes curl and makes me feel things that scare the hell out of me.

CHAPTER TWENTY-SEVEN

Josslyn

I SNEAK OUT OF HIS APARTMENT WHEN I'M SURE HE'S FALLEN ASLEEP, after we have sex for a third time. Back in my apartment, I press my back against my door, let my dangling heels fall to the floor, and bury my face in my hands. Considering it was a one-time thing, I feel like I got the Finn Barlow special. He took me slow and hard, putting me in positions I didn't even know existed. Unable to form coherent thoughts right now, I let my hands drop and grab a glass of water before heading to my room. I shower and fall asleep in record time.

It's not until my alarm goes off that everything that happened last night hits me. Even though I went into this with the awareness that this was a one-time thing, I can't help but overthink it. Should I have snuck out the way I did? We never discussed whether or not I was staying the night, but based on the way he was so adamant about this being a one-time thing and what I've heard about him, leaving felt like the right thing to do.

I groan and cover my face. Why didn't we just wait to have sex after tonight's fundraiser? Now we're going to be forced to see each other, share a table, and act totally nonchalant, like we didn't have the best sex of my entire life. I have no doubt Finn is capable of doing it. It's my lack of a poker face that I'm worried about. My thoughts hop from Finn to my meeting with Scarlet, and just like that, my post-sex high vanishes. Going back there had been worse than I thought it would be. I'd never be "over" Mallory's death, but I've always been remarkably good at compartmentalizing and figured I'd be fine. I didn't think it would feel like ripping open unhealed stitches.

"She used to come here every Saturday night," she'd said about Mallory. "It's when the groups meet."

I already knew she was meeting with a group, but she never told me what they did. It didn't take a rocket scientist to figure it out, though. The three things Mal was into were hard sex, bondage, and drugs. All of which led to her untimely death.

"John's group, which is the one your friend was a part of, provides complete discretion to a very high-profile clientele."

"Is John one of the owners of Onyx?"

"Yes, though there are three main owners, so he's not the only one," she said. "One of them lives in Dubai. John is the brains behind the sex group, though."

"I'm assuming you need to be invited to join?"

"Yes. Only an existing member can invite new ones. You have to pass background checks and pay fifty grand a month."

I balked. "Fifty grand a month?"

Scarlet nodded gravely.

"So Mal was paying that much money?" I whispered.

The fee itself didn't surprise me. Mal had always been a big spender. I'd never judged her for it, but she certainly judged Livie when she talked about possibly joining a sorority. She'd said, "I didn't realize you needed to pay for friends, Olivia." By then, Mal was … different.

Scarlet nodded and looked around quickly, as if trying to make sure no one could hear us. The only reason we were meeting there to begin with was so she could introduce me to some of Mallory's "friends."

"The group is small, from what I know, and they're all

very high-profile people who would rather not have their business out there."

That made sense.

"John should be here. He's the one I think you should meet," she said. "He liked your friend very much, so I think he might help."

Unless he had something to do with it. I don't say that, though. Scarlet already knows I don't think what happened was an accident, and she understands why I'm digging. She introduced me to John and an older man named Leo, who happens to be friends with my stepfather. *God, what a mess.* I should just give all of this information to Finn and call it a day, but what information? I don't think it would be that shocking to him that Mal was in some sort of sex group. I take a deep breath and exhale shakily, just as my phone starts to ring with a call from Olivia.

"How'd it go last night?" she asks, the moment I greet her.

"It went."

She exhales. "I figured it was bad when you said you weren't coming out with us afterward."

"It wasn't bad," I say. "It was just weird. Did you know she was in a fifty-grand-a-month sex club at Onyx?"

She's quiet for a beat. "Like a kink club?"

"I'm not sure. Maybe? It sounds like a very expensive hookup club."

She sighs. "Are you surprised?"

"I mean, you knew her much better than I did," I say.

"Yeah, but toward the end…"

"Yeah."

Toward the end, Olivia had all but cut Mallory out of her life. Their entire friendship had been rocky. When Livie introduced me to Mallory, they were on the mend from a major falling out, so I wasn't surprised when that cycle continued to repeat itself. Livie didn't like Mallory's mean streak, and Mallory didn't like the way Livie called her out on her shit.

"Anything else?" Livie asks. "Did she mention anyone specifically she was hanging out with a lot?"

"Not really."

"I take it you haven't asked Tiago anything?"

That makes my back stiffen. "There's nothing to ask him. He went there once, and gave me way too much information about what they did in there."

"What a mess." She exhales. "Are you ready for tonight?"

"I guess."

"Want to do my makeup?"

I laugh. "Sure. Come over soon, though."

I run through the checklist again: I called my mother, steamed my dress, washed and curled my hair, and finished my makeup. The last two I did on a live feed because I needed content to post today. Unlike the other times, I didn't answer any questions that popped up while I was speaking about the Alma Foundation, since all of them were asking if Finn was really my date for this. We have to be at the hotel in two hours and haven't spoken or texted, which means … well, I don't know what it means. By the time Livie gets to my place for me to do her makeup, I start to worry.

"When do you have to be there?"

"An hour and a half."

"Is Finn picking you up?" she asks, as I face her with the eyeshadow palette in my hand.

"I haven't spoken to him today."

"At all?" she asks in disbelief.

"Nope." My stomach tumbles, and I take a step back until her brown eyes are on mine. "We had sex last night."

Her mouth drops just for a second before she shrieks, "What?!"

"Yeah." My lips purse. "So I don't know if I should text or just … go by myself?"

"Um, I'm still trying to wrap my head around you having sex with Finn Fucking Barlow," she says, wide-eyed. "How was it?"

"It was good, but it's worth mentioning that Tate set the bar in hell…"

Livie snorts. "Which means anyone would have been good."

"Right." I feel myself smile. "It was really good though."

"But?" she asks expectantly.

"There's no but. Not really, anyway. I just hope things aren't weird now. Scratch that, they're already weird considering I haven't even been able to text him a simple question."

"Do you think you're catching feelings for him?" she asks quietly.

I think about that for a moment, then shake my head. "I think I could very easily fall for him though, which would be a mistake."

"Maybe."

I shoot her a look. "Definitely. Now shut up so I can finish doing your makeup."

She laughs and doesn't shut up, but at least the topic of Finn is over for now.

CHAPTER TWENTY-EIGHT

Josslyn

Me: do you want to meet there?

I stare as the little bubbles appear and disappear before his text finally comes through.

Finn: we live in the same building

Me: so...meet in the lobby?

I stare, and stare, and when he doesn't respond, I toss my phone aside with a huff and start putting essentials in the small clutch I'm taking. If he doesn't respond in the next ten minutes, I'm going downstairs, and if he's not there ten minutes after that, I'm leaving. He may be hot as hell and give great orgasms, but I've never sat around waiting for anyone and I'm not about to start now. Especially tonight.

We've been hosting fundraisers for the Alma Foundation for a few years now, and I'm usually fine going and mingling. Tonight, I'm giving a speech and even though I'm keeping it short, my nerves are still wrecked. Once I'm done gathering my things, I head to the door and come to a dead stop when I open it and find Finn standing on the other side. My heart skips a beat at the sight of him in his tux. His light brown hair is brushed back, he shaved the shadow of a beard he'd been rocking, which I would say is a pity if he didn't look so damn good this way as well, and his green eyes are dark and unreadable as he takes me in slowly.

I swallow hard as I take a step outside. "Hey."

"I was on my way down," he says, jaw clenching as he turns toward the elevator.

I hold my breath as I stare at his retreating form. I don't need him to tell me I look incredible, but complimenting the person you're on a date with is practically a requirement. Even if he doesn't go on dates, he should know that. I push the thought out of my mind as I sigh heavily and make myself go after him. *It's going to be a long freaking night.*

I'm not even sure how to handle this situation. The closest I've come is when I lost my virginity to a friend of mine. Things were a little awkward the next time we saw each other, until one of us cracked a joke and then it was back to normal. I don't have much hope of this going that way. Not because I don't think we can crack a joke, but because grumpy Finn probably wouldn't laugh.

We're quiet as we share the elevator with a couple and their two dogs. We're still quiet as we walk through the lobby, and when we get outside, I'm surprised to find a very fancy black car and a driver waiting for us.

"Do you always have a driver take you to events?" I ask, getting in the back seat after thanking the driver for holding the door open for us.

"My car's being washed."

It's all he says, which annoys me, though I refuse to let it show. I also refuse to be the only one sparking up a conversation, so I take my phone out and check my texts.

> **Mom:** If you or Finn are uncomfortable arriving together, just let him get out of the car first and give him a few seconds to walk in. Just giving you an alternative.

My grip tightens around my phone. Maybe that's why he's acting this way. He can't think I'm naive enough to believe last night meant anything to him, and I can't imagine it's about me leaving. It occurs to me that none of this is the norm for him. He's not used to seeing women the day after he's rocked their world or going out in public with anyone, and right now he's doing both of those things. I take a breath to rid myself of the pressure in my chest that comes with the reminder that I'm the woman he'd normally leave in the rearview.

> Me: Good idea. I'll wait in the car while he walks inside.
>
> Mom: I'll have someone go out there and escort him inside, and someone else will come get you

I force myself to stop being a coward and put my phone away. Finn does the same with his, tucking it inside his jacket pocket.

"Lang is on his way," he comments.

"He usually comes."

"He's a good agent."

"Not my agent." I raise my eyebrows and look at him. "College athlete, remember?"

He huffs out a laugh. "Those rules are so ridiculous. What do you call him, if not your agent?"

"My entertainment lawyer."

He shakes his head, but I see a hint of amusement in his eyes, and that helps settle my discomfort. The car stops in front of the hotel, and when the driver gets out and opens the door, Finn turns slightly to look at me.

"You go ahead. I have to fix my dress," I say.

His brows furrow slightly, but after a moment of searching my face, he steps out of the car. The driver shuts the door behind him, and I look out to see him button and adjust his jacket. He's standing next to the driver when Milly, one of Mom's employees, walks over and tells him something. Finn says something and points toward me with his thumb, but Milly shakes her head and grabs his arm.

I fix my dress as I watch him pull away from her. Whatever he says to Milly makes her shake her head in an exasperated way and walk away. When she's gone, Finn opens the door and slides back inside the car, shutting it behind him. The driver folds his arms and stands in front of it.

"What are you doing?"

"What are *you* doing?" he counters, eyes blazing, jaw clenched.

"I was fixing my dress."

His eyes narrow. "Don't play stupid, Josslyn."

I stare at him for a moment. "Fine. I was giving you an out."

"I don't need an out," he snaps. "Do you?"

"No," I scoff. "You're the one who doesn't like your picture taken, and you're being weird."

"*I'm* being weird?" He chuckles darkly. "I'm not the one who told her mother to send someone to walk us in separately."

I purse my lips. "I didn't do that. My mother offered and I figured it was for the best."

"For who? You or me?"

"You!"

He stares at me for a long moment. "Let's go."

"Fine. Let's go." I follow him out of the car.

CHAPTER TWENTY-NINE

Finn

If you want to feel invisible at a party, take Josslyn as your date. I've spent most of the evening trying not to let the amount of male attention she gets bother me. And consequently, trying not to think about *why* it bothers me. It's baffling. Maybe I *am* acting weird. I *feel* weird. Uncomfortable. When was the last time I felt uncomfortable? *If ever.*

When I woke up this morning and she was gone, I should have felt indifferent. Or relieved. Instead, I felt … strange. Empty. The feeling remained until I saw her again, looking like *that*, and it sent me into another tailspin. *What is she doing to me?* None of this was supposed to happen.

Being inside her last night … the way she moved, the sounds she made, the way she looked at me—fuck. I push the memories aside. The last thing I need is to sit across from her stepbrother who happens to be my teammate, with a hard-on. I fucking *knew* this would happen. I knew if anyone had the power to turn me inside out, it would be her.

I need to go back to the basics and find out who was in that room with my sister. The story the world has been told is that it was all a tragedy—that she got stuck inside Onyx during a fire. The lead detective has all but shut a lid on the whole thing, which I know is my father's doing. Richard Barlow would rather make it disappear and act like none of it happened. He'd rather pretend Mallory is in Europe. It worked for me while I was still living in Nevada, but being back here makes it impossible to deny her absence. Watching Josslyn live her life, posting videos and pictures, and going to parties as if nothing happened, makes it worse. A nearly blinding light shines on my face, and I blink in time to hear the click, click, click of the camera in front of me.

"One more," the photographer says, smiling. "Aren't you two the cutest?"

Another snap and then they're gone, and I take out my vibrating phone to see a call from my mother. Normally, I let it go to voicemail, but being in Fairview means I can run into her at any moment, so I excuse myself and answer it as I walk to the nearest door.

"I just received a call from Patricia Abbott telling me you're on a public date," she says by way of greeting.

"I'm at a charity event."

"With a date."

"Yes, for charity," I say, not bothering to bite back my irritation.

I knew I'd receive a call from her, but I didn't expect it to be while I was still here. I guess I shouldn't be surprised since I ran into Patricia earlier and she's been watching me since. Guaranteed she's already dug up whatever dirt she can find on Josslyn and determined she doesn't have an "impressive pedigree." It would explain my mother's urgency on the matter. She speaks about marriage like women are horses and I'm their prized stallion. It doesn't help that my mother and Patricia Abbott have been trying to set me up with her daughter our entire lives. Forget the fact that Traci has been in a committed relationship for five years and I have absolutely no interest in her.

"That woman you're with, was she the one who was Mallory's

friend? The one who spoke to the police and said she had no recollection of that night?"

My jaw tightens. "Yes."

"Hm."

"I have to go."

"You're still coming to the club for my birthday," she says, rather than asking.

"I'll be there."

"Good. It'll give you an opportunity to catch up with Traci," she says.

"Not going to happen, Mother."

"Maybe one of the Andrews girls then," she suggests.

"Not interested."

"Maybe…"

"See you Sunday, Mother."

I hang up before she can respond. I turn around to walk back to my table and stop short when I see Nate Crawford in my seat. He's leaning over Josslyn with a cocky-ass smirk on his face that further sours my mood. She laughs at whatever he says to her, and I ignore the way my eye twitches.

Before I get there, a familiar voice calls out my name. At the sound of it, Josslyn glances over and locks eyes with me. I'm not sure what she sees on my face, but she inches slightly away from Nate. I glance to my left and meet Lachlan and his brother halfway.

"Long time no see, man," Liam says.

"How've you been?" I greet him with a fist bump and quick hug. "I hear congratulations are in order," I add, remembering Lachlan mention his engagement.

"Thanks." Liam grins. "She's a die-hard Canucks fan, but she's also a huge fan of yours."

My brows rise. "She must be a keeper then."

"Lee made me get her your Owls jersey before they were even at the arena store," Lach says.

I feel my lips tug up. "I'll have to remember to send you a signed one." I look at Lachlan. "How's Lyla?"

"Uncomfortable," he says, looking at his phone quickly, as if his wife might magically call.

"She begged him to get out of the house," Liam says, laughing at the scowl it earns him.

"She wanted to spend time with her dad and best friends," Lachlan says.

"She wanted to get you out of her hair," Liam responds, then looks at me. "He doesn't let the woman breathe."

Lachlan rolls his eyes.

"How's Asher?" Liam asks me suddenly, which earns him a low growl from his brother that we can't help but laugh at.

"He's good. Having a baby, actually," I say.

"That's great," Lachlan responds, which makes Liam laugh again.

I shake my head. My soccer-playing cousin and Lyla met years ago when she was living in Rhodes and he showed up for one of her training sessions. Asher—who's very much like his brother Lucas, in that he can't help but flirt with everyone—paid too much attention to Lyla. Asher has been in a committed relationship for over five years now, and Lachlan is still not over it.

"I heard you're here with Josslyn," Lachlan says casually.

I nod my response and glance back to our table, where fuckboy Nate is still in my seat and Josslyn is currently rolling her eyes at whatever he's saying.

"That's quite a statement," he says, and I look at him again.

"It's for charity," I respond.

He raises an eyebrow. "The way you just murdered that guy sitting beside her with one look wasn't very charitable."

"She's a great girl," Liam says.

"She is." Lachlan nods and smiles. "Theo thinks he's going to marry her."

My chest tightens. "He's a little too young for her."

From the way Liam raises an eyebrow and the amused look Lachlan shoots me, I know I didn't imagine the bite in my tone.

Fuck. I look away again, this time my attention lands on Titus, who's surrounded by a group of men.

"Something going on between the two of you?" Lachlan asks.

I meet his eyes. "We're just friends."

"Friends," he says and looks in her direction. "That guy on the Blaze wants to be more than just friends with her."

"Didn't he call Dibs on her earlier?" Liam asks, shaking his head. "I can't believe they're still playing that stupid game."

Lachlan also shakes his head, his lips tugging slightly as he checks his phone again.

"Looks like he's going to make his move," Liam says.

My heart, so loud in my ears I can barely make out their words, pounds harder. I don't want to fall into the trap I know he's setting, but I can't help myself. I look. The sight of Nate's knee pressed against hers and his hand over hers on the table makes me see red, and I move before I know what I'm doing.

CHAPTER THIRTY

Josslyn

"Why are people saying Nate Crawford called Dibs on you?" Finn asks, his voice a quiet rumble that makes my heart skip.

I meet his intense gaze. "Because he did."

"Do you know what that is?"

"Everyone knows what it is." I laugh lightly. "Nate has probably called Dibs on thirty people by now."

He moves closer and presses his cheek against mine as he brings his lips to my ear. "I don't like it."

My stomach dips. "No?"

"Hell no." He presses the softest kiss just beneath my ear and my entire body heats.

Whatever he sees on my face as he pulls back makes him smirk, but I'm too lost in the moment to care about his arrogance. Ever since he took his seat back from Nate, he's been extra attentive—his arm on the back of my chair, his body moving closer to mine, his conversations reserved for my ears only. It's as if he's staking his claim on me, which is baffling. And thrilling. Every time a photographer comes around to take a picture, Finn confuses the hell out of all of us at the table by moving closer to me.

Damian and Will haven't stopped staring. Livie keeps biting her lip so she doesn't bust out laughing. Tiago hasn't stopped scowling. Nate doesn't give a shit, so he's been carrying the conversation. Between dinner and the auction, there's another break, and everyone gets up to mingle. Finn and I stay in our seats. I wait until Livie is gone before turning to him.

"What are you doing?" I ask quietly. He scoots his chair so close he might as well pull me onto his lap. I shoot him a warning look. "Finn."

"What do you mean?" he asks.

My eyes narrow. "You've been touching me all night."

"And that's a problem?"

I search his eyes for a moment because he has to be joking. He's not. "You realize they've taken a million pictures of us, right? Of you all over me."

He glances away and starts scanning the room.

"Finn."

His eyes snap to mine. I hate that he's so impossible to read. "I'm aware of the pictures," he says finally, looking completely unconcerned. "I didn't realize you cared."

"I don't, but I know you do." I set my elbows on the table and turn my face to look at him.

He doesn't respond, which drives me crazy. Tate was a no-show, so it can't have anything to do with pissing him off. We had sex, so it doesn't make sense for him to be acting this way unless there's a reason. He's been practically staking claim on me all night, and even though he never does that, I'm not going to kid myself into believing I'm special to him.

"Tell me about your dad," he says suddenly, and my stomach drops for a different reason.

I lick my lips. "What do you want to know?"

"Anything. Were you close?"

"Very." I smile softly. "He's the reason I got into basketball. He played pro for a few years."

"Really?" His brows rise.

"It was his life," I say quietly as I train my eyes on the white tablecloth.

"What happened?"

"He got hurt badly and … never recovered." I clear my throat to get rid of the knot forming there.

"Damn," he whispers.

"He used to go to all my games. Sometimes, Mom couldn't make it, but he was always there cheering me on, coaching my teams, driving me around…" I feel myself smile again at the memories.

"My parents have never seen me play."

My eyes snap back to his. "Never?"

"Not once," he says. "Not in person anyway."

"How can that be?" I search his face, looking for tells that he's joking, but he's dead serious.

"They never took it seriously. I had drivers take me to games and practices. My grandfather and uncle were usually there, so it's not like I had no family in the stands."

I instinctively reach out for his hand and cover it with mine.

He tenses. "I don't want your pity. Trust me, I was afforded many luxuries. Your pity would be lost on me."

"I'm allowed to feel sympathy for little Finn Alexander Barlow, who was probably the *cutest* kid on the ice." I run my thumb over his rough hand. "I would've loved to have been there."

He stares at me for a long time, his eyes cataloging my face before meeting my gaze. I can't read his expression, but when he turns his hand beneath mine and threads our fingers together, I feel like my heart might explode.

By the time we get home, pictures of me and Finn are everywhere. Thankfully, they mention the Alma Foundation, so the attention isn't wasted. The comments, of course, are all over the place. I ignore my notifications and make sure my sponsored post is scheduled, then set my phone on Do Not Disturb and put it away.

"Do you ever get tired of doing that?" Finn asks, as we step into the elevator in our building.

We haven't even been able to discuss the event since I was on the phone with my mom the entire car ride home, trying to explain that Finn and I aren't together as inconspicuously as I could with him beside me. I watch as he takes off his bow tie, stuffs it in his pants, and unbuttons the top two buttons of his crisp, white dress shirt. He looks mouthwatering like this. I make myself look away and focus on the doors.

"I like connecting with people and the brands pay me for these posts." I look at him again. "Do you get tired of it?"

He chuckles. "I don't connect with anyone. No one who follows me checks on whether or not they miss one of my posts."

I highly doubt that's true, but I don't say that. "That's because you only post professional pictures taken at games."

His eyes sparkle. "Stalking me, Josslyn?"

"No." I laugh quietly and look away again, hoping to hide the warmth on my cheeks.

Thankfully, the elevator doors open on my floor and I'm able to walk out before he sees my embarrassment. I'm almost at my door when he reaches out and takes my hand, sending my heart galloping. I figured he'd walk me to my door when we got here, but I don't know what to expect now that we're here. He has a serious expression when I turn to him, but there's something in his eyes that doesn't help the state of my heart or the strange, dumb hope that blooms inside me.

"You were the most beautiful woman in the room tonight," he says, voice low as he steps forward, backing me against my door.

"Thank you," I breathe.

"It took every ounce of willpower I have not to do this." He cups my face and tilts it with his free hand, bringing his mouth against mine.

It's a soft kiss. One that he deepens quickly, sweeping his tongue into my mouth as he pushes up against me. I instantly feel like I'm on fire. I let go of his hand and tug his jacket to bring him closer. There's no room left between us, but it still doesn't seem like it's close enough. I've wanted men before, but I've never wanted anyone as much as I want him. When he breaks the kiss, just as slowly and softly as he started, he sets his forehead against mine and lets out a harsh breath.

"One more night?" I ask quietly. Hopefully. *Stupidly.*

I should be terrified of even wanting that. The things I feel for him—that I've always felt when he's around—are terrifying. Despite everything, it would be so damn easy for me to fall for him. But one more night won't hurt. And I want him so badly. I want the scary, all-encompassing feeling he gives me. He nods, then pulls away and takes a step back, letting me open the door to my apartment. Once inside, I expect to end up with my back against the door, fumbling with his belt, but Finn takes a step inside and looks around, the way he did in my childhood bedroom.

I sit on the barstool and start unstrapping my heels, as he lifts one of the picture frames I have on my entrance table and looks at it. It's me and my dad at one of his games when I was around four years old. I have a lot of pictures with him around my place, and most are basketball-related. When Mom gave them to me as a housewarming gift and placed them all around my apartment, I thought I'd look at them all the time, but I rarely do. It's hard to see him smiling wide in all those pictures, knowing that he wasn't happy. I went to therapy long enough to understand that it had nothing to do with me, but it didn't make it any easier to understand.

I clear my throat. "He hung himself."

Finn's head whips toward me, a mix of sympathy and disbelief in his eyes. He sets down the frame but doesn't walk closer to me, which I appreciate. With the way he's looking at me, if he touches me right now, I know I'll cry. I always do. "Shit, Joss. I knew he'd ... but I didn't realize..."

"It's not something many people know. Titus was able to keep the sordid details out of the press and leave everything so vague."

He walks over to me now, gripping the armrests on either side of me, and leans in to kiss my forehead. It's a small gesture, a sweet one, and it makes my eyes sting with tears. I bring a hand up and dab the edges to keep them in. When I lower my hand again, Finn wraps both arms around me as best he can, and holds my face against his chest. I wrap my arms around him and take a deep inhale, relishing the way he smells. It's manly, fresh, and comforting. The latter so unlike what I thought he was.

But maybe that was my mistake. It's not like he's a loner. He has a friend group that he cares for. And though I'm sure he's not hugging Will or Lucas like *this*, he might be showing Ella this type of care. The thought makes my blood simmer. It's a ridiculous reaction, considering most of the people Ella dates are women, but it makes me realize how much I want this from him. How much I want *everything* from him. I squeeze my eyes shut in hopes of getting rid of that thought. I have him for now. I need to settle for that.

"Titus is a good man," I say against his chest.

His entire body stills, his arms a little tighter around me. I slide my hands from his muscular back to his sides, pushing him away a little—just enough to look up and see his face. He must think I want space, because he drops his arms, and I'm ashamed to say I instantly miss them.

"Look, I'm not going to read into whatever it is we're doing." I search his eyes, which are now hard and intense and completely unreadable. "I'm not going to ask why you're here or if this means something to you." I pause again, feeling like my next statement will either make or break whatever is happening tonight. "But I need you to not blackmail me anymore."

"I didn't blackmail you."

I shoot him a look. "You threatened to show those videos to my mother if I didn't help you."

"That was a mistake," he says. "Believe it or not, I've been trying really hard to not be an asshole around you."

I laugh. "You can't be serious."

"*To you.* I've been trying to not be an asshole to *you*," he clarifies, and my heart starts racing again.

"Why?" I whisper.

"I don't know."

I stare at him for another moment, before tearing my eyes from his and looking at the picture frames behind him that my dad's been immortalized in. My dad, who I could speak to anything about, and would probably love Finn Barlow, even if only for his protectiveness of me. I bite my lip and swallow to hold it together. This conversation isn't what he came here for. He's here to hook up with me and leave. I take a deep, settling breath and look at him again with that in mind. My gaze drops to his lips, and I stop thinking. I hop off the stool, get on the balls of my feet, and kiss him.

He groans against my mouth, arms instantly wrapping around me again, lowering them to my ass and picking me up. I wrap my legs around his waist, thankful for the slits of my dress, and sink my fingers in his hair as we deepen the kiss. I pull away and blink the hazy lust out of my eyes.

"My room's to the left," I say, and then my lips are back on his.

He sets me down when we get to the bedroom. I'd left one lamp on, which doesn't fully light the space, but it's enough. Finn looks around quickly, then brings his eyes to mine. My pulse quickens when I feel how hard he is as I reach between us and grab him.

"Fuck." He bites his lower lip and lets out a sound somewhere between a groan and a growl as he throws his head back slightly.

I take my hand off him and start undressing him as he kisses me and unzips my dress, letting it pool at my feet. He pulls back, looking like every single fantasy I've ever had of him—his jacket on the floor, shirt halfway unbuttoned, and hair mussed from my fingers running through it.

"You're so fucking hot," I say.

His lips curl into a seductive smile as he reaches behind me and deftly undoes my bra. His hooded eyes rake over me, stopping at my black thong for a moment before they meet mine again. He shakes his head but doesn't say anything as he takes my breasts in his hands, squeezing and licking one of my nipples while teasing the other.

I breathe shakily. "Finn."

He groans, teases the other, then kisses my sternum, and continues—down, down—tugging my underwear with him when he reaches it. His large hands grab my ass as he buries his face between my legs and licks, causing a shiver to run through me. I set my hands on his hair and tug until he glances up.

"I want you naked," I whisper.

His gaze darkens as he stands up slowly. I sit at the edge of the bed, and he keeps his eyes on mine as he continues undressing. I lower my gaze to drink in every inch of skin he exposes. It's not our first time doing this, but sometimes it feels like it. It feels special. He yanks his shirt off and tosses it to the side, pulls his pants and socks off, and then he's left in black boxer briefs. His desire for me is unmistakable, as is his size. I bite my lip at the thought of having him inside me. Unable to help myself, I reach out and hook a finger on the waistband. His abs flex and his cock twitches.

"Did you get these at Neiman?" I ask, smiling up at him.

His returning smile is sinful. He pulls my hand away from his waistband and tugs it so I'm standing, then takes a step back until I'm far enough that when he drops my hand, he can walk around me. The slow way in which he does it makes me feel more exposed than I've ever felt. Somehow, when he's finally in front of me, his eyes burning hotter than I've ever seen them, I find my voice.

"Do I pass inspection?" I ask breathily.

He drags his gaze up and down my body once more. "With flying colors."

His response makes my heart skip. He moves forward again until my knees hit the bed, which forces me onto my back. When he presses his fists on either side of me and lowers to hover over me, I think I stop breathing. He kisses my cheek and continues to press hot kisses down my body again until I'm writhing with need.

His large hands grip my thighs and spread my legs. He stands up, and for a moment, he takes me in, running a hand through his hair like he's overwhelmed and doesn't know where to start. Then, he's back on his knees and his mouth is on me, his tongue working me until I'm screaming and coming with his name on my lips. I'm still shaking when I feel his hands on the bed again. I force my eyes open and find him naked on top of me, a condom underneath his right hand.

Before he puts it on, I reach between us and grab him, stroking him once, twice. On the third stroke, he closes his hand around my wrist, and I look up with questioning eyes.

"I want to come while I'm inside you, and if you keep doing that…" He sets his forehead against mine with a shaky laugh and takes a moment to open the condom wrapper.

I take my eyes away from his to watch as he slides it on, growing wetter with each movement he makes. He grabs my thighs again and pushes my legs up as he sinks into me slowly—so, so slowly, I think I might die. Once he's fully inside me, he stops and blows out a harsh breath.

Hooded eyes meet mine again. "You good?"

I bite my lip and nod. And then he starts moving. He grips my thighs hard as he thrusts in and out of me, fast, hard, and with a look of concentration as he accommodates my legs and hips. It takes me a moment to realize he's going off my responses. He's studying every moan, every gasp, and adjusting so he's fucking me in a way that elicits that response. My core tightens, and I screw my eyes shut and moan again.

"Oh my god. Right there," I pant, as he lets go of my legs and grabs my hips, driving into me harder and harder.

"FUCK," he growls, and then I feel his fingers rubbing me, and it's all too much. "I want to see your eyes when you come for me."

My eyes pop open and my stomach bottoms out for a moment, just before I fall apart, shaking and writhing, and saying unintelligible things.

"Fuck, Josslyn." He thrusts once, twice, three times, his grip getting tighter on my waist, his eyes not leaving mine until he explodes in spurts I feel through the condom.

He lowers his face and kisses me—a long, passionate, toe-curling kiss that consumes me. When he pulls away, he tucks his face in my neck and lets himself fall against me. I gasp but realize I like it. I like the feel of his weight on me and his breath against my neck. *This is the last time.* Just one more night. I repeat the reminder again and again. It doesn't matter that he acted like tonight was a true date, laughing and talking to our friends as he set his hand on my thigh, an arm draped over the back of my chair. It doesn't matter that it felt good to have his undivided attention. It was one magical night, but it doesn't change anything.

CHAPTER THIRTY-ONE

Finn

I GOT NO SLEEP, BUT SOMEHOW I FEEL WIRED. IT'S JOSSLYN. IT'S ALWAYS fucking Josslyn. I rub my face and plop back on my bed with an exhale. She fell asleep after the third time we fucked, and I stayed and watched her until four in the morning. It took effort for me to walk out of her apartment, as if every cell in my body wanted me to stay. On the way up to the penthouse, I told myself it was because I wanted to fuck her again when her five a.m. alarm went off. Just *one last time.*

I remind myself that I was trying to get close to Josslyn to find out what happened the night Mallory died. I've been doing a shit job of it, which just further proves that I'm the worst brother. I'm aware of that, but my mind won't stop spinning with thoughts of her. It is now eight o'clock and I have golf with the guys in two hours. *And* I'm picking up Lachlan and his brother on the way there, which means I only have one hour to get a nap in. I wish I could, but every time my eyes shut, I see her, I smell her, I hear those little gasps and breathy moans in my ear, and I get hard again. God damn Josslyn.

I was supposed to be done by now. I was supposed to have

already fucked another woman, the palate cleanser I'd promised myself, and be finished with all thoughts of Josslyn. She's supposed to be long gone from my mind, like every other woman I fuck. She's not. If anything, she kicked her shoes off and settled in. I hate it. I hate thinking about her and wanting her, wishing I could see the way her eyes light up in defiance whenever she gets pissed off at me.

I only have myself to blame, but Josslyn was never going to be a faceless woman. I knew it from the moment I saw her that night in the hot pink dress. God, I'm an idiot. I pick up my phone. Before I left, I turned on the location on her phone and shared it with myself. Is it messed up? Maybe. Crazy? Depends who you ask. Illegal? Absolutely, which is why I'm not telling Lucas or Ham about it. The little dot says she's no longer home. I enlarge the map and toss my phone with a groan when I realize where she is. It's going to be a long fucking day.

An hour later, I'm in Lachlan's driveway looking at her car and cursing myself for agreeing to this. I should've told Lach to stop being a bitch and drive himself. What's the point of owning five cars if you don't drive them? I get out of my car and walk to the front door, nodding at the guard as I pass him. Liam opens the door before I can even knock.

"Hey, man," he smiles and bumps his fist against mine in greeting as I walk inside. "Lach's almost ready. He's making sure, for the hundredth time, that Lyla will be okay without him for a few hours." He rolls his eyes. "Lyla's probably going to throw a party when he leaves. He doesn't let her breathe."

That makes me laugh. I've never met a man as obsessed with his wife as Lachlan. I came into the league when he was on his way out, but the veterans used to say that even though Lach was single, he'd skip parties and dinners, and ignore the puck bunnies who threw themselves at him. Instead, he'd look for Lyla in every city they went to. Being from Fairview and hearing snippets of what happened to them, I understood why he was protective of her.

Having known them for years now, I can't imagine them ever

being apart. Then again, I feel that way about all of my friends with spouses. Probably because when I met them, they were already together. The only person I've witnessed go from player to devout husband is my cousin Asher, Lucas' older brother. Ash played professional soccer and was known to have women in many cities. None of us thought he'd ever settle down, but then he met Brit, and suddenly he only had eyes for her. It was weird and completely unrelatable.

But when I practically forced myself to leave Josslyn's side this morning ... Jesus. *What the fuck is wrong with me?* I'm out of sorts from a lack of sleep. It's the only explanation as to why I'm thinking about this at all. At the sound of a familiar voice, my entire body tenses and my heart pounds a little harder. Liam continues to guide me further into the house toward the voices. I haven't even seen her yet and my palms are sweating. I wipe them roughly against my pants, hoping to rid myself of these nerves. When was the last time I felt uncomfortable in front of a woman? Never. The answer is *never*. What have I gotten myself into? I swallow hard and focus on keeping my face blank and my heart rate reasonable.

"Can we go in the pool now, Joshlyn?" Theo asks.

They're in the kitchen, and I only have a few seconds to finish mentally preparing myself before Liam turns in their direction.

"The pool?" Liam asks. "I wasn't invited to this!"

Theo giggles, and I force myself to round the corner. My eyes instantly land on Josslyn, and I hear my audible inhale. From the knowing look Liam shoots over his shoulder, I know they heard it too.

"Hey!" Theo says excitedly as he rushes over and slams into my legs, making me stagger back a step. "You came back!"

I ruffle his hair and wink. "I told you I would."

"You said you would bring ice cream next time," Theo says, pulling back to cross his arms and pout.

"Theo," Josslyn warns, and my heart rate spikes again.

"I'll bring some when I come back." I keep my eyes on Theo, where it's safe.

The kid asks more questions than a standardized test, which can get exhausting, but I'll take them over having to face his babysitter. Suddenly, he jumps and turns around to run back over to her. Of course, today is the day he doesn't want to sit here and drill me about superheroes.

"Joshlyn! Finn's gonna bring us ice cream!" he says, making Josslyn laugh.

The sound makes my chest ache a little. I force myself to look at her, and once again, struggle to breathe. She's wearing a red one-piece bathing suit that dips to the valley of her breasts. It's a conservative swimsuit, one even my mom would wear. But dear God, on Josslyn, it looks obscene. Even more so now that I know every dip and curve underneath it. I try to fight myself from drinking her in, but I fail miserably. Fuck. Everything about this woman is…

"Here you go," Liam says suddenly, and tosses me a bottle of water. I catch it midair and thank him.

"Ice cream is for *after* we eat our lunch," she says sternly, looking at Theo before she glances over at me. "Hey, Finn."

"Hey." I clear my throat. She didn't miss me checking her out. "I didn't know you'd be here."

Jesus. What is wrong with me? I uncap the water bottle in my hand and take a small sip. Maybe drinking will keep me from saying stupid shit until one of us leaves the kitchen.

"I didn't know you'd be here either." Her eyes sparkle as she says it, and I swear, she's picking up on my discomfort. She smiles at me, then Liam. "Have fun golfing."

"Have fun pretending you're a mermaid."

She tilts her head. "How am I supposed to do that if Prince Charming is going golfing?"

I nearly choke on my water. *Is she referring to me?* I cap it and cough once, then twice, and finally, I clear my throat. Liam and Josslyn are both looking at me. Thankfully, Theo the inquisitor is busy putting his toys in a bag.

"I'll only be gone a few hours. Maybe we'll have time to role-play when I get back," he says, making her laugh hard.

I, on the other hand, am now glaring at him. *Role play?* This man is engaged! The words are on the tip of my tongue when Josslyn speaks again.

"I guess I know what I'm getting you and Sarah for your wedding."

"Oh, she'll love that." He laughs again.

I still don't find it funny.

Josslyn snorts a laugh and reaches her hand out. Theo automatically takes it with a huge smile on his face, and I realize he's completely enamored with her. Of course, he is. *Who the fuck isn't?*

"Let's go," she says. "The sun is beaming today and your mom wants us out before noon."

"Why?" Theo argues as they start walking to the back door.

"Because you get red as a tomato."

"So?"

"Sunburns hurt."

"Do you get sunburned?"

"Not as easily as you." She opens the door and Theo steps out, dropping a few toys, which she bends over to pick up. I'm going to die in this kitchen.

"Why not?" Theo asks.

"Because my skin is much darker than yours."

"Your skin isn't…" His words are cut off by the glass French door shutting between us, but I can't seem to tear my eyes away as I watch them.

When they get to the edge of the pool, Josslyn bends over and whips her hair forward to gather it. She puts it in a messy bun and starts laughing at whatever Theo is telling her. I watch as she lathers him up with sunscreen, even lifting his shirt before she applies some on herself. Everything she does is riveting—the way she laughs, talks, and reprimands him.

"Uh, Finn?"

I blink at the sound of my name and nearly jump out of my

skin when I notice that both Liam and Lachlan are standing there watching me. I shake myself out of the spell Josslyn clearly cast on me and greet Lachlan. It's not until we're at the front door that whatever is lodged in my chest loosens. Space. That's the cure for this.

"You've got it bad, bro." Lachlan laughs, shaking his head. "Look at you."

"I don't know what you're talking about." I try to lengthen my stride, but it's no use since we're about the same height.

"You should've seen his face when I told Joss we'd role-play later," Liam says, laughing his ass off, which of course makes Lach laugh his ass off.

I glare at both of them as I open the driver's door and pop the trunk for clubs. "I just thought it was an interesting choice of words, considering you're an engaged man now and too old for your nephew's babysitter."

They laugh harder. I turn the car on, my grip tight on the wheel as I back out of the driving space.

"Joss likes older men," Liam says, earning a glare from me.

Beside me, Lach, who's on his phone, laughs. She doesn't like *older* men. Tate's only four years older than her. *I'm* four years older than her.

"She's not just my nephew's babysitter," Liam adds, eyes sparkling in the rearview mirror. I wait for him to say something else that'll piss me off, but he says, "She's family," and adds, "and *Sarah's* the one who calls it role-playing when Joss and I play pretend with Theo. It's become a joke in our family."

Hilarious joke, I think bitterly, but don't voice it, since I know that'll only help the case they're trying to make.

"You have nothing to worry about," Lach says beside me as I start driving.

"I know I don't," I say. "You two are acting like the media and reading too much into this. We went to a *charity event* together, and we're just *friends*."

"Right," Lach says slowly. "But do you want to be *just friends?*"

"Is this because her brother will be your teammate soon?" Liam asks.

I frown. "No. It has nothing to do with that."

I'm pretty sure Damian wouldn't be opposed to me dating his sister if I wanted to, but I *don't*. I don't even know what dating entails. I must say that aloud, like a fucking moron, because the atmosphere grows serious.

"When I met Lyla…" Lachlan starts.

"Oh, God. Please don't," Liam interrupts. "You're obsessive and controlling and the last person anyone needs to take relationship advice from."

"Am I?" Lach shifts in his seat and raises an eyebrow at his brother. "We've been together a long time. Happy together. Blissful, even."

That makes me laugh. "Blissful?"

"Yes." He turns to face forward again. "I won't deny that I'm stupidly in love with my wife. There's nothing wrong with that."

"Obsessed," Liam says.

"In love, obsessed, whatever." Lach shrugs. "My point is, when we met, I was focused on hockey and getting a contract. Love was the last thing on my mind, but Lyla changed things for me. For the better."

"As heartwarming as that sounds, I can't relate," I say, my voice flat.

"With the love part or the obsessed part?" Liam asks, shrugging when I glance at him.

"Either."

"Sometimes they go hand in hand," Lach says.

"I guess," his brother reluctantly agrees.

"Lyles made me go to a therapist," Lach starts, ignoring his brother's praise for Lyla. "And the therapist—very smart lady, by the way, I can give you her info," he adds quickly, "made me work on myself and get over my hang-ups, which in turn helped me be less 'controlling' when it came to Lyla."

He pauses to shoot his brother a warning look. "She suggested

I get my own hobbies and hang out with friends *without* Lyla once in a while, and vice versa. I go golfing with friends and have dinner, and she does the same with hers. I'm not gonna lie, it's nice, but most of the time, I wish she was there."

He looks at me for a long moment, waiting until I finish parking the car at the course to meet his eyes before he continues, "I spent three years without her, which wasn't either of our faults, but those were the most miserable three years of my fucking life."

"As heartwarming as all of that is," I say after a moment. "And it is. You two are perfect together," I add seriously. "I don't understand what this has to do with me."

"I've never seen you with a girlfriend. I've heard rumors about how you operate." Lach shrugs. "Like Liam said, Joss is family. She's like a little sister to us. I've never seen her look at anyone the way she looked at you at the fundraiser … and I guess I see a lot of myself in you. I don't want you to fuck up your chance at the best thing you might ever have." He unlocks his door. "All right. Let's go golfing."

With those words, we get out of the car. I spend the rest of the morning getting to know my teammates. We golf, eat, drink, and talk shit, but Joss is never far from my mind. I loathe it, so decide it's time I start thinking about finding a palate cleanser. I own a goddamn sex club, for fuck's sake. With that in mind, I text my cousin to see if he'll be there tomorrow night.

CHAPTER THIRTY-TWO

Josslyn

"So, what's going on with you and Finn?" my mother asks, as she fries the croquetas I've been salivating over for months now.

My hands pause on the green plantain I'm peeling. "Nothing."

"Didn't look like *nothing* the other night," she says, and even though her back is facing me, I hear the smile in her voice.

"Whatever you think you saw was just an act." I swallow and focus on the plantain.

What am I supposed to say? That we've slept together twice now—which is more than he allegedly does with anyone else. My heart skips when I think about that, the flowers, and the way he gets all growly and possessive when other men show too much interest in me. All of those things combined would mean something, if he were someone else.

Maybe they do mean something, but I can't afford to get my hopes up. Even if he wanted more from me, I couldn't give it to him. Not with the Titus and Mallory thing hanging over our heads. He hasn't brought it up to me again, but I'm reminded of it every time I scroll through my pictures and find the footage. That's the main reason I'm going to meet with Mallory's friends at Onyx. Not only because I want to prove him wrong, but because the more I look at the footage and think about that night, the less sure I am about it being an accident like they claimed.

Shortly after it happened, when the cloud of sadness and anger lifted, I started asking questions. Why did only that part of the club catch fire? How did it even start? Why hadn't she fled? Why hadn't someone pulled her out of there? Surely, she wasn't by herself. I *knew* she wasn't. But who was she with? Someone horrible. It was the only explanation. Even if it had been an accident, they left her there to die. *We* left her there to die.

My chest tightens at the thought. I'm a professional compartmentalizer. It's the only way I know to survive the pain of losing a loved one. It's the only way I've been able to deal with what happened with Mal. I grieved and buried all of the negative things I've associated with that place and Mal. I've held onto the memory of the girl I became friends with—the one who was slow to trust and the life of the party. I was at a good place before Finn barged into my life with this mess, making me second-guess everything and think about that night.

A shiver rolls through me, as flashes of memories appear in my mind—the loud music during the car ride, the cute guy flirting with Livie, the way Mal smiled over her shoulder as she walked down that hall… that smile haunts me the most. I push it back into the box I've created for her, the one that sits on the shelf next to my father's. *Don't think about it right* now. The blunt end of the knife scrapes against my finger, snapping me out of my thoughts.

"The way he looks at you isn't an act. Not only that night, but when he was here as well," Mom says, eyes sparkling mischievously.

"Don't get your hopes up. He's not a relationship kind of guy."

"Who?" Damian asks, making us jump at his unexpected arrival.

My face is hot, but I manage to say "no one" at the same time my mother says "Finn."

Damian's brows shoot up and he blinks hard as he walks

toward the fridge. His reaction makes my stomach turn. They went golfing together yesterday and had practice together this morning. I suppose he'll hear things about Finn's private life that I probably don't want to know, if the face he made is any indication.

"How was golf?" Mom asks, and I sag in relief.

"It was nice." Dame sorts through the assortment of protein shakes and picks the strawberry.

"Was it only the guys?" she asks, moving her pot from the fire and setting another one in its place.

"Some wives and girlfriends went," he says, uncapping the protein shake and taking a huge gulp. He looks at me as he says, "Some singles."

My stomach dips again. I focus on picking up the plantain peels and stand to throw them out. I hate jumping to conclusions, but Dame makes it hard. Mom picks up on it too.

"And? Did any of them catch your eye?" she asks.

"I didn't really pay attention to them." He drinks the rest of the shake and tosses the carton into the recycling bin.

"That's new," Mom says, going back to her cooking. "What about Finn?"

My heart slams hard in its cage. I start cutting up the plantains into chunks, hoping I can hear his answer through the pounding in my ears.

"What about him?" Dame picks up a toston and blows on it before popping the whole thing into his mouth and muffling, "Oof. It's hot."

"I just took those out of the frying pan!" Mom picks up the kitchen towel and whips it at him. "Set the table. Your dad should be here any minute." After a moment, she shakes her head and asks, "Did Finn pay attention to any of them?"

Dame snorts a laugh. "Why are you so interested in Finn?"

"I think he has a thing for Josie."

I groan. "Oh my god, Mom. He accompanied me to a charity event. End of story."

"He's had a thing for Joss for years," Dame says.

My heart skips. "That's a lie."

"What?! I didn't know that!" Mom switches off the stove and starts plating the fried fish. "What happened? You lost touch?"

I throw my head back with a soft laugh. "We have the internet and smartphones. I don't think it's possible to 'lose touch.'"

"Finn's not the relationship type," Dame says, and I raise an eyebrow at my mother.

"When is your meet-and-greet?" I ask, trying to change the subject.

"Monday," he says. "No, Tuesday. Fuck, I can't remember."

"Men like him are never the relationship type until someone comes along and changes his mind," Mom says.

"Oh my god." I cover my face with my hands. "Make it stop."

"He was all over you the other night," Dame says, pursing his lips the way he does when he's trying not to say too much. "I'm sure people are asking you about the pictures."

"Yep."

As far as I know, only one picture is making the rounds, and we're not even touching in it. If it were anyone else, it would have gone unnoticed. Because it's us, people are now speculating like I knew they would. I don't care, though. I'm not the one with the aversion to dating or photographs.

"Why doesn't he like being seen with dates?" Mom asks.

Dame and I share a look. Finn doesn't exactly "date," but we're not going to tell my mom that. If she could, she'd ban boys from my apartment and girls from Damian's. She doesn't preach "sex before marriage is a sin" anymore, but she did for so long that we accepted our place in hell a long time ago.

"He's just a private person," Dame says after a moment. "Not many people know him."

I bite my lip and take out my phone to check my notifications. Anything to distract me from this conversation. I click on the notifications and sigh when I see how many times I've been tagged in the picture with Finn.

"And Joss is the opposite of that," Dame adds.

I look up from my phone. "How many times are we going to go over this? I'm a private person!"

Dame shoots a pointed look toward my phone.

I roll my eyes. "I told him our picture would end up on the internet."

Dame shakes his head and starts filling glasses with water.

"You're not touching, but you're looking at each other with such longing," Mom says, almost wistfully.

My eyes threaten to bulge out of their sockets. "What is *up with you* today?"

The door chime sounds before it opens and shuts, and there is the sound of keys hitting the dish on the entry table. Titus' dress shoes click against the hardwood as he walks in our direction. His expression is clouded with worry, but when he sees the three of us, he grins wide.

"I wasn't sure you'd make it," he tells Dame as he walks up to give him a tight hug.

"I have to go back later," Dame says. "Ice in the morning, work out in the afternoon."

"And you?" Titus glances at me as he goes up to my mom and kisses her lips before hugging her tightly as well.

"Did weight training this morning. I don't have anything going on for the rest of the day," I say, returning his hug when he reaches me.

"Tate asked me about you and Finn," he says, undoing the knot of his tie and tossing it over the jacket he'd set over the chair.

"I'm not surprised. What'd he say?"

"He … well…" Titus' brows rise. "He's not happy, that's for sure."

"He's a fucking asshole," Dame growls, crossing his arms over his chest.

"Has he called you?" Mom asks, picking up two plates and handing them to Dame.

"Yeah."

"I thought you blocked his number," Dame says as he sets

the plates down on the center of the table. I stand and pick up the bowl of salad to help set the table.

"I unblocked it."

He rolls his eyes.

"I'm surprised he didn't text me about it," I say.

"He really hates that guy," my stepfather says. "With good reason. And now this."

I roll my eyes. "I will never understand inherited drama."

"Finn made it personal," Titus says. "You remember that girl who died years back? Blair?"

"The one who drowned in the frozen lake?" Mom asks with a sad look in her eyes. "What a terrible tragedy."

An uneasy feeling skates down my spine. *What the hell does Finn have to do with that?* A part of me wants to cover my ears and not find out. I was in middle school at the time, but I remember the story. I think she was on her way home from a party when her car veered off the road and went into a lake. From pictures on the news, I know the girl was beautiful, with a tight-lipped smile and dazzling blue eyes.

"According to Tate, there was some sort of love triangle between them and Finn," Titus says. "He says Finn was there the night it happened."

My heart drops and I'm instantly ashamed of myself for being even remotely jealous of that poor girl. A love triangle hints at a relationship, though. It's not like I thought Finn never had a girlfriend, but he's made himself unavailable for so long that I hadn't really thought much of how, why, or when he became that way.

"Damn. I didn't know that," Dame says.

"Not many do," Titus responds. "The Barlows are good at covering their tracks. There's a reason Richard bought his lawyer a house beside his."

Dame whistles. I'm not sure if he's impressed or disturbed. I'm definitely both.

"He doesn't think Finn killed her, does he?" I ask, or say. I can't tell with the pounding in my head.

"No, that's not the impression I got. More like he blames him for whatever led to the accident," Titus says.

"He could just be saying this, since he knows you'll tell Josslyn," Mom says.

"Maybe." Titus shrugs and glances at me. "The point is, Tate asked and I told him last I heard, there was nothing going on between you and Finn. I assume that's still the case."

I nod.

Thankfully, the topic of Finn only lasts a few more minutes, and by the time we're sitting at the table, we're talking about sports and work. Titus' words remain at the front of my mind, though. Mallory's death was barely reported on. They acknowledged it, of course, but they never said she was at Onyx. In the official public story about Onyx, they call the woman Jane Doe. A couple of days later, they quickly reported on Mallory's "tragic, untimely passing." I knew it was her parent's doing. They wouldn't want their daughter associated with a sex club.

CHAPTER THIRTY-THREE

Josslyn

Blair Lowells. According to the news reports I found, there was no reason for them to think there was foul play involved, and no mention of Finn at all. Everything I found says Blair had been drunk, high, and speeding in her dad's Ferrari. It was a terrible tragedy. A terrible, untimely death, just like Mallory's. And much like Mallory's situation, the information about Blair's death is very limited. That doesn't mean anything, though.

Tate might be an asshole, but he's a smart guy. If he really thought Finn had any involvement, he would have outed him. Finn may be a Barlow, but even Barlows can't kill someone—purposely or not—without consequence. Were they together? Were he, Tate, and Blair in some kind of love triangle? Is that why he sent me those flowers that day? Fuck. I already know this is going to haunt me.

※

It's been days, and I've still heard nothing from Finn. I tell myself it's for the best but I can't deny my disappointment. I guess a part of me thought the other night meant something to him. Maybe

I thought I'd be different. My phone buzzes, and I expect it to be Olivia calling to let me know she arrived safely at her parents' beach house, but it's a text from Scarlet.

> **Scarlet: they just changed their venue from onyx to pearl**

My stomach churns. I'm supposed to speak to Leo and John to try to get information out of them. I couldn't start an interrogation right off the bat when I met them, so I told them I was interested in checking out the "pleasure club," as John called it. That led to a text from him inviting me tonight, but meeting at Pearl complicated things. Then again, Finn hasn't reached out. He obviously got what he wanted and has no interest in me, so it won't make a difference if his cousin happens to be there or finds out I was there. Besides, the club in the basement has nothing to do with the nightclub upstairs. I doubt Lucas will have a way of knowing I'm there.

Right now, I need to do this. I need to see the people she was hanging out with. I want to look each one of them in the eyes when I speak her name. I shut my eyes again, trying to conjure memories of that night, but as usual, they stop right at the moment I walked into Onyx. There has to be video footage of the rest of my night. It's something I thought about a lot, after the initial wave of grief lifted. No one knows what happened that night after I went back inside. I don't remember *any* of it, which is disconcerting. I went to the hospital the next day, and thankfully, they confirmed I hadn't been taken advantage of, but the fact that I had no memory was still unsettling. It was also something only two people knew about.

> **Me: thanks for letting me know**
>
> **Scarlet: are you going to go?**
>
> **Me: yeah**
>
> **Scarlet: you can't wait until next weekend? I don't want you to go alone**
>
> **Me: I'll be fine. Thank you!**
>
> **Scarlet: pls be careful around those people. I'm sure they're fine, but they'll sense your innocence and see you as prey**

My heart pounds harder.

Me: noted. Thanks

I set my phone down and take a deep breath. I wouldn't call myself innocent, but I know what she means. In this world, I might as well be a virgin. Leo definitely sees me as prey. Even after we figured out he knew my stepfather, he said he'd love to "teach me a few things" in a private room. He'd stared at me so intensely for so long that I started to fidget in my chair.

I think about Finn and how he looks at me. It's intense, for sure, but I crave it. I remember the way he looked at me at Lyla's house and my stupid heart speeds up again. My mom's words come back to me, and I feel a tiny spark of hope bloom in my chest, but I squash it down quickly. He hasn't reached out again, which means we're done. For real, this time.

And even if we weren't, we still have this Mallory thing looming over us. Unfortunately, I agree with him that it wasn't an accident. I don't know how I let myself believe it was. The more I think about it, the shadier it all is. For a second time, I squeeze my eyes shut and try to replay what I remember from that night, but I hit the same dead end.

I just need to prove that my stepfather had nothing to do with what happened that night. Yes, he was there, but he was only there to get an alibi for a client of his. I believe that to be true. I just hope I can convince Finn. I lift my phone and hold my breath as I type.

Me: what other "proof" do you have on Titus?

His response comes surprisingly fast.

Finn: I can't send it on here

Me: you sent footage on here

Finn: a lapse in judgment

I don't know why, but his words sink into my chest like a knife. It feels like he's saying that about me. About *us*. I'm probably just overthinking it since I'm hurt that he dropped me so quickly, but still. *A lapse in judgment.* I shouldn't have texted him. I set my phone down with shaky hands, but at the last minute, I pick it up and furiously type out a response.

> **Me: kind of how you feel about us then**

This time, I set my phone on Do Not Disturb mode where only a handful of people have access to interrupt me. None of which include Finn Barlow. In the shower, the knot in my throat gets bigger, and finally, the sob I'd been trying to hold back bursts out of me. Fuck him for making me cry. Fuck him for making me feel things. Ultimately, this is my fault, though.

I knew what this was when I went into it. I knew what it was four years ago, and I knew what it was the night of my birthday at Pure. And still, I feel this way. My head and my heart are at war and I'm the only one losing. I cry until I feel like I've purged him from my life, and then finish getting ready.

Once I'm dressed and my hair and makeup are done, I upload a video I shot yesterday when I was trying on activewear from one of my sponsors. I take a very deep breath and look for John's phone number.

"John speaking," he says after two rings.

"Hey, John," I say. "This is Josslyn. We met the other night at Onyx. Scarlet intro—"

"Yes, Josslyn. Of course. How could I forget?" he says, a smile in his voice. "What can I do for you?"

"You told me to call when I was interested in joining the group my friend was always raving about," I say.

It's a damn lie, but he doesn't need to know that.

"Of course," he says. "Unfortunately, Onyx is hosting a joint bachelor/bachelorette party tonight, so Leo reserved some rooms at the speakeasy at Pearl. Do you know where that is?"

"Yeah."

"I'll let Leo know you're going," he says. "A couple of them haven't been in a while, but most of the people your friend used to have fun with will be there."

"Okay. I'll be there." I can barely talk with my heart beating so wildly.

"Call Leo when you get there. I'll send you his information now," he says. "I hope you enjoy yourself. I'll be back next week and would love to see you."

There's no missing what he's hinting at, but as uncomfortable as it makes me, I make a pitiful attempt to laugh.

"Sure. Thanks, John."

I hang up before he gets another word in and rub my arms to rid myself of the goosebumps. I stare at my phone for a while, waiting for his text, when I remember I'm on Do Not Disturb. I add John to my list. I don't switch it out of that mode, out of fear that Finn responded to my text with something hurtful. I push the thought aside. If Livie were in my situation, I would have already told her to walk away and forget about him. I decide I'm going to take my own advice for once.

I knew he would be unforgettable from the start. I knew hooking up with him would lead to heartache. I knew it and I did it anyway, and when he kept coming back, I tried hard not to hope, but I lost that battle as well.

I take a couple of deep breaths and spend a few moments centering myself before I leave. When I'm ready, I roll my shoulders back, grab my purse, and head out.

I text Leo after handing my keys to the valet, then follow his instructions on how to get into the speakeasy. When I get to the door, he's already there waiting for me with a smile on his face. He's *really* hot for an old guy. He totally leans into the silver fox thing, and even though he's been wearing a suit both times I've seen him, I can tell he has a good body underneath it. He has a sparkle in his eyes and keeps three buttons of his dress shirt open to show a sliver of light brown skin.

"You look ravishing," he says, lifting my hand to his mouth and kissing the back of it, as he keeps his brown eyes on mine.

"It's nice to see you again," I respond, as I take my hand back and grip the chains of my purse with it. "Thanks for adding me to the list."

"Of course." He turns around and leads me inside.

Unsurprisingly, it's a dark hallway. I can't tell if the walls are dark red or black, but they're lined with gold sconces that light the way until we reach the end. As we make a right, I start to hear music, and Leo informs me about the group and the fee I'll have to pay if I decide to join.

"We were fond of Mallory, so your visit is our gift to you," he says when we reach a lobby, similar to the one in Onyx, with BDSM-style photos on the walls. We stop in front of the hostess. "Heather, this is my friend. She'll need to sign in and fill out a form." He turns to me. "This may take a little while, so I'll leave you to it and come get you shortly. We can have a drink, I'll explain things to you, and you can ask questions."

"That would be great." I smile. "I'll just have someone tell me where to go and meet you there. I don't want you to keep walking back and forth because of me. You've done so much already."

"I'll do much more if you want me to." The way his eyes darken is almost imperceptible with the bright smile he gives me. "Heather will tell you where to find me."

Somehow, despite how little that interests me and how uncomfortable it makes me, I manage to laugh as he walks away. This is a man who KNOWS MY STEPFATHER. Thankfully, he had the sense not to ask about him tonight. Otherwise, I would have either run away or thrown up. Or both. I turn to Heather with a smile, take the tablet she hands me, and have a seat on one of the black leather couches that's sort of hidden from both doorways. My heart is in my throat the entire time I fill out the questionnaire.

I filled one out for Mallory's birthday, that time, and Onyx still has it on record, but I barely paid attention to the questions then. I kind of skimmed, checked everything, and signed my name. Titus would have been so upset, but Tate read and summarized the contract for me, and I really didn't care enough to pay attention.

This time, I'm reading each word and analyzing the phrasing, because this isn't only Pearl's waiver and NDA, this is also for the sex group "Voluptatem et Dolorem," which I learn, after doing a quick search on my phone, means "Pleasure and Pain." I take a deep breath and exhale. *Fun times.*

I look up when I feel Heather's eyes on mine and smile. "I'm almost done, I think."

"No rush. Take your time." She smiles back. "I didn't take you for the voyeur type."

I bristle, gripping the stylus in my hand. My gaze drops to the questionnaire again, landing on "Do you like to get spanked?" Holy shit. How could I be so careless? I walked right by the line waiting to go into the nightclub portion of Pearl. What if someone saw me? What if they took pictures and posted them? My heart sinks. *I'm an adult.* I'm an adult, and I'm single. If I want to go to a sex club, I can go to a damn sex club.

"I don't mean that in a bad way," Heather says after I don't say anything. I bring my gaze back to her now worried blue eyes. "I just … I've been following you for a while, and … oh my god, please forget I said anything." She covers her face.

My shoulders slump. "It's okay. I know you didn't mean it in a bad way. It's just, I mean, I don't want people finding out that I'm here."

"Oh god, I would never." She lowers her hands with wide eyes. "I would never say anything. And we've all signed NDAs, and you will as well." She nods at my tablet. "This is a safe space."

I smile. "Thank you. But to answer your question, I've only been to one of these once, and I liked it. I didn't participate, but I thought it was cool."

She laughs. "It is cool, isn't it? My girlfriend DJs here, and since she's closer to the action, she gets home pretty…" Heather blushes. "Anyway, it's a cool place to have fun."

I laugh. "I bet."

I go back to the questions. There are SO MANY questions about spanking. It's not just a "yes." It's "yes" followed by "hands, paddles, or canes?" I'm so out of my element. I try to picture what Mal would have said here, and then smile when I think she'd probably say yes to everything. My smile fades. She should be here. She should be doing all of these things. I swallow, hoping tears don't fill my eyes. *Not now.*

"My friend used to…" I clear my throat and look at Heather. "My friend used to love going to Onyx."

"I've never been," she says. "I heard it's way bigger than this."

I nod and go back to the form, a knot forming in my stomach when I get to the part about ropes, whips, cuffs, and choking. I fly through the rest of the questions, checking "no" to everything, to the point that I'm sure Leo is going to laugh and ask me what I'm doing here, but I don't care. I was clear on wanting to check out the group to learn what kind of stuff they do, since my friend used to tell me I'd love it. I never said I'd participate.

"I think I'm ready," I say, walking over to Heather after I fill out the last question and sign all the papers. I glance over my shoulder. "I'm surprised no one has walked in while I've been here. Is it usually slow on Saturdays?"

"People who want rooms usually make reservations," she says, clicking things on the tablet. "Couples looking for a good time usually come in a little later."

"Hm." I look around again. "Do people use fake names?"

"They have to show us their IDs, so we always have the real names on file, but in there, you can go by whatever name you want."

I nod, hoping to get rid of the twisting in my stomach. Even if Lucas Barlow sees my name on the list, he wouldn't ban me. He may tell his cousin, but it won't matter. Finn won't care, and even if he does, it'll be too late. I take the optional mask Heather hands me and follow her instructions on where to find Leo. After taking a deep, calming breath, I head that way.

CHAPTER THIRTY-FOUR

Finn

I'VE CHECKED MY PHONE MORE THAN A DOZEN TIMES AFTER RESPONDING to Josslyn's text and she still hasn't replied. The silence is driving me fucking crazy. It's taken everything in me not to call or text or show up at her apartment. I really fucking wish I didn't take Lucas' advice to get my PI off her tail. Not seeing pictures of her or knowing what she's doing is proving to be more distracting than not.

"You know who hits hard? Wallace," Ryan says loudly. "Took me out last time I played against him."

Hamilton pipes up and regales everyone with his own story about Jared Wallace, who's arriving in a couple of days and everyone is happy to have on our side. I see their lips moving, I hear the noise of their voices, but I can't concentrate on anything. I barely touched my food, and I'm not sure how much longer I'll be able to feign interest in their conversations. Between that and the obvious glances Ryan's sister-in-law, Tasha, has been throwing my way since she sat in the chair across from me, it's a wonder I'm still sitting here at all.

We met at the golf course the other day, and ever since, Ryan has been not so subtly hinting that she's interested in me. Even if I wanted to fuck her, which I don't, I wouldn't. The teammate connection is a recipe for disaster. Why I don't feel that way about Josslyn is beyond me. I should. I should want to avoid her at all costs, which is what I've been doing, but somehow she's been on my mind every second of every day. I keep doing stupid shit like *wishing*. Wishing she was the one sitting across from me. Wishing she was next to me, so I could feel her jolt when I put a hand on her thigh, and she can give me that stern look that turns me the fuck on. God, I need to get over this. I should go to Pearl and fuck a faceless, nameless woman. *I should.* As if summoned by my thoughts, my phone buzzes with a call from Lucas.

"I have to take this. I'll be outside." I slap my napkin on the table and push my seat back.

"When are you getting here?" Lucas asks as soon as I answer.

"I didn't realize there was a curfew." I look at my watch. "What's up? You found someone for me?"

Even as I ask the question, Josslyn's face comes to mind and my stomach churns. I have a feeling that her face is what I'm going to be picturing on anyone I fuck.

After a pause, Lucas asks, "So you're really a hundred done with Josslyn?"

My jaw tenses. "I wouldn't be going over there if I wasn't."

"You're *sure* sure?" he asks, which annoys me.

No, I'm not fucking sure sure, but I'm not going to stand here and explain that this is what I need to do to get over her. I need to replace her moans with someone else's. Her touch, her smell, I need to erase all of it. I have a feeling it'll take more than one woman to replace all of those things.

"Finn," Lucas says. "I asked if you're sure."

"Why are you questioning me?" I snap. "Is it because I sent her flowers? I told you that was…"

"Josslyn's downstairs."

My stomach drops. "What?"

"Not that it matters, since you don't care what she does or who she—"

"What the fuck is she doing there?" I growl. "Who is she with? Has she gone into a private room?"

I go up to the valet and give him my ticket, waving it so he knows I'm in a hurry.

"She…" He clears his throat. "She was in one of the bigger private rooms."

My stomach churns again. Fuck, I'm going to be sick. "Who is she with?"

"Some guy. I just started looking through the list downstairs and when I saw her name, I checked the cameras."

Some guy. She has me in fucking knots and she's at *my* club with *some guy.*

"Fuck!" I tighten the grasp on my phone so I won't throw it. "Go down there!"

"And do what?"

"I don't fucking know, Luke. Show your face and entertain her until I get there."

"Entertain her? You sure you want me to do that?" he asks, and I can picture the smirk on his face.

"You better not fucking touch her."

He's quiet for a beat. "Weren't you saying you wanted a palate cleanser? Maybe this is hers. It's only fair."

"Fair?!" I shout. "Lucas, I swear to fucking god if you don't go down there…"

"I'll keep an eye on her via the cameras and find out who she's there with."

"That's not enough!" Heart racing, I hang up and start pacing. "Goddamnit!"

Where the fuck is my car? My fucking head is spinning, my stomach hurts, and my heart won't quit pounding in my ears. *Motherfucking Josslyn.* As I pace, I pull up her location, but nothing comes up, which means her phone is off. Jesus Christ. *Did she go* there by herself? Is Olivia with her? I look at the last text I sent her, the one that remains unanswered.

> **Me:** a lapse in judgment
>
> **Josslyn:** kind of how you feel about us then
>
> **Me:** i never said that

Fuck. I should've followed my gut and stayed at her place the other day. I should've called or texted. I thought a couple of days apart would bring clarity, but I know I'm only fooling myself. Time without her only brings misery. And thinking about her with another man. Moaning for him, coming for him … *fuck*.

I set a hand over my aching stomach. *Where the hell is the valet?* I take a deep, steadying breath, wishing I had someone to tell me that I'm not going to die and that what I'm feeling is normal. Hamilton's inside, but there's no way I'm involving him in this right now. Ella is on a yacht in Europe with some fucking lingerie model. And my cousin is being a fucking asshole. I laugh despite myself. None of them would know if this is normal.

"You're leaving without saying goodbye?" a soft female voice asks, pulling me from my thoughts.

I turn to find Tasha standing by the door. God, this is the last thing I need right now. "Something came up."

"I'll let them know. I just wanted to give you my number before you left." She smiles as she walks over with an exaggerated sway.

"I can't take it." I look toward the street again, willing my car to show up.

"I know about your one-night stand rule and NDA. I'm okay with both." She moves so she's in front of me and I have no choice but to look at her.

"I have a girlfriend." The words fly out of my mouth before I can stop them.

I'm sure I look as shocked as she does. *Where the fuck did that come from?* A girlfriend? I've never called anyone my *girlfriend*. I've always thought it was such a dumb word, but associating it with

Josslyn feels right. *I'm so fucked.* If there was any doubt about how I felt, this confirms it. Josslyn fucking owns me. Now that I've accepted it, I realize how many things I've already done wrong and my stomach twists again.

"Oh." Tasha takes a step back, eyes wide. "Oh. Oh my gosh. I'm so sorry. I had no idea. I just … I thought you didn't do the relationship thing."

I huff out a laugh. *I do now.* I keep that to myself.

"I thought it was just a rumor, but I'm assuming it's Josslyn?" she asks, and when I don't respond, she adds, "She's really pretty. I love her videos. They make me feel like we're besties."

"Yeah, she has that effect on people," I say, feeling my lips tug as I think about the way she lights up any room she's in.

And now she's lighting up as some other guy stuffs his cock inside her. The thought makes my heart drop hard.

The sound of my car behind me kicks my adrenaline back into high gear. I rush to the driver's side, not even bothering to say goodbye to Tasha as I give the guy a tip and floor it.

CHAPTER THIRTY-FIVE

Josslyn

"I REALLY AM SORRY FOR YOUR LOSS," LEO SAYS ACROSS FROM ME.

I give him a tight-lipped smile. As enlightening as the night has been, I'm no closer to getting answers than I was before I got here. It's why I ended up telling Leo—in a roundabout way—the reason I'm here, as I've been practically begging him to give me the names of everyone Mallory may have come into contact with at Onyx. I'm pretty sure that Titus is the only reason this man hasn't already tried to bribe me with sex for information. Not that he's said much about my stepdad, but he sang his praises when we first sat down and started talking, so that must be enough. Not enough to keep his eyes from staring at my cleavage, though.

"I just really need closure," I say after a moment.

"It's been, what, a year? Why now?" He takes a sip of his drink.

He says a year like that's enough time for someone to process and move on from something this big. I guess it is for some people. It probably should be for me, considering I didn't know Mal my entire life or anything. Grief doesn't work that way, though. *Guilt* doesn't work that way.

"I guess in the beginning, I was in shock, and then I filed it all away so I didn't have to think about it, but lately it's been haunting me."

"Understandable," he says, offering me a sad smile. "It was such a horrible accident."

"Were you there that night?"

"I was out of town. My brother-in-law and sister were there, but they left early." He takes another sip, eyes on the table like he's lost in memory.

"I was supposed to drive her home."

"Were you there when the fire started?" His eyes widen as he sets his glass down. "Do you remember what happened?"

The quick way in which he asks the questions makes me wonder if he's covering something up or has his own suspicions about what happened that night.

"I don't know." I press my lips together momentarily to gather my thoughts. "I don't remember."

He frowns. "What do you mean?"

"I think my brain blocked the night out," I say, not wanting to give him too many details. "That's part of why I want to speak to people she was close to. I guess I just want to understand what happened."

"You don't believe it was an accident." His brown eyes narrow slightly. "Do you believe she took her own life?"

I know I can't trust this man, and I'm scared that if I give away too much, he'll pull back and not help me at all, but I need to play this right.

"What do you believe?" I ask.

"I think there is a lot of mystery surrounding this. I know the rope was found intact. Do you know how they identified her?" he asks.

I nod, swallowing hard. "Her teeth."

They said it was so bad that the Barlows didn't even have a choice to have an open casket. No one ever spoke about it, but from the research I did, I don't think there was anything left of her but bones. The media said the rope that remained gave detectives a "clear understanding as to what probably happened." They reported that she took her own life, but I'll never believe that narrative. I probably should. It's not like I thought my father would ever take his own life, and he did, so why not Mal?

I clear my throat. "I don't think she committed suicide."

"We can't know that," he says, offering a sympathetic smile. "I know you want the list of people who were there that night, but there's the issue of privacy."

"I understand." I take a deep breath and look away. This is futile. I might as well just thank him for his time and get out of here.

"I'll see what I can do for you." He reaches over and sets a hand on mine. My stomach turns, but I try not to let my discomfort show on my face. "You're too young and beautiful to hold onto this much sadness. If it will help you get closure and move on, I'll try to get you the list you want or see if my brother-in-law has any videos put away somewhere, but I can't guarantee anything."

I offer him a small smile.

"Excuse me, Miss Santos?"

I snatch my hand back and look at the beautiful black woman standing there. She looks like a vintage pin-up model. Leo looks at her as well, licking his lips as he stares at her very ample chest. He's obviously a tit man, and hers look great. That beige corset dress hugs her voluptuous frame perfectly.

"Yes. That's me," I say, returning her smile.

"Someone is requesting your presence in room five."

My heart starts to race. "Who?"

"I don't have a name." She offers an apologetic smile.

I glance at Leo, who's still ogling the messenger. "Do you think it's one of your people?"

His gaze snaps to mine. "Possibly."

Fuck. I don't want to meet with anyone from this mix. Certainly not in a private room. Part of "welcoming a new face to the group" was to have a naked conversation, and even though I'm totally okay with nudity, the entire thing was weird. Because of my outfit, I had an excuse to not go fully nude. Still, in an attempt to fit in and make them comfortable, I unzipped the top of my jumpsuit, took my arms out of the long sleeves, and left it open to my belly button. I didn't get much information, but there's a guy named L.T. with clear blue eyes that looked at me extra carefully when Leo said Mallory had been a friend of mine.

"Well, I guess I should find out who it is." My stomach is in knots as I push my chair back and stand. "Thanks for everything."

"Of course. We'll be meeting at Onyx next Saturday, and a few other regulars will be there. I can't give you a list, but I can invite you to join us."

"For a fee," I say, smiling.

He chuckles. "For a fee, but if you want to hang with me, I'll cover your fee."

I force myself to continue smiling as I stand up, and when he stands, he takes my hand to kiss the back of it. When he drops it, his eyes are back on the woman in the corset, who's still waiting patiently.

"Lead the way," I say, and follow her out.

"I absolutely love your bodysuit," she says as we walk.

"Thanks." I grin. "I didn't really consider how difficult it would be to take off."

She laughs. "Wrong place to wear it."

I'm wearing what Livie and I call my, "Catwoman costume". I actually bought it for Halloween one year, but it's become my go-to when I need something sexy and don't want to wear a dress. It's a shiny leather bodysuit with a low neckline and a zipper that goes from my breasts to my crotch. It makes me feel sexy and powerful, but it's a pain in the ass to take off and put on.

I only had to unzip it to my belly button earlier, and I'm not planning to fully take it off until I get home, so that won't be an issue. I take a deep, shaky breath and try to swallow the unease rolling through me. Do I really want to go inside a room with a stranger? My immediate answer is no, but I need to at least look inside. Maybe I can have this woman wait for me.

"What's your name?" I ask as we walk.

"Lisa." She glances at me over her shoulder.

"Do you really not know who requested to see me?"

She shakes her head, her thick dark waves bouncing with the movement. "No, but it's room five, so I assume it's someone important."

My stomach twists again, and when we finally reach a red door with the number five on it, she punches in a code and turns the handle. I'm about to ask her to wait, but she pushes the door open and my jaw drops when I see who's waiting for me. I step inside, still gaping at Finn, and forget all about the door.

This room, unlike the previous one I'd been in, has a huge bed with black sheets, cuffs peeking out of the corners, and red walls covered with photographs of people in sexual positions. Finn's standing between the door and the bed, hands in his pockets, wearing a casual black suit with a white button-down and white sneakers. His hair is tousled and his green eyes are dark and inscrutable from where I stand. The pounding in my ears makes the click of the door shutting behind me sound far, far away.

"What are you doing here?" I ask when I manage to compose myself.

"Did you fuck him?"

I blink a few times. "What?"

"Did you fuck him?" He repeats the words a little slower, those dark, intense eyes pinned on mine as he takes slow strides toward me.

My heart slams harder with each measured step. He stops a couple of feet away. Close enough that I can fully see the hard set of his jaw. I chew on the side of my lip, but his gaze doesn't veer from mine as it normally would. No, this Finn Barlow means business. Somewhere in my jumbled mind, I realize a few things at once—*Finn is here* and he requested to meet me in this private room. Somewhere in my mind, I make sense of it. I know his cousin owns Pearl, but still. Finn being here can only mean that he probably came to use this place and found out I was here. I really shouldn't care that he's here to hook up with someone else, but thinking about it makes me feel sick.

"Josslyn."

I jolt a little and clear my throat. "Yeah."

"Yeah, you fucked him?" he asks, his voice a rasp.

I don't want to get any ideas, but I swear he looks like he's hurt by that. Considering I haven't heard from him in days, I doubt that's the case. I take a breath and try to clear this confused haze.

"Are you here because you're on your *jealous caveman* bullshit?" I ask.

"I'm here because I'm on my Josslyn bullshit."

My stomach flips. "What does that mean?"

When he stays quiet, I give him another once-over. He takes another step and my eyes drop to his clenched fists. He looks like he might be shaking.

I meet his eyes again, heart in my throat. "You look crazy right now."

His chuckle is dark. Sinful. "I *feel* crazy right now."

I swallow and take a step back, keeping my eyes on his. I'm not afraid of him, but my heart feels like it's going to leap out of my throat if I don't put distance between us. Finn has other ideas. He lowers his gaze and gives my body a slow perusal as he closes the distance between us.

I take another step back, gasping when my back hits the door. He stands in front of me and brings a hand up, splaying it over my collarbone. I'm certain he feels the way my pulse spikes against the pads of his fingers. He looks like he's torn between devouring me and choking me. Right now, I'll take both.

"Why are you here, Josslyn? Did you come here to get fucked?" he asks, his voice a low growl.

My breath hitches. "Did you?"

"I'm here because of you." He drags his hands down slowly until he reaches the zipper. His eyes drop to it and he pulls it down just a little.

"How'd you know I'd be here?" I ask, finding it harder to

breathe as he pulls the zipper again. He shoots me a look that I take as confirmation that his cousin must have called him. "You know that's illegal, right?"

"Is it?" He tilts his head. "You do know I own this place with my cousin, right?"

I watch him for a long time. "No, but I'm sure it's still illegal."

"I genuinely don't give a fuck if it is," he growls. "But if you want to discuss legality, I'm sure that creep you were with is into a plethora of illegal things."

I scoff softly. "The creep I was with."

"What else would you call him?"

"I'm not sure. What would you call someone who finds out you're at a sex club and shows up uninvited?"

His eyes dance. "A concerned citizen."

I can't help it. I throw my head back in laughter. It's cut short when I feel his hard body press against mine. I gasp and straighten quickly. The look in his eyes makes my breath stutter.

"You're so fucking beautiful," he says, his voice a low rumble against my skin. He kisses the side of my neck softly, and a full shiver runs through me. "So fucking hot." He presses a kiss on my collarbone. "So fucking perfect."

"Finn," I breathe. A plea. His eyes shoot to mine and he stops what he's doing. "I didn't fuck him. Or anyone."

The relief he shows is nearly imperceptible, but I see it. I *feel* it, and damn, if it doesn't make my toes curl. I grip his biceps and try to tug him closer, but he resists, eyes searching mine.

"Were you going to?" he asks, lowering the zipper a little more. "Did you come here, hoping to find someone who could erase the memory of me? Hoping I'd find out and come show you that you can't?" He leans in, his breath hot against my lips. "I won't let you."

I don't want to take that to mean more than he intends, but my heart is about to explode, and I can't take it anymore. I fist the front of his shirt and crash my lips against his. He growls against my mouth, the sound vibrating through me and pooling in my core. He keeps unzipping until I'm exposed from my belly button up. His tongue is exploring my mouth, warring against mine, as he brings both hands to cup my breasts, the rough pads of his thumbs flicking my nipples.

I gasp against his mouth, moving my hands to tug his hair as I push into him, trying to get rid of every bit of space between us. He keeps one hand on my right breast as he lowers the zipper as far as it can go. Long rough fingers dip into my underwear. I moan into his mouth and he breaks our kiss, breathing hard against me as he watches my reaction to his fingers running up and down my folds. My grip tightens on his hair. He pulls away and replaces the hand on my breast with his mouth, his tongue flicking as he dips a finger inside me.

"Finn," I gasp.

"Hm." His answering hum is appreciative and so fucking sexy. "So wet."

The back of my head hits the door with a thump when he flicks my clit with his thumb and my nipple with the tip of his tongue.

"Oh my god," I breathe.

"Is this for me, Josslyn?" he asks, licking my other nipple as his fingers continue to move. "Is this pretty pussy wet for me?" He brings his face back up to mine. "Or were you this soaked before I got here?" I shake my head vehemently. When he stops moving his fingers, I push into him, trying to get myself off, and he chuckles softly. "Tell me."

"It's for you. Only you," I pant, meeting his dark gaze and grinding my hips forward. "Please, Finn."

"Hm." He takes my mouth again, this time in a deep, slow kiss as he dips another finger inside me, then another, and another, eliciting a sharp gasp from me as I break the kiss and tilt my neck back with another moan.

Holy shit. His mouth lands on my neck, sucking and biting lightly as he continues to fuck me with his fingers, slowing down the ones inside me to add his thumb to my clit. My core clenches hard.

"Fuck, I'm going to come," I pant. "Finn. I'm going to…"

He drags his mouth back down to my breast and bites my nipple as he hooks his fingers inside me. "Scream my name when you come for me, baby."

And I do. I shatter, screaming his name over and over as my entire body shakes. He pulls his fingers out slowly, still moving against my folds, his thumb doing slow circles on my clit. It's a gentle touch, but no less effective.

"Look at me," he says, voice husky.

I do, through hazy eyes. It's not until I blink a few times and feel tears spilling out that I realize I'm crying. *Why am I crying?* Finn doesn't comment on it. He takes his hand away to suck his fingers before slinking into my panties once again and continuing his slow, tortuous motion.

"Are you going to come for me again, baby?" he asks, kissing along my jaw and laughing lightly against me when he dips his fingers into me and feels me clench around him. "So. Fucking. Perfect."

He lifts his head and watches me as he fingers me. The orgasm that sweeps through me feels more intense than the last, but with his eyes locked on mine, the words get lodged in my throat. I bite my lip hard, making a soft whimpered sound when I find my release. And then his lips are on mine again.

CHAPTER THIRTY-SIX

Finn

After promising Josslyn I'd have someone drive her car home, I usher her to mine. There are a million things I want to ask, and I can tell there are just as many things she wants to say, but neither of us speaks. Every once in a while, I glance over and find her chewing on her lip, appearing to be lost deep in thought, but I don't dare interrupt the silence. Not when I'm still trying to process my own emotions. The relief I felt when she said she didn't fuck anyone was all the confirmation I needed to confirm how far gone I am for her. And yet, I have no idea how I'm going to say that to her. We're still quiet when we get to our building, and we ride the elevator up to her floor and get to her apartment. She turns around before unlocking her door with a frown on her face.

"Are you … is this … are you coming in?"

"That's the idea."

She turns toward me again and presses her back against the door. She looks down the hall to the right, to the left, down at the black carpet, and across at the wooden panels. Anywhere … everywhere but at me. I bite back my annoyance and push down the urge to snap. I wait and wait, and fucking finally, she clears her throat and looks at me again.

"I can't do this anymore."

My stomach sinks. Jesus. I didn't know five little words could have such an impact. She's only been my girlfriend—unbeknownst to her—for a couple of hours and she's already breaking up with me.

"Do what?" I ask.

"This." She signals between us. "Whatever this is. I don't want to do it anymore."

Fuck. That. The only reason I don't say that outright is because she already looks wary and I want to know why. I have a feeling it has to do with her stepfather, which is a lead that has gone nowhere. The only things I have are the footage of him arguing with Josslyn outside of Onyx that night, my sister's journal entries, and pictures my PI has taken of him doing mundane things with mundane people. None of that would hold up in a court of law. Worse, I have a feeling that Josslyn is going to give me an ultimatum: her or justice for Mal, and if it comes to that ... *fuck*.

"Why?" I manage to ask after a moment of silence.

"I don't want to..." She looks away briefly. When her eyes land on mine, my chest squeezes. "What is this, hookup number four? Am I supposed to just—"

"I'm not counting," I say, interrupting her. "I've never kept count with you."

"What is that supposed to mean?" she whispers, eyes wide.

"Can we have this conversation inside?"

She swallows and turns to open the door. Inside, I watch her take off her heels and shrink about four inches.

"Do you..." She clears her voice. "Do you want something to drink?"

"I'll take water, please." I toss my folded jacket on the back of the couch and roll my sleeves up, as I debate where I should sit.

I walk around, glancing at the pictures I saw the other day as I make my way to the couch. I'm glad I'm sitting down, because when she heads my way, I have to bite my tongue so I don't swallow it. She's already my walking wet dream, but in that catsuit, she's my teenage fantasy come to life. She hands me a glass of water and sits down on the opposite end of the couch. My eyes drop to her chest, then travel lower. Fuck, that outfit of hers is distracting. It's so tight, I know I'll have to peel it off. Slowly.

"Finn."

I blink. "I'm waiting for you to start talking."

She raises an eyebrow. "It looks like you're checking me out."

"I am. While I wait."

She bites back a smile. "You know, I knew I shouldn't have hooked up with you. I knew it at that party. I knew it the day after when you showed up at Onyx. I knew it in the bathroom on my birthday."

"But you did it anyway."

"But I did it anyway." She shrugs, a sly smile playing on her beautiful lips. "I would say it was a lapse in judgment, but I'm pretty sure that excuse went out the window after the second time."

The constraints on my chest loosen a bit when I smile back and see the look on her face. It's hard not to feel special when she looks at me like that, cataloging each of my features as if I were a work of art. I know how I look. I've been admired by women and men my entire life. I've used that to my advantage on many occasions. No one has ever made me feel the way she does when she looks at me.

"I felt the same way," I say, shaking my head as I add, "And after that night at Onyx, I knew I was in trouble."

She frowns. "You disappeared after that."

"You had a boyfriend, remember?"

Her brow lifts. "Yeah, you seemed real concerned about that when you told me to get on my knees."

My stomach tightens. "Are you really going to sit there looking like that and remind me how you look on your knees? I thought you wanted to talk."

Her lips part slightly and her eyes darken, as they drop to my very obvious hard-on. I know without a doubt she's wet right now, but I force myself to stay on track. This conversation needs to happen. We need to get past the bullshit and lay it all out there. Maybe not *all*.

"What were you doing at Pearl?" I ask finally.

She licks her lips. "I went to Onyx the other day…"

"By yourself?" I snap, unable to keep myself from interrupting. Now that she's said it, I can finally express the anger I've been harboring since I followed her in there that night.

"Well, yeah. I wasn't there for sex," she says. "I thought if I could prove Titus had nothing to do with it *and* find the person who might have done it, you could get your closure."

My jaw tenses. "And? How's your investigative work panning out?"

She shoots me a sour look. "Not great, and you interrupted a conversation that may have gotten me somewhere."

I scoff. "That conversation would only have led to him trying to get in your pants, and that wasn't going to fucking happen."

She rolls her eyes.

"Why were you in a private room?"

She blinks hard and laughs. "Of course, you know about that."

"Are you going to answer the question?"

Her eyes narrow. "Are you going to stop being an asshole?"

I take a breath and let it out slowly. "I'm trying."

"Mal…" She bites her lip and sets the glass of water on the coffee table. "Your sister…" She takes a deep breath and shuts her eyes, as if trying to regain her thoughts.

"Just tell me," I say, trying to keep my voice gentle despite the building pressure in my chest.

"How often did you talk to her?" she asks.

Now, I'm the one who looks away. My eyes land on the picture frames and stay there for a moment. Me being a terrible brother wasn't what I wanted to discuss tonight, but that's the root of this, isn't it?

"I'm not asking because I'm judging you," she adds softly, with sympathy in those beautiful brown eyes of hers I don't deserve.

"Not as often as I should have," I say.

"I'm not sure what she had to say about me, if anything, but I can't imagine it was good—"

My light laugh cuts her off. "I found her journal. It's one of the reasons I knew to look into Titus. Most of the entries are about you and how incredible you are."

The pain in her eyes is unmistakable, but she looks away, biting down on her trembling lip. I clench my fists to restrain myself from reaching for her.

"We didn't speak for months before that night," she says quietly, bringing her eyes to mine. She must see the shock on my face, and the way my eyes widen when she adds, "Livie hadn't spoken to her in a year. I…" Her lip trembles again, but she bites down on it quickly and continues.

"I failed her that night, and every night after." She bats away stray tears and clears her throat. "In the very beginning, I came to the same conclusion as you. Surely, it couldn't have been an accident, and even if it was, who was with her? I asked, and asked, but then your parents made us sign those papers and—"

"What papers?"

She shrugs. "An NDA of sorts. We weren't allowed to speak about Mallory or post anything. I had to remove any posts she might have appeared in, even if she was in the background."

I sit back, processing that information. It doesn't surprise me. It's the Barlow way, after all. Everything we do involves contracts.

"Can I ask you something?" she asks after a quiet moment. I stare at her, waiting. "Who was Blair Lowell to you?"

My stomach turns. "How do you know about her?"

In typical Josslyn fashion, she's searching my face for answers she won't find. After a moment of her scrutiny, I set my elbows on my knees and glance between my legs, eyes on the blue and white area rug. I refuse to let this be the reason she walks away from me. If she does, I will fucking *murder* Tate Foster and bury him in an unmarked grave.

CHAPTER THIRTY-SEVEN

Finn

"WAS SHE YOUR GIRLFRIEND?" SHE ASKS.

I take a breath. "It was complicated, but no, not really."

"Did you love her?" she asks, her voice so soft, I almost miss the question.

My head lifts and I meet her eyes. "Why are you asking me about her? What did Tate say?"

"He..." She licks her lips, and I realize she's scared of what my reaction will be. I nearly laugh.

"You can speak your mind. I won't harm your perfect little ex-boyfriend." *Much.*

"He blames you for her death."

An uncomfortable weight lands on my chest. "He wouldn't be the only one."

God, I hadn't heard Blair's name in ages. I'm ashamed to say I haven't even thought about her in a very long time. All of that feels like it was ten lifetimes ago. I'm not sure how long we sit in silence before the couch shifts and Josslyn is at my side, her hand on mine over my knee. It's so warm and unexpected, I nearly jump out of my skin. I stare at it, so small over mine it almost looks fragile. I don't deserve the comfort or the peace it brings me, but I'm a selfish man. I turn my hand and thread our fingers together.

"Tell me," she says quietly.

"I was a sophomore at the time. I'd known Blair since ... forever. We ran in the same circles, went to the same schools. Same as Tate." I look at her again, my lips twisting. "She always liked me, but she started dating Tate. The girls had this bet on who could tame me, and Blair didn't want any of her friends to get with me..."

An unamused chuckle leaves my lips as I shake my head. We were so fucking stupid back then.

"What happened?" she asks quietly.

"The first time she tried to fuck me, Tate found out and threw a fit. We were on the same team at the time," I say.

Her eyes widen. "I didn't know that."

"He had a lot of reasons to hate me," I admit. "His family lost a lot of money because of my father. I was better than him at everything. He finally got the girl he'd been in love with his entire life, and she wanted me."

"That's why he said you were only with me to get back at him," she says. "What happened with Blair?"

"That night, we were at a party. I was leaving for hockey camp the next day. I guess she thought it would be a good time to finally get me to fuck her again."

She tenses. "Again?"

"We'd hooked up a few times before she got with Tate," I say. She tenses again. "Oh."

"I wasn't always like this," I say, amused at her reaction. "I've had girlfriends."

This time, she tries to wiggle her fingers away from mine, but I hold on and bring our joint hands to my chest. It probably shouldn't make me feel this good to know she might be jealous. I wait until she looks at me again before continuing.

"That night at that party, Blair came on strong. She usually did, but for some reason, that was the night I let her drag me to the bathroom," I say, feeling a hint of amusement when Josslyn tries to pull away again.

"After that, we got into a huge argument. She started drinking and getting belligerent. She kept saying she'd broken up with Tate to be with me. I finally snapped and told her I didn't ask her to do that. I think I called her a slut." I flinch, ashamed of the things I'd said. "It got heated quickly. Blair left, and I made my exit a few minutes later with Ella. Police were all over the bridge, so we knew whatever had happened was bad, but we didn't find out until the following day. So, I guess Tate isn't wrong to think what he does."

"That wasn't your fault," she says. "You were a teenage boy."

"It was the last time I made that kind of teenage boy mistake."

"You were a kid."

"I was old enough to know better."

She blinks. "No, you weren't."

"It doesn't matter. None of it should've happened. Blair shouldn't have died like that. I shouldn't have said all of those things to her. I shouldn't have gone to that bathroom with her."

"What happened after?" she asks. "Tate blames you, but there's no mention of you in the two articles and blog post I found. There's barely any information about it at all."

My smile feels forced. "I'm a Barlow, remember?"

This time, when she pulls her hand away, I let her. She sits back and looks at the floor. I do the same. That accident was the real reason Tate's family was ousted. After Blair died, he wouldn't stop attacking me publicly. He only had himself to blame for the downfall. Even after he was told to shut up, he kept going, and eventually it caught up to him. You can't go for the king's throat and expect to keep your own.

"Do you blame yourself for it?" she asks quietly.

"I did for a while. I haven't thought about that in a very long time," I say, which probably sounds callous, but it's the truth.

"It explains why Tate hates you," she whispers. "He lost the girl he loved, and he had to watch you succeed in everything."

I stare at her for a long moment. "Why were you at Pearl tonight?"

"When I heard how Mallory was found, I couldn't stop seeing images of my dad and how I found him. Some people said the woman found there did it to herself, others said she was murdered, but the police said it was a tragic accident, and since she was a Jane Doe on the news, everyone accepted that answer." She frowns. "I just always knew there was something off about that night."

"Who told you?" I ask. "How she was found, I mean."

My parents, who didn't want a sex club tarnishing the family name, pulled a lot of strings to make sure my sister remained Jane Doe in the media, but most people knew it was her. The club may require an NDA, but people still talk, and too many had seen Mallory there. Every time I thought about how often she went, I felt another blow to my chest. Josslyn's brows pull together. I don't know what memory flashes through her mind, but whatever it is shakes her.

She clears her throat and finally says, "I don't remember."

I don't believe that for a moment, but I let it go for now.

"What did you do when you went back inside? Were you there for the fire?" I ask, and I swear it's as if she stops breathing.

Her reaction makes an uneasy feeling skate down my spine. I need to get the rest of the footage from that night. I don't believe for a fucking second that the cameras weren't working. Even if the ones inside had been damaged, there are six cameras recording everything outside. I've considered that maybe Rustin got rid of the evidence, but … something doesn't add up. He's not a close friend of ours, but he's an acquaintance we grew up seeing at parties, and we've known him for a long time.

"I'll get to that," she says. "In the beginning, I tried to find out who she was with. It was the only way to get through the grief and guilt. I wanted to see the footage. The guest list. Anything. Tate helped for a while," she says, biting her lip as she looked away. "It was one of the many reasons we broke up. After three months of watching me cry, he just…" she shrugs.

"He's a spineless piece of shit."

"He is who he is."

"You always looked so normal online, as if none of it affected you," I say and instantly regret giving away that information.

Her brows shoot up. "You follow my page?"

My lips purse. "I lurk on your page."

"So you tell women not to contact you anywhere, but you stalk their social media?"

"Josslyn." I sigh heavily, glancing away momentarily. When I look at her again, she has an expectant expression on her face that makes my jaw tense, but I answer her stupid question, "You're the only person I've ever done that with."

The shock on her face is priceless and fucking adorable.

"Anyway." She clears her throat. "Your parents made us sign a ton of papers, which seems to be their M.O. That's why I asked about Blair."

I feel my lips twist, as I nod.

"I was depressed for months after. I will never understand how life just keeps going after someone dies. It's like we're expected to grieve for a socially acceptable time and then move on." She shakes her head. "I did what I had to do with Dad. I filed it away and dissociated. But then you came to Mal's funeral and made me feel like shit." I flinch, but she keeps going. "I understood it though, and I understand your need for answers." She wraps her arms around herself and rubs them as if she's cold. "I had to find out the truth. *Have to.* So, I went to the only person at Onyx who would help me." She smiles sadly. "And that's how I ended up in a private room at Pearl with my tits out in a room full of naked strangers."

It takes me a moment to process her words. I think I stopped listening when she said the words "private room," but the moment my brain processes her statement…

"YOU WHAT?" I roar, shooting out of my seat.

CHAPTER THIRTY-EIGHT

Josslyn

I WATCH AS HE TAKES IN THAT BIT OF NEWS, AND WONDER IF I SHOULD even continue.

"Maybe we should go back to the part about why I went to Onyx with her that night," I suggest quietly.

His jaw sets. "Oh, we're going back to that, as soon as you tell me how the fuck you ended up naked."

"Only from the waist up," I point out. He scowls, so I keep talking. "Mal met up with a group of people at Onyx on Saturdays. It's this whole thing." I wave a hand. "There's a steep membership fee and it's very hush-hush. The other night, Scarlet introduced me to these guys and they invited me to go tonight—"

"And you fucking went," he says, eyes narrowed, his voice low and hoarse. "You went to a sex club, *my* sex club, to meet with a group of swingers *by yourself*."

"To be fair, I didn't know about the change in venue until the last minute, so it's not like I *wanted* to go to Pearl."

"So you would've gone to Onyx instead." His jaw clenches again.

"Yes."

"Why the fuck…" He shuts his eyes and pinches the bridge of his nose for a moment before he looks at me again. "Why would you do that?"

"I already told you! Because you think my stepfather was having an affair with your sister, and you threatened to ruin his life!" I shout. "And I realized that you actually could, because, despite his stellar reputation, he's not a fucking Barlow and this conversation just further proves how much weight your name has here!"

He stares at me for a moment, jaw still tight. "Did they force you to get naked?"

The fact that he didn't dispute wanting to ruin Titus' reputation and went back to the nudity thing makes my blood boil. I sit on my hands to keep from shaking.

"They didn't force me to do anything," I say between my teeth. "It's not a sex thing. It's a trust and being on equal ground thing. The group does it each time they meet."

"Right." He scoffs. "Did you learn anything worth writing down in your handy dandy fucking notebook?"

This motherfucker. Maybe it's the sarcasm, or everything that happened tonight, or the weight of it all crashing down on me, but my entire body is *shaking* when I stand up and walk over to glare at him. I've never hit anyone in my life, but this man. I take a breath and huff it out, surprised that fire doesn't spill out of me.

"Fuck you, Finneas. Do you think I *enjoy* people's lascivious looks or being propositioned by older men? Do you think I was comfortable when I walked into that private room? I did it because you trying to bring Titus into this is making me sick. I did it to *help you*. If you don't like the extreme measures I had to take, you can fuck right off."

"While you were living your best life and fucking your way through Vegas, I was here dealing with your sister's bullshit. You know why she stopped talking to me?" I ask, hating how my voice breaks and the hot tears blur my vision. "Because after driving to my apartment drunk and high at three in the morning multiple times, I got concerned and called your mother. Mal…" I shake my head, batting away the tears that come with the memories I've tried to bury.

"And then you show up talking all this shit about Titus and calling me a liar and send me footage that seems so foreign to me, I can barely recognize myself," I add, seething. "I have no recollection of that night after I went back inside. My last memory is waking up the next morning on my couch and hearing what happened." I unclench my fists and point at myself. "I drove her there because I was in town and didn't have a game, and couldn't let her drive home like that again. I was supposed to make sure she was safe and…"

The sob that rattles through me is so loud that I don't get to finish my sentence. I rush to my room, slamming the door behind me, and go to the bathroom, doing the same and locking it. The wood panels on the door are rough against my back as I slide down and bury my face in my hands. I am so freaking tired. I hate him for making me relive this.

I hate these memories and the reminder that I failed someone else who needed help. Hearing so many people say they think she did that to herself is tearing me apart. I hate that I have no recollection of what happened that night after my argument with Titus. I hate that I gave my stepfather my word to not tell anyone who he was there to see, because it's an open case he's working on.

When I'm done crying, I wipe my face, stand up, turn the lights on, and switch on the shower. My head throbs with a massive headache that makes peeling off the leather jumpsuit more difficult than usual. I get in the shower and start washing, but my shaky knees force me to sit down under the spray. I know I locked the door, so when I hear it open and shut, it's clear that Finn picked the lock.

Right now, I don't have the energy to care. I keep my head down and my eyes closed. After a moment, the shower door opens and shuts, and long muscular legs and arms encase mine as he sits behind me. He moves my wet hair and kisses the back of my neck.

I hate the shiver that rocks through me. I hate the way my stomach dips. I hate how good—how right—being in his arms feels.

"You should leave," I manage to say. My voice is so hoarse and quiet, I wouldn't be surprised if he doesn't hear me.

"I'm sorry," he says against my skin and wraps his arms around me.

His tenderness makes me cry harder, and I hate that too. When I'm done crying, I take a few deep breaths until they're less shaky.

"I wish I'd called her more often," he says when he finally speaks. "Ham told me he was worried about her. I should've listened."

I keep my eyes on the white tiles in front of me. "Will knew?"

"He said she was partying more than usual, but I figured she was just doing the college thing."

He kisses my shoulder blade and lets go of me. Even though the water is lukewarm, I feel like I'm freezing without his touch. I hear him open a bottle behind me and then his hands are lathering shampoo into my hair. I shut my eyes, trying to fight a new wave of tears at the unexpected tenderness. He continues washing my hair in silence.

"Everyone warned me about her, you know? Mostly Livie, but even Dame was worried."

His fingers stop for a moment. "What did they say?"

"Livie said Mal treated her friends like possessions, and she was right. She'd get pissed off when I had too many away games or hung out with Livie, Dame, or Tate more than her. I probably shouldn't have let her back in my life." He helps me stand, and I squeeze my eyes shut as he washes off the conditioner. "But she was so lost, and I wanted to help her."

"Of course you did." He smiles with a soft expression I've never seen on his face.

For a moment, I think he'll kiss me, but he reaches for the soap and starts cleaning himself. By the time we finish showering, the water is freezing. He switches it off and we get out to dry ourselves. My stomach dips when I catch him staring at me, as I'm wringing water from my hair over the sink.

I let go of my hair and stand up straight. "What?"

"You're so beautiful," he says quietly, as he closes the distance between us. He brings his hand down, his long fingers fanning the back of my neck as he runs his calloused thumb over my cheek. For a moment, he just gets lost in staring, and my stomach dips repeatedly. He brings his lips to mine in a slow, lingering kiss that makes a million butterflies take flight deep in my belly. When he pulls away, he sets his forehead against mine and exhales.

"Thank you for helping me," he says.

My heart swells. I didn't realize how much I needed to hear those words. I swallow the knot in my throat and will the tears from forming again. I nod, moving both our heads. We're quiet as we finish drying off.

He picks up my jumpsuit and shakes his head. "I was looking forward to stripping this off you."

I laugh and open my mouth, but I shut it quickly. What am I supposed to say? You can do it another day? Despite all of this, I'm not sure what to think. I put on the underwear and oversized t-shirt I'd left out earlier, and start blow-drying my hair, trying not to ogle him when he whips off his towel. He pulls on a pair of black briefs and tosses a gray t-shirt with the Owls logo over his shoulder. I know I don't own one of those yet.

I frown. "Where'd you get that?"

"My apartment."

"When did you…" I stop myself from finishing, when I realize he must have gone up while I was crying on the bathroom floor. Still, why would he… *"Oh."*

Does he mean to stay here tonight? I hope he knows sex is out of the question. Between my headache and the exhaustion from the day, I just want to sleep. I look away from him and keep drying my hair, but in the mirror, I see him put toothpaste on a toothbrush I've never seen. My heart skips. He's definitely staying. I switch off the blow-dryer and study the puffy mess that is my hair. I hate sleeping with my hair in my face, so despite my headache, I pull it into a loose bun at the top of my head.

"Did you take something for your headache?" he asks.

"How do you know I have a headache?"

"You hissed and flinched when I was washing your hair and applied too much pressure."

"Oh." I feel myself frown. He really pays attention. "I'll be fine. I just need to close my eyes in a dark room."

He smiles and my heart stops beating. "Lucky for us, we just need to turn off the lights."

I don't respond, because I know my words will be a stuttering mess. He grabs the t-shirt on his shoulder and pulls it on as we walk toward the bed.

"I'm not having sex with you," I say, meeting his gaze warily.

"I'm offended that you thought I'd expect you to."

"I…" I shake my head and release an exhale. I can't do this right now.

He waits for me to pick a side of the bed before he walks to the opposite side and gets in and under the covers like this is normal. My heart pounds as he switches off the lamp on the nightstand. The bed dips as he moves until he's behind me. I get on my side and let him wrap an arm around me and pull me against his chest. I don't move for a moment. I don't breathe. With the darkness enveloping us, I find my words.

"Finn?"

"Hm." It's a rumble against my back, a breath against my neck.

"What is happening right now?"

He chuckles, a deep sound that slithers through me and grips my core. "I was under the impression that we were going to sleep."

I elbow him lightly. "You know what I mean."

"I thought we should finish our conversation in the morning since I made you cry and you have a headache."

"But … why are you here now?"

His arms tense around me. "Do you not want me here?"

It's dark, so it doesn't really matter, but I turn around to face him. "I didn't say that. I'm just surprised."

"I want to be with you." The conviction with which he says it takes my breath away. He kisses my forehead. "Go to sleep. We'll talk more about why I'm here in a few hours."

My heart is threatening to pop out of my chest as I turn around. I should be terrified of what this could mean. What I feel for him, what I've always felt despite everything, should terrify me. It doesn't. It just feels … right. After a few minutes, I get hot, throw his arm off, and scoot away from him. He doesn't say anything, but when he starts running his fingers softly through my hair and over my scalp, I'm convinced I've somehow jumped into an alternate dimension.

CHAPTER THIRTY-NINE

Josslyn

Tate: heads up, it looks like I'll be at your parents' house on Titus' bday

I FEEL MYSELF FROWN. TITUS' BIRTHDAYS ARE EITHER DINNER AT FANCY restaurants or ordering takeout at the house before he disappears into his office to work. He's been so busy lately that I just assumed the latter would be happening, and since it's not until a couple of weeks from now, I haven't even brought it up.

Me: ????

Tate: two big cases. meeting over dinner

I groan as I set my phone down and focus on the espresso I'm making on the stove. Titus has a one-track mind when it comes to his cases, and if he's working on two right now, this checks out. When he's extra stressed, he literally brings his job home and holes up in his home office with his employees and sometimes partners, depending on the case. At the end of the day, it doesn't matter. Tate and I were civil when we broke up the first time. Then again, there was no bad blood between us then.

I'm whipping up sugar as the espresso finishes brewing, when

Finn appears. My eyes nearly bulge out of their sockets. He's in shorts and a t-shirt, tapping his phone as he brings a muscled arm up to run his fingers through his unruly hair. The sliver of skin between his shirt and the elastic of his boxers makes my mouth go dry. The sound of the espresso brew finishing snaps my attention back to the stove. My heart is pounding, my hands shaking, as I focus on my task.

The two boyfriends I had before Tate were both athletes. I'm used to toned bodies. I'm used to muscles. I don't stare at the guys in the park when they take off their shirts. But this guy … I find everything about him annoyingly sexy. I hear when he sets his phone on the counter, and from the corner of my eye, I see him walking up to me. He wraps his arms around me and kisses my head.

"How's your headache?"

Even his groggy morning voice is sexy as fuck. I'm not sure my libido can handle this. I should really kick him out and end this right now. I clear my throat and set everything in my hands down, as I turn in his arms.

"Gone," I say.

The warmth in his eyes makes me take a step away from him. I can't have him act this way and this just be a casual hookup. I can't play house with him if it's not real. My guard is already down, and if I keep falling for him and he breaks it off, I think it might kill me. He frowns.

"Why are you being like this?"

"Like what?" he asks, but his expression is wary, his guard up.

"Nice," I say. When he doesn't respond, I add, "I can't figure out if this is some sort of prank, or if you got hit hard at practice."

He opens his mouth, shuts it, opens it again, and glances over my head. "Is that coffee?"

I press my lips together and stare at him for a moment before sighing and turning around to pour our coffee. It takes me longer to explain the difference between a cortadito and café con leche than it would have been for him to answer my question, but I do it anyway. When I'm done, I bring out overnight oats—which he also has questions about—and fruit, which is thankfully self-explanatory. Finally, we take a seat on the barstools—me with my café con leche and him with just straight-up coffee. He drinks his in two sips and starts eyeing the espresso maker.

"You know you're going to be wired all day, right?"

"Because of this?" He laughs, looking at the cup. "I drink black coffee every morning."

"Cuban coffee hits different."

He raises an eyebrow. "You have a full-size mug."

"*With milk.* We went over this already." I take a sip, lower my mug, and watch Finn stand up and pour himself another cup. He really has no idea how potent this stuff is. He remains standing, so I pivot my chair toward him.

"So," I say. "We should talk."

"Every time you use those phrases—'we should talk' and 'I can't do this anymore'—my chest tightens," he says quietly, almost as if he doesn't want to admit it.

I inhale sharply and place my mug on the counter so I don't drop it.

"I don't know what to make of that," I respond.

"I was at dinner last night when I found out where you were," he says.

My stomach caves in. He could've been at dinner with anyone, but Damian told me they'd all made plans to have dinner together the day before at the golf course. All of them. "Single women included," Damian pointed out when he told me. Which, under normal circumstances, I wouldn't think twice about, but he'd already told me one was flirting with Finn. Thinking about him flirting back or considering taking one of them home makes me feel sick.

I lick my lips. "Were you with a woman?"

"There were several women."

I feel that tightness in my chest he was describing, but I push on. "And?"

"It was a group dinner," he says. "But one of them tried to give me her number."

My pulse quickens, but I don't trust myself to speak.

"You know what I told her?" he asks.

"What?" I ask with a bite in my tone that seems to amuse him.

"I told her I have a girlfriend."

I stop breathing. I open and shut my mouth a couple of times and I think I make a sound, but words fail me.

"After the incident, when that woman snuck into my apartment, I stopped taking women home. Most of the time, I go to a hotel. It makes things easier anyway. Either I leave or they leave at the end of the night. There's never that sleeping over and cuddling bullshit. Some have begged—"

"Can you get to the point? I really don't want to hear about you fucking other women."

He looks at me for a moment, before his lips tilt into a devilish smile. I roll my eyes and cross my arms, which apparently amuses him even more.

"The other night when you left, I felt…" He frowns, as if looking for the right word.

"How did you feel?" I ask, when I feel like he's taking too long.

"Empty."

My heart dips. "You can't say things like that, Finn."

"I don't know how else to do this, Josslyn." He runs his hand through his hair and exhales as he paces the small space. "I don't know how to play this game. I don't know what to say or not say."

"It's not a game! Just say what you feel."

He stops pacing and walks over to me, his thighs brushing against my knees. The way he's looking at me … I think I might die.

"I want *you*." He runs the back of his hand along my cheek. "I want to be with you. I want more than just sex."

I inhale sharply. I'm not sure what I was expecting. I thought he'd say he has feelings for me or apologize again or something, but…

"That sounds like a relationship," I manage to say, pulse throbbing in my ears.

"What if that's what I want?"

For a moment, I just stare at him. "You want a relationship?"

"With you, yes."

"And you figured this out because you heard I was at Pearl and you thought I was hooking up with someone else?"

"I think I figured it out when I was sitting across from you at the barbecue," he says but sounds unsure.

"You mean when you were jealous of Tiago?" I ask. "It sounds like what you want is to possess me."

"No. It's not like that," he says, scowling.

"Then tell me what it's like. Tell me what you want."

"Maybe that's what it took for me to finally snap out of it, but I want *you*," he says. "I want the Josslyn people don't get to see. The one who gets mad and cries and laughs with abandon. The one who makes my heart beat so fast I can hardly stand it." He holds my hand in his and brings it up to his chest as if to show me. "I want all of you."

Somehow, I force myself to breathe. "That's a big ask, Finneas."

"I know." He moves closer so he's standing between my legs, still holding my hands on my thighs. "I want to take you to dinner and watch stupid movies with you. I don't care what we do. I just want to *be* with you."

My heart skips a few beats. I want that. I want it so badly, but I don't know…

"People pay attention to my whereabouts. They'll take pictures, they'll talk, they'll speculate," I say. "That picture of us at the fundraiser was literally examined and talked about by a person who reads body language."

His brows shoot up. "That's … interesting."

"My point is, you'll give up a lot of your privacy, and if you…" I swallow hard and look down, focusing on our linked hands. "If you cheat on me or something—"

"Are you fucking kidding me right now?" He lets go of one of my hands and lifts my face with it, eyes blazing. "I would never do that to you. Never."

"You don't know—"

"I *do know*. Do you think I'm some fucking kid who needs to fuck all the time? Or that I accept every proposition I get?" he asks, his eyes hard. "That's not me. I've been hyperfocused on my career and haven't had a serious relationship, so maybe I'll fuck up, but never like that."

I know I can't blame the entire male population for one cheating bastard, but it's easier said than done. Especially when it comes to Finn. He's every hetero woman's fantasy.

"What you went through was shitty, but I'm asking you to trust me." He sighs, grabs my face, and touches his forehead to mine. "You're my fucking fantasy, my dream girl. Do you really think I'd be stupid enough to hurt you like that?"

"Oh my God," I whisper. "I'm going to have a heart attack if you keep saying things like that."

He chuckles against my lips and kisses me softly but pulls away quickly.

"You'd lose your privacy," I reiterate.

"But I'd gain you."

I take a shaky breath. "Are you going to complain about my guy friends?"

His eyes narrow. "Define guy friends."

I laugh. "*Guy friends*. Like Tiago."

"I don't expect you to ditch your friends, but he likes you as more than just a friend."

"He doesn't, and you have nothing to worry about because I'd never do anything to hurt you either."

"He's always touching you. I don't like it."

"I think I understand," I say. "I was jealous of Ella, and you and I weren't even together."

He frowns. "Why?"

"You were always at events together. I thought maybe…" I shrug. "It shouldn't have mattered since we weren't together, but I hated seeing those pictures."

He cups my face and tilts my head again. "You have nothing to worry about. Ever. I mean that. And not just with Ella, who's a lesbian, by the way. If anything, I'll be the one annoyed as fuck if she keeps checking you out the way she does."

I smile. "You don't have to worry about anyone either. I'll definitely speak to Tiago, but he's like that with everyone. I told you, he's a touchy-feely guy."

"Yeah, well, he can touch and feel someone who's not my fucking girlfriend," he growls, his grip tightening on my thighs.

I stop breathing. "Girlfriend?"

"Girlfriend, partner, whatever." He bites my bottom lip. "As long as you're mine."

"And you'll be mine?"

His mouth quirks. "I think I've been yours for a long time."

My heart skips. *Again.* I search his face—for what, I don't know. It's not like I have to think about it. Things have always been different with him. It's as if we have a magnetic pull we can't repel. After a moment, I nod.

"Yes?" he asks.

"Yes."

He grins and kisses me as his hands slide underneath my oversized t-shirt, leaving goosebumps in their wake while he explores. My hands go to his hair and I tighten the grip of my legs around him until he moves forward and I feel him getting hard between my legs. He groans against my mouth and pulls away from me to whip my shirt over my head and throw it. His hooded eyes, hot and lustful, drink me in, as he cups both my breasts in his hands, playing with my nipples in a way that shoots straight between my legs.

His lips pull into a slow, sensual smile that makes me clench my thighs harder and grind against him. His smile drops and he hisses through his teeth, letting go of my breasts to remove my underwear and his clothes. I grip the counter and watch his cock bounce as he takes off his briefs. I bite my lip, and he makes a little growling sound that goes straight to my core. He slides his hands from my knees to the insides of my thighs, and then pushes them open wider so he can duck down and give a long lick between my folds. I grip the counter harder and throw my head back as he does it again, and then he starts to move his tongue in ways that make an orgasm quickly build.

I let go of the counter with one hand and curl my fingers into his hair as I move against him. His appreciative rumble vibrates through me, and when he starts dipping fingers inside me and matching them to the tempo of his tongue, my legs start to shake hard.

"Finn! I'm going to … fuck. I'm going to…" I gasp, searching for air that's quickly sucked out of my lungs as an orgasm shoots through me.

He doesn't even let me fully come down from the orgasm when he lifts me, walks to the couch, and sits down so I'm straddling him. His length is right beneath me, and I gasp when I slide against him, chasing another orgasm.

"Fuck. Yes, baby," he hisses, hands squeezing my ass so he can take control of my movements, cursing each time I moan. "You look so beautiful grinding on my cock like this. You're going to let me fuck you like this, aren't you, baby? With nothing between us."

A shiver ripples through me. "Yes. Oh, God, yes."

He keeps the motion slow, putting his thumb right where I stop each time to add more tension, and bringing his lips down to each of my breasts. My body starts to shake from sensory overload, and I feel the familiar tightening in my core.

"That's it. Just like that," he says, his voice strained. He pulls back and twists my nipple while his other hand presses my clit each time I slide up to it. "Fuck. Yes. That's it. Use my cock to make yourself come. Just like that. Fuck, you're going to make me come, Josslyn."

His words are too much. The tightness in my stomach returns and I squeeze my eyes shut, throwing my head back as I scream his name. I straighten to look at him as he throws his head back and shouts a curse, jets of cum landing on his taut stomach.

"That was…" I pant, unable to find words.

"I know." He kisses me and pulls me closer, his sticky stomach pressing against mine as he carries me to the shower.

CHAPTER FORTY

Josslyn

An uneasy feeling curls in the pit of my stomach as I flip through the pages of Mallory's journal. A few days ago, I finally convinced Finn to take Titus off his list of suspects, but he insisted I see this. I really wish I hadn't. I put a hand over my stomach, regretting the lasagna I had after my training session. I feel Finn's stare, but I can't bring myself to look at him. No matter how dysfunctional their relationship was, she was his sister.

What would I say anyway? The journal entries remind me of things I used to write in middle school about my crushes. But I wasn't Mallory's crush. *Was I?* Oh, God. Could I have missed that somehow? Anxiety threatens to grip me, but I breathe through it. *I will not overthink this.* How can I not, though? I flip through the catalog of memories we'd created, but they're hazy and nothing stands out. I need to speak to Livie about this.

I bite my lip and finally look at Finn. His dark green eyes search mine, but I can't read the expression on his face. Some of the entries say "I want out!" Others talk about someone she was seeing, but most of them are about me. It's beyond uncomfortable.

Livie comes to mind instantly, since she'd tried to warn me a few times about the way Mallory treated me. But this is a lot.

"Would it be okay for me to show this to Olivia?" I ask. "It's okay if you don't want me to. I just … she might be able to figure out who she's talking about here, or why she's … talking about me like this."

"As long as she comes here."

I nod and send Livie a quick text.

"I'm sure she'll be thrilled. She's been dying to 'see us together,'" I say, hoping to lighten the mood and lift the boulder in the pit of my stomach.

He smirks. "Did you tell her you're hiding me like a dirty little secret?"

My jaw drops. "I am not!"

He laughs as he stands up and tugs me out of my seat. When we're in the living room, he sits and pulls me down so I'm straddling him. I push back my unease about the journal and settle into the moment. Every moment with him is cherished. Not only because we've been busy during the day, but because being with him makes me so damn happy.

"I don't mind being your dirty little secret," he says against my lips.

"Stop saying that. You're not."

He keeps joking about that since we haven't gone out together, but between the semester finally starting, my brand sponsorships, his training camp, and the rest of his hectic schedule, we've had no free time. By the time we get home, we just want to shower, eat, chill on the couch for a little while, and go to bed.

According to Finn, training camp for the Owls is longer and tougher than usual since it's a brand new team, and "everyone has to get their shit together." Since we want to spend the little free time we have together, we've been staying over at each other's places. Mostly Finn's, though, since he has a better view and a plush king-size bed. Just the thought of getting ready to go out to eat is exhausting. The other day, I had to do a late shoot for a smoothie company and when I got home, I texted him that I didn't have energy for sex. He showed up thirty minutes later with an overnight bag.

Still, it's not a secret. Livie and Damian know. My mom knows, and Titus knows by default. My teammates know. His teammates know. We both got an earful from Lyla and Lachlan about it. It's not a secret *at all*. Personally, I think he's upset that I posted pictures with Tate and not him, but I was very clear that I wouldn't post anything about anyone until I knew it meant forever. That seemed to piss him off even more, but I don't care. He has my trust, but I learned my lesson about being too open on the internet.

"Hm." He bites my lower lip and kisses me. "Let's go out to dinner tomorrow."

"Don't you have practice?" I run my fingers through his hair and search his eyes. I don't think I'll ever get tired of his eyes or the way he looks at me.

"No. We have a meet-and-greet signing event with season ticket holders. I'll be done early." He kisses my jaw and the side of my neck. "Josslyn."

"What?" I gasp when he pulls away, cupping my left breast and tweaking my nipple. "Oh my God."

"I think you should move in with me."

"Wait. *What?*" I push myself away from him and sit up straight.

"You think it's too soon," he states rather than asks.

"Umm … yeah."

"We already have a key to each other's apartments and sleep together every night. What's the difference?"

My stomach dips. "Not too long ago, you were insisting this was a one-time hookup. *You were upset that you were attracted to me*—"

"Because I knew this was inevitable and part of me didn't want to accept that since we had that…" he waves a hand in the direction of the dining area, "to deal with."

"We still have that…" I mimic his hand gesture, "to deal with."

"But we're dealing with it together." He runs his hands up and down my sides with a hungry expression on his face that makes me wiggle on his lap.

"You were also totally against relationships."

He brings one of his hands to the side of my face and caresses it softly. "That was before. I already told you, I want everything with you, and that includes waking up with you in my arms every morning. We've done great so far."

"We haven't even gone out in public," I point out.

He raises an eyebrow. "And whose fault is that?"

"Your mother doesn't even know about us!"

He rolls his eyes. "Who cares? I'll tell her the next time I speak to her."

"Well, I kind of care, since I know for a fact she's not going to approve of me."

"I'm not sure that's true, but, again, who cares?"

My lips purse. "Is it true she has a list of potential wives for you?"

He laughs. "She probably does, but this isn't the 1800s, Joss."

The doorbell rings, and I push myself off him. He stands and as I turn to go, he grabs my hand and looks at me with one of his intense, serious expressions.

"This conversation isn't over."

I nod, take my hand back, and practically speed walk to the door. I've never been more grateful for Livie's impeccable timing.

CHAPTER FORTY-ONE

Josslyn

I watch Livie's brows rise and dip as she reads each entry. She walked in, looked at the two of us, laughed, asked for a drink, and hasn't spoken since. From the expression on her face, I know she has the same uneasy feeling in the pit of her stomach. When she looks up at us from across the dining table, her dark brown eyes are wide.

"Did your parents see this?" Livie says after a moment and looks at Finn.

He nods. My stomach twists again. I can't even imagine what they must have thought about this. *About me.*

Livie and I look at each other for a long moment, having a wordless conversation. I plead with her not to make a big deal about the entries about me and only focus on the others, and she responds that she absolutely will make a big deal about it.

"Well, I can't say I'm surprised by this," she says finally, as she takes a sip of wine.

"Do you have any idea who she might be talking about?" Finn asks. "Who was picking her up?"

"No. I hadn't spoken to Mallory in like nine months before that night."

"But you were around her at Josslyn's house," he says.

She glances at me and searches my face. From the way her expression falls, I know I won't like whatever she's going to say next. She looks at Finn again. "You don't think it was an accident."

"No."

Her eyes jump to mine. "No. You're not doing this again."

I squeeze Finn's hand. "Even if it was an accident, someone was in there with her."

She looks at Finn. "You can't drag Josslyn into this!"

"He's not dragging me into anything!"

Her eyes pierce mine. "You're not doing this to yourself again." She glances at Finn. "Do you understand what you're doing to her? When your sister died, Josslyn missed two months of games. She barely left her apartment. You can't make her re—"

"He's not making me do anything," I tell Livie, my voice surprisingly calm.

"I thought your parents made it clear they didn't want anyone looking into this," she says, looking at Finn again.

"They did." His hand tenses beneath mine. "They're convinced it was suicide."

My face whips to his. "What?"

"In the beginning, my parents asked if it could have been suicide and the detectives said anything was possible. That was when my parents forced them to shut down the investigation."

"How could they force the police to…" I pause, frowning. "They can't possibly have that much power. This is the legal system!"

"This is Fairview," he says simply.

I slide my hand away from his and sit back in my chair. I guess I shouldn't be surprised, considering everything I know has happened here and was swept under the rug, but still.

"Why would you bring Josslyn into this? You already know she didn't lie to you about anything. She told you everything she knows about that sex group your sister was involved with. Can't you leave her the fuck—"

"He's not dragging me into anything, Liv. Maybe his parents are okay with sweeping things under the rug, but he deserves peace. Mal deserves justice."

"Mallory was SICK, Josslyn!" She slaps a hand on the table, her eyes flashing from me to Finn. "I'm not saying your sister deserved to die or that you shouldn't find your peace, but Josslyn definitely doesn't deserve to have her mental health fucked with over this. Not over Mallory!"

"Livie," I warn.

Beside me, Finn tenses. "What does that mean?"

She glances at him, then looks back at me with a pointed look on her face that makes my stomach drop. I shake my head slowly, pleading.

"What does that mean?" Finn demands. "Why are you looking at her like that?"

"It doesn't mean anything," I say quietly.

"Oh, fuck off, Josslyn!" She holds up a few pages and shakes them. "You can't tell me I'm full of it after seeing these. She was obsessed with you!"

My stomach clenches again. I sit on my hands to hide the shaking.

"Did she … was she in love with you?" Finn asks, his voice a hoarse whisper.

A knot climbs to my throat, and I don't dare look at him, let alone answer. Not that I'd know what to say if I could.

"Do you need more proof?" Livie asks, still holding the papers and looking at me. "I fucking told you."

"You're making her uncomfortable," Finn says, voice low. "Either speak clearly or get out."

He has that unreadable look on his face that I can't stand, and even though I am uncomfortable and my hands are shaking, I feel the need to slide my hands from under me and reach for his. He glances at me, eyes softening, as he threads our fingers together.

When he looks at Livie again, his expression shifts right back to indifference. It's scary that he can switch off like that in a blink.

Livie straightens, shock clear on her face for a moment before she starts speaking. "Mal and I ran into each other at one of your mom's country club parties a while back. It was the usual group of people. Somehow the conversation turned to Joss. When I said we were good friends, Mallory freaked out and asked me to introduce them. I hadn't seen her in years, but I'd never known Mallory to want to meet someone. *Ever.*"

"Yeah, me either," Finn mutters beside me. I run my thumb over the back of his hand.

"After I introduced them, Mal started acting like Joss belonged to her," she says, pursing her lips. "It was little things. Like one day, she came over while Joss was showing me pictures of a bathing suit shoot she did for a sports magazine. Mallory looked at them and went crazy. She called her a whore for sharing her body with the entire world and demanded she not post the pictures."

This is so fucking uncomfortable. I already know it's going to get worse. I wish I could cover Finn's ears. I wish I could cover mine. I try to comfort him again, running my thumb over his hand, but this time, he pulls his hand away from mine. I'm surprised at how much it hurts. It's worse when I look at him and he doesn't meet my eyes. I cross my arms and sink back in my seat.

"Mal would trash everyone she knew and try to get me to conspire in pushing them out of Josslyn's life." She takes a sip of wine. "She wanted to isolate her and keep her to herself."

"That's not true," I say quietly. "I was always in practice and games and hanging out with you guys."

Liv stares at me for a moment. "She hated when I was around. She hated Tate, which … fine. None of us liked him. She barely liked Damian. She fucking *hated* when Tiago was around."

"Okay. That's a lie. She fucked him, so I don't think she hated it as much as you think," I say sharply.

"Jesus Christ," Finn mumbles quietly.

"Tiago always liked YOU, Josslyn!"

"Oh my fucking—"

"No. Stop denying it. Why do you think Tate hated him?"

"Tate doesn't like anyone who isn't rich or can't help him get ahead," I snap, hating how long it took me to realize that.

"Did she or did she *not* invite you to have a threesome with her and Tiago?"

"OH MY GOD." I bury my face in my hands. "That's not even relevant."

"It kind of is," she says softly. I glance up and she smiles sadly at me. "Did you tell Finn why you were at Onyx that night?"

I swallow the lump in my throat. "Yeah."

"Did you tell him how Mallory used to show up at your apartment in the middle of the night?"

"You need to stop, Liv," I say shakily.

"Did you tell him about the night she was literally naked on your couch waiting for you to come home, only to find that—surprise—you weren't alone, and Damian and I were in tow?" she asks, ignoring me.

Finn inhales sharply. I look away, hoping to get rid of the knot in my throat and hide the heat on my face. OF COURSE, I didn't tell him that. I try my best not to even remember that, but it was *one time*, when she was high and kept saying everything felt so good on her skin.

"She wasn't waiting *for me*," I say, finally. "She was high."

"Did you tell—"

"OH MY GOD, THAT'S ENOUGH!" I pound a fist on the table and lower my voice. "He's heard enough. Are you going to try to remember who was around back then, or do you want to just sit here embarrassing me?"

"I'm not trying to embarrass you!" Her eyes widen. She looks at Finn. "I'm sure this is a lot, but your sister was very sick, and the last thing Joss needs is to be involved in this. She's been through enough."

"I agree," he says, jaw ticking. "If only Josslyn had a friend who didn't abandon her at sex clubs."

"That's not fair," she whispers.

"How could you do that?!" he growls. "She could have been hurt. She could have been…" He stops talking and swallows hard.

"I know! Don't you think that haunts me every fucking day?!" she says, eyes glossy. "But it doesn't change the fact that your sister was sick and had a sick obsession with Joss. I wish I'd never introduced them." The three of us are quiet until Livie speaks again. "I can only think of a few people whose name starts with 'T' and I'm sure they're already on your list, *but* just because she was seeing someone doesn't mean that person was the one responsible for what happened. That's something to consider."

I glance at Finn hoping he looks back at me. When he doesn't, I feel my shoulders slump. Livie stands up, says some other things about wishing she could be of more help, and warns me not to get involved. I stand and follow her to the door.

She searches my face when we get there. "You're mad at me."

"No shit, I'm mad at you!" I whisper-shout. "How do you think he feels right now?"

"He needs to hear the truth about his sister, and the last thing you need is to fall into another bout of depression over this," she says. "She was not a good person, Joss."

I swallow hard. "That doesn't mean she deserved to die."

"Of course not," she says. "But it's *not your fault* that she did."

"I know."

"Please be careful." She gives me a kiss and a hug that I don't return. "Maybe you can make a list of who was at Titus' birthday that year."

I let out a laugh. "Everyone was there."

"Including T," she says pointedly as she pulls away.

"Stop bringing Tiago into this."

Her eyes fill with tears. "You think I *want* to think that about him? I'm just saying, it's very weird. He was always around before, then he stopped coming, and now he's kind of back again? Every time I ask him why he was MIA, he gets weird."

"He's been going through a lot with his mom," I say, swallowing the knot in my throat.

When she leaves, I take a moment to regain my composure. "T" could technically be another letter. Like "I." It's not like Mal had the best penmanship. And like Olivia said, the person she wrote about isn't necessarily the person responsible for what happened. The only real way to find out who was there that night is from Leo. Or John. I wish there was a way to convince them to show me their guest list for that night. I walk back to the dining room and find Finn in the same spot.

When he hears me approach, he turns in his seat. My heart drops when I take in his expression. This past week, I've gotten used to having a version of him no one else gets. One who laughs, smiles, and doesn't act like he has to hold himself a certain way because of who he is or the family he comes from. Someone who looks genuinely happy for once. The look on his face right now … is not that.

"Why didn't you tell me any of this?" he asks quietly.

"Any of what?" I ask as I walk closer.

"That my sister did those things. That she tried to get you to … that she waited for you…" He swallows hard.

My stomach turns. "Why would I tell you that?"

"What do you mean *why would you*? You don't think this is something I should know?"

"No! Besides, I didn't know any of this." I point at the papers. "She didn't give me a reason for me to think she felt this way. I had no idea."

"How could you not?" He stands up and jabs a finger toward the paper. "It's pretty fucking obvious! And after everything Olivia said?!"

"What Livie described were *isolated* incidents that happened over a long stretch of time while Mal was out of her mind."

"You should have told me." His jaw ticks, anger hot in his eyes.

"When? How!?" I ask, blinking and trying hard to clear the knot from my throat and stop tears from filling my eyes. "I called your mother and told her, and Mallory called me a traitor and stormed out of my life, and you know what, Finn?" I say, leaning into my anger. "I should have never let her back in, but she was alone, and I couldn't be yet another person who just ignored her," I say and watch him flinch.

I wait until he says something. When he doesn't, I'm filled with a new sense of disappointment and pain. My lips start to tremble, but I manage to say, "I'll be at my place."

I turn around and head to the door, trying to push down the sob forming in my chest. I could turn around and point out a plethora of things that would make him feel like shit, but I don't. Not only is it not in my nature to purposely hurt someone, but doing it to him makes me feel sick. If he wants to blame me for something, fine, but I won't sit here and pretend I knew this was how Mallory felt. And I won't let myself feel bad for not seeing it.

With my hand on the handle, I say, "For what it's worth, I'm sorry."

I don't even know what the fuck I'm apologizing for, but it's the most I can do. I make it all the way to the elevator before I break down.

CHAPTER FORTY-TWO

Josslyn

I'm not sure how long I've been asleep, when I feel my bed shift and the warmth of Finn's body behind me. He tucks an arm under me and wraps the other one over me to pull me flush against his chest. For a moment, I think I'm dreaming. I touch him, inhale his scent, and turn to look at him before shutting my eyes and settling against him.

"I shouldn't have screamed at you," he murmurs against my ear.

"You're right, you shouldn't have. I understand your frustration, but I really didn't know any of this."

"I know. Even if you did, you had no reason to tell me, and even if you had, it probably wouldn't change anything."

"Can we not talk about this right now?" I whisper, feeling new tears build in my eyes.

"Okay." He sighs, his breath tickling the nape of my neck. "Is your mom the only one who calls you Josie?"

My eyes pop open. "Yeah. My dad started calling me that as a joke when I told him some kids at school were taunting me with it. I used to hate it so much."

"Why?"

"I don't know. It just wasn't my name. 'Joss' was fine because at least it sounds like Josslyn, but Josie just pissed me off." I laugh a little. "He kept calling me that and then Mom joined in, but they're the only ones who were ever allowed to."

"Really? Not even Dame or Titus get to call you that?"

"No." I laugh a little. "Damian did once and I gave him a black eye."

His laughter shakes my entire body. "You hate it that much?"

"No, but he was taunting me. He never did it again. I'm not even sure I'd care if he or Titus did it now, since they'd probably use it the way Mom does, but I think they figure it's something between me and my parents."

"Did they get along? Titus and your dad?"

"Oh my god, yeah," I say. "Dad even joked that he wished Titus would have fallen for him instead of Mom. We never had that awkward stage between our families. It was pretty cool."

"What about Damian? I can't imagine he never had a secret crush on you," he says and begrudgingly adds, "or you on him."

I roll my eyes. "Our friends have always *loved* to romanticize the stepsibling thing, which is annoying. Dame blames porn."

He chuckles lightly. "I have to agree."

"Either way, no. We were very brother-sisterly from the start."

"What about his mom?"

I feel myself stiffen. "She passed away when he was young. We don't really talk about it," I say, and add, "She was killed by a boyfriend. It was very disturbing and tragic. Titus blamed himself for a long time. At least, according to Mom. He never speaks about it either. We do have pictures of her throughout the house, though. Mom wanted to make sure Dame knew she wasn't trying to replace her."

He's quiet for a moment. "You have a good family."

"I know." I lick my lips. "Dame was there when I found Dad. We were on our way to school and I kept saying I had a really bad feeling, so Dame drove to my dad's instead of school." I swallow hard. "He waited in the car while I went inside. I blocked most of it out, but I do remember him carrying me out of the house."

Finn squeezes me tighter. "That sounds awful."

"It was."

We're quiet for a long time before he takes my hand and links our fingers together. "I didn't like it when you left."

I feel my lips tug. "Really? It seems like it took you a while to realize that."

"I needed time to process," he says. "I thought I could wait until tomorrow, but when I went to bed, I realized pretty quickly that I didn't want to sleep without you. I *couldn't* sleep without you."

My heart skips. "And here I was thinking that this was the perfect example of why we can't move in together."

His arms tighten. "I fucked up, Joss. I told you I don't know what I'm doing."

"You're doing better than most," I say, lifting the hand linked with mine up to kiss it. "You know, if you were 'playing the game,' you would have ghosted me for a day or two."

He scoffs. "Fuck that. I play to win."

I close my eyes again. "I would have never pegged you for a cuddler."

"I'm not sure I am."

I laugh. "You're always touching me."

"You said you like touchy-feely guys," he murmurs, his breath tickling my neck. "I'm trying to be that guy for you."

My breath catches. "You know I like everything about you, right?" I ask. "You don't have to be anything other than yourself."

He kisses my neck. "Go to sleep, Josslyn."

※

I'm getting out of class when my phone buzzes with a call from my mom.

"How does it feel to be back on campus?" she asks.

"Pretty good, actually." I smile as I walk out of the building.

"Has anyone bothered you?"

"They don't bother me, Mom, but no," I say. "I'm wearing Dad's San Francisco Giants hat."

"Ah, that explains it," she says, and I can hear the smile in her voice.

"Anyway, I was calling to let you know that we're singing happy birthday to Titus at 6 p.m. He wants to get it out of the way so—"

"Okay. I'll be there."

She pauses. "What's going on with Damian?"

"What do you mean?"

"He's been MIA lately."

"I mean, he's playing *professional* hockey now, and it's not like he was around a ton when he was playing for the Blaze."

"I know. I just worry about him sometimes," she says. "When he goes MIA like this, and lately he's been … very distant."

"He's fine." I clear my throat. "The Owls are a brand new team, and he's new to the league and has to fight for his position on the ice," I say. "That's word-for-word what he told me."

"So you've spoken to him?"

"Yeah, he sends me memes like five times a day."

"So that's it? You communicate through the memes?"

"No. We actually text in between the memes. He's fine."

"That's good," she says quietly. "Is Finn coming with you tonight?"

My heart skips. "I'm not sure. Tate will be there, so…"

"Who cares? If he's going to be in your life, they'll have to get used to seeing each other once in a while," she says. "Just bring him."

My stomach flips. "We'll see."

"Are you smiling?" she asks, obviously smiling. "You know, I haven't seen any pictures of you two online. I thought I'd have an ESPN alert by now."

I laugh. "We haven't been out together."

A pause. "Does he not want to be seen out with you? Honey, if that's the case—"

"That's not the case at all. I promise," I say, finally reaching the parking lot. I spot Tiago and some of his teammates walking in my direction. "I gotta go, Mom. See you later. Love you."

"Okay. Love you too."

"Are you trying to be incognito?" Tiago asks with a laugh.

"You're taking on-campus classes this semester?" Reggie asks, eyes wide.

"Yup." I smile at Reggie and greet the rest of the guys before I look at T again. "And yes, I am incognito."

"With a hat?" He laughs.

"I don't know why you're laughing. It's as foolproof as Clark Kent's glasses."

They laugh and we talk about the upcoming season for a little bit, comparing our schedules to figure out if we're traveling together. After a few more minutes, we say goodbye and they start walking toward campus. Tiago and I stay in the same spot.

"So, you and Finn, huh?"

I smile, biting my lip, and nod.

"I'm pretty sure he hates me, but as long as you're happy, I'm happy," he says, pulling me into a hug.

I laugh against his chest. "He doesn't hate you. He just doesn't like that you're always touching me."

"Oh my God." He laughs, dropping his hands as he pulls away. "Does he know I'm Brazilian?"

"I explained that."

He shakes his head, looking amused as he looks away. "I hope this doesn't mean we won't have our one-on-ones anymore."

"Practice starts soon, so I'm sure we won't have time," I say. "But Finn doesn't care about our one-on-one games."

He raises an eyebrow. "When you were with Tate—"

"That was different."

"For your sake, I hope so," he says, pressing his lips together.

"So." I clear my throat and look at my sneakers for a moment. "I have a strange question for you."

He raises an eyebrow and waits.

"Did you ever go to Onyx with Mal?"

The surprise on his face is obvious, but he recovers quickly. "Why are you asking?"

"I found an old journal of hers and some of the things she wrote about were pretty intense. I'm wondering if it was an exaggeration," I lie.

"I…" He looks away, bringing a hand up to squeeze the back of his neck. "I only went once. She rented out a floor and invited a group of us."

"Did you meet anyone she knew from there?"

His lips purse as he thinks about it. "Only one guy. John, I think?"

I swallow and nod.

"I didn't go there to hook up," he says. "I was just curious about the place."

I stay quiet for a moment. "She told me you guys hooked up."

His brows hike up. "Really? That is … wow." He shakes his head and huffs out a laugh.

"What?" I frown.

"Nothing." He shakes his head and exhales. "Can we talk about this later? I don't want to be late to class."

"Yeah, of course." I try to smile and fail.

We hug quickly and start walking in opposite directions. I hate the feeling in the pit of my stomach. I know Tiago had nothing to do with this, I do. Why is he acting so weird, though? Ugh. I'm almost to my car when I hear the pounding steps of a runner behind me. When I turn, I see Tiago. My heart climbs to my throat. I've never been afraid of being left alone with him, but I'm feeling a little uneasy now. He is breathing heavily by the time he reaches me.

"I don't remember much about that night at Onyx, but the next morning, I woke up in her bed," he says, exhaling. "I didn't want you to find out, so I told her to keep it quiet."

"Why didn't you want me to find out?"

"I guess I didn't want you to…" He glances up at the sky and exhales before looking at me again. "I thought … I don't know. I didn't want to ruin things between us in case I had a shot with you."

"So you thought you'd hide the fact that you hooked up with my friend?" I ask, frowning.

"I know," he says. "Not my proudest moment. I really don't remember being with her, though."

"Why didn't you just tell me how you felt?"

He rolls his eyes. "It was pretty fucking obvious how I felt. Everyone knew."

"You could've just told me."

"Would it have made a difference?" he asks, raising an eyebrow. When I don't respond, he shrugs. "You only ever saw me as your friend, and that's fine. I know we're better off like this." He looks toward campus again. "I just wanted to tell you that in case you read anything else about me in those pages."

He turns and runs back to where he came from, without letting me get a word in. In case I read anything else? *What the hell does that even mean?*

CHAPTER FORTY-THREE

Josslyn

I spent most of my day debating whether or not I should tell Finn about my conversation with Tiago. In the end, I decide it's not important enough to talk about before our first official date. I'm wearing a taupe dress that goes down to my ankles. It's form-fitting, with a slit, and cut-outs in the shoulder and waist. I model it for my followers and start doing my makeup in front of the camera as I read incoming comments.

"Hey, Shannon! Good to see you here again." I grin and pause to apply lip liner and lipstick. "To answer your question—I have a date tonight."

I laugh when consecutive comments start popping up asking if it's Finn, but never answer before logging off. At the sound of the door opening and shutting, I gasp and shoot out of my chair. The butterflies in my stomach multiply, as I grab my purse and head out of my room.

When I see him, my mouth goes dry. He's wearing a charcoal suit, white dress shirt with the top buttons undone, and white sneakers. His light brown hair is tousled and his freshly shaved face emphasizes his sharp jaw. There isn't a thing about him that I don't find sexy, and the fact that he's actually mine is almost impossible to believe. My heart skips a beat when I look at his face and find his gaze burning into me. He takes a breath and releases it, as he walks over and wraps an arm around me.

"You…" He sighs, shaking his head as he brings his lips to mine for a quick kiss. "You're so fucking beautiful."

"And you're so fucking handsome." My cheeks feel hot as I lick my lips. "I was just thinking that I can't believe you're mine."

His eyes darken and he pulls me flush against him to give me another kiss, a slower, deeper one that I feel all the way down to my toes. When he breaks the kiss, his face stays inches from mine.

"I love hearing you say I'm yours."

I wrinkle my nose and smile. "Really?"

"Really." He kisses me one more time and straightens, shaking his head again as his gaze drops down my body in another slow perusal. "If we don't leave right now, I might take you back to the room."

"You're the one who wants to go out," I say, smiling at his quick strides to the door.

"Which is why I'm trying to resist temptation."

I smile and follow behind him. When we reach the kitchen, I spot a beautiful arrangement of sunflowers and smile wider. "You got me flowers."

"Ella suggested I get you red roses for our first date, since they symbolize passion."

"I see you took her advice," I say, laughing as I take my phone out and snap a picture before we walk out.

He holds my hand on the way to the elevator. When we're inside, I press the button to the lobby and push him against the wall. His eyes are burning with a heat I feel in my core. I wrap my arms around his neck and pull him down to kiss him quickly.

"Thank you for the sunflowers," I say against his lips. "Seeing them makes me smile."

"You make me smile," he says, squeezing my hips and kissing me lightly again.

"I also make you very hard, apparently," I whisper.

"Always, baby."

The doors open and I turn to face the newcomers, but keep my back against Finn's chest as he wraps his arms around me. I smile at the gray-haired man and his cute beagle. When we reach the lobby, we let them get out and Finn adjusts his pants.

He checks me out again and exhales as he grabs my hand. "It's going to be a long fucking night."

"You know, the first time you sent me flowers, I figured you only wanted to one-up Tate. I was kind of surprised you didn't just send me double the roses he gave me or something," I say, as he holds the door open for me and leads me to his car. "Maybe that was why you sent them, but your note was really sweet."

"Because I said they remind me of you?" he asks once we're in the car. He glances over as he starts the car. "They do. They're bright and always face the sun, like you."

"Do you think anyone would believe me if I told them how incredibly sweet you are?" I joke, smiling.

He chuckles as he starts driving. "No, because I'm only like this with you."

My heart skips a beat and I set my hand over his on the gear shift. "Will this be weird for you again?"

He spreads his fingers so mine fall between them. "What?"

"Going to my house. I know it was weird for you last time."

He glances at me. "It'll be different now."

"Because you finally believe me when I say he had nothing to do with this?" I ask. "You do believe me, right?"

"You told me you couldn't be with me if I didn't," he points out.

"Does that mean you lied just to get me to be with you?"

"No, but you were right." His lips purse. He squeezes my fingers a little. "His story checks out."

"Checks out?" My brows rise. "You fact-checked me?"

"I don't trust blindly," he says, squeezing my fingers when I try to move my hand away. "I'm not talking about you, Joss. You know I'll take your word over anyone's."

"Why?" I ask as we stop at a red light.

"You're just … you." He glances at me, his eyes taking in every inch of my face. "You're different."

"Different from whom?"

"Everyone I know." He shifts gears and starts driving again.

"You mean the girls you grew up with?"

"Everyone," he says and glances at me briefly. "What was your impression of Mallory's friends from high school?"

I frown. "Elizabeth seemed nice."

"And the rest?"

"Well, you know how I feel about Gracie."

"Fuck Gracie."

That makes me smile.

"What's her problem anyway?" he asks. "She's always been a bitch, but she seems more vindictive when it comes to you."

"Long story short, in junior year, she dated a baseball player from my school who happened to be my first boyfriend," I add quickly. "She showed up at his birthday party and called him trash in front of everyone, so I went off on her and kicked her out, which I guess no one had ever done." I pause, biting my lip before I add. "Aaaand Lance made out with me in front of her out of spite."

Finn scowls. "You could've left that part out."

I laugh. "It's the whole story."

"Where is this Lance guy now?" he asks, still scowling.

"New York. He plays in the majors."

He hums.

I shrug. "So that's the story. I understand that we've had different life experiences, but she thinks she's superior to everyone. Then again, Mallory was like that before I started bringing her to my family events."

"Do you think I'm like that?" he asks, his voice oddly quiet as he pulls into the driveway.

"I think you can come off as an arrogant asshole sometimes,

but I wouldn't say superior." I pause. "Unless you're using your last name for gain."

"I only do that here."

"Ah." I smile. "So you're only an arrogant asshole when you're in Fairview? Is it too soon to talk to Lach about a trade?"

He narrows his eyes at me. "You can't get rid of me. Besides, I'm retiring as an Owl."

"I figured." I lower the visor and check my makeup as he pulls into my mom's driveway. "You're too old to play much longer."

"*Old?*"

I bite back a laugh. He's not too old, but I knew he wouldn't like that joke and the scowl on his face is hilarious.

"Just a little." I wink at him. "Don't worry, I'll accept you no matter what."

Once he parks and turns the car off, he turns to me with a grin. I inhale sharply when he brings his face closer to mine.

"Do you know what sunflowers represent?" he asks.

"No," I whisper.

"Loyalty, longevity," he says, coming closer, until he's only a breath away. "And adoration."

He presses his lips against mine in a soft kiss that leaves me breathless, and gets out of the car.

CHAPTER FORTY-FOUR

Josslyn

Finn and Titus have a faceoff when Titus opens the door for us. But after Finn gives him a cigar and a bottle of scotch, Titus pats him on the shoulder and thanks him. As we walk inside, I hear the familiar voices of my stepfather's colleagues. He and two roommates from law school own the firm, and most of their employees have been there for a long time now. I look around quickly and spot Tate outside. He glances up from his phone and locks eyes with me. He looks at Finn, and when he looks back at me, I see sadness in his eyes. I shouldn't care, but I can't not. He visibly swallows, gives me an almost imperceptible nod, and goes back to his phone.

We say hi to my mom, Dame, and the young lanky kid he's speaking to, whose eyes nearly pop out of their sockets when he sees us. He's tongue-tied as he tries to introduce himself, so Dame puts him out of his misery, patting him on the shoulder.

"This is Nathan, Luis' nephew. He's interning."

"Nice to meet you, Nathan," I say. "I'm Josslyn, and this is Finn."

I introduce Finn out of courtesy. With the way he's acting,

I'm sure he knows who Finn is. It's pretty heartwarming to see. Nathan looks from Finn to me.

"I … holy shit," he breathes and clears his throat. "Yeah. I know who both of you are."

His uncle, who's leaning over a mountain of files and papers, stands up with a laugh. "I'm not sure if that reaction is for Finn or Josslyn."

"Probably Josslyn," Titus' secretary, Bertha, says with a wink.

I smile at her and walk over to greet them, introducing them each to Finn as we go. I don't give him a label, I just say his name. He's Damian's teammate, but with the way Finn's hand is practically branding my lower back, they can't possibly miss that we're together.

"I got season tickets but couldn't go to the meet-and-greet because of this." Nathan waves a hand in the general direction of where the firm employees are. "Do you think you can sign my jersey?"

"Nathan! We're in a private setting. I'm sure Finn just wants to kick back and relax," his uncle says.

"It's fine. I'm happy to sign it," Finn says.

Nathan practically sprints outside. Everyone laughs and makes jokes about his reaction, and Finn and I walk closer to where my mom is standing by the kitchen island. She hands us each a glass of red wine and shoots me a look that says, "Just try it."

Dame walks closer to us with an amused look on his face as he glances at Finn. "He was talking about you for ten minutes straight. I should've been ready to record his reaction when he saw you."

"He's cute," I say with a laugh, and when I feel Finn's arm stiffen against mine, I shoot him a bewildered look and add, "Not *like that*. His enthusiasm is cute, though."

Finn grunts out his response, his face impossibly unreadable, the way it usually is in public settings. Nathan comes back inside with his jersey. While Finn signs it, my eyes flick toward the patio, where Tate is now sitting down and talking on the phone. I know it's too much to ask for, but I wish he'd stay outside. It's not like I want them to be friends, but I wish he and Finn would just make amends so this doesn't have to be as weird as it is. But that's way, *way* too much to ask for. *How the hell did I unknowingly get caught up in the middle of a family feud?*

"I follow you online," Nathan blurts out, blushing deeply, and then glances at Finn. "Only because my ex-girlfriend was always talking about the makeup you use and it made it easier to buy her presents."

"Sure, keep telling yourself that, pal," Jimmy says from the couch, making everyone laugh, and Nathan's cheeks turn redder, if possible.

My heart skips a beat when Finn's fingers graze mine before he laces our hands together.

"I can't wait to see both of you on the ice," Nathan says quickly. "I went to some Blaze games to watch Dame and he's a solid winger."

"I agree," Finn says.

"I don't know how the two of you are going to walk around Fairview together," Luis says, walking over and serving himself a plate of cheese and crackers. He's stabbing a toothpick into the bowl of olives, glancing at Finn. "Brace yourself, because everyone in town tries to hit on her."

"Let them fucking try," he growls.

"Finneas!" I hiss, squeezing his hand.

He leans over until his mouth is near my ear. "Careful, baby. You know what that does to me."

A full shiver runs through my body. I shoot him a glare and mouth, "I'm going to kill you." My face is burning when he smiles at me—that slow, wide, sensual smile that's only for me.

Luis ignores that and points his toothpick outside. "That one over there is an idiot. *You're* far better suited for each other."

"I agree," Finn says.

Nathan snickers. "I told him he's an idiot for what he did and letting her go. If she were mine—" He flinches as he looks at Finn. "I'm sorry, dude. I word vomit when I'm nervous."

Finn lets go of my hand and slides it up the side of my body slowly until he reaches the cutout of my dress. He brushes his thumb up and down my exposed skin. *Oh my God.* I'm going to kill him.

"No, you're right," he says. "Unfortunately for you and everyone else in the entire galaxy, she's *mine* and I'm not an idiot."

My gaze snaps to his and my heart does a little free fall when I see the intensity in his eyes.

"Let's eat some cake!" Dame says, clapping his hands loudly and setting everyone in motion.

I'm still rooted to my spot, lost in the endless forest that sits inside of Finn's green eyes. My mom calls my name and I nearly jump out of my skin. Finn chuckles so quietly I'm sure only I can hear it. His eyes twinkle and he winks at me as he pulls me toward the cake that I'm no longer hungry for.

Tate walks back inside to sing happy birthday, but keeps his distance. When Finn and I move to the dining area to share a slice of cake, we're joined by my mom and Dame. Everyone else goes back to their papers, discussing depositions and trials.

A few hours later, at the restaurant, the hostess smiles at us and looks at Finn. "Your usual table?"

He shakes his head and points at an empty table smack in the middle of the dining area. "I want that one."

Her light blonde eyebrows shoot up. She glances at me and grins wide, a knowing twinkle in her blue eyes. I can't help but laugh.

"Follow me!" she says brightly and leads us to our table.

"Is your 'usual table' where you take your fuck buddies?" I ask when she walks away, my tone a little snappier than I intend.

His lips curve into a shadow of a smile. "I don't have fuck buddies, and for the record, I haven't touched anyone in Fairview since sophomore or junior year of high school."

"Oh." I pick up my menu and feel myself frown as I process that. I set it down again. "What about me?"

He lowers his menu. "You're an outlier."

"But ... why?" I ask. "And I'm not asking you because I want you to shower me with compliments. I'm just trying to understand."

"I'm not sure if I can explain it."

The server comes by to take our order. We both stick with water and put in our food orders. Well, Finn does, since he's been here and wants me to try four different dishes. When he leaves, I focus on him again.

"Try," I say.

He laughs lightly. It's not an amused laugh, though, and doesn't reach his eyes. It's his public laugh, and it makes me wonder if he's nervous. I reach out and just before I set my hand over his, he flips his over to welcome mine.

"Just try."

"Fine, but I want to make it very clear that I don't believe in love at first sight," he says, very seriously. I give a nod. "When I got to Pearl that night for my sister's birthday, I said hi to her and walked over to where Ella and Ham were. Ham was already leaving, so I turned to say goodbye to him and I saw you."

"I saw you when you walked in," I admit.

"Oh, really?" He brings his hand up and bites the tip of my pinky before he sucks it into his mouth. My gasp stays stuck in my throat. His eyes twinkle with mischief as he sets my hand down again, but he lets go when some of our food comes.

"What did you think when you saw me?" he asks.

I roll my eyes. "What do you think I thought?"

"That I was the sexiest, most alluring man you'd ever laid eyes on?"

"Oh. Wow." I laugh, serving myself some lobster mash. "You are way too full of yourself. Please continue the story."

"You caught my eye right away. The hot pink dress you were wearing, which was fucking sinful by the way," he says, dropping his voice. "I lost count of how many times I jerked off to the image of fucking you in that dress, remembering the sounds you made and the look on your face when you came."

"Finn!" I whisper-shout, looking around quickly.

He leans forward, eyes burning with desire, as he reaches out and sets his hand on my forearm. His long fingers cover it as his thumbs brush over my pulse point, which is racing.

"If we were sitting in a booth," he says, his eyes briefly dropping to my parted lips. "I'd take care of you right now."

"Please stop," I whisper shakily, shifting again.

He lets me go and sits back a little, a smug look on his face. My heart is still racing and my hands are shaking, as I reach for my water.

"So you thought I looked hot," I say when I set down the glass.

"Obviously, but it was more than that. It was your mannerisms, your smile, that fucking laugh that lights me up inside, the way you looked at people when you spoke to them, like they mattered, and…" He frowns. "I wanted you to look at me like that."

"People always look at you like that," I point out, serving myself another spoonful of food.

"Not like that. Not the way *you* do," he says quietly. I look up from my food, my heart skipping for the millionth time. "People have conversations, but they don't listen. You listen."

"And … you wanted to fuck me because I listen?"

"No." He laughs once, like it's ridiculous, and shakes his head the way he does when he's genuinely at a loss for words. "I couldn't stop looking at you. I think I was unknowingly trying to lure you over with my eyes, but you never looked. Then Gracie came over with her usual Gracie bullshit—"

My stomach tightens. "Which is?"

"Does it matter?"

"No, but tell me anyway," I say.

"She tried talking shit about you and got mad when I defended you even though I had no idea who you were," he says. "I mean, Mal had mentioned you, but I, like most people, don't listen." He pauses. "Except when you talk to me."

I smile. "You don't have to sweet talk me, Finneas. I'm going home with you no matter what."

His eyes darken. "Do you want to box this up so we can go?"

I laugh. "No! Finish the story!"

"I finally went up to you, which was nerve-wracking, by the way—"

"No way!"

"Do you know how long it's been since I approached a woman?" he asks, frowning. "Fuck, I can't even think of a time when I did that."

I roll my eyes. "Okay, Finn Barlow, God's gift to women. Please continue the story."

He chuckles. "You were so fucking beautiful and hot as fuck, of course, but your energy is magnetic." He pauses. "I wanted you and I justified why I could break my rule for you."

I sit back and look at him. "What about the night of my birthday?"

"I was watching you from the second story."

My eyes widen. "That's not creepy at all."

He glances away briefly and eats some food and chews it before he looks at me again.

"My friends kept talking about you, which pissed me off since I was already having a hard time staying away," he says. "And as you know, I broke another rule for you."

"By hooking up with me a second time."

"Yeah. I told myself we hadn't had sex yet," he says. "Ella kept telling me you were single. The other two idiots kept saying how hot you were. I didn't even tell them about our time at Onyx, but just from our interaction at Mallory's party, they said they knew."

I blink. "Because you spoke to me?"

"Because I approached you, and because you made me laugh." He tilts his head slightly. "That's the story. Can we go home so I can fuck you now?"

I laugh. We package our food, pay, and head out hand in hand. A few people take not-so-sneaky pictures, others take obvious ones that I smile for, and I'm amazed at how *right* it all feels.

CHAPTER FORTY-FIVE

Finn

"IF YOU DO THAT, YOU WON'T HAVE TIME TO CLEAR THE PUCK!" I shout. Preseason starts next week, and even though it's out of town, it'll be the Owls' first game ever. Two days later, we'll be back here and have our inaugural home opener. Growing up, I never thought Fairview would get a professional hockey team. Definitely not while I was still playing. Win or lose, this game will be in the history books, and that's something the entire team seems to be very aware of. For a group that hasn't played together before, we're pretty in sync.

"If you can't stop there, you need to drop the pass," Coach P says to Gally, who's a first-year player.

A lot of these kids are. Hamilton and I are amongst the three oldest players on the team.

"Or I can flip pass," Gally says, and I resist the urge to roll my eyes.

He loves trying out fancy passes that are great in practice but may not work during a game.

"That would only work if you're able to get it to me," I say and skate back to the cones on the other side. "Let's go again."

"Let's switch up the line," Coach P says. "Hamilton! Fletcher! Get over here. Gallagher, move to right defense."

I almost breathe out a sigh of relief. I've been trying to keep my opinions to a minimum, since I'm not the coach and Coach P has proven his worth on every team he's worked for. It's hard, though. Especially when I know Gally would be a better grinder than wingman. All of our practices flow better when Ham and Dame are my wings. We're playing against the rest of our teammates, which has also been helpful.

"Jefferson was a swingman in college. He played both positions well," Coach P says.

I feel my mouth tip up. "Trying to replace me already?"

He laughs. "I'd never dream of it. He's one to watch though."

"He definitely has the speed," I say. "Maybe we should try him at left D."

Coach nods and writes something down on his pad. We spend the next two hours going over our plays on the ice, and a third watching film of our practice. By the time we finish and hang up our gear for the equipment managers to clean, the sun is already setting.

"I'm assuming you're going to your mom's birthday thing," Hamilton says as we walk to our cars.

"I told her I'd swing by. I don't want to be there longer than I have to."

"Are you taking Joss?"

"I'm hoping she goes. She's not really looking forward to dealing with that group of people."

"I don't blame her," he says. "You know everyone goes to your mom's birthday parties. *Everyone.*"

"You mean Gracie?"

"Yep. I can't imagine that'll go over well."

"Fuck Gracie." I feel myself scowl.

"It's not really about her. I'm sure you don't want Joss to feel uncomfortable."

"Of course not, but she'll be with me."

He shrugs. "I'm going to drop by with Ella. Let me know when you head over there, so we can be there at the same time."

I bump his fist and we go our separate ways. I have to find a way to convince Joss to go with me. It's not only because her being there will finally get my mother off my back about setting me up with someone. I want her there. I want to be around her all the fucking time.

"I can't believe you talked me into this," Josslyn whisper-shouts as we walk toward the country club.

"Who knew orgasms were the way to your heart," I say.

"Finneas," she hisses and looks around.

I squeeze her to my side. "You're so fucking cute."

"I've only spoken to your mother once and it was to tell her about Mallory. I highly doubt she has a good impression of me."

I stop walking and pull away so she can see my face. "I already told you I don't care what impression she has of you. You're mine and if she doesn't like you, she can fuck right off."

Her eyes widen. "Finn!"

So fucking cute. I feel my lips tip up as I grab her hand in mine and continue walking.

"I know you don't have the best relationship with her, but you should speak to her. Maybe invite her to a game?" she suggests quietly.

"That's not happening."

"*If* she brings it up, you should extend an invitation." She shrugs. "If she doesn't, then she can fuck right off."

I chuckle and kiss her temple.

"Is Lucas coming? Are Will and Ella here already?" she asks quietly, as we reach the open doors that lead to the event area.

"They should be here soon."

"Okay, good." She takes a deep breath and lets it out, squeezing my hand as we walk inside.

I spot my father right away with a group of his friends. He only spares me a quick look before he focuses on Josslyn, admiring her a little too much for my liking. Because of the small space between the chairs, I'm forced to let go of her hand as we walk over.

"I'm glad you made it," my father says, patting me on the back before shifting his eyes back to Josslyn.

I wrap my arm around her, my fingers possessively splayed over her hip as I pull her into me.

"This is my girlfriend, Josslyn," I say. "Joss, this is my father, Richard."

My father doesn't even bother to hide his surprise as he looks between the two of us. His brows shoot up, his green eyes finding mine again. There's no dismay or disapproval, which is what I was unfortunately expecting from my parents. He just looks surprised. Whether it's because he saw her name all over my sister's journal or because I've never brought a woman around—much less introduced one as my girlfriend—I'm not sure. He turns to Josslyn again and takes the hand she offers him.

"It's nice to officially meet you, Josslyn," he says, lifting her hand and kissing the back of it.

My grip instinctively tightens on her hip. My father is quite charming, especially when he wants to get a woman in bed. Not that Josslyn would ever do that—to me or herself. Still, it's annoying to know he and his friends are going to talk about her the moment we walk away. The dress she's wearing isn't even form-fitting or revealing, but that won't matter.

"It's nice to meet you as well, Mr. Barlow," she responds with a smile as she takes her hand back.

We greet the other three men, who, unlike my father, at least have the decency to wait until we're not in front of them to check her out. We speak to them for a couple of minutes, about the Owls and Titus—who's friends with two of them—and we walk away to look for my mother.

"That wasn't terrible," she says quietly.

"It was torturous."

"If that's the case, you should never go to one of Titus' law firm parties." She laughs and rolls her eyes, as she adds, "At least they didn't call me 'exotic.'"

That makes me laugh under my breath. When we finally find my mother, I'm expecting a repeat of what happened with my father, but she shocks the shit out of me by pulling Josslyn into a hug. A warm hug. It's very quick, but still. My mother has never been much of a hugger.

"I've been meaning to thank you," she says to Josslyn. "I just … I haven't been able to … I—"

"It's okay," Josslyn says quietly and grabs my mother's hand. "I understand."

My mother smiles sadly, gratefully—I'm not really sure which, since I haven't seen enough of her smiles to tell them apart. I stand there dumbfounded. There's no denying that Josslyn has a gift. I grab her hand again and intertwine our fingers. My mother takes note of it and glances up at me, her eyes widening a touch. Ella, Hamilton, and Lucas walk inside and Josslyn starts wiggling her hand out of my grasp.

"I'll be right back," Josslyn says, shooting me a look that tells me I should speak to my mother.

I watch her until she reaches them and narrow my eyes at Ella, who fully checks her out. Lucas, as well. At least Hamilton knows better.

"I didn't realize she was the one you were on a date with at that fundraiser until I saw the photographs," my mother says. "She's not like us, you know?"

My eyes narrow. I brace myself for the inevitable talk about our different social classes and backgrounds.

"There's a calmness to her. A kindness," she says instead.

I swallow hard and give a nod when words fail me. That's exactly what I thought about, the first time I saw Josslyn. Her spirit is a balm on my cracked interior, healing and soothing the underlying pain buried there.

"I suppose you thought I'd try to talk you out of it," she says.

When I don't speak, she continues. "I won't. I've done a lot of reflecting this past year. Our family was broken long before I became pregnant with you. Your father and I longed to be with other people and felt trapped when we married," she says.

"I love your father. Over the years, we've become great friends, and that was my hope for you, but after Mallory…" She clears her throat. "The episode with your sister opened my eyes to many things. The Hamiltons tried to tell us. Your aunt and uncle tried to tell us. If I'd listened, if I'd been more like them … I hope one day, you'll forgive me for failing you and your sister."

"There's nothing to forgive," I say.

I open my mouth to say the biting words that have been on the tip of my tongue, as I've waited years for a moment like this, but I stop when Josslyn's hand motions to grab my attention. My friends and cousin are laughing at whatever she's saying. Genuinely laughing. The cold anger I'd been harboring is replaced by a warm feeling that slithers down my body.

"You're serious about her," my mother says after a moment.

"Very," I respond, meeting her gaze.

"I'm glad for you."

She glances past me and dons a placating smile to face whomever is walking over.

"Finn! I was hoping you'd be here!" Gracie sets a hand on my arm.

I stiffen and look up, thankful that Josslyn's still turned away from us. Ella catches my attention, and her eyes widen in concern.

I glare at Gracie. "Get your hand off me."

Her expression sours, but she drops her hand and looks. "I was hoping to speak to you," she says, smiling at my mother. "And I guess this is the perfect time to ask what your thoughts about Finn *slumming it* are." Her eyes flick between me and my mother. "I mean, after all those years of talking about the list of hopeful matches you had for him, and he decides to bring around—"

"Don't finish that sentence," I say, jaw clenched. The last thing

I want is to give her a reaction, but I can't help it. "If you have nothing nice to say about my girlfriend, I suggest you leave now."

She gasps, eyes wide. She looks at my mother again, waiting for her to jump in and back her up.

My mother lifts her chin. "I think Josslyn is a great match for Finneas."

My brows rise a little. That's high praise coming from Eliza Barlow.

"You can't be serious," Gracie says, frowning. "Just the other day you were saying you were looking for a good match for him."

"I was," my mother says. "But Finneas surprised me by choosing someone I know he'll be happy with."

"Happy." Gracie scoffs, waving a hand around the room. "As if anyone is happily married."

"It's about time we change that, don't you think?" my mother responds. "It doesn't matter now, but you should know, you were never on the list of contenders for my son." When Gracie's jaw drops, my mother continues. "Did you expect to be? After the awful way you treated my daughter?"

I catch movement and glance over to see Josslyn walking over. Ella is next to her, and Ham and Lucas are walking behind them. The three of them have stoic expressions on their faces, but I know better. We were all taught to keep our composure and our emotions from showing in any situation. It's something that has helped me immensely in life, and one of the things I'm actually grateful to my parents for. My eyes lock with Josslyn's, and even though I know my mother and Gracie are chatting, I no longer hear them. The only thing I see is Josslyn. The only thing I *feel* is Josslyn. When they finally reach us, my friends and cousin greet my mother, and I wrap an arm around Josslyn. That familiar comforting warmth I feel when she's near envelops me as she wraps an arm around my waist.

"I should go," Gracie says, glaring at Josslyn before her eyes meet mine. "I hope you enjoy Tate's sloppy seconds."

"Rest assured, I am." I pull Josslyn closer. "Everyone knows leftovers always taste better."

She finally walks away. My jaw hurts from the way I've been clenching it. I'm not a violent person. I've only been in one fight my entire life. On the ice, I hip check and I'm aggressive, of course, but I've never been in a brawl. There's no doubt in my mind that if Gracie were a man, I would have knocked him out for that display.

"Well, that was fun," Josslyn says after a moment. The playfulness in her tone makes my anger dissipate.

"She's such a bitch," Ella says.

"I hope you won't take that personally," my mother says to Josslyn.

"Oh, I don't. She's been trying to get under my skin for six years now," she responds with a small shrug. "My silence cuts deeper than her words."

I run my hand up and down her arm. My mother looks at me and does a double-take when she sees the grin on my face.

"I'm glad you're here," my mother says, and with that, she gives each of us a smile and walks away.

"Did I just imagine that?" Lucas asks, eyes wide. "Eliza Barlow thanked Josslyn for being here?"

"People are saying the end of the world is near," Hamilton says.

"Yeah, I don't know what to make of that." Ella laughs, shaking her head with an exhale. "Can we get out of here now? I need a real drink. Preferably without stuffy assholes."

Josslyn laughs. "Hell yes."

"I have to introduce her to a few people," I say. "My godfather will kill me if I don't."

Ella rolls her eyes. "I guess I should find my parents."

"You haven't seen Mom?" Hamilton asks as they walk away.

"Asher's in town, so my parents are skipping this," Lucas says. "I guess I'll be your third wheel."

For the next half hour, we go through the motions with my

family and family friends—the small talk, introductions to my girlfriend, more stunned looks and questions, rinse and repeat.

"I probably have an imprint of your hand on my hip," Josslyn says as we walk toward the door.

"Good." I pause our walk, cup her face, and kiss her.

Her eyes are wide when I break the kiss and pull away, tugging her hand to keep walking.

"You really wanted to shock people tonight, huh?" she asks, laughing.

"I think you gave Mrs. Rensselaer a heart attack back there," Ella says behind us.

"You might have given me one," Lucas says. "What the fuck did you do to my cousin, Josslyn?"

"Sometimes I wonder the same thing. Do you think he's a clone?" she asks, laughing.

"I think we need to call national security," Hamilton says.

I roll my eyes as they joke around, but their jokes are just a reminder that I have her, and that they don't bother me in the least.

CHAPTER FORTY-SIX

Josslyn

Finn brought more pages from Mallory's journal for me to see. Even though they're not about me, they're no less disturbing than the rest.

I told him I want to stop. Stop or come clean. I can't do this to Joss anymore.

I saw him again tonight. He took me to a secluded farm and we lay on the bed of his truck. I love the way he makes me feel. FML.

There's a spot in their yard that the cameras can't get to. It's become our secret cove when I go over and 'go to the bathroom.' I hate myself so much. I know I need to stop.

That last one really makes my stomach turn. She could be talking about anyone's yard, but deep down, I know it's my mother's. In high school, when Dame and I invited people over for pool parties or to hang out at night, the little area near the outdoor bathroom was known as "the make-out nook." The lovely thing about it was that the cameras couldn't reach it. There was one that pointed at it, but Damian got on a ladder one day and directed it the other way. It seemed like a good idea at the time. Now, not so much. My mom's neighbor has cameras, though, so I'm hoping he can help.

"Joshlyn!" Theo says, yanking my hand.

"Yeah." I blink away from my thoughts and look at him.

"*I said*, did you know there are *five whole layers* under the ice?" he asks excitedly. "Five whole layers!"

"I didn't know that. I'm very impressed that you do," I say and smile when he beams at me, as we're led to our seats.

As much as I'm hoping my presence here is a surprise, I have a feeling Finn knows I'm coming. It's a preseason game, but it's the Owls' first home game ever. He spent the entire week talking about it, but I told him I'd have to miss it since I'd had plans to babysit Theo so his parents could be here. I mean, I wasn't lying. I *am* babysitting Theo. But while his dad and very pregnant mom are upstairs in their box, I'm sitting in the first row with Theo, Liam, and Marissa—Lyla's best friend. Having three adults with Theo should be enough, but Lachlan also made Patrick, his head of security, sit directly behind us.

As soon as we're in our row, I have Marissa take a picture of me wearing the replica of Finn's Fairview Owls jersey. It took two weeks for me to get my hands on it, because even though I'm Finn's girlfriend, jersey sales come first and it was sold out everywhere.

"Finn's there!" Theo says, jumping up and down and pointing at the other side of the rink, where Finn and a teammate are talking while stretching.

"Yes, he is," I say, smiling as I take some pictures of him.

"I love sitting near the penalty box," Marissa says, smiling.

Liam snorts a laugh.

"I can't even remember the last time I went to a hockey game," I say as I look around.

Everyone isn't even in their seats and it already looks like a full house. Well, it will be. Lyla said within fifteen minutes of the tickets going live, they sold out for the entire season. The arena is a sea of white and blue jerseys with the signature Owl in the middle. The game hasn't even started and already, the atmosphere is full of energy.

"Oh my gosh, Josslyn! I love you so much!" a teenage girl says, as she takes her seat in the row behind me.

I smile. "Thank you so much. What's your name?"

"Laura." She grins. Her friend is blushing and waves. "This is Rina."

Rina starts signing, and Laura translates, "She says she especially loves your basketball videos."

I sign, "Thank you, Rina."

It's about as much ASL as I know, but Rina's smile makes it worth it. I pose for a selfie with them and turn back around just as the guys start skating. I wave at Damian when he skates near us, and he comes over to stand in front of us.

"Uncle Dame!" Theo says excitedly.

"Hey, buddy. Whose jersey are you wearing?" Dame shouts through the plexi with a grin.

Theo turns around and shows him his personalized jersey. It says Duke and has the number ten—his dad's old number. And his mom's.

"That's nice, Thee," Dame says and nods at Marissa and Liam. He looks at me again. "He still doesn't know you're here?"

"Not unless you told him."

He shoots me a look and skates away toward where Finn is still stretching.

"Dad said there's cotton candy here," Theo announces.

"We'll get you some later," Liam says. "The game is starting soon."

"Okay." Theo hops off my lap and slaps the plexiglass. "Let's go, Finn! Let's go, Finn!" He glances at me over his shoulder. "He stretches a lot."

I laugh. "He has to."

I glance up and see Damian skating next to Finn, and I can tell he's trying not to be obvious as he herds him in this direction. The surprise on Finn's face as he skates up is worth gold. He smiles wide when he reaches me and puts a gloved hand on the plexi. I stand, hauling Theo up with me as I get closer.

"Finn!" Theo slaps the glass near the glove as if giving him a high five.

"I like your jersey," he tells Theo. His gaze drops down my body when he looks at me again, his expression darkening. "I love yours."

I smile. "Did I surprise you, or did you know I was coming?"

"I was hoping," he says, glancing at Theo as I set him down. "Try to behave for my girlfriend, Theo."

Theo's little jaw drops and he frowns. "Joshlyn was *my* girlfriend first."

"Yeah, well, she's my girlfriend now, and I'm the last boyfriend she'll ever have." He winks at me and skates off.

My heart skips a beat and my stomach dips as I watch him skate away. He makes statements similar to that all the time and every time, I'm shocked.

"That was practically a proposal," Patrick says behind us.

"He can't possibly be jealous of a child," Liam says, laughing. "Fuck, he really is like my brother."

"I don't know if I should congratulate you or feel sorry for you," Marissa says as she starts laughing. "At least he's cute and can get away with it."

Theo crosses his little arms and glares toward the ice. "Tell Finn he's not your boyfriend, Joshlyn."

Even Patrick laughs at that one.

"I'll tell him," I say, picking him up and setting him on my lap again as we watch everyone get off the ice.

Soon, the announcer starts talking and the arena goes dark as the strobe lights switch on. Smoke pops up from each corner, and the announcer starts going on about the team and the history being made tonight. The crowd goes wild and continues as each player is announced. When Will skates out, they get louder. When Finn skates out, it gets so loud, I'm pretty sure I'll need to borrow the ear protectors I put on Theo.

The place calms down as the game starts, and I'm enthralled watching Finn at the faceoff. He gets the puck and the crowd goes wild again. My heartbeat is competing with the cacophony of the game around us. Marissa gets up and goes with Patrick and Theo to get cotton candy.

"They play so well together," I say to Liam.

"I know. I'm impressed," he says, flinching when someone hip checks Damian right in front of us.

"I feel like this is the only team sport where you can hit opponents like this and not start a riot," I say, jumping out of my seat as Finn gets near the puck and passes it to Will, who scores.

"WILL HAMILTON!" the announcer shouts.

Liam and I jump up and down like lunatics. The crowd roars. The announcers get louder and more excited. As loud as I'm screaming, I'm pretty sure my voice is going to be gone by tomorrow. The other team gets close a few times, but our goalie stops each puck, and the Owls get most of the possessions. Finn scores his first goal, and between my wildly beating heart and my screaming, I think I might faint. My phone buzzes and I look down to see a text from Marissa, along with a picture of Theo with his parents up in the box.

Marissa: Theo wanted to come see his mom

Me: LOL I'll be up in a minute

Marissa: no! Stay. I got this.

Me: you sure?

Marissa: positive. Watch your man!

I grin and set my phone away. "They went upstairs because Theo wanted to see his mom."

"Of course, he did." Liam chuckles. "I don't know what she's going to do if Rosa is a mommy's girl."

I sputter a laugh. "Rosa is going to be the ultimate daddy's girl. I almost feel sorry for Lach."

He laughs and nods in agreement. "If she's anything like her mother, I have a feeling we're all fucked."

I laugh and hold my breath as Damian, Will, and Finn get near the goal. I don't even know how they do it, but they pass it between the three of them and Finn gets it and taps it in right between the goalie's left leg and the post.

"HOLY SHIT!" I shout, screaming again.

"He's so fucking fun to watch," Liam says, laughing.

We watch the rest of the game like that. We win 3–1. Liam and I go upstairs to celebrate with the rest of them, until the arena mostly clears out and Prescott, Banks, Lachlan, his dad, and Lang say they want to go downstairs and all of us follow.

"I think tonight is the night," Lyla says, holding her stomach.

I gasp. "Contractions?!"

"How far apart?!" Marissa asks.

Lachlan, who is carrying Theo and talking to the rest of the guys, somehow hears this and turns around. "What's going on?"

"My contractions are getting stronger," Lyla says.

"We need to go to the hospital," Lachlan says.

"Not yet, Lach." She sets a hand on his arm. "They're not that bad or that close."

"Lyla James…"

"I'll tell you." She smiles, and it only widens when Theo leans down and wraps his little arms around her neck. She kisses him, then her husband, and everyone keeps walking.

I hold onto her left arm and Marissa holds her right. It's not like she needs help walking, but it's the only thing I can think to do. With the measured steps Lachlan is taking, I can tell it's taking everything in him not to set his son down and carry Lyla instead. By the time we get to the back and pass security, the guys are spilling out of the lockers with their regular clothes on.

They stop and say hi. A few wives are waiting around. I look at the women a few times, trying to figure out which one, if any, is the one I should be thanking for being the reason Finn got his head out of his ass.

When Finn walks out, he spots me immediately and walks over. One of the women, I'm pretty sure the goalie's wife, calls out his name, but he doesn't even look in her direction. It's like he has blinders on and only sees me. When he reaches me, he lifts me up and puts his hands under my butt, so I have to wrap my arms and legs around him.

"You did so good," I say, grinning.

He gives me a peck on the lips, and another, and another. "I can't believe you're here."

"I wasn't going to miss your first game," I say, sinking my fingers into his damp hair.

"Where'd you get the jersey?" he asks. "I thought they were sold out."

"They were, but I know a guy." I wink at him, and he smiles and squeezes me tighter as he kisses me again.

"Dad, tell Finn that Joshlyn's my girlfriend first," Theo pouts.

Finn fully wraps his arms around me, and I laugh. "Don't be mean, Finneas."

He groans into the crook of my neck. "You're mine and I've been waiting days to see you."

"You're going to see me all night," I whisper into his ear.

"I don't think your words are doing what you intend them to do," he murmurs.

I laugh again. "Let me down."

He finally does and I give Theo a kiss on the cheek and ruffle his hair. We all say our goodbyes and I make Lyla promise to let me know if she needs me to go over. On our way to the car, Finn wraps his arm around me and doesn't let go of my hand the entire way home.

CHAPTER FORTY-SEVEN

Josslyn

"Come closer, baby," Finn says, curling an arm around me to pull me closer until I'm straddling him.

His hands move up my thighs to my waist.

"Fuck," he says when he finds that I have nothing on underneath his jersey. "You just want to kill me, huh?"

"If I kill you, I can't fuck you," I say. "And that doesn't sound very fun."

His eyes darken as he wraps a hand behind my neck and pulls my face near his. He bites my bottom lip and sucks it into his mouth with a groan. "I missed you so much. I want to fucking devour you."

"I want you to, but first…" I scoot back slightly and grab his hard length over his dress pants, making him hiss.

I slide down his body, unbuttoning his dress shirt as I go, and kissing each sliver of skin I see. He had two road games and the days he was gone felt like an eternity. He likes to joke that I've bewitched him, but he's done the same to me.

He slides his fingers into my hair and grips it, making me gasp at the sting.

"I've been thinking about this since you left," I say as I undo his belt.

He growls when I lick and bite his lower abs, and grips my hair tighter. My stomach does a little swoosh when I look up and see the hunger in his eyes. I focus on undressing him, and once he's fully naked, I get on my knees and settle between his legs again, setting my hands on his muscled thighs and squeeze. He groans. I move my hands up, looking at his thick erection, and lick my lips when it jolts.

"Fuck, Josslyn," he says, voice raspy. I glance up at him and my heart skips a beat again. When his hands close over my arms, I sit back on my heels quickly.

"No touching."

His brows hike up. "You're kidding, right?" he asks, but lets his hands drop to the bed.

"Not kidding." I kiss his left knee and every inch of his inner thigh as I make my way up.

He fists the sheets. "Fuck. You really do want to kill me."

I lick his balls and smile up at him. "I already told you, that doesn't sound very fun."

I keep teasing him, licking up his full length, then the sides, but never closing my mouth where he wants it. Finn's breath picks up as I start kissing his abs, stopping at each muscle. I lick the dip of his throat and kiss his neck. I set my hands on either side of his face and look at him. He'd been out of town for two days before today's home game and I've been missing him, but I hadn't realized how much until this moment.

"I missed you," I say quietly, and kiss him.

I mean for it to be a soft kiss, but Finn wraps his arms around me and takes over, his tongue delving into my mouth as he devours me. I break the kiss when I feel him shift, because I know he intends to flip us over and I don't want that yet. I'm breathing heavily as I push myself up.

"Hands on the bed," I say.

He growls, grabbing my ass hard and earning a loud gasp from me before doing as he's told.

"So the entire time I was gone, the only thing you thought about was torturing me?" he asks, a rumble against my lips.

I smile and continue, kissing the path down his chest until I reach where I want to be, and this time, after I lick the sides of his length, I take him into my mouth slowly.

"Oh, fuuuuuck," he hisses. The fitted corner of the fitted sheet snaps up as it comes undone with his grasp. "God damn it, Josslyn. Fuck. Fuck."

I continue licking and sucking and massaging his balls as his hips push off the bed. I nearly laugh because I know what I'm going to say next is really going to drive him crazy, but I suck twice more before I let him go. His eyes are wild as he searches my face, panting as he waits.

"Can I touch you now?" he asks, his voice a croak.

I smile and move up a little, pressing my weight against him until my mouth reaches his ear so I can whisper, "You can touch me, but I want you to fuck my face."

He stops breathing. But when I pull back and see the look in his eyes, I'm the one who stops breathing.

"I am so going to fucking keep you," he says, eyes blazing as he positions us so he's sitting at the edge of the bed and I'm kneeling before him.

He takes off the jersey I'm wearing and tosses it aside, and I don't wait for instructions before taking him in my mouth again, inhaling sharply when he wraps my hair around his hand and pulls so hard, my eyes start to tear up. I continue licking and sucking as I condition my mouth to take him deeper. My thighs clench with each growl from his lips, each thrust of his hips. He hits the back of my throat, and the urge to gag makes me want to stop what I'm doing, but he doesn't give me any reprieve.

"Breathe through your nose. Just like that," he says. "Fuck yes. You take me so well, baby. So fucking perfect for me."

His words shoot a wave of need through my body and I start clenching my thighs to make friction between my legs.

"Fuck," he hisses. "Touch yourself for me. Touch yourself while I fuck your mouth."

I continue to grip one of his hips while I lower my other hand. He groans, thrusting harder as my fingers dance between my legs.

He brings a hand down to cup my breast and pinch my nipples, and I moan around his cock.

"That's it, baby. Keep playing with that pretty pussy," he growls, thrusting faster.

He lets go of my hair and starts to play with both of my breasts. My fingers quicken to match the tempo of his thrusts, and I moan again, louder, as my core tightens and the familiar sensation whips through me. I start to shake as my orgasm consumes me. Finn pulls out completely, and through hooded eyes, I watch as he continues to pump his cock in his grip.

The sight keeps my hand moving and pulls another orgasm from me—so intense, I feel tears build in my eyes. I try to keep them open and on him. He gasps, throwing his head back with a roar, as he shoots cum all over my face and chest. We're both panting by the time we finish. He lets go of himself and lowers his face to look at me, heat still flaring in those intense eyes of his.

"You have no idea how beautiful you look right now with my cum all over you," he says hoarsely.

Later that night, we're lying in bed watching highlights of some games, including his. When he's home, our days are pretty structured. We're both gone the entire day, and whoever gets home first makes or orders dinner. We talk, shower, have sex, talk some more, watch TV, and just lie here.

"You leave again soon," I say sadly.

"We have a few days." He kisses my temple.

"What are we going to do when my season starts?" I ask, already dreading it.

"We'll figure it out," he says, slowly running a hand over my hair. "What are you going to do when you get your degree?"

"I want to keep developing the Alma Foundation. There are so many more people we can reach and help. My mom's done a great job with the annual fundraiser and raising money throughout the year…" I stop talking because I don't know how to express that it's not enough.

"But it's not enough," he says, somehow reading my thoughts.

He pulls back slightly to look at my face. "You don't want to keep playing basketball?"

"I started playing basketball because of my dad. I was a total daddy's girl." I smile when his eyes soften. "I love it. I've played for as long as I can remember. I broke the all-time 3-point record at Fairview University. I mean, it's not like I'm Caitlin Clark or anything, but I *am* good," I say.

He looks amused as he leans in and kisses me. "I know you are."

"*But* playing college and playing professionally are completely different. I'm a great college player, but the women in the WNBA are next-level good." I lick my lips. "Besides, basketball isn't my life. It never has been. It's just a sport I play that makes me feel closer to my dad. I don't think… I don't think I need it anymore. Not for that."

"I understand."

My eyes rise. "Do you, though?"

He's next-level good, and it's not like hockey is something that ties him to his parents. If anything, it's the opposite.

"Priorities change," he says, looking back at the television. "I love hockey. I excel at it and I know if I'm healthy, I can play another eight, maybe even ten years, but when I picture life ten years from now, it's not what I see." He glances at me again.

My stomach dips. The last man I dated love-bombed me and repeatedly told me he wanted to marry me, and that didn't turn out very well. I don't need Finn to verbally confirm his emotions to know what he's feeling. The way he holds me, treats me, and acts around me is enough. But nothing compares to the way he looks at me. Not when he's checking me out or telling me I'm beautiful the way guys before him have. He looks at me like I'm precious *to him.*

CHAPTER FORTY-EIGHT

Josslyn

I TOLD HIM I WANT TO STOP. STOP OR COME CLEAN. I CAN'T DO THIS TO JOSS anymore.

  I saw him again tonight. He took me to a secluded farm and we lay on the bed of his truck. I love the way he makes me feel. FML.

  There's a spot in their yard that the cameras can't get to. It's become our secret cove when I go over and 'go to the bathroom.' I hate myself so much. I know I need to stop.

  I push the pages away and stare at the computer, willing it to load faster. From the amount of updates I've had to run, it's clear Finn hasn't used it in a while. *If ever.* Maybe if I weren't in a rush to turn in the assignment, it wouldn't bother me, but I am. I'm supposed to go to Lyla's house to see the baby and give Theo the "big brother" present I got for him. As I thrum my fingers on the desk, my phone buzzes with a text from Leo. Even though he's now second place on my list of anticipated texts, I jump at the sight of his name.

  The other person I'm anxiously waiting to hear from is my mom's neighbor. They have a camera that points at my mom's backyard, which may have a clear view of the nook Mallory is talking about in her journal entries. Since his dad is paranoid and a hoarder, I'm hoping he can find saved footage from last year. Just the thought of what I might see makes my stomach turn. Doubt has been consuming me lately. I think about Tiago and what he could be hiding. Not that the "T" person Mallory mentioned has to be the same person from my mother's house, but what if it is?

Tate was no longer around at the time, so I've ruled him out. Titus...well, I don't want to think about that being a possibility, but the more I think about it, the less sure I am. Damian would have no reason to hide hooking up with Mallory, so I know it's not him. It could be one of his friends, though. Maybe someone on the Blaze.

> Leo: I have something you might want to see
>
> Me: the list?
>
> Leo: yes

I take a breath and lower my phone.

> Leo: we'd have to meet in person
>
> Me: when can you meet?
>
> Leo: I'll be available friday

I stare at the words. I have class and practice on Friday, but I'll do anything to make this work.

> Me: not at Onyx
>
> Leo: my place?

I scoff. Fat chance of that happening.

> Me: somewhere public. A coffee shop. I'll send you the location. It has to be between 1-4

He sends me a wink emoji that I immediately want to delete, but decide not to. If I was dating Tate, I would have, since he would have gone through my phone and found a way to make me feel like I was doing something wrong. I set the phone down and open the school portal. After turning in my assignment, I click around to make sure I'm up to date on everything else, and an email pops up at the top of the screen. I see my last name and click it before I even process that this isn't my computer and the email isn't *for* me.

TOM FRAGA <tomfragaPI@gmail.com>

Subject: RE: Santos/Fletcher

My last invoice is attached.

I glance at the subject line again, and at the signature in the email that says this Tom guy is a private investigator. As I try to wrap my head around what this could mean, I scroll down what seems to be an endless email chain. My stomach twists when I open candid pictures of me, and then candid pictures of Titus. One set of pictures in particular catches my attention. Not unlike some others, it's me sitting at my favorite coffee shop down the street. Unlike the others, I'm looking at my phone with an angered, shocked expression on my face. I know from what I'm wearing that it was the moment I saw the videos circulating of Tate and Gracie making out.

I set a hand on my stomach, hoping it will lessen the sick feeling in it. I keep scrolling until I find the first email, which dates back to just after Mallory's closed-casket funeral. What. The. Fuck. I note that Finn hasn't responded to any of these emails, but he's definitely seen them. I can imagine him getting them on his phone and scrolling through to see the pictures and updates this guy sends him. The invoice is from over a month ago and it says "last invoice," so I have to assume he's no longer having this guy following me around. It doesn't make me feel any better though.

I look through the pictures again. Seeing pictures of myself doing everyday things like running at the park, playing pick-up basketball games with Tiago and Olivia, hanging out with Damian, pulling up at my mother and Titus' house, makes me feel ... exposed. He was having us followed for an entire year. A shiver runs down my spine at the thought. After sitting there for a while, I take a picture of the screen and send it to Finn. I don't even bother texting words. I just want him to know that I know. I assume he'll understand why this would upset me.

I sit at the edge of the bed as Lyla nurses the baby. Rosa James Duke. Apparently, Lachlan insisted on the middle name. I think it's cute. Lyla thinks it's corny, but smiles when she talks about it, so I think she secretly likes that they all have the same middle name.

"What's on your mind?" she asks.

I stop staring at the top of the baby's head and glance up at Lyla. "I don't even know how to talk about it."

"Well, let me know if you do," she says, then adds, "Is it about Finn?"

"Baby, do you want…" Lachlan begins to interrupt, but stops short and looks at me. "What about Finn?"

I bristle. "I don't want to tell you."

"Why not?" He frowns as he sits down in the chair beside his wife and smiles at the baby.

"Because you'll make a big fuss."

"If you tell Lyla about it, I'll make her tell me, and the outcome will be the same," he says, setting a cloth on his shoulder and taking the baby from Lyla's chest to start burping her.

"You've already said too much. You know how nosey he is," Lyla says, rolling her eyes.

"Fine, but don't say anything to him," I say, shooting a pointed look at Lachlan, who looks too excited to be in on the gossip. "I was on the computer doing homework and an email of his popped up. I would have ignored it, but my name was on the subject line."

"What did it say?" Lyla asks, eyes narrowed.

"There are endless candid pictures of me from a PI that go back *over a year*."

Rosa's burp was the only reaction I got out of the three of them.

"Hello?" I say, my wide eyes jumping between them. "He was stalking me for over a year!"

"That's what's bothering you?" Lachlan asks, frowning.

"I mean, yeah, shouldn't it bother me?"

"I'm sorry." Lyla laughs. "We're the wrong crowd for this. Lachlan stalked the fuck out of me."

"And I'd do it again," he says, grinning at her as he taps Rosa's back.

"I don't mean sneaky social media stalking. I mean legit stalking, with a PI," I clarify again.

"I tried to get people to use facial recognition on some guy she went on a date with once," Lachlan says, like it's something he's proud of.

"And we weren't even together," Lyla adds. Lachlan shoots her an annoyed look.

My jaw drops for a moment. "That is *not* normal."

Lachlan frowns. "Who wants normal?"

"Right? Is it even love if there's no stalking involved?" Lyla asks in a deadpan tone and smiles at Lachlan when he smirks at her. She shakes her head and looks at me again. "Have you spoken to him about it?"

"No. I just found out a couple of hours ago."

"Is it a make it or break it kind of thing?" Lyla asks.

Even as I'm frowning, I'm shaking my head, which only further proves how far gone I am for this man. It bothers me, yes, but I know I won't leave him because of it. Crazy as it may be—and it *is* crazy—I trust him.

"I have to be honest," Lachlan says, standing up and putting Rosa James in her bassinet near Lyla's side of the bed. "I'm kind of surprised Finn would do this."

"Because he's so reserved?" Lyla asks.

"I guess. And I've never even seen him look at the same woman twice. Definitely not after they hook up." He flinches a little. "Sorry, Joss."

"Nothing to be sorry about." I shrug. "I know his history."

He chuckles. "I swear his eye twitches every time Theo says you're his girlfriend."

"Jealous of a child? He sounds insane," Lyla says, shooting Lachlan an amused glance.

He rolls his eyes as he leans down and kisses her. When he pulls away, he gazes at her with so much love that I have to look away. Isn't that what I said I always wanted? Their kind of love? Finn looks at me the way they look at each other, and I'm sure I reciprocate it.

"Thank you," I say, smiling at them. "This was helpful. Weird, but helpful."

They laugh as I stand up and begin saying my goodbyes to them. "I'm going to see if Tia Nina needs help with Theo, and then I'm heading out."

By the time I leave, I feel a little lighter, at least on this front. I haven't stopped thinking about what Leo could possibly have to show me.

CHAPTER FORTY-NINE

Finn

I LET OUT A HARSH BREATH AS I WALK TOWARD THE LOCKER ROOM. Cameras and journalists are already piled up outside of the door, waiting to pounce the first chance they get. I've always made it very clear that I won't speak to them. Especially before, during, or after games, but part of my contract with the Owls—the part that makes me a minority owner—says I need to play nice and speak to them. It'll be difficult to do, especially after our first loss of the season. As we get near the cameras, I glance at our goalie, who's been brooding since the game-winning puck slid under his glove during the last ten seconds of the game.

"I knew I should've gone left," he grumbles when he catches me looking.

"It's in the past now. Get your head ready for tomorrow," I say, repeating the advice I got when I was a first-year player and I lost my first game.

We walk inside, where our coaches are waiting. Coach P gives his usual pep talk, but unlike the last handful of games that we've played and won, the championship belt the team has been passing around is nowhere to be seen. We made a decision after our first preseason game to only celebrate wins. I know better than anyone how long the season is and that losses are inevitable, so we won't sit around moping about them. The WWE-style championship belt will only be handed out to our MVP after a win.

They wait a few minutes after the pep talk to let cameras inside. A group of them catches me and I decide to answer their questions quickly—we'll be fine for tomorrow, there was nothing we could do to stop that last puck, we should have been more aggressive, blah blah blah bullshit. Once I'm done playing nice, I walk toward my stuff.

"Yeah, basketball practice started already," I hear Damian say to someone as I walk by, and my ears instantly perk up. "She says she won't try to play professionally."

I glance over and see him talking to Max Gomez, a tall, dark-skinned guy with light brown eyes and a buzz cut. He's one of the wingers on the team we just played. I've met him a couple of times at different youth camps over the years, but this is his first year in the league. He grew up in Fairview, so I'm not surprised Damian knows him. I just don't understand why I'm hearing my girlfriend's name coming out of his mouth for a fourth time in as many minutes.

"She always said she only wanted to play college ball," Gomez says. "What will she do now?"

"More work for the Alma Foundation. She wants to expand on the mental health thing and also start providing sports equipment to underprivileged kids."

My heart swells with the same pride I hear in Damian's voice as he speaks about Josslyn's goals.

"Damn, good for her," Gomez responds. "She's gotten a lot of sponsorship deals."

"Yeah. I'm pretty sure she's still one of the highest paid college athletes," Damian responds.

"I swear, breaking up with her was the stupidest shit I've ever done."

Damian laughs. My hands freeze on my laces. I feel myself

scowl and glance over my shoulder again. This time, I look at Max a little closer. He's tall and dark-skinned, with light brown eyes and a buzz cut. He has a carefree smile and a wistful expression on his chiseled face that makes an uncomfortable feeling curl in the pit of my stomach. I've been trying to pretend Josslyn had no guys in her life before me, but I guess it's unavoidable.

"Does she still hate when people call her Josie?"

Damian scoffs. "I wouldn't know. I haven't tried since the time she punched me in the nose."

"Yeah, she gave me the silent treatment for two days when I did it," Gomez says, smiling. "I heard a rumor that she's dating Barlow now."

I turn back around quickly and keep undressing.

"Yeah. It's the happiest I've ever seen her," Damian says. "No offense."

"Nah, she deserves it." Gomez laughs. "It was good to see you, brother. Let Joss know I asked about her."

I reach for my phone. She's been on my mind all day, as usual. The only reprieve I get from thoughts of her is during games, and even then, when I'm on the bench, I wonder if she's watching from home, and if so, where she's sitting and what she's wearing. My smile drops and my stomach twists painfully when I unlock my phone and find a picture of my emails from Tom. God damnit. *How am I going to explain this to her?*

It's only a fifteen-minute ride to the airport and our flight will take off shortly after we arrive, so I call Josslyn as soon as I get on the bus. I've tried to figure out what I'll say to her, and keep coming up short. I can explain why I did it, but I can't apologize for my actions. It would be equal to a lie, and I promised her I wouldn't lie to her.

"Calling *your girlfriend* already?" Hamilton jokes, and laughs when I flash him my middle finger as I keep walking to the back of the bus.

"Hello?" she says. It's noisy wherever she is.

"I got your texts."

"Yeah." She exhales. "Are you going to apologize?"

"No."

She's quiet for a moment. "You know what, I respect that."

"Are you upset?"

"About the stalking? What do you think?"

I sit down and shut my eyes as I lean against the wall. "Where are you?"

"I just got home from practice," she says, moving further from the noise. "There's a mom with like six kids in the lobby right now. All under ten. It's insane."

I feel my lips tug. "Do you want kids?"

"Yeah." Her tone makes me uneasy, but I'm afraid to address it.

"How many?" I ask instead.

"I'm not sure. I guess it depends on who I have them with."

My eyes pop open as a wave of anger rushes through me. It takes me a moment to push it down. Every time she says things like that or suggests I might want to date someone else at some point, I want to shake her. I don't know what else to say or do to make her see that there will be no one else. Ever.

"I told Theo I'm going to be your last boyfriend. You can't have me lying to a kid," I say, hoping it sounds like a joke despite the pressure on my chest.

"Sorry to break it to you, but he's rooting against you."

I roll my eyes. At myself. At the kid. I don't even know anymore. Everything about this conversation is off-putting.

"Are you at my place or yours?" I ask when I hear a door open and shut.

Another sore subject. I've been asking her to move in with me every day and she still hasn't caved, even though we've only slept apart a handful of times.

"Mine. Livie's supposed to come over soon," she says, her voice still drawn. Distant. I can't fucking stand it.

"Are you going to leave me?" I ask quietly, as I screw my eyes shut and hold my breath, waiting for her response.

"Leave you?"

"Yes."

Another pause. "What would you do if I said yes?"

My chest squeezes painfully. "I don't know, Josslyn." I swallow hard. "Cry." I let out a short laugh. "Scream. Get on my knees and beg you to reconsider."

"And if I don't reconsider?" she asks quietly.

"You will."

"Oh, really?" She laughs, and it sounds light enough that I feel some of the pressure in my chest loosen. "How do you know?"

"Because I'm not letting you go."

"Would you have me followed again if I broke up with you?"

"Yes."

"No hesitation, huh?"

"Nope." I open my eyes and stretch my legs out on the empty seats beside me. "I'd probably retire and do it myself."

"No, you wouldn't." She laughs louder, and I feel my mouth twitch.

"You underestimate how much I want you in my life."

It's not even a matter of *want* at this point. She's as vital to me as water. As air.

"I'm not going to leave you," she says. "I'm a little weirded out about the stalking, but I think I can get over it. I just have a lot on my mind."

I nod, even though she can't see me, and I clear my throat. "I didn't know you dated Max Gomez."

"You saw … oh, that's right! I forgot he was playing for Carolina," she says. "I'm assuming he's still good."

The obvious smile in her voice makes me scowl. "He's fine."

"Just fine?" she asks, teasing.

"How long were you together?"

"God…" She pauses to think. "Like a year? He was my first boyfriend."

"Hm." It's all I can say as a wave of jealousy crashes through me.

I try to remind myself once again that I'll be her last boyfriend and none of them matter, but when it comes to Josslyn, there's not one rational bone in my body. Suddenly, I wish I could turn back time and go back into that locker room.

"Please tell me you're not jealous," she says, obviously amused.

"What do you think?"

"It was a long time ago," she says quietly.

"Do any more of your exes play in the league?"

"No. Not hockey anyway."

My jaw tightens. "How many boyfriends have you had?"

"Hmm … actual boyfriends? Three, including Tate. Gomez plays hockey, as you know, and Russ is a tight end at Fairview, but he'll be drafted in April."

I remain silent. There's not much for me to say on the matter anyway. It's in the past, and even if I could turn back time and meet her before she started dating any of those clowns, I wouldn't. I would've been too old for her back then, and too focused on hockey. I'm self-aware enough to know nothing would have changed.

I still would have wanted to escape Fairview and free myself from the expectations that come with being a Barlow—working in the family business, schmoozing people in positions of power, and settling down with a woman my parents approved of. Still, I wonder how my life would have turned out if the circumstances had been different and I'd met Josslyn sooner.

"Do you think I like the idea of you being with other women?" she asks after a moment. "There are blogs and accounts on social media dedicated to your one-night stands, which people tag me in, by the way, so if you ever get any ideas while you're on the—"

"Don't finish that sentence." I straighten in my seat, a new kind of annoyance consuming me. "I told you I'd never do that to you. You're the only one I want."

"For now."

"ForEVER." I throw my head back and look at the roof of the bus, as if it'll reveal a way I can get this through her head.

I've never paid much attention to those accounts. Some are

just fan accounts, which I don't mind, but the ones that are about my lack of a love life are ridiculous. They make it seem like I fuck every woman I see. A handful of times I was pictured having lunch and dinner with my cousin's wife, and it became a whole thing since we'd met up multiple times. When they found out who she was, it went from "the woman who tamed Finn Barlow" to "Finn Barlow is having an affair with his cousin's wife." Fucking ridiculous.

Thankfully, Asher is a smart, secure man who knows I would never do that, but *what the fuck?* Then, there's the fact that one of my lawyers is a woman. And my money manager. My accountant's daughter had to deal with the circus multiple times. It's fucking ridiculous, but I've never cared enough to do something about it. Right now, I wish I could. Right now, I wish I could—if only to give Josslyn one less thing to doubt. Though if she's keeping up with them, she'll soon realize she's the only one in any pictures with me.

"I can't believe you were having me followed for so long," she says after a moment. "I feel like you know me so much better than I know you."

"That's not true."

"It is, Finn. You have pictures of some pretty intimate moments," she says. "And for someone who claims he's jealous of my exes, you sure looked at a lot of pictures of me and Tate."

My jaw tics. I fucking hated seeing those pictures. "It was my personal hell," I tell her.

"I just don't understand what you thought you'd find. I get that you thought I was hiding something, but what would following me accomplish?"

"I had a PI on Titus. I thought maybe I'd find him with another young girl or … I don't know. Something. But then I saw you in some pictures when you were out to dinner as a family and I just…" I exhale, completely aware that this is making me sound like a creep.

"You just what?"

"I told myself I was having you followed because I wanted to find out what you were hiding, but I just wanted more of you. Even if it meant seeing you with that asshole. Those one-night stands I had were nameless. Faceless. I never looked at any of them again. But you? You, I couldn't stop—can't stop—looking at or thinking about or wanting."

"God, Finn," she whispers. "I hate it when you say stuff like that."

I bark out a laugh that I'm sure startles some of the guys in front of me. "What? The truth?" We're both quiet for a long time before I say, "Look, we're adults. We each have a past. It's probably good that you've dated those idiots, so you can see they're nothing compared to me."

She makes a *psh* sound. "You're so arrogant."

"So you've said."

"Hey, Finn," she says quietly.

I shut my eyes and take a breath. I love it when she says that to me in that soothing tone. "Yeah."

"I miss you. A lot."

My breath gets caught in my throat. "I miss you too, baby. So fucking much."

"Good."

My lip twitches. "So, you're not leaving me?"

"I'm not leaving you."

All of my annoyance melts away at once. *She's not going to leave me over this.* I shut my eyes and take a breath, wishing I could reach through the phone and lift her into my arms. When I feel the bus come to a stop, I say my goodbyes and promise I'll call her when I get to the hotel in Toronto. I've never missed a game, but the way I'm feeling right now, I wish I could take a flight home instead.

It certainly gives me a new appreciation for my friends with families. They go home to be with their wives for the birth of their children and come right back to keep playing, as if their lives hadn't forever been altered. That's exactly what Josslyn is—life-altering—and there's no way in hell I'm ever letting her go.

CHAPTER FIFTY

Josslyn

I didn't tell Finn that I'm meeting Leo at the coffee shop. I haven't told him about Leo at all. I don't know that there will be anything to tell him, and I don't want to distract him from his games. I asked Olivia to accompany me, though, and she's sitting at a separate table doing homework while I sit with Leo. So far, I've got nothing. He was on a call when I got here, and he's still on it five minutes later. I sip my coffee and look outside to watch the people walking by during their lunch breaks.

"I'm sorry about that," Leo says, as he hangs up and puts his phone in the inside pocket of his jacket. "You look different today."

I laugh. "Yeah."

Different is an understatement. We're going to basketball practice in a few hours, so I'm wearing a t-shirt and basketball shorts, and my hair is up in a ponytail. A far cry from the Josslyn he's seen at Onyx and Pearl.

"You look younger like this." His eyes are warm as he looks at me. After a moment, he reaches into his briefcase and sets some papers on the table. He locks eyes with me again. "No one knows

I'm doing this. Johnny would have me killed if he finds out, so I trust you won't say a word."

"I won't," I say. "And I can't thank you enough for doing this for me."

He gives a nod and slides the papers over. "This is the guest list for the club and for our group that night. The list is long, but only the ones with check marks beside their names were there. The rest reserved a spot and most likely didn't show up."

My heart is going a mile a minute as I pore over the list. It's pretty long. People had reservations from six o'clock in the afternoon until four in the morning. I'm trying to focus on the check-marked names, wishing this list was in alphabetical order when I freeze on one. Titus Fletcher. Knowing he was there is one thing, but what gets me is seeing that he's on this list at all. My heart stops for a moment.

"If someone just showed up, would they be on this list?"

"If they were granted entry, yes."

I let out a relieved breath. Four names above Titus', I see his client's name—the one he was dragging out of there—and let out another relieved breath. I knew he wasn't lying, but having solid proof makes me feel a little better.

I glance up and find Leo looking at me, which gives me pause for a moment, before I ask, "Is there any way to get footage of this night? Right before or after the fire?"

"I tried," he says.

I tear my gaze from his and look at the side of the industrial coffee machine. I'd already told him I didn't remember anything, but I feel like I should tell him the reason for my lapse in memory. Being drugged is something I've thought about sharing with my followers multiple times. I haven't, because I hate bringing people down and sometimes what I'm going through would do exactly that. The drug thing feels like something that's important to share.

The issue is I don't remember what happened, and sharing my experience would lead to questions I don't have answers for. My stomach twists when I think about Tate. He said he'd been drugged the night he ran into Gracie, and after forcing myself to watch the video again, I believe him.

"I was drugged that night," I say, looking at Leo, whose eyes widen. "That's why I don't remember it."

"Are you okay? Did anything happen?" he asks, and he seems genuinely concerned.

"I don't think anything happened," I say.

It's another thing that would drive me crazy if I think about it too much. The rape kit proved I wasn't raped, but that doesn't mean other things didn't happen. The thought makes me want to throw up. This is why I don't dwell on it.

He frowns. "You don't think anything happened?"

"There's no telling. I really don't remember any of it. I was at the bar at Onyx drinking water, and that's as far as my memory goes. That's why I want the footage."

He's still frowning as he nods slowly. "I'll get it for you."

"I thought you said—"

He waves a hand, suddenly looking determined. "I'll get it for you."

"Thank you." I offer a small smile and go back to the papers.

Johnny Matthews
Paul Rose
Erin Cain
Laura Erickson
Tate Ford

My breath catches.

"Did you see one you recognize?" Leo asks.

My heart is in my throat, in my ears, as I nod. I flip the pages in a daze until I finally reach the guest list for their exclusive group, and bring both shaking hands up to cover my mouth when I see Mallory's and Tate's names on the list.

"What is it?" Leo asks urgently, sliding the papers so he can see.

I look around for Olivia, but I only see her bag and laptop. I spot her outside on the phone. I lower my hands and point a shaky finger to Tate's name.

"Do you know him?"

"Of course. He used to go all the time." He frowns as he looks at me. "You're shaking. Are you okay?"

I swallow hard, trying to maintain my composure, even though my eyes are burning with unshed tears that I know will fall any minute. What does this mean? Do I even want to know? My thoughts are scrambling as I think about Mal's journal entries. "T" picking her up, someone looking at her from across the table, the truck. Tate's red fucking truck.

"Oh my God, I'm going to be sick," I whisper hoarsely.

I bury my face in my hands, and suddenly everything feels like too much. My skin feels too tight and my heart is galloping too hard, too loudly in my ears. My vision starts to tunnel and I know without a doubt that I'm on the verge of fainting.

"Oh my God!" Livie's voice is near. I feel hands on my shoulders. "What's going on? What did you tell her?"

"I didn't say anything. She was looking at the paper and saw a name that upset her."

"What the fuck?" Livie hisses. "Let me see."

"No. These are confidential. I did this as a favor to your friend."

"Yeah, real fucking favor."

There's more talking, but it all sounds muffled when my head begins to spin.

"I think I'm going to…" is all I can get out before everything goes dark.

CHAPTER FIFTY-ONE

Josslyn

"WHAT THE FUCK, OLIVIA?! YOU JUST LET HIM LEAVE?! WHO WAS IT?!"

I frown at the sound of that voice.

"What was I supposed to do? Tie him to the chair?!"

"YES, GODDAMNIT!"

I open my eyes and blink rapidly, trying to clear the black and white dots in my vision. It's only then that I realize I'm no longer on a chair, but on a couch, and I'm sitting on a person's lap. I blink, and blink again, frowning when I turn my face and see Tiago staring back at me.

"What the…" I start, but Livie rushes forward and grabs my face in her hands.

"You scared the fuck out of me!" she says, her voice catching.

I couldn't have been out for that long. As a teenager, I had fainting spells often. Usually, it was a low blood sugar thing and I was only out for two to three minutes at the most.

"How long was I out?" I ask, frowning, and look at Tiago. "What are you doing here?"

"Studying," he says, like it's the most obvious thing in the world. I look over his shoulder and see two guys from the team and a pretty black girl I've never seen. "What the hell happened? Who were you talking to before?"

"None of your business," Livie says.

"Fuck you, Olivia." Tiago scowls. "She's my friend too."

She covers her face and starts to pace. "Oh my God, I almost had a heart attack." When she lowers her hands and looks toward the front door, her eyes nearly bulge out of their sockets. "Oh, shit. We're all going to die."

I frown and open my mouth to ask her what the hell she's talking about.

"What the hell happened?!" Finn roars from somewhere behind me. When I look over Tiago's shoulder and he spots me on his lap, his expression turns murderous. "What the *fuck* is going on?!"

"Is everything okay?" Damian asks, panting, as he walks through the door.

They were both due home today, and this is down the block from our building, but what the hell? How many people did Olivia call? Finn finally reaches us and I swear, if he could make thunder with his fingertips, he would have already obliterated me and Tiago. I start to get up, slowly swinging my legs from Tiago's lap. Finn helps me and once I'm standing, I crash into his chest. The feel of his arms around me and his familiar scent instantly soothe me. I make a noise in the back of my throat that sounds a lot like a sob, though I'm not crying. Damian is asking Olivia a million questions as Finn pulls back and cups my face with both hands.

"What happened? Olivia said you fainted."

I nod and lick my lips. The concern in his green eyes makes mine water. I open my mouth to speak, but my lower lip wobbles, and another sob escapes me. I bite my lip hard.

"Let's go home, baby." He kisses my forehead and pulls away to tuck me into his side. It's then that I realize he's shaking. "You're lucky she's my priority right now. Otherwise, you'd be headed to the ER with a concussion and a broken arm. Don't touch my fucking girlfriend again unless you want that threat to become a promise."

"I WAS HELPING!" Tiago shouts. "You should be fucking thanking me!"

Finn starts to walk, but I stop him and look at Tiago. "Thank you."

He's still glaring, but gives a sharp nod.

"What the hell were you thinking, Josslyn?" Damian seethes as we walk out of the coffee shop. "Why would you meet up with a sleazebag from a sex club?"

Finn's entire body tenses, but he keeps an arm around me. "What?"

"I was talking to Leo about—"

"You were what?!" Finn stops walking, drops his arm, and looks at me. "Why didn't I know about this?"

"You were at a game!"

"You knew I was coming home today! Whatever it was could've waited a couple of hours!"

I bring my hands to cover my face. "Can we not do this right now? I have a headache."

"Fuck your headache!" he shouts. "You need to tell me exactly what happened in the next three seconds. Otherwise, I'm going to find Leo and end up in jail tonight."

I drop my hands, eyes wide. He looks like he means it too. His cheeks are slightly flushed and his ears are red. His arms are crossed and his expression is hard, screaming murder. I've never seen him this upset before. My eyes swing to Dame and Livie, who both look worried and angry.

"Uh, Finn, is that your car that's about to get towed?" Livie asks warily.

Finn keeps staring at me, but I take a step and look behind him, my eyes widening again when I see his sleek black car parked in the right lane. Not on the curb or illegally parallel parked. He parked in the *middle of the street*. I bring a hand up and set it on Finn's arm, but he uncrosses his arms, making my hand drop.

"They're towing your car," I say hoarsely.

"I don't give a fuck about my car! Speak or I go find Leo."

"He didn't do anything! He showed me some papers. That's it."

His jaw tics. Damian runs toward the tow truck with Olivia at his heels.

"Tate was there," I say, swallowing hard. "The guy she was writing about in her journal has to be Tate."

His face falls. "No."

Tears fill my eyes as I nod, but I blink them away and wait until my lip stops trembling.

"It has to be. He has a red truck. His name starts with the letter T. It has to be him." I press my hands over my stomach, feeling sick again, but I keep talking because I do owe Finn an explanation. "I'm sorry I didn't tell you about Leo. The other night when we spoke after your game in North Carolina, my brain was just—"

"He'd already contacted you when we spoke?" he bites out.

"Earlier that day," I say. "He told me he had the guest list for that night and that he'd show it to me if we met up. I didn't want to tell you since our conversation was already…" I bite my lip and look away. "Awkward enough, I guess."

He brings a hand up and pinches my chin lightly as he turns my face to his. "You knew I'd object to this."

"I don't need your permission, Finneas." My eyes narrow and he mirrors the action. "And I took precautions. We met at a coffee shop and I took Livie with me."

"I still don't like it." He drops his hand and looks away, taking a deep breath and shaking his head. "Tate?"

My stomach rumbles again as I nod. *How long had they been hooking up behind my back?* I think about Mallory and how much she loathed Tate; and Tate, who never wanted to hang out with her and stayed home if he knew she'd be around. I bite my lip and blink away hot, angry tears as I start walking toward our building. Who knows how many people saw the spectacle at the coffee shop, or us arguing on the sidewalk? *Fuck.* Being tagged in pictures is the absolute last thing I need to worry about, but I can't help it.

The walk to my apartment is a blur. Before I know it, I'm in the elevator and Finn is beside me. He pushes the button to shut the doors quickly—the button to his floor, not mine.

"I think I need to be alone right now," I whisper, looking at my sneakers.

"Tough. I'm not letting you out of my fucking sight."

My head snaps up. He's looking at the doors, his shoulders bunched with tension. He looks like he's ready to burst and I already know if he yells at me again, I'm walking out. As the doors open, my phone buzzes with a call from Damian.

"Where are you?" he asks.

"Going to Finn's."

"I'm on my way to pick up his car at the lot with Liv, but I'll be over as soon as we get back. I don't know what you've gotten yourself into, and I know I don't have to tell you how motherfucking pissed off I am that you didn't come to me about it, but I'm telling you anyway."

"You've been busy," I say, my voice flat, as I slip my shoes off by the door when I walk into the apartment.

"Don't use that lame-ass excuse. You know I'm never too busy for you! I'll see you in an hour." He hangs up before I can get another word in, and I toss the phone on the kitchen counter.

I turn around and find Finn staring at me with a dark expression I can't decipher. I get that he's upset since he hates Tate and loved his sister, but I just found out my friend and my ex-boyfriend of two years were sleeping together. My heart stops when he closes the distance between us in two strides. For a split second, we just stare at each other, and then his fist is grabbing the front of my shirt and his lips are crashing down on mine.

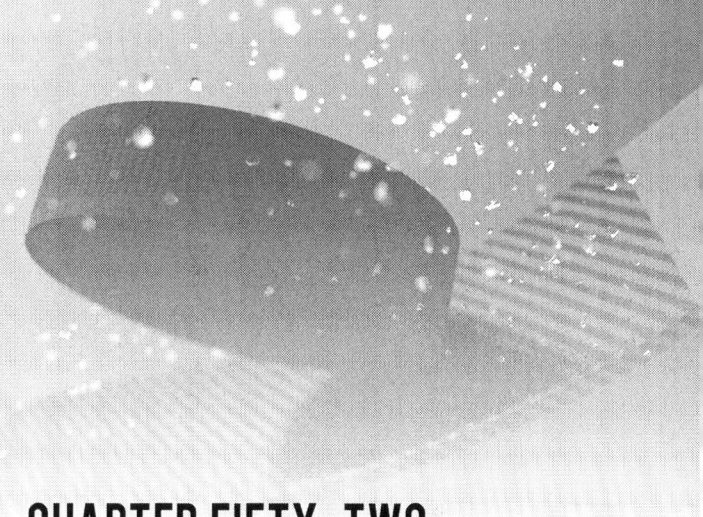

CHAPTER FIFTY-TWO

Finn

I KISS HER IN A DESPERATE FRENZY, MY TONGUE PLUNGING DEEP INTO her mouth. I tuck my hands underneath her shirt and splay them over her ribcage. My hands slide up, needing to feel every inch of her skin to make sure she's real, that she's actually here … and actually mine. When I reach her breasts, I pause and break the kiss.

"No bra?" I ask, breathing heavily.

"I don't usually have one on when I wear oversized shirts."

"Good to know."

I kiss her again, my hands covering her breasts. She breaks the kiss and throws her head back with a gasp when I tease her nipples. She's so fucking sexy. I take a step back and lower her to her feet so I can yank the t-shirt over her head. We undress quickly, like we're trying to break a record. Once we're naked, I hoist her up and push her against the wall again, my lips on hers as one hand plays with her tits and the other slips between us.

She breaks the kiss and digs her fingers into my shoulders when I find her slit. "Oh my … Finn…"

"That's right, baby. *Your* Finn."

I lift her a little higher to suck a nipple into my mouth, biting it as I let go. That earns me a yelp. I do it again and dip a finger inside her, groaning when I find her wet already. Normally, I would spend adequate time on foreplay and making her come before I fuck her, but I'm desperate for her, so I line my cock to her pussy and thrust hard.

The way she screams my name, moans, and gasps are my favorite sounds of all time. I grip her ass as I fuck her wildly with abandon, pouring all my anger and the magnitude of what I feel for her into my thrusts.

"Fuck, baby," I groan, throwing my head back when she starts to squeeze me. "You feel so fucking good on my cock. So perfect."

"Oh, fuck. I'm gonna…"

I lower my head in time to watch her fall apart. The way the rush of her orgasm drenches my cock makes it hard not to come right along with her, but I want this to last. I need to be inside her a little longer. Something about her taps into a primal part of me I never knew existed. I constantly have the urge to mark my territory and remind her and myself that she's mine and no one else's. I slam into her harder and faster, my stomach tightening with the feel of her.

"Finn," she says hoarsely, squeezing me as she starts to come again. "Oh my God. Finneas!"

My orgasm climbs higher and I try to hold back, but it's impossible with my name on her lips and her pussy squeezing me like a vice grip. I thrust harder, knocking down a frame on the wall. It gives me pause for only half a second, and then I'm coming.

"Fuck, Josslyn!" I throw my head back, panting as I slow my thrusts.

Her legs are shaking, her breaths coming out in spurts as she rests her head on the wall. I lean in and suck her exposed neck, then push her up a little until her breasts are in front of my mouth. I lick her nipples again and Josslyn shivers. She sinks her fingers into my hair and lifts my face slightly. We hold eye contact for what feels like an eternity. I see so many emotions that reflect mine in her beautiful brown eyes. I slip out of her slowly, but keep her hoisted against the wall as I lean in and kiss her softly. When I pull away, I set my forehead against hers.

"You own me, Josslyn. I don't think you realize it, but you fucking own me," I say as I take a breath.

She smiles, the first real smile I've seen from her in days, and kisses me as I lift her and start walking to the bathroom. After we shower, we lay in silence for a while.

"I'm sorry I didn't tell you about Leo," she says quietly, her voice breaking when she adds, "When I saw Tate's name on the paper ... You don't think Tate ... I mean, Tate wouldn't..."

She starts crying before she can finish her sentence. I pull her closer and shut my eyes, breathing out slowly. Tate might be an asshole, but he's not capable of doing something like this. Not committing murder or leaving my sister there, assuming he was there with her. That doesn't mean he doesn't *know* something. It definitely doesn't mean I don't want to fucking kill him. He's fucked up too many times for me to ignore this slight. It's not only that he was sleeping with my sister, but he hurt Josslyn and I can't—*won't*—stand for that.

All this time, I had Tom following Titus and Josslyn for nothing. For a short time, Tate was on that list, but every time I saw a picture of him, my blood pressure began to rise, so I stopped. I couldn't stand to see his smiles or know he was going to see Josslyn. Knowing he had her—period. I should've known then that my visceral reaction to anything Josslyn-related was more than just a need to fuck her once.

She sits up and covers her face with her hands. "I missed practice."

"You don't need to worry about that right now," I say, sitting up and cupping her face.

I can't stand the glassiness in her eyes or the pain I know she's feeling. For a moment, I feel like an asshole for not comforting her the moment I walked into the coffee shop, but when I found her on Tiago's lap, I just reacted. And I know if I had to turn back time, I'd do it all over again. All of the self-restraint I've practiced my entire life goes out the window when it comes to her. I pull her into my arms and kiss the top of her head as she cries softly.

"I feel so stupid," she whispers. "How could I be so blind?"

"You're not stupid."

She trusts too easily and is too good to undeserving people. Including me. I won't point that out, though, because it wouldn't make a difference. I'm not good enough for her, but I'm not letting her go. Besides, I'm trying to be better. Every day I make a conscious effort to be the man she deserves.

"You're not stupid," I repeat, kissing her. "You're beautiful." I kiss her again. "And kind." Another kiss. "And loving." Another kiss. "And mine."

"Would you let me go through your phone right now?" she asks, her voice wavering.

"Yes," I say, no hesitation.

She pulls away further and studies my face. "Really?"

I reach for my phone on the nightstand, hand it to her, and give her my passcode. She blinks rapidly a few times, as if she can't believe I'm trusting her with this, which annoys me to no end, but I don't let it show. Fuck Tate for planting seeds of doubt in her head. I watch as she goes through my texts, which are boring as fuck. She glances at me and the spark of amusement in her eyes makes my stomach dip.

"Am I the only one you have normal conversations with?"

"Probably."

Next, she opens my social media accounts and looks at my DMs, which I rarely check, let alone respond to. Her face pulls in disgust.

"Some of these women are so desperate," she says. "They're hot though. You really never respond to any of them?"

"No."

"Why?" she asks, frowning at me.

"Why would I?"

"I mean before me," she clarifies.

"Paranoia, I guess."

"How were you finding your one-night stands?"

I raise an eyebrow. "Despite what you believe, I didn't fuck my way through Vegas. Most were models or sex workers I met at events or nights out."

"Really?" she asks, her surprise obvious. When I don't say anything, she adds, "I'm not judging. I'm just surprised. According to that account with the sneaky pictures of you, you used to take them out to eat."

"Sex workers eat too, you know." I feel myself smile when she rolls her eyes. "But you're right. The women in those pictures are family and people I work with."

"Even the blonde?" she asks, pursing her lips.

Maybe it's messed up, but my heart skips a beat at the thought of her being jealous. Nevertheless, I'm quick to put her at ease. "The blonde is my cousin Asher's wife. She works on the strip, so we'd grab lunch sometimes."

"Is Asher the soccer player?"

"Was. He coaches the professional team in Vegas now."

She goes back to my phone. "I'm not judging, but why sex workers? Is it just easier since you know there's no expectations with them?"

"Pretty much. To them, I'm just a job assignment," I say.

"And the models?"

"They aren't looking for anything serious." I shrug.

"What about the woman who snuck into your apartment?"

"We met at a party. I got paranoid after that experience."

She glances up from my phone. "Is that why you've never had sex without a condom?"

"That, and I don't trust anyone. The thought of getting some random woman pregnant and being stuck with them forever is not appealing."

She frowns. "But you and I—"

"I know," I interrupt, cupping her face. "I don't mind being stuck with you for an eternity."

The surprise on her face as she searches my eyes kills me. I lean in and kiss her again just because I can, and fuck, what a privilege. She goes back to my phone. After searching and searching for something she'll never find, she tosses it on the bed and lays her head back down. I do the same and turn when she faces me.

"Do you think you still would have pursued me if we'd gone all the way at Onyx that night?"

That's something I think about often, and always come up with the same answer. "I think so. You've always been an outlier. No one else exists when you're around."

"Finn," she whispers, blinking fast.

I smooth her hair away from her face. "Are you going to tell me not to say things like that?"

"No." She scoots closer. "I was going to tell you that I love you."

For a moment, time stops. My heart feels like it's going to burst in my chest. The emotion is so overwhelming—so powerful—that I'm not sure I'll survive it. How can anyone? I pull her against me and search her face for a sign that she's joking, that she's going to take it back. Because even though I knew I felt that way, and I had a feeling she might, hearing her say it is unreal. *She's* unreal.

"No one's ever said that to me," I manage to say despite the emotion that clogs my throat.

Her smile is slow and beautiful. "Then I'll make sure to tell you every single day."

Fuck. I shut my eyes trying to regain a semblance of composure. When I open them, I find her watching me with that warmth I want to cocoon myself in.

"I love you, Josslyn," I say, smiling when her eyes widen as if she wasn't expecting to hear the words from me. "I love you so fucking much."

I kiss her again, wishing we could stay in this bubble forever.

CHAPTER FIFTY-THREE

Josslyn

I'M TRYING TO FOLLOW THE DIRECTION OF THE MAN'S SCREAMS AS I RUN through the corn maze, but I hear him everywhere and it's impossible to know what direction to go in. He yells again, as if he's in agony, and I pick up the pace.

"Josslyn! Josslyn! Get away! Leave!" the man says in guttural moans.

My ankle rolls when I step on an uneven surface, and my foot gets caught on the next. My hands and knees break my fall and I look around in the dark, trying to figure out what's beneath me. I push myself into a crouch and realize it's rope. Manila rope, like the kind my father had in his garage. Like the kind he used…

Something soft touches my shoulder and my eyes fly open in a gasp.

"I didn't mean to wake you," Finn says, sitting down beside me, as he runs a hand over my hair and lifts the silk scarf I had covering it.

It must have come undone while I was tossing and turning. God, that dream. I shiver thinking about it.

"Another bad dream?" he asks.

I nod and grab his forearm, hugging it against my chest. For the last two nights, my sleep has been interrupted by multiple nightmares. I think I've only slept five hours max, and when I've napped, I'm right back in the nightmares, so I stopped trying. Thankfully, Finn has had home games and been sleeping beside me, but he leaves today. My eyes swing to the clock. He leaves right now, actually. Tears fill my eyes and I squeeze his forearm tighter. He pulls it away and lifts the covers so he can get in bed and wrap his arm around me. His cologne envelops me and I shut my eyes, trying to pretend we can stay like this the rest of the day, but he's already wearing his dress shirt and slacks.

"What was it about this time?" he asks against my hair.

"I was running in a maze and tripped over ropes like the one my dad used…" the words get caught in my throat, and I lick my dry lips as he squeezes me tighter and links our fingers together.

"Maybe I should stay," he says for the hundredth time.

"You can't. You know you can't." Tears build in my eyes and I bring up our joined hands to kiss his rough knuckles.

His heavy exhale ripples through my hair and tickles my ear. I don't know all the rules of hockey, but I know if his coach puts him in the lineup and he doesn't show up, they'd be one player short, which would lead to major consequences for Finn. For a year after my dad's death, every time I closed my eyes, I relived the way he looked when I found him—his eyes black and bulging out of their sockets, his swollen tongue sticking out of his mouth, the vivid rope marks around his neck, the feces. My eyes squeeze shut as I try to push the image away now.

Somehow, I stopped having nightmares about it, but the rope continued to haunt me. Maybe because in the beginning, I wanted so badly to believe it wasn't suicide. There was no way my father would take his life. No way he would abandon me like that. No way a rope could hold the weight of such a large man.

After years of not having them, after I'd heard Mallory was involved in some kind of rope play, the nightmares had come back. Every time I had closed my eyes, my father's face had been replaced by hers. Things between me and Tate had been very rocky by then, but after she died, he was there for me. My memories look different when I think back on it now.

He'd been clingy in the aftermath, but not even a week later, he was telling me that I needed to move on. He'd suggested therapy, which I went to, and when that didn't magically take away my nightmares or lift my depression, he suggested everything from soothing teas to drugs. Everything became an argument, and every argument turned into a screaming match until I finally couldn't take it anymore and broke things off.

Finn's phone vibrates in his pocket and he sighs again but doesn't move.

"You have to go," I say, my voice a broken whisper.

"I can't, Josie," he murmurs against my hair. "I can't leave you like this."

"I'll be fine. They're just nightmares. It's nothing I haven't already been through."

His arms loosen as he pulls back to look at me. "You shouldn't have to go through this alone."

"I've done it before."

"You didn't have me before," he says and kisses my cheek. "Invite Olivia to stay here with you while I'm gone."

My brows rise. "That's a big switch for someone who hates having her over."

"I can only handle people in small doses." He smirks. "Except for you, of course."

"I don't know how you play a team sport at a professional level."

"It's work," he says. "And my teammates are alright."

"Would you want to have them over for dinner one night?"

His face pulls, but he says, "Not particularly, but I guess we can."

That makes me laugh. I lean in and kiss him. "Go. I'll be fine."

He sighs and gets out of bed, taking his vibrating phone out of his pocket and answering with a snap, "What?" He pauses. "I'll be there in two minutes."

He hangs up and shoves it back in his pocket, turning to me. "Damian is waiting for me downstairs."

"Be nice. He got your car back for you."

He makes a little grunt of acknowledgement and grabs the handle of his small suitcase. "Do you want me to open the blinds?"

"Nah. I think I'm going to skip my morning run. I'll probably go to my mom's later and hang out with her for a while."

He takes a step toward me and curses when his phone starts vibrating again. He leans down and kisses me one last time.

"I love you," I say, smiling up at him.

"I love you more."

He leaves and answers his phone again on his way out, cursing at Damian, I assume. When I turn my phone on, I have a slew of texts from multiple people—Damian, Livie, my mother, and Leo. My stomach hurts when I see that one and I open it first.

> **Leo:** I apologize about yesterday. I hope you understand why I could not show your friend those papers and why I rushed out of there the way I did. I'm looking for the video now. I'll let you know.

I read his text again. Finn, Olivia, and now Damian have planted important questions in my head, "Why is he helping you? What does he get out of it?" That was a conversation that ended up with me feeling like crap. "You're too trusting," "You care too much," "Not everyone is like you. People don't do things out of the kindness of their hearts." All true statements. Sad, but true. I open and respond to the rest of the texts and save my mother's for last.

> **Mom:** making mangú and queso frito for breakfast tomorrow after church

That makes me grin. It's not a signature dish in her culture, but it is in my dad's—plus it's my favorite—so she makes it from time to time when she can find good green plantains. I let her know I'll be there and stay in bed a little longer, focusing on Finn's scent on the sheets and pushing away the darkness that threatens to take me under.

CHAPTER FIFTY-FOUR

Josslyn

My phone buzzes for the third time with a call from Titus and I rush out of the quiet floor in the library.

"Hey."

"Did you ever speak to Tate?"

I frown. "No. Why?"

"He didn't show up at court today."

My stomach drops. "What?"

"He's not answering my calls. I don't know what to think." He lets out a breath, and I can tell he's walking briskly. Probably at the courthouse. "I went by his place the other day after you called and it looked like he had company, so I kept driving."

I walk to a column and lean against it for support. My very first thought is Onyx, then Mallory. There's no way Tate knows that we suspect anything. He never returned my calls, and the texts I sent were just asking him to call me back. This is very unlike Tate, though.

"I'll call his mom," I say.

"Keep me posted. I'm at the courthouse now covering for him." He hangs up.

I call Tate's mother, but it goes straight to voicemail.

"Hey, Virginia, it's Josslyn. I was just wondering if you know where Tate is. He didn't show up for work today and we're worried. Please call me back." I hang up and stay pressed against the wall for a few minutes.

Tate's parents are always traveling, which could explain the call going straight to voicemail. She's probably on a flight. Even as I tell myself that, something feels wrong. My knees are shaky when I start to walk to my car, but I manage to drive home. When I get to my building, I start moving my clothes to Finn's apartment. It's absolutely crazy, and fast, but moving in with him feels right. Oddly enough, my mother, the woman who, to this day, doesn't allow me to be alone with boys in my room, was the one who convinced me to do this.

I'm multitasking—carrying clothes in one hand and scheduling posts for my social media in the other—when I decide to do a live video. It's been a while since I've done one, and I feel like this is a milestone worth sharing. I haven't confirmed any rumors about me and Finn, but there are pictures of us everywhere now.

I hit record and start filling them in on what's happening, starting with basketball practice being on again. I answer some of the questions that pop up and keep talking. Finally, I leave my clothes on the bed and walk to the couch.

"So, I'm moving in with someone," I say, unable to fight my grin. "I've never lived with anyone before, so it'll be interesting, but when you know, you know, right?" I bite my lip. "Any advice?"

Comments start coming in so quickly, I barely have a chance to read them.

Is it Finn?

OMG IT'S FINN

DID HE PROPOSE?

HOLY SHIT YOU'RE MOVING IN WITH FINN BARLOW!! HOW DOES IT FEEL TO LIVE MY DREAM LIFE?!

That one makes me laugh.

"I'm not confirming," I say, "OR denying anything." I wink and laugh as I keep reading comments.

PLS LET IT BE FINN

WHAT DOES TIAGO THINK OF THIS?!

Josslyn Barlow has a nice ring to it!

I smile at that one and respond, "It does, doesn't it?"

I instantly wish I could take it back. Not because I don't mean it, but because they'll definitely think we're engaged. With so many comments coming in at once, I'm hoping most people will miss what I'm referring to. I tell them I'll update them again soon and log off. Finn won't see the video, since I have it set to disappear immediately and he's playing right now. I'm sure parts of it will be circulating later, but by then, his notifications will probably be inundated with tags on the picture of us I posted on my page. If I hadn't already told him I loved him, that would have been a declaration in itself.

I thought about doing that, but I don't like leaving those words unsaid. At first, when he told me nobody had ever said them to him, I thought he meant women he's been with, which makes sense. But the way his eyes light up and the way he holds me when I tell him I love him make me think he really meant nobody. That breaks my heart. He grew up with everything except the one thing money can't buy, which is the most important gift of all. I think about Mallory and my mood instantly sours. I click on the text message window with her name on it and read the last texts I sent.

> Me: i can't fucking believe you
>
> Me: i hate you
>
> Me: HATE YOU
>
> Me: you were supposed to be my friend
>
> Me: tate!?!?!?! Really, mallory?!?!!?!? FUCK YOUUUU

It only felt good to get that off my chest for a few minutes, and then I felt like shit, because even though her actions disgust me, her life was taken too soon. As if summoned, my mom's neighbor sends me a text.

Jack: it took forever but I found something. This is the clearest one I have. There are a LOT. Popular corner, huh? LOL

He attaches the video with the text. If he knew who I was looking for and why, he wouldn't find it so humorous, but I didn't give him any information to go on. I take a deep breath and play the video. There's a bug obstructing the view so I can barely see anything. I do see Mallory walking over there though. My stomach clenches at the sight.

It's eerie to see her alive and know this was just a few months before it all happened. A few months before she cut me out of her life for calling her mother. I wait and wait, and finally, the bug moves. It's still kind of hazy because of the rain, so I bring my phone closer to my face, as if that'll make a difference. My heart stops when I see her outfit—a short white dress with brown sandals.

I remember the exact day she wore that, because Tate and I got into a massive argument after this barbecue. My stomach coils as I watch her walk into the little nook. She waits, twisting her hands and doing a little shimmy like she can't contain her excitement. My stomach starts to hurt. I probably shouldn't watch this now that I know who she was hooking up with, but my morbid curiosity doesn't let me set it down.

I see a shadow on the ground before Tate appears and walks into the nook. His back is facing me, but I can still see when she throws herself at him and wraps her legs around his waist. *Oh my God.* It feels like all of the air has been sucked out of my lungs. I can't breathe, but I keep watching. He turns so they're sideways as he sets her down and presses his back against the wall. The phone starts to shake vigorously in my hands. I tell myself, plead with myself, to stop watching, but I can't.

Tate shakes his head, but she presses against him, pulls his face down to hers, and kisses him. Bile climbs up my throat and I cover my mouth quickly. Between the rain on the lens and the tears in my eyes, I can barely make out what's happening, but I see her put her hand between his legs. He pushes her away slightly and says something, but she goes right back to doing what she was doing. I never thought a heart could actually break, but it's what I feel mine doing.

The phone falls out of my hand and bangs against the hardwood. The betrayal is so strong. I've never felt anything like it. Not even when I saw him with Gracie in those videos, which he claims he was drugged in, but he's not drugged here. He's perfectly sober. They both are. Surprisingly, despite the ache in my chest, the tears never fall. I pick my phone back up, thank Jack, and send the video to Finn with a warning of what it's about. I jolt when my phone starts to vibrate in my hands and quickly answer the call from Tate's mom.

CHAPTER FIFTY-FIVE

Josslyn

VIRGINIA SOUNDS CONFUSED AND DESPERATE WHEN I ASK ABOUT Tate. Confused because she doesn't know where he is, and desperate because he'd never miss work.

"When was the last time you spoke to him?" I ask.

"Friday afternoon, I think. Maybe Saturday morning. I can't remember," she says, her voice nearly a whisper. "I would say he's ignoring your calls, but for him to not show up at work? Oh God, should we call the police?" she asks, panicked, and quickly adds, "He'd be so upset and embarrassed if we did that."

My heart pounds hard against my rib cage. I'm so glad I'm sitting down. *Should we call the cops?* My instinct is yes, but she's not wrong. If Tate is fine and on some kind of drug binge somewhere and the police and media got involved, he'd be mortified.

A week ago, I would have laughed if anyone told me Tate was doing recreational drugs, but now I'm not so sure. If I'm being honest, I don't give a fuck if he's mortified over this. I want him to be mortified for what he did to me. Virginia starts to cry, and my chest squeezes. His parents are good people and they've already been through so much.

"I'll call you back," she says quickly. "I'm going to try calling now."

She hangs up before I can say another word, and I wait with my heart in my throat. *Fuck*. Dame, Livie, and Finn were right. I am too nice, and I do care too much, but I refuse to believe that's a bad thing. The world is full of assholes and I refuse to be one of them. Besides, Virginia is the kind of person who cries during commercials. I may get emotional about some things, but not even I do that. When my phone buzzes with a call, my stomach sinks. That was too quick for a phone call.

"It went straight to voicemail," she says. "I don't know what to do. I'm going to take the first flight available."

"I think we should call the cops," I say.

"He'd hate that. You know he'd hate that."

"I know, but what if something happened to him?" I ask quietly, not wanting to stress her out more.

Of course, that makes her cry harder. I hate it. I can't even imagine being a mother and having to deal with this.

"Can you go by his house?" she asks. "I know it's a lot to ask of you after what happened, but—"

"I'll drive there right now."

"Please call me back," she says, her voice breaking.

"I will."

※

There's a sinking feeling in the pit of my stomach as I drive to Tate's townhouse. I know he won't be there, unless ... I shiver and push the thought aside. Please God, don't let this be a repeat of my father. Please, *please*, I plead internally as tears fill my eyes. It's been a while since I believed in anything, which horrifies my mother, but right now, it's the only thing I can think to do. Everything in me is telling me to call the cops, but I'm going to honor Virginia's wishes. For now. I get to his house and park behind his car. After I locate the hidden key, I take a breath and walk inside quickly. It's not like I have time to mentally prepare myself for anything.

"Tate?" I call out as I walk around. "TATE?"

I look everywhere and find nothing, which brings me comfort and unease. I even check the shower but it doesn't look like he's used it today. His bed is perfectly made, but it always is unless he's in it. Thoughts of me in bed with him immediately lead to thoughts of Mallory in bed with him and I get that sick feeling in my stomach again. I rush down the stairs, but something catches my eye when I walk toward the door and makes me pause. I was in such a rush, I didn't even notice that he still has pictures of us together hanging on the wall. I'd framed them one night and put them up myself, because his walls were so bare and he was waiting for the "perfect painting." In one picture, we're both smiling at the camera with our snowsuits on. It was taken during a family trip to Colorado.

My mother got a big cabin and didn't allow us to share a room. As if that was going to stop Tate from sneaking in at night. Below it, he's spinning me around in the middle of a dance floor at a wedding we attended. The last is from his grandfather's farm. I'm dressed in overalls and a red, plaid shirt, donning pigtails and a cowboy hat I borrowed from his grandpa.

Despite everything, it makes me smile. I'd never been to a working farm before and I recorded some of my time there, which of course meant I needed to dress the part. It's the same picture I'd posted on social media and took down when the Gracie thing surfaced. A quick calculation tells me he was already hooking up with Mallory when we took this, and that instantly sours my mood again. I tear my eyes away and start calling his mother as I walk back to my car.

"Are your parents home?" I ask Virginia, after I tell her I found nothing here.

She gasps. "They're in Florida, but Tate could be there! Sometimes he goes over there to decompress!"

I've been parked in the driveway staring at his car for the last five minutes. He normally keeps his red truck in his one-car garage, but it's empty. And he never drives his beloved Porsche to the backcountry.

"I'll call Joe," she says and hangs up.

If I remember correctly, the farm has about twenty employees and they're usually around. Unease continues to grip my gut. Even if Tate went over there, it's not like him to stay. It's definitely not like him to disappear. I shut my eyes and lean back in my seat. I look at the time and curse. I can't miss practice today, but this feels important. Too important.

I think about the last conversation I had with him and panic rises in my chest again. Mostly, he recounted what he remembered about the night those videos were taken of him and Gracie. It wasn't something I necessarily wanted to hear, but he did clarify that nothing had happened between them before, and that he didn't think he would have done anything that night if he'd been sober. Obviously, that's bullshit. I look at the time again, slam a hand on the steering wheel, and start driving toward the farm.

CHAPTER FIFTY-SIX

Josslyn

PRACTICE STARTS IN FOUR HOURS, WHICH GIVES ME PLENTY OF TIME to go to the farm, look around, ask the employees about Tate, and come back. For everyone's sake, I hope he's there. I try to think of places he could be. Maybe Onyx? My stomach twists at the thought, but I push it aside. I can be angry after I know he's okay. It takes about thirty-five minutes to get there. The cows and most of the other animals are about half a mile from the house itself. I spot two trucks that I assume belong to employees and keep driving until I see the road that leads to the main house.

I turn into the driveway, but stop when that uneasy feeling coils in the pit of my stomach again. I look at my phone. Finn and Damian are at their game, which is only about an hour away. I grab my phone to text Finn, but my fingers are shaking so hard I don't even know what I type, so I call Olivia instead as I drive further in. Goosebumps ripple through me when I see the familiar red truck. Part of me wants to leave and let Virginia deal with this, but my gut tells me I can't.

"What's up?" she says. "You wanna ride—"

"Livie." I cut her off sharply, the phone shaking hard in my hands. "I'm going to share my location with you right now. If I don't call you in thirty minutes, call the police and have them come here."

She doesn't speak for a moment. "Josslyn, what the fuck are you talking about?! Where are you?!"

"Just do it. Thirty minutes. No more than thirty minutes," I say and hang up.

I would call now, but I don't know if there's anything to call about. As soon as I put the car in park, I get out and walk briskly to the truck, which is empty. I rush to the front door, try the knob and find it locked, so I start knocking. It takes me pounding about ten times before it finally opens. My jaw drops and I practically jump back when I see Tate. A messy beard covers his face, and he appears to be pale and sweaty.

His eyes are puffy and bloodshot, and the left one has a purplish ring around it. For a moment, I can't breathe. I can't move. As far as I know, Tate has never been in a fight. And the clothes he's wearing … an oversized t-shirt that's been ripped on the left side, revealing a large cloth that looks like it's covering a wound. His arms are covered in scratches, but it's the rope marks on his neck that terrify me.

"What are you doing here?!" he seethes in a harsh whisper.

"What happened to you?!" I ask, my eyes wide as I glance at his wound. "What happened?!" I demand again.

He jaw tics and as he glares, he whisper-shouts. "Keep your fucking voice down."

My stomach drops. I blink at his tone and the fear in his expression. I lower my voice and ask, "What happened—"

"You need to get the fuck out of here *now*," he demands quietly. "Leave, Joss. Leave." He inhales shakily and his blue eyes fill with unshed tears. "Please leave. Go!"

My heart is slamming so hard inside my chest, I can barely breathe. Every bone in my body is telling me to heed his warning and leave, but he looks tattered. Suddenly, I'm wishing I'd told Livie ten minutes instead of thirty. I study him again.

"Go!" he urges again, eyes wide.

I take another step back, hoping my eyes convey what I'm thinking, "I'm going to go get help. I'll get you out of whatever this is."

I'm turning around when I hear a familiar voice say, "Are you fucking kidding? You promised you'd stay put!"

My entire body goes rigid. So many things happen at once—my jaw drops, my palms start to sweat, and my heart pounds even harder. So hard that I think it'll truly give out on me. I tell myself to react. To turn around or scream or do something, but my body remains frozen. I hear them arguing. I don't know how much time passes before I'm finally able to move, but when I do, I'm staring straight into Mallory's brown eyes.

CHAPTER FIFTY-SEVEN

Josslyn

I don't understand what the fuck I'm looking at right now. An apparition, maybe, because there's no way ... there's *no fucking way*. She looks different—her long, straight dirty blonde hair is dyed black and cut to her chin, and her clothes are baggy and casual—but it's definitely Mallory.

"You died," I say, mouth hanging open.

I look at Tate, who looks miserable and terrified.

He shakes his head. "I didn't know."

"Come inside," Mallory says, pushing Tate out of the way and opening the door for me like I'm here for fucking lunch.

Even in my dumbfounded state, I know that's not a good idea. The way Tate looked when he opened the door and told me to leave demands I go get help. The fear in his expression begs me to run. Heart in my throat, I glance to the driveway and back, trying to calculate how many steps there are between me and my car, but Mallory takes a step forward and lifts a gun to Tate's temple.

"Come inside or he dies," she says simply.

Tate's entire body visibly starts to shake and I stop breathing and walk inside. She slams the door and I turn so my back isn't facing her. Someone clears their throat, and my eyes fly in that direction. My stomach hollows when I see the man sitting there. *John.*

"Joss, you know John," Mallory says with a hint of amusement.

He's dressed in jeans and a t-shirt. When his eyes meet mine, he doesn't look pleased, which gives me nothing to work with. Is he also her hostage? No. Tate is a hostage. He's wounded and looks like he could pass out at any moment. John is holding a magazine. He looks … fine. Worried, but fine.

"Why?" I ask in a horrified whisper. John looks at the magazine in his hands.

"Have a seat," Mallory says, waving the gun at the loveseat near the door.

My entire body shakes as I sit down. Tate hisses in pain as he sits beside me and I cross my arms tightly to keep from shaking. It occurs to me as I glance over at him that he's been here with her for a while now. Hours? Days?

I look at the bloody gauze on his abdomen, and look at Mallory. "He needs help."

"So sweet of you to worry about him even now," she says, sitting in the chair across from us. "Don't worry, I didn't shoot him and it's not as bad as it looks."

"He needs help!" I say, shouting at John, who flicks his gaze up and ignores me.

"What the fuck is wrong with you?!"

Mallory points the gun in my direction, and I jolt with a gasp. "Don't speak to him."

She lowers the gun and sets it on her knee, pointing it toward us. Heart in my throat, I eye it warily, then look up to find her staring at me. She looks sober, which somehow makes this all the more terrifying. So many questions pop into my mind at once, but when I open my mouth, only one comes out.

"How?" I ask. "They identified you. They used your *teeth* to identify you!"

"Yes, I know. You'd be surprised how cheap it is to get them replaced in Europe." The proud smile she wears, showing all of her teeth are intact, makes my stomach turn.

"*Why?*" I whisper.

Tate inhales sharply as he adjusts in the seat beside me, and my heart stops for a moment when I glance over. He looks so uncomfortable.

"Can I have water?" he asks hoarsely. "Please?"

John shuts the magazine and leaves. He has two water bottles in his hands when he comes back and hands one to each of us. I thank him automatically. Tate grunts his disapproval, but uncaps it and starts drinking. I notice they've already been uncapped, and lower mine. I don't trust them not to have drugged them. Maybe that's why Tate looks that way. John takes a seat again and wordlessly goes back to his magazine.

"Is he making you do this?" I ask Mallory as John sits down and picks up the magazine.

She scoffs. "God, no. Let's just say we have a mutually beneficial understanding."

"Why would you do this?" I ask. "Do you know how difficult this has been on us?"

"Yes, I received all your lovely texts," Mallory says. My stomach sinks. She smiles. "You were pretty upset to learn about me and Tate."

"Tell her what you did," Tate says between gritted teeth.

Mallory looks at him. "Which part?"

"About Gracie! About the drugs!"

She rolls her eyes. "Tate was drugged the night he made out with Gracie. She was an easy target. God, she hates you so much."

"Gracie knew?!"

"No!" Mallory laughs. "John was there that night and got in her ear about how hurt you'd be if she went after Tate," she says.

I look at John again, hoping my glare burns holes through his stupid face.

"I told you," Tate says.

"Oh, shut up! Don't act like you were a fucking saint," Mallory says, eyes narrowed on him. "You let her kiss you before the drugs even kicked in. You always were an easy lay."

Despite everything, her words make my stomach turn.

"You ruined everything!" he shouts.

"She never loved you!" she screams. "I gave you everything she wouldn't and you still chose her!"

I inhale sharply. "Is that what this is about?"

"You used me!" Tate shouts. "You blackmailed me into hooking up with you!"

"I didn't blackmail you into joining Onyx! I didn't blackmail you into fucking those girls!" she shouts. "You loved every fucking second you spent with me!"

I press the bottle of water to my stomach and my other hand over my mouth, suddenly feeling very sick.

"I was going to marry her!" Tate shouts back, and I hold my breath now, thinking she might point that gun at him and shoot him.

Her jaw clenches. "She loves my brother, you fucking idiot!"

I gag and press my hand tighter over my mouth. Oh God. Finn. This is going to destroy Finn. He's been living with so much guilt.

"How could you do this to us? To Finn?" I ask when I finally regain my composure. "He was trying to get justice for you. We both were!"

"And, what, you found justice in his dick?" she spits, eyes narrowed. The venom in her tone and the way her grip tightens on the gun make me freeze. "You felt guilty for leaving me there to die so you turned to him for comfort?"

"That's not what happened." I wipe my eyes.

"Maybe not." She purses her lips. "My brother has only ever cared about four people. He *never* cares about women, but of course, he had to fall for you. It's like you have us all under a fucking spell."

"You act like I planned this!"

"That's the thing, Josslyn. You don't have to plan anything. Everything just works out perfectly for you. Always."

Anger hits me with a force and I shudder. "You're a fucking BARLOW, Mallory. YOU COULD HAVE HAD EVERYTHING! You HAD everything!"

"You know, my brother didn't miss a game after I died," she says, ignoring me. "He missed two practices when he flew home and went right back to Vegas like it was nothing."

I wipe tears away again. "What do you want from me?"

"You got too close to the truth," she says, glancing at John briefly. "We have a plan. I was going to disappear and John was going to file an insurance claim. Everything was fine until Leo started sniffing around and sending you footage of that night."

"Mallory," John warns. It's the first thing he's said since I got here.

"I don't understand," I say. "If this is about me getting too close, why not go to my apartment? Why not get rid of Leo?"

She laughs. "You do know my brother has had a private investigator following you around for almost two years now, right?"

I feel the color drain from my face. I don't even ask how she knows that. She seems to know too much about everything.

"I knew you'd come running when Tate didn't show up for work," she says when no one speaks. "I mean, it was either that or the police, but I just knew you'd come here." She laughs again. "Does my brother know where you are?"

That seems like a trick question. If I say yes, she'll know I've already alerted the police. I take a sip of water to ease the dryness in my throat.

"What are you going to do to me?" I ask.

"I'm not sure yet," she says. "I'm not sure I can bring myself to kill you." She looks at John. "But he will." John's grip tightens on the magazine, but he doesn't look up. "I have too much dirt on John and too much money for him to disobey me. Maybe I am a Barlow, after all."

"You were my friend. I loved you. I—"

"Not enough!" she shouts and bangs the gun against her knee, making me flinch.

"What is enough for you, Mallory?" I demand. "I invited you into my home, I took you to my mother's house for the holidays, I listened to you and comforted you and—"

"I WANTED MORE! I wanted you to notice me!" she yells, her voice shaking slightly with emotion.

"I didn't know!" I respond and stop talking when my tongue starts to feel heavy.

I lift my hand to wipe my face again, but it feels like I'm trying to move a boulder. Panic spreads through me. This can't be happening. *This can't be happening.* I turn my face and notice Tate is slumped against the couch, passed out. Everything is spinning and seems to be going in slow motion, but I manage to look at Mallory again.

"I had to drug the water to keep you from trying to leave," she says, answering my question. "Don't worry, you won't lose consciousness this time."

This time. *This time.* A tingle spreads through my body, leaving goosebumps on my flesh. A sob threatens to shut my airways.

"It was you," I whisper. "You were the one who drugged me at Onyx that night."

The expression on her face confirms it. I feel so sick. I pitch forward as I start to heave. Nothing but spit comes out, but my movements propel me off the couch, toward the coffee table. I fall in a thump, but I don't feel it. I don't feel anything. My vision blurs with new tears. I think about all the times I tried to be a good friend to her. All those nights I declined to go out with my teammates because she was having a bad day and needed a friend. The times I bailed on Tate because she was depressed and didn't want to see anyone.

"I took you home," Mallory says, her voice far, far away. "Got you there safely and didn't touch you. Much."

I feel queasy and heave again. And again. Nothing comes out.

"Don't worry, I didn't do anything too crazy," she says. "I guess you've bewitched us all, Joss."

"People only like the *idea of me*," I say, or try to say. My words come out garbled. Still, I try again. "People only like the idea of me. *You have to know that.*"

I can't make out her response, and soon, everything goes dark.

CHAPTER FIFTY-EIGHT

Finn

I STAND UP AFTER TYING MY SKATES AND HOP ONCE, THEN AGAIN. I haven't been able to check my phone all day, and I smile when I see a text Josslyn sent me a few hours ago.

Josslyn: Indidfudhf

I frown and try to decipher it. It has to be some kind of acronym. After a moment, I text back.

Me: is that an acronym?

Me: coach is walking in. i'll call you when i finish. I love you

Coach P starts talking, so I put my phone down and check the tape on my stick as I turn around to listen. He gives us the usual rundown, pep talk, and we're off. We haven't lost a game since Carolina, so we're in a winning mindset. I score Bar Down right out of the gate, and not long after, Hammie scores. At intermission, we're winning 3–0 and feeling pretty confident.

"Barlow cheesed the fuck out of the goalie," one of my teammates says laughing.

WHEN WE LIED

"Don't take your eyes off 85," Coach P says. "He can dangle and he had that deke on you, Fletch."

Dame nods. "I'll stay on him."

Another teammate laughs. "85 has eggs in his pockets."

"Coach P is right," I say after downing the drink I'm given. "He can dangle. His passing execution is off, though."

"Yeah, it's like he loses concentration when he's right in front of Lundy."

We talk strategy for a couple of minutes before everyone goes off to do their own thing—retape, bathroom, etc. Once I'm done with my tape, I check my phone. I don't always do it during intermission, but I had no one to check on before.

"Dude, it's official-official," Lundy says behind me. "Barlow's off the market."

I frown and shoot him a questioning look over my shoulder.

He laughs. "Do you not look at your girlfriend's accounts?"

"He doesn't stalk her like Froggy," another player says, and I automatically look for Froggy because what the fuck?

"Bathroom break," Hammie says, grinning as he looks at his phone. "Holy shit. Good picture, too."

My pulse quickens as I reach for my phone. I have seven missed calls from an unknown number, but I ignore them and go to Josslyn's page. There, at the top, is a picture of us together. The guys keep talking and joking about our wedding, but I'm too caught up in the fact that she made this official. OFFICIAL. I don't even bother smothering the smile that plays on my lips. To my left, I hear a commotion and see Damian drop his bucket and stick, and practically run out of the room.

"Someone needs the bathroom," one of the guys says.

They laugh again, but my mind is still on Josslyn's last post. From the moment I got social media, I've probably only commented on a handful of posts, but my fingers fly as I comment on hers now. I repost the picture on my own page with a simple caption: MINE. Once I exit out of the app, I look at my missed calls and texts.

Unknown number: it's olivia. Call me NOW

Unknown number: call me as soon as you see this

Unknown number: emergency

My stomach drops. I press her number and listen to it ring once, twice, three times. Finally, she answers.

"Ohmygodthankgod," she says in a rush. The background is loud wherever she is. "Josslyn…" Her words break and my stomach twists harder than ever before.

She hasn't even finished her sentence and I'm already sitting down and taking off my skates.

"What happened? Where is she?" I ask, trying to keep calm despite the chaos inside me.

"She … she went to Tate's," she says, and my skin suddenly feels impossibly tight. When she speaks again, she does so quickly, "She called me earlier and told me that if she didn't call her in thirty minutes, I should call 911. She sent me her location, and I searched and it's Tate's family farm. The police have been there but … she's been in the house for a while and they're calling this a hostage situation." Her voice breaks.

I stop breathing. Stop moving. Stop existing, as all of that sinks in. She went to Tate's farm and now he's holding her hostage? I can barely wrap my head around that. *Why would she go there?* Why the fuck…

"Send me the location," I demand and hang up the phone.

I call Josslyn. I know it won't do any good, but I call anyway. Behind me, I hear my teammates talking, but their words are just noise. Anything that isn't about her is just noise. A body crashes into me and I startle and look at Damian sitting beside me. He has the same worried expression on his face I'm sure I'm wearing.

"Did you…"

"Olivia called." I focus on taking off my gear.

"Barlow, what the hell are you doing?" Coach P asks,

walking up to me. He looks at me, then Dame, and back at me. "What the hell is going on? Why are you—"

"I need to go."

"We're in the middle of a game!"

"This is an emergency." I stand up, whip my undershirt over my head, and spray deodorant before putting on another one.

"What…"

"My sister's being held hostage by her ex-boyfriend," Damian manages as he takes off his skates.

Coach P gapes at him. For a moment, I think he's going to complain about being down two men, but he blinks and asks, "Is she okay?"

"We don't know," Damian says, while I say, "She better be."

My stomach turns. *She better be.*

"Well…" Coach shakes his head and looks over at our teammates who have stopped talking. "Family emergency!" he shouts and starts clapping. "Let's go. Let's go." He sets a hand on my shoulder and squeezes it before he walks away.

I pick up the pace, grab my shit, and catch Hamilton's eye as he walks out of the bathroom. He frowns when he sees me, and looks at Damian behind me.

"Josslyn," I say simply and start walking to the door.

He runs over, his skates thumping on the carpet. He grabs my arm when he reaches me. "Is she okay?"

I swallow hard. I can't even look at him because if I see the sympathy on his face right now, I'll fucking lose it. Instead, I nod and walk out. Damian follows. I see the shocked faces from our opposing team and keep walking. Some ask if we're okay, but we ignore them. I've never, not once, missed or walked out on a game.

Not even when I was playing for the world's biggest asshole of a coach who benched me—even though I was the best player—for saying I could coach better than he could. I didn't even miss a game when Mallory died. I felt guilty as fuck in the aftermath. But Josslyn? I don't even know the full story, but it doesn't matter. They can write me off for the rest of the year, or kick me off the team, and I won't care.

Dread pools in my gut as we step outside. I'm trying very hard to not let my mind go to a dark place or think about all the lovers' quarrels that have led to murder-suicides. I swallow down all of that uncertainty and shut my eyes briefly. She'll be fine. Everything will be fine. It has to be. There's no universe in which I exist without her.

CHAPTER FIFTY-NINE

Finn

WE STAND OUTSIDE AND LOOK AROUND LIKE A CAR IS GOING TO magically appear for us.

"I'll get a car," Damian says after a moment.

While he does that, I call the one person I swore to myself I'd never ask a favor from. Funny how in times of need, everything becomes water under a bridge.

"Finn?" he says, his surprise obvious.

"I need the heli."

"Where are you?"

I tell him where I am, and he starts yelling out orders and telling them to get the helicopter to me. He tells me where to go, and I tell Damian, who informs the very small car that just arrived.

"What's going on?" my father asks.

"Josslyn's being held hostage." I swallow hard to get rid of the knot in my throat, but it doesn't seem to be going anywhere.

He's quiet for a moment. "Do you know where?"

"The Ford farm," I say. "Police are there now." I shut my eyes for a moment and swallow the knot in my throat and what's left of my pride. "I don't have Ruiz's number. Can you—"

"I'll call him and tell him the helicopter is landing on the property," my father says. "You know they have their protocols."

"Yeah, well, they can fuck right off with those."

He chuckles. "Spoken like a true Barlow."

"We'll be at the airport in four minutes," I say.

"Hugh will be there in ten."

We hang up at the same time and the pain in my stomach worsens.

"I just don't understand how this happened," I say quietly as I stare at my phone.

"What the fuck was she doing there?! God, my sister's a fucking idiot," Damian seethes.

Under different circumstances, I would jump to her defense because Josslyn's not an idiot, but this is an undoubtedly idiotic thing to do. *Why did she go there? Why not wait for me?* I asked her to wait for me before she did anything. I've only been gone two fucking days. I can only assume this means Tate was responsible for my sister's death, but if she believed that, why would she be there alone? I rub the pain in my chest in hopes that it'll lessen. It doesn't.

"Dad said Tate didn't show up to work this morning. He had court," Dame says, looking at his phone and answering when it buzzes. "Yeah. We're on our way. Me and Finn. In a helicopter." He pauses to listen. "Well, he's her boyfriend." He exhales. "I'll see you when I get there."

My jaw clenches. There's no doubt in my mind his father was asking why I'm involved.

"Titus better get used to seeing me around," I say when he hangs up.

Dame's brows rise. "We're overprotective of her."

"Trust me, I've noticed," I mutter. "Though you haven't given me any issues."

He looks at me for a moment, and I can see there's a slew of things he's holding back from saying.

"You love her," he says finally. "But if it turns out this is about your quest for vengeance and my sister gets hurt, we're going to be having a very different conversation."

I swallow hard and look away. I don't bother telling him that I won't survive it if something happens to her. Josslyn told him mostly everything about Mallory and the things we've found so far. She left out the parts that would make me look bad, because that's the kind of person she is. She accepts me for who I am and doesn't hold my mistakes against me. *God, let her be okay. I'll do anything. Any fucking thing. Just let her be okay.*

Everything happens in a blur and suddenly we're in the helicopter on our way to the farm. The sun has already set, but there's enough light for us to see the fall leaves underneath us. Even if Hugh hadn't said we were here, the scene beneath us—the rows of police cars and lights and camera crews—would have alerted us. As we land, my phone buzzes and I open Olivia's texts.

> **Olivia Nassir:** one of the employees told me the house is always unlocked. And the back lock is broken and doesn't shut properly. Police haven't done shit to go in there

"Mr. Barlow," Hugh says once he lands, and turns to me with a suit jacket. "Your father asked me to give this to you."

It takes me a moment to process what he's handing me, and another to put it on. Hamilton told me once that Damian had a dark past, and he was there when Josslyn found her father, so I know he's seen some shit, which is probably why he doesn't give the gun a second glance.

We hop out of the helicopter and start walking fast. It's pitch black here, but they have a bright light pointed at the house that helps illuminate our way. Despite that, I nearly stumble when a man on a megaphone starts bargaining for Josslyn's freedom. A handful of police officers storm us, making us halt. I'm about to shoulder past them, when a man in a suit walks up from behind them.

"Finn," Chief Rivera says with a sharp nod.

I look toward the house. "What's happening?"

"Are they ... have you seen Josslyn?" Dame asks.

"She stood by the window an hour ago and they've assured us she's unharmed."

"An hour ago? How long has she been here?" Damian asks.

"Since one thirty or two."

I blink, a rush of disbelief and pain shooting through me. "One thirty *or two*? You don't even know?"

"She called—"

"She's been in there for eight hours, and you guys are still out here!? Have you even tried to go inside?!" I ask, my voice rising.

"Our officers—"

"I don't give a fuck about your officers and your goddamn protocols!"

Damian answers his phone and tells whoever it is that we just got here. "Yeah, I'll be right over."

"Go be with your parents," I say.

"I'll be right back," he responds and starts jogging toward the front of the house with two officers at his sides.

I look at Captain Rivera. "What the hell have you been doing all day?!"

"These things take time," he says, "But we know she's safe in there. We have audio around the house." He takes out his phone at the same time that a man starts speaking into a megaphone.

"Why is he addressing them like they're both involved?" I ask when the megaphone shuts off. "Josslyn is being held captive in there!"

He raises an eyebrow. "You know that for sure?"

"Of course I…" I take a step back, frowning. "You think she's part of this?!"

"There are three people in there right now. I don't know what to think, but in my experience, if it was only the ex-boyfriend who was going to kill her, he already would have, and by now, he would've turned the gun on himself as well."

He looks apologetic, but the way he speaks about it is chilling. Four people? What the motherfucking fuck. I instantly think of Onyx. If Tate brought that sex group here … I clench my fists. I'm going to fucking murder him. I brush past Rivera and start walking, not even pausing when I hear the click-clacks of their holsters behind me. If they draw their guns and aim for me, I'll be dead, and they'll be fucked.

"I don't think any of you wants to find out what happens if you shoot a Barlow in this fucking city," I say loudly without even looking back.

I hear a string of curses and suddenly Rivera is beside me, grabbing my arm.

"Jesus Christ. Is that a gun underneath your jacket?" Rivera asks, eyes wide.

I yank my arm away and glare at him. "I will fucking *end you* if you try to stop me from going in there."

He knows it's true. My father is the only reason he's the chief of police. He's the reason he's on this farm. My last name is the only reason I was able to land a fucking helicopter here while this is happening. In any other city, they would've put me in handcuffs and in the back of a car. Not in Fairview, though. We have dirt on every single person of importance in this city.

We make and break careers. And while I don't normally use my last name for gain, since my presence does the job for me, I will proudly use it to swing my dick around right now. We walk until we're a few feet from the house and I stop to study it. Goddamn it. If this was a movie, I'd barge in there, kill Tate, and take Josslyn. I need to be smart about this, though. I know I won't be able to accurately shoot him if he uses Josslyn as a shield, or takes off running. I've been to the gun range many times, but shooting a piece of paper and a moving target are wildly different. I take another step, but Rivera stops me by telling me he has something to show me.

"We have ears," he says and plays an audio clip.

My heart stops beating when I hear Josslyn speaking. "Seriously, you don't have to do this. I don't understand what you want!" she says. The sound of her desperation and tears makes my heart break. "I did so much for you. I tried to help you. I tried to…" She starts to cry. "JUST TELL ME WHAT YOU WANT!"

No response.

"At least let Tate out! His wound will get infected! He'll die if he doesn't get help!" Josslyn shouts.

Wait. *What the fuck?* My stomach sinks. If Tate is hurt and she's pleading, he's definitely not behind this. *But who the hell is?* My mind goes back to the people at Onyx. I think about the way Leo looked at her and my pulse starts ringing in my ears.

"Please let him go," Josslyn cries.

"It really is so sweet of you to care about him even after he cheated on you," a female voice says.

My blood runs cold.

"LET HIM GO!" Josslyn shouts. "PLEASE!"

"Are you willing to do anything for his freedom?" the female asks.

My heart is pounding so hard and I swear I'm hearing things. I must be.

Josslyn stays quiet.

The female laughs. "Are you willing to … let me fuck you?"

My breath gets caught in my throat. One minute I'm standing upright, and the next my hands are on my knees and I'm gasping for air. She speaks again, and my stomach clenches hard. I glance up at Rivera.

"That's my sister," I manage through gulps of air.

He frowns deeply. "What?"

"That woman speaking is my sister."

"Are you going to let me touch you?" Mallory asks. "Willingly."

"Please don't," Josslyn says brokenly.

My head is spinning. Everything hits me at once—my sister is alive. My sister, who is obsessed with Josslyn, is alive and threatening to … oh fuck. I push away the sick feeling that threatens to overtake me, and start running toward the house.

CHAPTER SIXTY

Finn

I TAKE MY SHOES OFF AND TOSS THEM ON THE GRASS, IGNORING RIVERA calling my name as I try the door. As Olivia said, it's unlocked and barely even shut. Anger shoots through me, and I glance over my shoulder to glare at the sorry-ass captain. Protocol or not, the fact that they stand out there twiddling their thumbs while my girlfriend could be injured is fucking maddening.

I lift my jacket, grab the gun, and click off the safety after I shut the door as quietly as I can. Bile climbs up my throat when I hear my sister's voice and I'm forced to take a deep breath, and another to get rid of my nerves. I can't see them, but Rivera said there are three people in here, so I prepare myself to shoot, the way I do at the range. They say, if you aim a gun at someone, you have to be prepared to shoot. Under different circumstances, this would be a no-brainer, but *my sister*? If it comes down to that, I know I'd choose Josslyn. Always. Any day. Over anyone.

A wave of guilt crashes through me and I swallow hard thinking about the way I've failed Mallory time and time again. The guilt is quickly replaced by anger, and I breathe through it and go to the place in my mind that only allows rational thought. Finally, I turn the corner and stand at the threshold. I take in everything—Tate and Josslyn on the couch. Tate's head is lolled on Josslyn's shoulder. My sister is kneeling between Josslyn's legs, and John is sitting on the opposite couch. Mallory cut and dyed her hair the way she had it when she went through a quick rebellious goth phase in middle school. My heart squeezes painfully. All this time ... HOW is this even possible?!

"I'll make it good for you. I promise," Mallory coos as she runs her hands up Josslyn's legs, and I see fucking red.

No one gets to touch Josslyn that way. *No one.*

"GET THE FUCK AWAY FROM HER. NOW!" I shout pointing the gun at the back of my sister's head.

Mallory turns around, wide-eyed, with a loud gasp, and picks up the gun next to her as she stands and faces me. John sits up suddenly, and I position myself in a way that I can keep an eye on him and aim if he moves.

"Finn." My sister's eyes go wider as she looks at the gun I'm aiming at her. "Are you going to shoot me?" she asks, her voice a whisper.

Her big brown eyes fill with tears, and for a moment, images of her at every stage flash through my mind. That doe-eyed look has gotten her many things over the years. I glance at Josslyn and my heart sinks. Her wobbling lip, the sadness in her eyes. There's no doubt in my mind that if something happens to this girl, I'll die. Literally, physically, and metaphorically, I will cease to exist.

The megaphone turns on and the man starts speaking again. "Please call us. We will give you anything. Everything will be okay."

"What the *fuck*, Mallory?!"

For a moment, she just stares. "Did you really care that I died or were you just using it as an excuse to get close to *my* friend?"

"Are you fucking..." I say, and pause. Is that what this is about? *Attention?* "Of course I fucking cared! How could you ... why would you ... they identified your body."

"I know," she says, chin wobbling. "I ... I had to have my teeth knocked out."

My head starts to spin again. "Why? why would you do this?"

"I wanted out!" she wails.

"Out of what!?" I shout, my anger overpowering my disbelief. My heart launches into my throat when the gun at her side slips a little before she grips it tightly again. "Put the gun down, Mal."

"What are you even doing here?" she asks, her eyes filling with tears. "You're supposed to be out of town! You're supposed to be in the middle of a game! You NEVER leave games!"

From the couch, Josslyn makes a light whimpering sound. I don't dare take my eyes off my sister. I try to think of something to say that might appease her, but come up short because what she's saying is true. I don't leave games or practices or meetings, but for Josslyn … I'd leave the league in a fucking heartbeat. My breath hitches when Mallory shakily moves the gun and points it at my chest. Josslyn wails for her to stop. Stoic mindset and all, being on the other side of a gun is fucking terrifying, especially when the person holding it is unhinged.

"Come on, Mal," I coax despite the riot of emotions inside me. "Put the gun down."

"You first," she says, hands shaking wildly now. "You put yours down first."

"You *know* I don't want to shoot you."

"But you would?" she squeaks. "You'd choose her over me?"

I'd choose her over anyone, I want to shout, but don't.

"This isn't a competition," I say instead.

Mallory blinks hard and fast, new tears streaming down her face. "I just wanted a fresh start," she says, her lip wobbling. "I just wanted a break from this life. From Mom and Dad. From Fairview society," she cries, the gun shaking harder.

"You can have that. I'll help you. I know you hate it, but you must have come back for a reason," I manage to say, even though I don't think I've breathed in five minutes.

"I didn't *want* to come back," she sobs, lowering the gun to her side. I take a step forward, but her eyes narrow and she starts to lift it again, so I step back again. "I didn't want to come back, but then Josslyn got back together with Tate, and then … then you…" She glares through her tears. "How could you do that to me?!"

"Do what?"

"Fall for her!"

Fuck. *How could I not?*

I swallow back those words. "My relationship with Josslyn has nothing to do with you."

"You took her from me!" she shouts.

"I was never yours!" Josslyn shouts, her voice hoarse from screaming.

"YOU WOULD HAVE BEEN!" Mallory roars, her expression angry as she glances momentarily at Josslyn. "I just needed time! I needed time!"

Fear chokes me. I've read enough horrifying accounts of jealous murder-suicides to know nothing good can come from this. There's no doubt in my mind that if she wasn't my sister, I would have already put a bullet in her chest.

"Time for what?" I ask warily, wanting to keep her talking.

"Please get Tate out of here. He's going to die," Josslyn pleads brokenly as tears fall down her face. Her eyes move to mine. "Finn. Please get him out."

I glance at my sister. "Let him go, Mal."

"You hate him," she sneers. "Why do you care whether or not he dies?"

"*You* don't hate him," I respond. "I read your journal. You love him. You don't want him to die."

"He wants her!" she shouts.

"WELL, HE CAN'T HAVE HER!" I roar.

That seems to take her by surprise.

"Mallory, I can take—" John starts.

"He went back to her after I died!" Mallory shouts, ignoring him.

"You didn't fucking die," I say through gritted teeth.

"He thought you were dead," Josslyn says. "Tate loved you. He grieved for you. We weren't even together then."

"I told you I did," Tate says hoarsely, his eyes opening and shutting heavily as the side of his body crashes against Josslyn's.

The movement lifts his shirt and I see a large white cloth on his side covered in blood. I'm not sure what kind of injury that is, but from the look of him, I know he won't make it through the night if he stays here. My sister's not wrong. I wouldn't necessarily care if he survives, but Josslyn would, and the last thing I want is for her to try to take the blame for another death.

"Mallory. Let him go," I say sternly.

"Please, Mal," Tate rasps.

Mallory's face falls. She lowers the gun, but keeps her grip firm on it. "You chose her," she says, turning slightly to Tate with new tears forming in her eyes. "If you hadn't cheated with Gracie, you'd still be together."

My jaw clenches.

"You had me drugged and set me up that night with Gracie," Tate slurs.

My brows shoot up as understanding of what she did to Tate dawns on me. That's actually … pretty clever.

"If you hadn't left maybe—" Tate says, his voice hoarse.

"You'd still be together!" my sister shouts. "And I'd still be second choice! I was always second choice!"

"Joss and I broke up before you died in that fire. If you hadn't been high all the time, we could have tried," he says, grinding his teeth as a lone tear trickles down his face.

My sister's eyes widen, suddenly she looks stricken and confused. I guess she didn't know that. I only know because ending up on Josslyn's list of ex-boyfriends isn't an option and I made her tell me what each of them did wrong. They all made the same idiotic mistake of not putting her first. Tate begs again and I look at John, who's been quiet this entire time.

"John, take Tate outside," Mallory says finally. "I swear to God, if either of you lets the cops in here, I will shoot Josslyn. I can't guarantee that I won't do it anyway."

My stomach dips. For nearly two years, I blamed myself for

not being there for my sister. I spent time and resources trying to find the person responsible for her death, or at the very least, someone who could give me clarity of what happened that night. Never in that time did I think I'd have a second chance to right my wrongs. Never in that time did I think I'd have a gun aimed at her chest and a finger on the trigger, ready to shoot. I don't know what the fuck is going to happen here tonight, but I know it'll change everything.

CHAPTER SIXTY-ONE

Finn

MY ATTENTION VACILLATES BETWEEN MALLORY AND JOHN AS HE stands and walks over to Tate. He helps him up and Tate groans and leans on him as they walk. Josslyn doesn't shift or move her arms as the weight lifts from the couch. She just slumps over against the armrest and lets out what sounds like a relieved breath. I glance back at my sister and the door, where John is shouting and putting a hand up so no one will shoot. He shuts the door behind them and a slew of shouts erupt outside.

"She has a gun!" John shouts. "If you go near the house, she'll kill them both!"

Screams ring out and the megaphone starts up again, telling 'whoever is in here' to come out.

"If I hadn't ripped her and Tate apart, she would have stayed with him," Mallory says, obviously still thinking about what he said.

I don't respond. What's the point? I can stand here and tell her that sooner or later, I would have looked for Josslyn and taken her from Tate. I can confess that from the moment I spoke to her, we were inevitable. I didn't believe it back then. I didn't even believe it when I was keeping track of her movements. It doesn't matter, though. Josslyn may have been with him back then, but I've belonged to her from the moment she called me out on my arrogance.

"Did John help you with all of this?" I ask, finally lowering the gun when she does.

With him gone, it's just my sister I need to worry about, and everything about her posture tells me she's tired.

"Yes," she says.

"Did anyone else know about it?" I ask.

"Mom knew."

My stomach hollows. I stare at her, waiting for her to start laughing, but I know that expression well. She's serious. I shake my head anyway. There's no fucking way. It's just not possible. She has to be lying. My brain runs a mile a minute, trying to find clues that my mom may have slipped up, but there's nothing.

Then, I remember her words at the country club. "Your sister's episode." *Episode*, she'd said. Even then the word stood out, but I let it go. I think about the days that followed Mallory's supposed death—how much my mother cried, how vehemently she placed the blame on me, and then ... nothing. By the time I was on the airplane flying to my next game, Mom was "much better" and nearly every trace of Mallory was gone. After being told the Jane Doe at Onyx was a sex worker, no more questions were posed.

"Did Dad know?" I ask, my gaze going to Josslyn, who's still lying there.

"No," she says. "But he was easily convinced when Mom told him to put a gag order on everyone. He just went along with it. It's like no one cared to get—"

"*I* cared," I say, swallowing hard to prevent a knot of emotion from clogging my throat. "I wanted justice for you."

"You waited over a year! My own brother!"

"It was a lot to process!"

"You were trying to pretend it didn't happen!" Mallory

shouts and tears begin streaming down her face. "You didn't even miss a fucking game!"

I look at Josslyn again and my chest squeezes. Something is wrong with her. Why isn't she sitting up? Why isn't she doing *anything*? I need her to sit up and get ready to run.

My eyes fly back to my sister. "What did you do to her?

"Gave her a paralytic," she responds nonchalantly. "Nothing too serious."

"She drugged me at Onyx that night," Josslyn says with a scratchy voice. "She was the one who drugged me and took me home."

It takes a moment for that to sink in, and after what I saw when I walked in here... "What did you do to her?" I demand. "Did you touch her?!"

My sister's brows shoot up. "So testy about her. What, you can't share with your sister?"

I take a step forward, and she lifts the gun. I don't know where the fuck she's aiming, but I'm close enough that if she shoots me, she'll hit something. My shoulder, my arm, my heart, I don't know. Right now, I'm so fucking enraged at the thought that my sister did something to Josslyn, that I don't care.

"Leave!" Mallory shouts, her voice cracking. "Please go. I don't want to hurt you!"

"You think I'm going to leave her?!" I ask, my hands shaking at my sides. "*You* leave. Go back to wherever the fuck you came from!"

"I'M NOT LEAVING WITHOUT HER!" she roars.

I open my mouth to scream at her when the megaphone goes off again.

"We are coming in! Please put your weapon down and surrender, Miss Barlow!"

Her eyes widen as if she's just now—hours later—understanding the gravity of this. Her awareness quickly turns into panic. I know that look well. It's the same look she had when I forced her to go on rollercoasters. It's obvious my sister needs help, and I would feel sorry for her, if she wasn't holding my girlfriend hostage. Loud footsteps and demands get closer as we stand there, and I bring the gun back up and point it at her.

"Put the gun down, Mallory!" I plead. "This is your last chance. Put it down!"

Footsteps pound on the porch. Everything happens in a fraction of a second, but it plays out in slow motion in front of me. Gun still raised, Mallory turns her body toward Josslyn, and I pull the trigger.

Bang.

Bang.

The door bangs open, crashing into the glass cabinet behind it and shattering it with the full force of it. Guns are pointed at me and Mallory is splayed out on the floor lying in a pool of blood. She makes a sound and someone rushes over to her and starts yelling for medics.

"PUT YOUR WEAPON DOWN!" one of them shouts, and I realize I'm still holding the gun in shooting position.

I lower my arms and crouch to set it on the ground, kicking it over to them. My attention flies to the couch where Josslyn is still motionless. I take a step toward her, and when I see the blood seeping through her shirt, I stop breathing. *No.* Oh, God. No. For a second, I'm frozen again, and then the chaos inside me snaps.

"NO!" I yell, lurching forward. "JOSSLYN!"

An officer holds me back, and I push him to the side. Another comes, and I fight him as well.

"JOSSLYN!" I yell, yanking my arms away from them until I'm free.

I take another step, a third man runs over to hold me back, and then a fourth. I watch as the medics rush inside with gurneys, taking my sister away while the others run to Josslyn.

"JOSSLYN! PLEASE!" I scream again, as they lift her up and check her vitals. "SHE'S NOT MOVING. WHY IS SHE NOT MOVING?!"

The voices around me are muted by the pounding in my ears. I keep saying Josslyn's name and fighting the officers holding me back, as I watch paramedics lift the gurney she's on. Her head lolls to the side again and my chest grips tighter than ever before. Tears sting my eyes as I shout her name, begging her to be okay, pleading that she'll stay alive. She can't die. She can't fucking die on me. My throat burns, but I keep fighting and screaming as they carry her out of the house.

CHAPTER SIXTY-TWO

Finn

"**M**OVE OR I BURY YOU WHEN THIS IS OVER," I YELL at the men surrounding me.

"Let him go," Chief Rivera demands from somewhere behind them.

They do, and I don't look twice; I just take off running. Out front, there are camera crews and news helicopters. People are being held on the other side of a barricade. I hear my name called out, but I'm zoned in on the paramedic truck that's taking Josslyn. I run faster when they're about to shut the door, pull it open, and jump inside.

"Sir—"

"DRIVE!" I bellow. "FUCKING DRIVE!"

They do, and I launch myself at her and hold her hand while they start checking vitals and doing all kinds of shit.

"Is she okay?" I ask desperately, squeezing her hand as tears fill my eyes. "Is she okay?!"

"She's alive," the paramedic says. "You're going to have to back up and let us work." When I don't do it, she pierces me with a glare. "Do you want her to survive or not?!"

I drop her hand and sit back, my knee bouncing as I watch them work. When we get to the hospital, I let them hop out first and follow them as they wheel her in. I'm following, watching for any sign of movement while they speak to a doctor, when we reach a door and they tell me I can't go any further.

"Fuck that," I say and charge forward.

Two security guards come out of nowhere and hold me until the doctor and nurses are on the other side of the door, then they let me go. I pull on the handles and find them locked.

"No," I say, looking through the window. I slam the door. "NO!" I turn swiftly and see a nurse approaching me. "Where are they taking her?!"

"Sir, I'll lead you to—"

"WHERE ARE THEY TAKING HER?"

She flinches. "Surgery. If you'll allow me, I'll lead you to the waiting area where the doctor will come and give you an update."

My body is vibrating as I follow the nurse. The two security guards come with us. We walk into the waiting area and I head to the chair closest to the doors and stagger into one of them, barely catching myself from missing the seat.

"Are you hurt?" the nurse asks once I'm sitting down.

I nod, then shake my head. "I'm fine."

But I'm not fine. Everything hurts. *Everything.* But all my pain is internal.

I hear stomping and drop my hands from my face to see Damian walking over. Behind him are Josslyn's mom and Titus. Behind them, Ella and Lucas. I don't stand up. I don't think I could even if I wanted to. Damian's eyes are bloodshot and I can tell he's been crying. So are Jackie's and Titus'. So are Ella's. Lucas looks fierce, the way he used to on the football field all those years ago. My stomach feels so fucking hollow.

"She's in surgery," I say, my voice hoarse.

"Oh, God." Jackie covers her mouth and sobs, as Titus wraps an arm around her.

"How long has she been in there?" Titus asks.

I shake my head. I'm about to answer that she's been in there too long, but I stop myself. "Thirty minutes."

"Fuck." Damian exhales.

"Are you okay?!" Jackie asks, wiping her eyes.

I nod, wishing I was the one in surgery and not Josslyn. Ella runs up to me, tears running down her face, as she wraps her arms around me, over my arms, locking me into a hug. Lucas follows and sets a hand on my shoulder, squeezing.

"Is…" I swallow hard. "Mallory."

"Surgery," Ella says quietly as she backs away and wipes her tears.

My body locks. "In this hospital?"

"Yes," she says. My nerves must show, because she adds, "There are officers all over the floor she's on though. They won't let her out of their sight."

She doesn't deserve to breathe the same air as Josslyn. I hate myself for thinking it about my own fucking sister, but it's undeniable. She doesn't deserve a second chance after what she did. She tried to take her from me. I take a shaky breath. She better be okay.

"Tate's also here," Ella adds.

"What happened in there?" Damian asks quietly as he walks over. He wipes his eyes, his Adam's apple moving as he swallows. "I thought … fuck, I didn't know what to think. I tried to go back, but they put me in handcuffs."

"Oh my god, where is she? Is she okay? Is she in surgery?" Olivia says frantically as she runs over, wiping tears. "I tried to get here faster but everything was blocked off."

I sit down again, setting my elbows on my knees and dropping my head for a moment to take a breath. It does nothing to lessen the pain inside my chest.

"Finn?" Ella whispers, setting her hand on my head and scratching lightly.

The way Josslyn does. My heart hurts so fucking much. I sit up so she's forced to drop her hand. I love Ella like a sister, but I don't want her comfort. I want Josslyn. I want her fingers in my hair. I want her to be here rolling her eyes at me and pretending she doesn't like my possessiveness. I want her to berate me using my full name when I do something that shocks her. I want her to whisper, "Hey, Finn," the way she does when she's about to say something sweet. I swallow hard, and this time, I can't do anything to stop the tears that have been building. I want to hold her hand and watch the stupid television shows she likes. I feel arms around me, and my shoulders start to shake. I can't lose her. I can't.

The door opens, and we all straighten. I wipe my face and take a breath.

"Who is Josslyn Santos' next of kin?" he asks, looking at all of us.

"She's my daughter," Jackie says, rushing forward.

"Is she okay?" I ask and step forward as well.

"She's stable."

My heart squeezes and my eyes fill again, but this time, with nothing but gratitude.

"She was lucky. And I mean *lucky*," he says. "The bullet went straight through her arm and missed a major artery and organs. She definitely had someone watching over her," he says, shaking his head. "I haven't seen a case like this in years."

"Can we see her?" Jackie asks desperately.

"She's sleeping. She won't be awake for a long time. When she got here, she was already out of it, and with the anesthesia we gave her..." He shakes his head. "She'll be sleeping for a while."

"Can we see her?" I ask, probably a little too forcefully.

"Are you her husband?" he asks, glancing at me like he knows I'm not.

My heart pounds harder. "Not yet."

I feel every eye on me, but mine remain on the surgeon.

"Let her parents go in first," he says after a moment. "Two at a time."

My heart sinks. I swallow hard. I don't think I can handle waiting any longer, but I remain silent. I know her mother needs to see her. I know Titus and Damian are family. I know all of this, but it doesn't make it any easier to stay put. I watch her mother and Titus go, and kick the nearest chair when I turn around. Fuck this place. My phone buzzes, and I take it out to hopefully take my mind off the fact that I'm not at Josslyn's side right now. When I see my father's name, I answer.

"Did you know?" I ask.

"No," he says, his voice quiet. "I didn't. Is … is Josslyn okay?"

"NO, SHE'S NOT OKAY! SHE WAS SHOT!" I yell, my chest rattling. Out of the corner of my eye, I see a security guard and lower my voice.

"Is she alive?"

"Yes."

He exhales. "I don't know why your mother would keep this from us. All this time…"

I stay quiet and try to get a grip on the anger I feel rising when I think of my mother. Josslyn called her to warn her about Mallory. She *hugged her* at her birthday.

"If there's anything you need, let me know," he says.

"Do you donate to SPH?" I ask.

"Yes. We helped fund their new cancer center."

I can't believe I'm asking him for another favor. "They're only letting two people visit at a time."

"Did you tell them who you are?"

"No." I let out a single laugh. "I don't think the surgeon cares who I am."

"He should!" my father says, his voice fierce. "I'll make a call, but you should tell them your name is Finneas Barlow. Our last name is on the street that leads to the cancer building, for fuck's sake!" He hangs up and I lower my phone but keep it in hand.

"What happened in the house?" Lucas asks quietly. Damian, Ella, and Olivia are right behind him waiting.

"Mallory shot Josslyn, so I shot her," I say. "I didn't think she'd do it. If I thought she would … and I couldn't…" My voice breaks.

"She's your sister," Ella says quietly.

I look at her. "If I knew she was capable of using that gun on Josslyn, I would have killed her on sight."

Her eyes widen.

The doors open again and a nurse appears. We're the only ones in the waiting room, so I step forward.

"Is she okay?" I ask quickly.

The nurse smiles. "Yes. She's been moved to the private suite and can take more visitors."

My heart skips.

"I'll wait here," Lucas says before I start walking.

I turn to him. "Thanks for coming. You don't have to stay. I won't be leaving her room until she does."

He stares at me. "You have games."

I shrug. "Let them fire me. I don't care."

"I'll get you some clothes," he says.

"I'll go with you," Ella says and looks at me. "I'll be back, and I'll fill Will in on everything."

I give them a grateful nod and follow the nurse with Damian and Olivia on my heels. My phone buzzes in my hand with a call from my father again.

"Thank you," I say upon answering. "I…" I swallow hard. "Thank you for everything."

He's quiet on the other end. After a moment, he clears his throat and says. "Any time."

I put my phone away.

"You're really going to miss the next game?" Damian asks.

I look at him. "Yes, but you should go. She's stable, and the bullet didn't hit anything vital."

He nods. In his eyes, I can see what he's not saying. She's stable, and the bullet didn't hit anything important, so why aren't *you* going? I wasn't kidding about getting fired. Hockey was my first love for a long time, but nothing compares to what I feel for her.

CHAPTER SIXTY-THREE

Finn

I RUSH INTO THE ROOM AND FREEZE WHEN I SEE NURSES SURROUNDING Josslyn, and Jackie standing off to the side with a hand over her mouth. Behind me, Damian and Olivia gasp at the state-of-the-art suite. My heart pounds hard, in tandem with my steps as I close the distance. The nurses pause when they see me, but don't say anything as they move away from her and step out of the room. The relief that rushes over me when I see her makes my knees go weak. I grip the bed rail to keep from falling and swallow hard as I take her in.

She has a bandage on her left shoulder and an IV on her right hand. She looks pale and her hair is a mess, but she's alive. *She's alive.* I mean to just lean down, but I end up on my knees with my eyes shut and my head resting on her arm. My throat closes and I grip the bed rail hard as tears start spilling out. I've cried more today than I have my entire life, and the reason is obvious. I've never loved anything or anyone the way I love her. Not even close.

"God, baby," I whisper, inhaling shakily. "I'm so fucking sorry."

"They just took out the breathing tube," Jackie explains.

"Fuck," Damian says behind me.

"Why is she not awake?" Olivia asks, slightly panicked.

"She's heavily sedated. She already was before she got here," Titus answers. "The nurse said it could be days before she wakes up fully."

My head snaps up. *"Days?"*

"It could be hours," he says. "But she told us not to be alarmed if it takes a couple of days."

"Oh my God," Olivia whispers.

"They said talking might help," Jackie says.

I look at Josslyn again. My Josslyn. My heart. My world. The rest of them keep talking and discussing the physical therapy she'll need and how she may or may not get to play this season. My heart breaks a little at that possibility. She says basketball isn't her life, but I know she was looking forward to playing one more season.

"I know you have games—" Titus says.

"I'm not leaving," I respond, looking at him as I stand up.

"Joss will be fine," he says. "Jackie will stay overnight."

I stare at him. Hard. "Well, then I guess we'll be roommates, because I'm. Not. Leaving."

His brows shoot up, but he doesn't challenge me.

"I'm sure Josslyn will appreciate having you here when she wakes up," Jackie says, smiling softly. "There are two pull-out couches in the living room area."

We stay there for a while, before Titus goes to visit Tate and Jackie leaves to get a change of clothes. Hammie calls Dame on video and we speak to him and Coach P briefly. Dame agrees to head out tonight for tomorrow's game. Olivia says she'll be back in the morning. And finally, it's just me and Josslyn. I pull up the chair and take her hand slowly, kissing the back of it and stroking it with my thumb. I lean in closer and move the tips of my fingers softly on her scalp.

"I need you to wake up, baby," I whisper, swallowing past the knot in my throat. "I miss you too much."

A loud sound makes me jump out of my sleep and blink. It takes me a second to remember everything—Mallory, the guns, the blood, the hospital. The nurse on the other side of the bed smiles warmly.

"Sorry to wake you. I'm just checking her vitals."

I drag a hand over my face. "What time is it?"

"Eight," she says. "I don't know if you had a chance to look over the menu or explore the suite, but you should find everything you need here. If you need anything else, let me know." She walks over to the board and writes her name down, Shawnell, and looks at me again. "You know there are two pull-out beds right over there, right? I'm sure they're more comfortable than that flimsy chair you barely fit in."

I feel my mouth twitch. "I'm sure they are, but I'll be staying right here, unless you're going to let me move her to one of those beds."

She laughs and shakes her head as she walks away. I stretch my back and look around, surprised to see I'm alone. There are a few flower arrangements in the seating area and a familiar duffel bag next to one of the couches. I sag with relief, silently thanking my cousin for always having my back. At some point while Dame and Olivia were still here, one of the nurses brought me a pair of sweatpants and one of his t-shirts for me to change into. I was grateful to be able to shower and change out of the bloody clothes I was wearing.

Despite the clean clothes, I feel like I need another shower and to change into my own things. I pick up Josslyn's hand and kiss it softly as I stand up. I kiss her cheek first, and place my forehead against hers.

"Wake up, Josie," I whisper. "Please."

Maybe pissing her off will wake her up.

The bathroom looks and smells brand new. I didn't notice much of it last night when I was trying to hurry up and go right back to Josslyn's side. The morning brings new hope, though. As I take the clothes off, I look around and wonder if my father is planning to get sick and live out the rest of his days here. Whoever maintains this place thought of everything. There are towels and robes and new toothbrushes and toothpaste.

After I'm finished cleaning up, I stand under the shower spray for a few more seconds. It usually helps me relax. Today, all it does is bring back awful memories. I switch it off and get dressed. I wonder if my sister is alive, and if so, where she is. I'm not sure how I feel about seeing her ever again, but if she survives this, I'll make sure she ends up in a prison or mental institution.

There's no doubt in my mind that this too will soon become another skeleton in the Barlow closet, but unlike the times in the past when family members got off with a slap on the wrist, Mallory will answer for what she's done. If Tate doesn't survive, she's fucked anyway. Our last name goes a long way in Fairview, but this was public and there's no way people will let her forget what she did.

"I ordered breakfast," Jackie says when I step out of the bathroom and drop my bag by the couch. She hands me a cup of coffee. "I don't know how you take it, so I didn't add anything in. There's sugar and creamer in the bag, though."

"This is fine. Thank you." I take a sip and walk over to Josslyn again to touch her hair and her face.

To remind myself that she's alive and well.

"You really love her," Jackie says.

"With everything I am."

"And you were serious about marrying her," she says.

"One hundred percent," I say, looking over at her. "And after the whole, 'next of kin' thing yesterday, I plan on doing it very soon."

Jackie laughs and takes a sip of coffee as she takes a seat in the chair on the other side of Josslyn's bed. I take a seat as well.

"You know, Tate asked her to marry him," she says, lowering her coffee. My jaw tics. "Not officially," she adds, "Unofficially. He didn't give her a ring or anything, though he said he bought one. He must have asked about six times."

I scowl. "He's an asshole."

"He is." She nods. "He's alive, by the way. I'm not sure if you care."

I nod and take another sip of my coffee. I doubt I'll ever like the guy, but he's been through a lot—most of it at the hands of my family—so I'm glad he's alive.

"She always said no to him," Jackie continues. "Straight up 'no.' Not even an 'I'll think about it,'" she says, laughing and shaking her head.

My lips purse. "She should've never been with him."

"She probably wouldn't have if I hadn't pushed her," she says, and my eyes snap back to her. "I was raised to seek safety, not butterflies. Josslyn was always reluctant about that. She wanted the butterflies and the fireworks." Jackie smiles looking at her daughter. "Good for her."

"Yeah." I feel my chest loosen a bit.

"I'm curious as to how she'll react when you ask her."

"You and me both," I say, but I'm not worried. I freeze when Josslyn's fingers twitch in my hand. I shoot out of my hair, setting the coffee down on the tray behind me. "She just moved. Joss?"

Her fingers twitch again. Jackie sets her coffee down and rushes over to the button. Nurses show up almost immediately. It takes what feels like an eternity, but is probably just a couple of minutes, before Josslyn blinks and moans.

"Is she in pain? Does she have something for pain?" I ask.

One of the nurses clicks something on the IV and keeps checking her vitals. I wait with bated breath for Josslyn to fully open her eyes. When she does, she instantly finds me. Relief hits me like a punch in the gut. Jackie goes to the other side of the bed, but

Josslyn keeps her eyes on me. The nurses ask questions, and she nods and shakes her head as she answers. Finally, they leave to get the doctor.

"My God," Jackie says, crying as she touches her daughter's other hand, but Josslyn is still staring at me.

"You called me Josie," she says, her voice hoarse.

It takes me a moment to process that and bark out a laugh. "I knew that would wake you up."

She smiles, or tries to, but flinches. I freeze again. "My lips are cracked," she says. "Mom—"

Jackie ignores whatever she's going to say and starts telling her how worried she was and how many people in the family chat are praying for her. Josslyn listens, but every few seconds, she glances at me.

"Mom, can you ask if I can have water please?" she says, clearing her throat.

"Of course." Jackie's eyes widen and she runs off.

I sit back down, scoot the chair closer, and press my lips against the back of Josslyn's hand. The soft smile she gives me is one that always brings me to my knees.

"You own me, you know that?" I say against her hand.

"Finn," she whispers, her eyes filling with tears. She tries to shift her body and flinches. "Fuck, that hurt."

"Don't move," I say, looking at her bandaged arm to make sure it's still intact.

"I want you closer," she says, blinking away tears. I stand and kiss her lips ever so softly.

"I'm serious, Josslyn. You own me," I repeat, my voice hoarse. "My love for you is a living thing inside me. You're everywhere all the time—on my mind, in my blood, in my bones. I don't think we can get much closer than that."

She tugs me closer and I get as close as I can without hurting her. "I love you," she whispers as she starts to cry. "So much."

I wrap a hand around her head and bring my chest closer so she's against my beating heart.

"Hey, Finn," she whispers after a moment.

My lips twitch as I pull away. "Yeah."

"You know there are actual living things inside your body," she says, scrunching her nose. "Like bacteria and fungi."

I stare at her for a moment before I start to laugh. Fucking Josslyn.

CHAPTER SIXTY-FOUR

Finn

3 Days Later

I continue to stare at Leo. He's been apologetic and helpful these last few days, but I still don't trust him.

"I really am sorry I didn't do more to help," he says for the third time since we sat down across from each other at the coffee shop.

"I don't want your apology," I snap.

"We understand," Hamilton says calmly, setting a hand on my forearm and squeezing so I shut the fuck up. "We just want the footage you promised and we'll be on our way."

I almost snort out a laugh. I swear he missed his calling as a lawyer. He and Damian insisted in coming along and I didn't have the energy to tell them to fuck off. Josslyn was sent home from the hospital late last night, and our apartment currently looks like a birthday celebration with the amount of people, balloons, and flowers. It took more willpower than I knew I had to not kick them all out.

After an eternity, Leo slides his phone across the table. I pick it up and press play. Hamilton and Dame lean closer to watch. The video starts out with the three of them—Josslyn, Olivia, and my sister—walking into Onyx. Seeing my sister makes my skin crawl. The quality of this video is better than the one I have, and I'm able to pay close attention to the expression on their faces. Josslyn looks concerned. Olivia looks like she doesn't want to be there. My sister looks strange, with huge pupils and an expression that borders on deranged. My stomach twists. Beside me, Damian mutters a quiet curse and Hamilton shifts closer.

In this video, I see Josslyn and Olivia walk toward the bar, and my sister takes a right. The next shot is of her walking into that room I saw her disappear into in the footage I have. She smiles and waves at someone off camera. She walks into the room, and shortly after, a man wearing a mask walks inside as well. The video skips to him walking out, and I know from having watched the footage of the rest of the club that Josslyn is outside with Titus and Olivia is gone.

The timestamp up top skips to three hours later, when the door opens again, and my sister walks out. My heart pounds hard and loud in my ears as I watch her walk toward the bar, give something to the same man with the mask that had been inside the room with her. He takes a small envelope from her hand and starts arguing with her, but Mallory shrugs and glances into the bar. My stomach turns.

Thirty minutes pass and people start leaving the club. I hadn't noticed when I watched the footage before, but there weren't many people there that night.

"Is it usually that dead on a Saturday night?" I ask, keeping my eyes on the phone screen.

"No. It closed early that night. Everyone who made a reservation had to be out by midnight."

"Is that normal?" Damian asks.

"No."

I press pause on the video and glance up, waiting for him to explain himself.

"Mallory rented out Onyx quite a few times," Leo says.

"Normally, when people do that, we keep a record of it. That night, there is no record. I found the guest list that I showed Josslyn, but no record of anyone renting the entire club."

My jaw clenches and I press play again. A man walks inside with a body bag hanging over his shoulder and steps into the room Mallory vacated. At first, I figure she's inside there, but the video cuts to the empty bar, where Josslyn is sitting with her head down on the bar as if she's taking a nap.

"Fuck," I whisper, my stomach curling. I don't know if I can watch this.

"I can watch it for you," Hamilton suggests, but I shake my head.

Mallory walks into the bar and heads straight to Josslyn. I watch as she pushes her hair away from her face gently and brings her face closer. I stop breathing.

"Finn, I'm serious. I can watch it," Hamilton says, his voice a little wary.

Mallory backs away suddenly and looks toward the door. She looks at Josslyn one more time before she starts walking in that direction. The next frame cuts to my sister walking out of the room she'd been in with both hands over her mouth. She crouches and lands on her knees as if in fathomless pain.

How she went through with all of this is beyond me. My sister could barely get a scratch without crying like she was dying, so for her to have her teeth knocked out … it just makes all of this more sick and twisted. The last thing shown is John carrying Josslyn out of Onyx with Mallory beside them. They both stop walking and glance to the left at the same time, and then start walking faster until they disappear from the frame. I set the phone down and stare at the blank screen.

"You took Joss to the hospital the day after this?" I ask Damian, my flat voice reflecting the numbness I feel inside.

"Yeah, they said she hadn't been…" he says, letting his words trail off.

"Jesus," Hamilton says on an exhale.

"You understand why I didn't want to send this to Josslyn," Leo says across from us as he takes back his phone.

"She doesn't need to see that," I respond.

The unknown would be too much for her. It's enough to haunt me for the rest of my days, especially after my sister insinuated she did something to her while she was unconscious.

"Do you have enough to prove what John did without this video?" Damian asks Leo.

"I believe so."

"Whatever happens, his life is over," I say with conviction.

He's either going to jail or he's going to die. I don't care what his reasons were for being involved in the fire. I don't care if my sister paid him a shitload of money or bribed him or whatever the fuck happened.

The details don't matter. He was there that night, he helped take an unconscious Josslyn home, and he helped my sister and held Josslyn hostage. As long as I'm breathing, there's no way John will walk around as a free man.

"The only way Joss would ever see this is if Mallory survives, since they'd need it in court," Damian says to me.

I swallow hard and nod. Mallory's in critical condition. The bullet damaged some organs, so they're not sure she'll survive. After seeing this footage, I don't know if I have it in me to let her.

CHAPTER SIXTY-FIVE

Josslyn

1 month later

A MYRIAD OF EMOTIONS FLITTER THROUGH ME WHEN I GET THE CALL about Mallory's death, before I'm overcome with sadness. Painful sobs press down in my chest, and I make myself go to the bathroom and shut the door. I turn on the shower but before I can even start taking off my clothes, I double over and start to cry. My only hope is that the water drowns out the sounds. The last thing I want is for Finn to hear about this and worry more than he already has been.

I don't even understand why I feel this way. It's not like Mallory had a chance at a regular life after everything she did. It's not like I wanted her to have one. But still. Death is so final. How will Finn feel about all of this? I try not to think about his mother, but it's impossible. Finn says he hates her and that he'll never forgive her for what she did, and I get it. I'm not her biggest fan right now, but a part of me understands why she did it.

It wasn't like she thought Mallory was roaming around freely. She'd sent her to a mental institution overseas in hopes that she would get better. I'm sure she didn't think Mal would have her phone on her at all times or that she'd break free and end up back in the place she swore she wanted to get away from. Nevertheless, her actions cost her greatly.

Her son wants nothing to do with her and her husband is planning to file for divorce—something a Barlow never does. It's not like she had a great relationship with Finn or her husband to begin with, but it's got to hurt, and now her daughter is gone for good. That thought sticks with me as I shower and dress again. *Is she gone for good?*

I know John is. I got the call from Scarlet a couple of weeks ago saying they found his body a few days after he'd been hit with a handful of lawsuits. Scarlet didn't go into details and I didn't ask for any, but it sounded like he'd committed suicide. Normally, that's a triggering subject for me, but I can't bring myself to think about him much, let alone care. It's not like I knew him, but he'd also been helpful with the whole Mallory thing.

It's a lot to wrap my head around. Dealing with people is exhausting enough without questioning their motives, and this situation has proven to be damn near draining. Loud pounding on my bedroom door makes me nearly jump out of my skin as I step out of the bathroom.

"Miss Josslyn," Tamara says from the other side. "Mr. Barlow is on the phone. He says you haven't answered his calls and he's worried."

I let out a breath as I unlock and open my bedroom door. Even with the three bodyguards Finn hired for me—the only reason he even agreed to go back to work—I can't help feeling paranoid. The only time I leave the house is to go to basketball practice, and that's only because our coach refuses to bring the practice to me.

The only personal post I've made on social media was one written on a black background letting people know I'm okay and thanking them for their well wishes. Everything else has been sponsored posts from brands that I'd previously set up. Maybe someday I'll get back to sharing my life with the world, but I'm still too shaken up to do it.

Mallory betrayed my trust in so many ways, but what bothers me the most is the doubts she planted in my head. I can't look at anyone—even my own teammates—without second-guessing their motives, and it's not fair. Tamara gives me a comforting smile as she hands me her phone, and I thank her as I take it and set it to my ear.

"Hello?"

He exhales heavily. "I've been calling you."

I turn away from Tamara. "I was in the shower. Can I call you from my phone or are you at the arena already?"

"Call me." He hangs up and I hand Tamara back her phone.

"I'll leave the door unlocked," I tell her, walking back into my room and shutting the door.

"Did you hear?" Finn asks quietly when I call him back.

"Yeah." I swallow hard and sit on his side of the unmade bed. "How are you feeling?"

"Not good," he confesses in a whisper.

"I'm sorry," I say and bite my lip hard to keep from crying again. It doesn't work. "I'm so sorry."

"No. You don't…" He stops talking for a moment. "Don't apologize, Josie."

I swallow hard again and nod as I bat away tears.

"I'm glad she's gone," he says and pauses again as if to gauge my reaction. When I don't say anything, he adds, "I know I should feel shitty about that."

"It's okay to feel angry, sad and relieved, you know?"

"Is it?" he asks, chuckling darkly. "I didn't know that was an option."

"Of course." I smile, hoping he can hear it in my voice. "Your feelings are valid no matter what they are."

He's quiet for a long moment. "I love you."

My stomach dips and I shift to lay my head on his pillow. "I wish you were here."

He sighs. "Josslyn."

"I'm glad you're playing again. *I want you to be there,*" I say, hoping he hears the conviction in my voice. "But I also wish you were here. Maybe I'll clone you."

He chuckles. "I don't think that's a good idea."

"Why? You don't think I can handle two Finn Barlows?"

"I can't handle thinking about you with two Finn Barlows."

That makes me laugh. "But it would kind of be you."

"I kind of don't care. You're mine and only mine," he growls.

My heart skips again. "I love you, Finneas."

Another sigh. "I have to go kick this team's ass."

"Go do your thing, Barlow. I'll be watching from your side of the bed."

He groans and mutters a few dirty things before we hang up. As soon as I'm alone again, I start thinking and a wave of sadness comes over me again when I think of Tate. According to my mom, his stab wound wasn't deep and didn't hit any vital organs, but the infection he got from leaving it unattended could have been fatal. Thankfully, they were able to help him and send him home. We both got lucky, I guess.

I haven't spoken to him at all since everything went down, but he did send me a long text apologizing and telling me how things between him and Mallory started. My response was a thumbs up emoji. What else is there to say? Now, I'm the one who picks up the phone and sends him a text.

Me: I'm sorry about mal

I know everyone in my life—with the exception of my mother—would be opposed to me sending this, but I can't help it. I'll never like him or willingly hang out with him, but I hate knowing anyone is suffering alone. His response comes as I'm setting my phone to charge.

Tate: i am as well. How are you holding up? Finn?

My brows shoot up.

Me: the whole thing is fucked up, but we're okay. At least, we will be

Tate: I believe that. Thank him for me. I'm pretty sure he saved my life that night

Me: I will. Take care of yourself

Tate: you too

I close out his text and check the rest, responding quickly to Dame, Livie, Tiago, Cassie, and some of my other teammates before I toss my phone aside and walk to the kitchen to talk to Tamara and Oak while I heat up some food my mom left for us earlier in the day. When we're done eating, I excuse myself and go back to my room where I do some stretches for my shoulder before I tune into Finn's game.

CHAPTER SIXTY-SIX

Josslyn

THE BED DIPS BEHIND ME, AND I STARTLE AWAKE. AS SOON AS I SMELL him and his strong arms wrap around me, my body sags. I'd never admit it to him, but I cried while I watched his game earlier. And after we hung up when he called me afterward.

"I thought you were coming back tomorrow," I say, looking at the time on the alarm clock.

"I flew back right after the game," he says, nuzzling into my neck. "I missed you so fucking much."

"I missed you too." I turn in his arms and give him a quick peck on the lips. "I thought the team had a media thing in the morning?"

"Hm." He kisses me, a slow, deep kiss that leaves me slightly breathless when I pull away.

"Was it canceled?"

"No." He tries to kiss me again, but I set my hands on his chest. He sighs. "I took a private flight home."

That both warms my heart and makes me want to slap him. "You can't keep missing important things."

"Nothing is more important than you," he says, cupping my face and running his thumb over my lower lip. "Nothing."

I blink back the tears that threaten and lean in again, kissing him slowly in hopes that it encompasses all the things I feel for him. It won't. I doubt anything can. Our kisses turn desperate, and we start tugging each other's hair and biting each other's lips. He moves to position himself over me and his hands slide underneath my oversized t-shirt—his shirt.

"This is a shirt I approve of," he growls against my mouth, plunging his tongue into my mouth as he slides down my panties and helps me sit up to pull off the shirt.

He takes off his own and lowers his head to draw my left nipple into his mouth, and then the other. Heat shoots through me and I nearly bow off the bed when he bites them and kneads my breasts, as he continues to pepper kisses on my face, my chin, and my neck. I reach out and start pulling down his boxer briefs, shivering when I feel his large thick erection, hot and hard in my hand.

"Fuck." A shudder rolls through him and his hips thrust into my hand once. "I'll take my time with you later, but if I don't get inside you right now, I'll die."

I moan and let him push me until I'm on my back. His hand moves between us and he touches me, groaning when he finds me wet and ready for him. He grabs himself in his hand and looks down as he ever so slowly slides inside me. I gasp at the feel of his girth stretching me and tilt my pelvis with a moan when he's fully inside me. He pauses there, his gaze lifting to mine. What I find in his eyes leaves me breathless prematurely, and then he pulls out to the tip, not taking his eyes off me as he slams back in, hard and deep. My legs wrap around his waist in encouragement, and I grip the sheets tight when he does it again, and again.

"Lift your legs, baby," he rasps. I do and he lowers himself and thrusts so deep I feel my breath go out of me. A wave of heat spreads through me and I clench around him, pulling a deep groan from his lips. "Goddamn it, Josie."

My stomach flutters and my climax hits me like a freight train.

Hard, fast, and impossible to contain. He shudders over me, his arms trembling as he throws his head back and pumps into me a few times, moaning out my name as he comes. He lowers himself, pressing his weight on me as he kisses my neck and breaths hard against me.

"I love you so fucking much," he says against my cheek.

I sigh against him as I let him lift and carry me to the shower, where he takes me again against the wall.

"Do you want to talk about it?"

He exhales. "What is there to say?"

"I'm not sure," I say quietly. "I can't stop thinking about it. Could I have done something different? What if—"

"No." He shifts so I'm flat on my back and he's propped up on his elbow looking down at me with a frown on his face. "You couldn't have done anything different. None of this is your fault."

"I know it's not my fault, but—"

"No, Josslyn. I won't let you feel guilty over something my…" He pauses and swallows. "Over something a person did who clearly needed help—the kind of help you could not have provided."

Unbidden tears fill my eyes and I blink rapidly, turning my face to rub my shoulder before any fall. Finn breathes heavily and cups my face so I'm looking up at him again, and brings his forehead to mine.

"I could have lost you," he says hoarsely. "I could have lost you before we even…" He slides his hand from my face to the nape of my neck, gripping it gently. "You couldn't have changed anything. I won't let either of us feel guilty about things we weren't responsible for."

"Okay," I whisper as I kiss him. When I pull away, his eyes are still closed. "What about your mother?"

His eyes pop open. "What about her?"

"Will you forgive her?"

He pulls away and lies on his back with a heavy sigh. I scoot closer, placing my head on his chest. "I doubt it."

"She was doing the best she could."

He scoffs. "That's a stretch."

"I'm not agreeing with it, but our actions are a reflection of our experiences, and your parents are … messed up."

"We'll have to disagree on that," he says, running his fingers on my scalp. "You can argue that I'm messed up and I would never do what my mother did."

"How can you know that?" I ask, shifting to look him in the eye. "You don't know what you would have done. What she did was wrong. There's no argument there, but her daughter was sick and she thought locking her up in an institution overseas would help her get better. There was no reason for her to think she'd get out or come back."

"Josie." He sighs. "There's no reality in which I would be okay with this. Maybe if you hadn't been in danger. Maybe if you hadn't gotten hurt. *Maybe*. And still, I don't know. I'm not the forgiving type. I'm not you."

I stare at him for a long moment, and silently concede. He's right. He's not me, and I accept him for exactly who he is. My own experiences give me a different perspective in this situation, but it doesn't mean I'm right. I imagine my mother would probably have taken the same course of action as his, but she wouldn't have lied to our loved ones about it. She would have sought help for me while making me own up to what I'd done. But then again, my mother is nothing like Eliza Barlow.

My mind replays the expression on her face when she thanked me the day of her birthday, and for the millionth time, I wonder if it was a lie. I don't think it was. She seemed thrown off by my presence and a little confused by her own reaction to me. She messed up, but I know she felt it was her only option.

If Finn doesn't want to have a relationship with her, I won't push it. It's not like they were close to begin with. No matter what happens, I'm on his side. No one else's. I place a kiss on his pec and turn around in his arms to lie on my side. We lie there for a long time before he breaks the comfortable silence between us.

"What would you say if I asked you to marry me?" Finn asks, dropping a soft kiss on my shoulder.

My heart stops. "Are you proposing?"

"No." He smiles against my skin. "I'm just wondering what you'd say if I did."

"Doesn't that take the fun out of it?" I ask as I tilt my face to look at him.

His eyes narrow slightly. "No."

I laugh and turn in his arms. "What do you think I'd say?"

"Yes. *Obviously.*"

"You're so certain." I lean in to kiss him, but he backs away. "I love that for you."

He stares at me. "You'd say no?"

"I guess you'll have to find out when you actually propose," I say, barely holding back my amusement.

"But you love me," he says slowly, cautiously, as if scared I'd take those words back.

"I do."

"And we live together now."

"We do."

He frowns. "So, why wouldn't you say yes?"

"A lot of people love each other and live together and never get married."

He scowls. "That's bullshit."

"It is not bullshit." I laugh. "Some people don't want to get married. I'm shocked you would."

"Do you?"

"Yeah. I mean, I don't need a lavish wedding or anything, but I'd like to marry the person I'm going to have kids with."

"Which is me."

"So sure about yourself," I say, yelping when he leans in and bites my lip. "Finneas!"

His eyes darken. "I'm going to fuck you until you admit it."

"Hm." I shift and stretch, smiling up at him when he lifts up and cuffs my wrists over my head. "We'll see."

He dips his face and growls as he crashes his mouth against mine and kisses the sense out of me. I have no doubt he'll manage to convince me to say yes by the end of this. Not that he has to. I'd say yes in a heartbeat if he actually asked.

CHAPTER SIXTY-SEVEN

Josslyn

1 month later

I ROUND MY SHOULDERS AND STRETCH MY NECK AS I WATCH MY teammates take practice shots during our pre-game warmup. It's my first game back and I'm so nervous, I actually threw up in the bathroom before coming out here. As I stand there, I look at the seats in the arena, which are filling up little by little, and smile wide when I spot Lyla and Theo courtside sitting next to my mom and Titus. When Theo looks up from his bag of cotton candy, he sees me and hops out of his seat. Lyla holds his little shoulders before he takes a step and whispers something in his ear that makes him scowl and sit back down.

Behind them, Patrick, their head of security, laughs and makes a comment that makes them all laugh as well. I start walking and stop a ball that bounces next to me. Without thinking much of it, I turn, shoot, drain it, and wink at Cassie and the rest of my teammates who cheer me on for it. They've been the best source of motivation for me while I've been recovering from my injury.

Thanks to them—especially Lyla, who called one of her best physical therapists to help me—I have full mobility and can play.

Not to say I'm not sore as hell, especially when I push myself, but it's better than sitting out my last season. When I reach my family and Theo hops out of his seat again, Lyla lets him run to me. I'm not even fully crouched down when he lunges at me and knocks me on my ass.

"Theodore!" Lyla scolds.

I laugh and return his tight hug. "I'm so happy you're here, buddy."

"Me too!" he says, tightening his hold around my neck before pulling away. "Look! We're wearing the same jersey!"

"We are!" I smile wide and lower my voice to a whisper. "You think you can go out there and play for me if I get tired?"

His entire face lights up with his laugh. "You're so silly, Joshlyn!"

I kiss his forehead and stand up to greet his mom and mine—who are also wearing my jersey—and Titus and Patrick. I thank them for coming, and they all roll their eyes and tell me to stop being ridiculous. Mom points behind the basket to tell me where my aunt and Lyla's dad are sitting.

"Have you seen any highlights of the Owls game?" Titus asks.

"I saw Dame scored a nice little 'Bar Down' in the first ten minutes," I say, smiling as I air quote the term.

Even after all these years, I don't know hockey terms, but that's one I'm familiar with now. I guess I better be since it's what most of Finn's teammates call him. I have to admit, it is a pretty cool goal to see.

"Barlow scored when they got back from intermission," Patrick says.

My smile grows. "I'll have to watch the highlights."

We talk a little more and land on the topic of Christmas Eve—"real Christmas" for half of us—which is coming up in a few days.

"Finn thinks it's weird," I say to them after we discuss it.

Lyla laughs. "Lach thought it was so weird, but then he smelled that roasted pork and had a change of heart."

Titus laughs. "Can't blame him. Same thing happened to me the first time my father-in-law made one."

We come to an agreement on what we're going to do before I'm called away by a journalist who's a former player for the team Fairview is playing against tonight. We catch up quickly and she asks me questions about being back, how I feel, and what the future holds. I give my usual honest answers and thank her before walking back to my teammates.

Livie bumps her hip against mine after coming down from a shot. "How you feeling?"

"Good. Great." I smile and step away from her to take another three-point shot.

"We got shooters!" Cassie shouts and the rest of the girls do our typical celebratory dance and hand gestures to celebrate when one of us is on fire.

We talk to some of the girls on the other team and then go back to the locker room to get into game-mode. By the time we come back out, the stands are full. They announce the starters for the other team, and then, since it's a home game, lower the lights and make a show of announcing us.

When they announce my name, the arena goes wild and even though I fight to hold back tears of gratitude, they fall anyway. I'm always grateful for their love, but it means more than ever tonight because they're not cheering for me for my popularity or because they like me as a player. They're cheering for me as a person and celebrating that I'm okay, and that means everything.

The game starts and I tune out the crowd, focus on my teammates, and work on getting the ball away from my opponents and into the basket. At the half, our coaches and trainers check in with me and give me the option to sit out, but I laugh.

"Uh-uh. Cassi's getting her triple-double tonight," I say, winking at my coach.

"Or maybe you are," Aaliyah quips.

"Somebody on this team is," I say with confidence, even

though unless I turn into a superhero out there, I know it won't be me.

Livie laughs and pats my back. "She's back."

"We've been up fifteen all game, but you know they like to come out strong in the second half so we can't take our foot off the gas," Coach Ogu says.

"Stay on Buck," I tell Cassie and look at Livie. "Keep applying pressure on Gianna. She chokes at the corner."

"I'll try to keep Elaine away from you," Aaliyah says.

"We got this." I finish the rest of my water and we all stand up, huddle, and disperse.

"Yo, did you see your boyfriend's post?" Cassie asks me as she changes her sneakers.

"You follow Finn?" I ask, laughing, and take the phone she's handing me. I frown when I click it. "There's nothing here."

She takes the phone back and frowns at the screen. "Weird. He must have deleted it."

"What was it?"

"Just you."

"Okay…" I say, and when she doesn't expand on that, I go back to what I was doing.

I walk by my family on my way back to our bench and freeze when I see Finn, Damian, Lachlan, and Will sitting there. They've all rearranged seats, so Finn is courtside, sitting where Lyla was before, and she's in the row behind with her husband. Theo's still sitting courtside between Damian and Finn—who's wearing my jersey. His eyes light up with mischief when he sees the shock on my face. Now I can say I fully understand how he feels when he sees me wearing his jersey.

Somehow, despite being acutely aware of his presence, I manage to have an amazing rest of the game. When we finish, I shower quickly and change before walking back out.

CHAPTER SIXTY-EIGHT

Finn

A few months later (March)

THE ATMOSPHERE AT OUR HOME GAMES IS ALWAYS ELECTRIC, BUT it's intense now that we're in the finals. Not many thought we would be, since we're a brand new team. But with the players, the coaching staff, and the solid ownership, the Owls have a shot at winning the Cup. I sit down and start stretching next to Damian.

"Have you seen Josie?" I ask.

Dame snorts a laugh. "I can't believe she lets you call her that."

I ignore him. "Lach told her to stay in the box since Lyla's coming later with Theo, but Joss told him she was going to sit in the stands."

"I heard."

I look at him mid-stretch. "You knew?"

"Maybe," he says, rotating his hip and sinking into the stretch as he laughs. "I don't know why it matters whether she sits up there or down here."

"Was she able to get a seat for Tamara?" I ask.

Even though Josslyn loves Tamara, she's still uncomfortable with having a security detail.

"I'm sure she did. She knows you'd be distracted if you saw her there without security," Dame says.

Some of the anxiety building in my chest loosens. He makes a good point. Josslyn is aware of my paranoia and understands how important it is to be in the zone during a game.

"I just saw Joss," Hammie says as he skates up to us.

The look on his face makes my eyes narrow. I stop stretching. "Where is she and why do you look like that?"

"Luke and Ella are there, and she brought like half the basketball team. Women and men," he says and laughs at the look on my face. "They mic'd up Tiago and some other guy."

"Lovely," I mutter and stand up.

With the amount of times Tiago and the other guys on the team have talked about coming to an Owls game, I should've known they'd be here. Both Fairview teams are deep into March Madness, but have a couple of days of rest before their next games. Not being able to support each other at games is my only gripe about us both being athletes and our schedules coinciding.

I start skating to the other side of the ice and notice them right away. Ham wasn't kidding. They take up the entire section. As I skate, I nearly trip, and do a double and then a triple-take when I see Josslyn. It's not her that makes me falter though. It's the person sitting beside her that makes me nearly keel over. I skate up to them and she smiles brightly as she stands in front of me. The man next to her stands as well.

"Surprised?" he asks, smiling like this is a normal occurrence.

A knot of emotion launches into my throat. I've spent my entire life wishing my parents attended one of my games, but gave up on that dream many, many years ago. Seeing my father here—wearing my fucking jersey—is a lot to wrap my head around at once. We've spoken and seen each other more the last few months than we have since I was ten, and it's all Josslyn's doing.

She invited him over for Christmas Eve, and then New Year's Eve, and sent a cake to his office on his birthday from the two of us—unbeknownst to me, of course. In the grand scheme of things, they're small gestures, but they all things that initiated phone calls, texts, and most recently, getting together for golf.

Being around him made me realize my father and I didn't know each other at all, and even though I've had reason to dislike him, I now understand some of his actions. I still don't necessarily agree with them, but I understand. He grew up under his father's thumb, doing everything asked of him to ensure he was in his favor.

He gave up his dreams of playing professional golf, broke up with the woman he was in love with, married my mother, and continued to make decisions based on expectations rather than personal fulfillment. He hasn't said it, but I know part of him is proud of me for defying him at every turn and going after what I want.

My mouth is still hanging open when I see Josslyn's hand on the plexiglass. Finally, I tear my eyes away from my dad's and look at her. The amount of love in her eyes nearly brings me to my knees.

"I hope you don't mind the crowd I brought," she says loudly, eyes twinkling. "None of them have been to a hockey game before, which is just preposterous, don't you think?"

I feel my lip twitch. "I didn't know you were such a fan."

"I prefer basketball," she responds with a shrug. "But hockey's pretty cool."

"She bought us all jerseys," Tiago shouts beside her.

I hadn't even noticed him. I realize he's wearing Dame's jersey before I glance at the rest of them. They're *all* wearing jerseys. A lot are mine, some are Dame's, and the rest are other players on the team.

"I opted for the one with my last name on it. I had to convince her to match me until it becomes her last name as well," my dad says, making Josslyn laugh.

My heart feels like it might burst in my chest.

"That, and I'm kind of in love with number seventeen," she says, grinning.

It's something I'll never tire of hearing her say, especially when she announces it to the world like this.

"Go kick some ass," Dad says, slapping the plexi.

"Yeah." I clear my throat. "I'll see you after the game." I lock eyes with Josslyn. "I love you."

She responds by making a heart with her hands and blows me a kiss. I'm still in a trance as I skate away, still processing that my father is actually *at my game*. I have no doubt that if things were different, my mother would be here as well. My father won't outright say it, the general consensus is that he forced my mother to go on a long journey of self-discovery. When she called me last month, I finally caved and answered the phone.

I'd been ready for confrontation, but I got none. Instead, she apologized and asked how things were going—something my mother never cared about in the past. I don't think I'll ever truly forgive her for her role in what happened with my sister, but it doesn't matter. I'm content with how things are.

❦

"Why does everyone think we're married?" Josslyn asks, glancing at me when we get to our floor. "By the time the third security guard congratulated me, I had to ask what it was about. Imagine my surprise—and your father's—when they informed me I'd gotten married."

I fight a smile as I open the door and let her walk inside. My eyes trail down her back and land on her perfect, round ass. I pick up the pace and grab one ass cheek before wrapping my arms around her and kissing her neck.

"That's because I call you my wife when I talk about you."

She laughs. "But I'm not your wife."

"*Yet.*"

"Yet," she agrees, and my hands, which were making their way down her body, freeze.

Heart pounding, I set them on her shoulders and turn her around. The conversation I had with her mom at the hospital haunts me, especially since the few times I've brought up marriage, Joss hasn't jump out of her seat with excitement. She's never said she wouldn't say yes if I ask, but she's never confirmed it either, and it drives me crazy.

I'd never been unsure of anything until Josslyn walked into my life and turned my world on its axis. Living with her isn't enough. I know she's happy with me. I make sure of it. But it's not enough. I want more assurances. The thought crosses my mind more than it should.

I search her eyes. "Yeah?"

"You can't possibly doubt it," she says, wrapping her arms around my neck. "You own me, Finn Barlow."

My heart skips and I shut my eyes briefly, savoring the moment. When I open my eyes, I lift her into my arms and grab her ass as she wraps her legs around my waist.

"I own you?" I ask as I walk to our bedroom.

"Yeah," she says breathlessly, her eyes darkening with the same lust I feel.

I set her down in front of our bed and sit at the edge. I tip my chin. "Strip. I want you to show me what's mine."

She lifts a brow and starts undressing. I bite my lip and clench my hands on my thighs as I watch her seductive movements—the brush of her hands over her stomach as she lifts the jersey over her head. She turns around as she slowly drags the jeans down her body, and it takes everything in me to stay put and enjoy the show. When she faces me again, she looks like a wet dream in a pale pink lace bra and matching underwear.

My eyes greedily devour every inch of her flawless golden brown skin and for the millionth time, I'm struck with a series of thoughts. Will there ever be a time when seeing her like this won't take my breath away? Will I ever fully grasp that I somehow managed to pull this incredibly sexy, selfless, beautiful woman? Will the fact that she's mine ever sink in? It's almost enough to make my heart burst out of my chest. This woman is *mine*.

"Fuck," I whisper when she turns around to show me how she looks from all angles. "Come here, baby."

Her eyes are blazing as she saunters over until she's standing between my legs, her tits right in front of my eyes. I lean in and bite the thin material that holds the cups together before dragging my lips over every inch of her skin.

"Finn!" she gasps and sinks her fingers into my hair when I bite her side.

"I own you, remember?" I say, sliding my hands over her thighs and squeezing her butt.

"You do," she says breathily.

I pull away and glance up at her as I move my hands toward the middle of her ass cheeks. "All of you?"

Her eyes widen in understanding and she swallows visibly as she nods. Fuck, that's such a turn-on. "I've never done that," she says quietly.

My hands still. "Do you want to?"

"I've never even considered it, but with you, I would."

The words are barely out of her mouth before I pull her over, sit her on my lap and kiss her. It's a harsh, demanding kiss—all tongue and teeth and moans and whimpers. As we kiss, I unclasp her bra and lift her slightly to take off her thong. I can't find a way to take it off without her getting off my lap, so I bunch it together. Just as I'm about to pull, Josslyn pushes me away and scrambles off my lap. She takes it off and tosses it aside before climbing on my lap again.

"You're wearing too many clothes," she murmurs against my lips.

I slide a hand between us and cup her pussy, dipping a finger inside her and groaning when I find her wet and ready. She throws her head back as I move my hand, so I take advantage, leaning in to kiss and suck her tits and neck. She grips my hair with one hand and my shirt with the other, as she rocks her hips to the tempo of my fingers.

"So fucking hot," I say against her neck. "Are you going to come for me?"

"Y-yes," she says, gasping. "Please don't stop."

I smile as I pull back and watch her fall apart on my fingers.

"Fuck, Finn," she screams, tugging my hair so hard my eyes water.

I hum as I take my fingers out and slide them lazily over her folds, making her twitch again.

"I can't," she whimpers.

"You can. You're already doing it," I say, sliding two fingers back inside her and playing teasing her clit with my thumb.

"Oh, fuck."

"That's it," I coax and watch her come again. I take my drenched fingers out of her and kiss her deeply before I pull away to look at her. "You're so fucking beautiful, Josie."

Her eyes light up. "As are you, Finneas. And you're still wearing too many clothes and hiding what you claim belongs to me."

"Everything I have and everything I am belongs to you," I say and chuckle when her eyes fill with tears. *God, I love this girl.*

"I love you," she whispers.

"I love you more," I respond against her lips.

She kisses me quickly and climbs off to undress me. Once I'm naked, she pushes me back down on the bed and climbs over me. She starts kissing my neck, my shoulders, and my chest, and then moves down my body painfully slowly. She enjoys torturing me like this, and I let her, because even though I'm aching to be inside her, I love everything she does to me.

When she finally reaches my cock and takes it in her mouth, my hips bow off the bed with all my pent-up need. I let her lick and suck me once, twice, three times, before I grab her hair and pull her away from me. She glances up with those big brown eyes that look so innocent but are so fucking not.

"Why'd you stop me?" she pouts.

My grip tightens, but I loosen it when she winces. "I need you to come back up here."

She bites her lip as she moves to straddle me. "Now what?"

"Now." I grab her, flip us over so she's under me, and push inside her in a quick, hard thrust that makes her scream. "Now I'm going to fuck you into the mattress until the only words coming out of your mouth are, 'Yes, Finn, I'll marry you.'"

Her laughter is cut short when I start making good on my promise.

EPILOGUE

Josslyn

THE UNCHARACTERISTICALLY GLOOMY WEATHER MATCHES MY SOLEMN mood. It's been years since I've visited my dad's grave. His funeral is still a blur, but I'll never forget staring at his casket. My paternal grandmother and my mother had been very adamant about the burial. For them, it was tradition. For me, the finality of it all had been crippling.

I've only visited twice since that day. I don't need a plot of land to feel my father's presence, but now that basketball is over for good, I'm scared I won't feel that way. For so long, every time I picked up the ball, I felt him beside me guiding my movements. Maybe the fear of no longer feeling his presence is the reason I'm here.

I'm so lost in thought that it takes me a moment to realize someone is standing over his grave. It takes me another second to process that it's Finn, wearing the shorts and polo he had on this morning when he left to go golfing. As if feeling my arrival, he turns to me and flashes that sexy smile that makes my heart lurch every time.

"What are you doing here?" I ask as I reach him.

He stares down at me for a long moment before cupping my face and giving me a soft, long kiss that makes my toes curl. I drop the umbrella in my hand and grab his arms to keep from swaying. After a moment, I breathlessly pull away and search his eyes. It's not until he smiles that it hits me. He chuckles when my eyes widen.

"Finn," I breathe and swallow the knot already forming in my throat.

"Admittedly, this is not the place I envisioned doing this," he says with a chuckle. "But it's the only way I could think of to let the first man in your life know that I'll be your last."

He smiles as he searches my already watery eyes.

"Honestly, Josslyn, if the sun could take a mortal form, it would look and feel like you," he says. "There's nothing I wouldn't do to keep that warmth, to keep *you*, by my side."

I gasp and bring a shaky hand to my mouth as he sinks down on one knee and picks up a little black box from the ground I hadn't noticed. Thunder rings out and a few drops of rain join the tears that begin to trickle down my face. Finn glances up momentarily and shakes his head before he opens the box and takes my trembling left hand in his.

"You're the first and last person I think about every day. The *only* person I think about every day. Your love is a privilege I'll never take for granted," he says as he begins to slide the ring on my finger. "You're the love of my life, my best friend, the person I have the most fun with, and the only future I see. Marry me. Marry me and let me spend the rest of my life showing you how much I cherish you, how much I love you."

I nod wildly and wipe away the mix of tears and rain on my face as he finishes sliding the ring on my finger. Unbeknownst to him, I've looked at countless rings, but the one he chose blows them all out of the water. It's the most beautiful silver ring with a large oval stone in the center and a halo around it that has gold accents that make it look like rays. It reminds me of...

"It looks like the sun," I whisper in awe, bringing my eyes back to his.

"It looks like you."

My heart skips. "Finneas," I say shakily, as he stands up and wipes away the hair stuck on my forehead. "You know, you didn't actually ask me."

The corner of his mouth lifts. "That's because there's nothing to ask."

"I'm pretty sure there is, but it doesn't matter, because I'd say yes to you a million times over."

"Fucking finally," he says, right before he kisses me.

It's a slow, all-consuming, toe-curling kiss that leaves us both breathless by the time we pull away.

"I love you, Finneas."

"I love you more, my Josie, my love, my heart, my sun, my everything," he responds, kissing me again before he wraps his arms around me. "You own me. I think you have from the moment I heard you laugh."

"Hey, Finn," I say, my words slightly muffled against his chest.

He chuckles. "Yes?"

"Do you believe in divine timing now?" I ask, pulling away slightly so I can look up at him.

He searches my eyes with such intensity that I nearly forget how to breathe. "Every second I'm with you," he says softly as he bends his head to kiss me again.

ALSO BY CLAIRE

ClaireContrerasbooks.com

TikTok:

clairecontreraswrites

Insta:

ClaireContreras

Facebook:

www.facebook.com/groups/ClaireContrerasBooks

Printed in Dunstable, United Kingdom